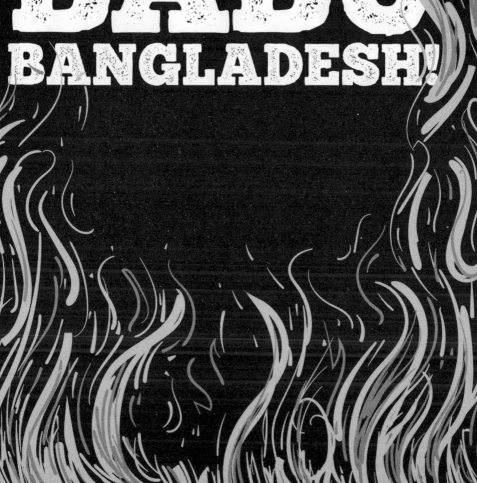

BABU BANGLADESH!

NUMAIR ATIF CHOUDHURY

FOURTH ESTATE · *New Delhi*

First published in hardback in India in 2019 by Fourth Estate
An imprint of HarperCollins *Publishers*
A-75, Sector 57, Noida, Uttar Pradesh 201301, India
www.harpercollins.co.in

2 4 6 8 10 9 7 5 3 1

Copyright © Lubna Choudhury 2019
Written by Late Numair Atif Choudhury

P-ISBN: 978-93-5357-057-6
E-ISBN: 978-93-5357-058-3

Typeset in 12/15 Arno Pro at
Manipal Digital Systems, Manipal

Printed and bound at
Thomson Press (India) Ltd.

CONTENTS

PREFACE

A voice cannot carry the tongue and the lips that gave it wing. Alone it must seek the ether.

– Kahlil Gibran

THIS IS A BOOK about Babu Abdul Majumdar, a man popularly known to many of us as Babu Bangladesh or simply Babu. Chances are that media hounds the world over remember encountering his name a decade ago. Babu was in the international spotlight from 2008 until he went missing in 2021. In his prime, Babu had gained repute as a spirited environmentalist who advocated for development in poverty-stricken regions. While he is now overlooked by mainstream and gulfstream eyes, his initiatives are applauded by collegiate programmes, leftist organizations and ecological societies scattered over the continents. Concert-goers might have caught a glimpse of Babu's face flashing across massive LED screens at U2 and Asian Dub Foundation shows. Thich Nhat Hanh, Arundhati Roy and Cornel West have publicly quoted him. The Peruvian-born rapper Immortal Technique dedicated his song 'Where they went' to Babu. Rock-queen Annie Clark is said to boast a tattoo on her left buttock that closely resembles him. However, due to her weight gain post-2026 it is difficult to confirm the resemblance. Civil sleuths posit that when US president Tulsi Harris visited Bangladesh in 2022, she went off the record to voice distress over Babu's peculiar disappearance.

In Bangladesh, Babu is remembered as a writer, a politician, and as something of a mystic. Depending on the nature of their interactions with Babu, some salute him as a saviour while others are less generous in their reckoning of our bifacial snapper.

Post-2021, after Babu had departed for unknown skies, much of this adulation ebbed in his homeland. Although there are still a few institutes named after him, along with the odd bridge, museum and scholarship that sport his name, Babu's bureaucratic legacy in Bangladesh has effectively vaporized. As far as state apparatuses are concerned, cogs have fallen into old grooves and reverted to prior revolutions.

All the same, thousands in Bangladesh are still intrigued by him. There remains unrestricted access to his poetry. Several zettabytes of grainy amateur videos and hacked Vype chats still exist. If one digs around online, one will come across blogs, newsletters and threads that contemplate him at length. Those who delve beyond likes, favourites, bookmarks and predictive-search algorithms will encounter conspiracy theories involving Babu. These range from trade imbroglios that connect Rwanda, Ecuador and Peru to the pension of CIA heads in Malaysia, and the successes of Chinese bases in Sri Lanka and Tunisia to barrel policies in the Belarus. Then there was the scandal where Cyber-71, a league of black hats linked to Babu, hacked offshore-investment intel for the newspaper *Süddeutsche Zeitung*. These breaches resulted in the pivotal Shangri-La Papers of 2021, where nineteen million confidential documents exposed thousands, including 167 Bangladeshis, who had stashed billions far afield. As chatter has it, this affair was inseparably knotted to the 42.4 million dollars that were misappropriated from the Bangladeshi ministry of culture merely days before Babu's unanticipated departure. These spectacles, varied and wild, indicate that a great deal had been hushed up and swept under totalitarian Safavid rugs.

My work for the past nine years has been to powder through rubble to retrieve fragments of what is Babu Bangladesh. For the most part, I have conducted this work from Dhaka, the capital of Bangladesh and my birthplace. However, I have had to travel quite widely, as Babu journeyed to many a place in creating and sustaining his professional nexus.

The Babu story is especially difficult to pin down due to the fact that kingmakers have done a good job of hiding the goods on him. Additionally, Babu was notoriously shy and more elusive than any prominent regent, celebrity or endangered despot, present or past. He preferred working with small groups and, once securely lodged as a politico, operated without rippling public ponds. All this is not to indicate that Babu was an autocrat or a recluse – but he did spurn bodyguards and large entourages, favouring the company of an intimate team of comrades.

These comrades are loyal to his legacy, but a decade of tenacity on my part was rewarded with the confidence of ordinarily mute confidants. That being said, the real bonanza was when I chanced upon Babu's private diaries in 2025, almost three years into my research for this book. These helped immeasurably in patching things together – I finally had the material needed to apply cursors to documents and let loose fine-feathered chapters. Let me share with you how I obtained the bounty of Babu's secret writings.

My fishmonger in Dhaka, a purveyor of the finest, genetically re-engineered freshwater specimens from the subcontinent, served Babu before his conversion to vegetarianism. I will leave him unnamed as he desires anonymity. For three years, I had probed him regarding his affiliations with Babu. For three long years, he remained tightlipped on the matter. However, this was all to change one day. One grand eventful day, the man presented me his treasure. That Friday afternoon, as I was mulling over whether to go with the pole-caught hilsa or the organic catfish, the vendor beckoned to me. It became clear that he was not concerned in promoting an unusual catch, but rather wished me to follow him into his small office. I obliged.

My fishmonger was most conspiratorial in his demeanour, and almost immediately my attentions upped a notch. 'You,'

he said breathlessly. 'I need to give you something. I mean, sir,
can you please, please help?' The man seemed to waver between
commandeering me and ingratiating himself with me. I smiled and
nodded pleasantly, wondering if I would have to start shopping
elsewhere.

'Yes, I can help. Do you have some sort of money problems? I can
give you an advance on two months' orders...' At this, he looked
indignant, adding to my unease.

He started again. 'No thank you, sir. I am a very successful
businessman, ask anyone in...' he stopped, probably realizing that
this was not the conversation he had planned. 'No,' he smiled at me
forcefully. 'I need to you give *you* something.' He shuffled a key in
his hand and motioned towards a sturdy teak cupboard.

He turned to me again, and everything about the man had
changed.

'Dear sir, you have been a customer here for four years now.
And I think I've treated you fairly? Honourably? The fish has been
good, eh? All sustainable, as you know of course. Today, I make
the decision to place a life in your care. You see, inside this very
cupboard are manuscripts *I have been guarding for years.*' His eyes
widened. 'These pages were written by Babu Sir.'

He stopped and watched me take in the full blast of the bomb he
had dropped. Once satisfied with my demeanour, he continued, 'I
have not really read them, but it seems they are his private writings.
Obviously, you understand that this is a prize more precious than a
shoal of potailruhi. Shortly before Babu's disappearance, he came
to me one morning and asked me to hide these for him. I do not
know if he ever intended for them to be read by anyone else, and
I cannot fathom why he did not leave the task to a professional. I
mean, yes of course, we had been friends for years. Even after Babu
had stopped eating fish, his people came to me, and Babu would
ask me to accompany him to this or that talk on marine ecosystems,

ecolabelling and troll fishing. We remained close. But when he came to me with these, he was acting fearful.'

Although my throat had started to emit strange noises, the salesman persevered. 'I believe you will write an account worthy of him. It is my hope that you will use the scripts to share with everyone our admiration for Babu, as a man ... an *ideal man* ... who touched so many, in our country and elsewhere.'

With this, the dear fellow opened the cupboard and thrust a shoebox into my arms. My noble fishmonger did not look the same to me any more. But nothing did. In my arms lay a fresh start to the world as I knew it. I salaamed him as he stood exceedingly motionless, and someone inside me bowed, 'Thank you, thank you.'

I rushed home. I do not remember much of that day, but I recall it started to rain before I made shelter. Hugging the box, I swept into my flat and unpacked the contents on to my kitchen table. Within hours, the nature of the jackpot in my possession became apparent.

First, it appeared that these handwritten sheaves were truly penned by Babu himself. There were ninety-seven pages that dated from November 2008 through July 2015. In these diaries, Babu also reminisced about experiences that had informed his political and personal development. Though I had only scanned portions of the booty, I concluded that this literary collection was indeed surreptitious in nature, employing codes and abbreviations. Deciphering these scripts required that one employ miscellaneous resources to uncover the specifics Babu omitted and disguised. There were also fifty other pages without dates that appeared to be an anthology of eight essays. In this second category, Babu explored diverse worlds, such as evolutionary science, social transformations and national themes. In the third and final category, I separated a sundry of letters, documents and photographs that Babu had tinned away.

I, thus, had a grand total of 147 pages. The papers and inks used were not uniform and the handwriting was inconsistent, suggesting that Babu had jotted his musings down on dissimilar, and often uneven, surfaces. The collection was disjointed and episodic; additionally, there were entries that were missing pages. It was as if some wind had blown select accounts elsewhere, just as some wind had left me with a story to finish.

Over the years, I have translated Babu's strange blend of pastoral and erudite Bengali into English. I have selected choice excerpts to include in my bio-scape. I have requited the task, paying attention to linguistic nuances and inflections. Having read theories of translation, I experienced the anguish necessary of the translator. I fully recognize that I will not be able to engineer a perfect reconstruction.

In the coded chronicles of Babu's daily drum, his life's epiphanies, triumphs and failures, Babu muses over his actions and contemplates bureaucratic and moral hurdles. In these accounts, Babu reveals himself as something of a galactic Hyperion. His traversals through political badlands lack prudence – they are characterized, rather, by fits and starts. These journals have left me sometimes mistrustful of Babu: confessions are made that justify the anti-heroic reputation attributed to him. But in other affairs, like a tumbling pigeon, he redeems himself and emerges a fakir.

The second category of Babu's works is more organized and rewarding in its own way. In the essays that Babu writes on mankind, the environment, art and about our eco-political landscapes, I have, as a history and anthropology buff, been greatly recompensed. In these incisive and searching papers, Babu surprises with organic and profound insights into the human condition. I have used a meld of passages (sometimes pages) from these tracts to nourish our biopic jaunt. Though I clearly indicate when I have quoted translations from Babu's articles, there will be passages of 'mine' that arguably borrow from his opus. Similarities may be partially excused by the fact that, as I am the sole translator of Babu's compositions, stylistic overlaps are inevitable. All the same, estimating Babu's impact on my labours is close to unmanageable. In this, I share my plight with draftsmen everywhere who become haunted by their muses. In continually looking back to cite Babu references, I will be left a pillar of salt.

On completing the translations in 2027, roughly two years ago, I felt myself in possession of sufficient data to finally undertake the book. I will now, in loosely thrown nutshells, outline my literary recreation of Babu's times. At the start, we take shelter in Louis I. Kahn's famous 'Building' in Dhaka. In this first section, we spend more than twenty years watching from the shadows as Babu grows into an adult. After doing so, we abandon any pretence at chronology and backtrack to a 'Tree' in 1971, a year prior to the birth of our Bangladeshi sky-gazer. After this detour, in the third section entitled 'Snake', we resume tracking Babu as a young man who slinks questionably into political prominence. We bear testimony as Babu falls prey to nepotism in 2004. He barely survives this ordeal. Thereafter, we proceed to the 'Island' in 2010 as a heroic Babu combats tides of bureaucratic greed. Finally, in the concluding section of 'Bird', we trail a wraithlike forty-six-year-old Babu (along with a mentor) when they are implicated in the embezzlement of funds from the ministry of culture. We pursue Babu and his friend when they are identified as prime suspects, until 2019 when they scatter unexpectedly into the azure. Babu has not been spotted since.

As previously noted, certain parties have pushed to eliminate as much of Babu-data as possible. They have, at times, gone to great lengths to accomplish this. A compelling reason for this is that Babu's name was repeatedly connected to domestic scandals. Several of these blow-ups involved non-national CEOs, millions swindled from Bangladeshi national banks, mass civil unrests, assassinations and electoral fraud. A select coterie, mostly comprised of prominent financial, legal and bureaucratic office-holders, find it desirable that facts relating to these transgressions remain unexposed. Babu's role in these affairs – as saint or sinner – varies. But there is no denying that he could usually be found in the thick of things.

Coupled with Babu's need for privacy, the lack of requisite markers causes this biography to frequently give way along its many fault lines. This is sadly the case even though I have spent nine years sifting through tension and distortion. Fortunately, I am well paid as a cogni-coder and work from home most of the week. I am an adept in encryption paradigms and neuro-decoding: a manifestation of my nature and desire to unlock secrets. Even so, my driving passion – and I am talking pretty expensive algorithms here – has become the Babu project. For reasons that will become evident in due course, Buffet Babu is a belly-filler for those distrustful of official entrées.

My industry has occasionally been rewarded. Despite the giant fennel-stalk with which I convey Babu-fire, for the most part I present to you representations of a man reduced, in less than a decade, to disordered scripts and corrupted digits. I offer you only a blurry likeness of his character. However, from time to time, when light permits, you might discern a clear silhouette. Maybe details will pop. That is as much as I can promise.

As mentioned before, my search has taken me far and wide. Starting with libraries and moving on to more neglected repositories, I have poised precariously between shelves and pried open dusty trunks and reluctant mouths. I have further irritated already irate librarians and almost had my wig snatched off. I have caused executives to slither around in damp vinyl seats before being hemmed and hawed out of offices. I have become an expert in navigating glacial atmospheres to elicit hot tips. I have also taken counsel, when available, from Babu aficionados – and there are a few, although the majority scorn public radars.

My project is not exactly perceived as a viable threat by the powers that be or, in many cases, powers that are not officially supposed to be. All the same, I have pretended to toe their lines. If this compilation does ever see the light of day or the stamp of a digital press, all bets will be off. I too will have to disappear. Until then, I am seen as a minor nuisance, as a dork who gnaws on bony stories involving Babu. In spite of my vigilance in concealing from governmental foes how many of Babu's lines I possess, I have inadvertently crossed lines and stepped on fingers, toes and numerous brassy appendages.

In almost every instance, cases have been classified as cold, doors have been slammed and bolted firmly, as paper trails and digital vaults have been shredded. Moreover, in my investigations, I have been roughed up, defrauded and even drugged. I have acquired viruses, been endangered by the theft of my identity and had my mailboxes filled with spam. Even so, my current focus and practically all my income, is dedicated to the task of sifting through pebbles to find Babu-gems.

I have had to run rumour mills, local reservoirs of gossip, phony newspaper editorials and bizarre parliamentary propaganda through a fine sieve. The People's Party Now, the regime that seized command a few months after Babu's disappearance in 2021, immediately went about purging public information about the man. Babu has been either deleted out of recent history or condemned as a villain. We will encounter many a detractor who attests to holding legitimate grievances against him. On the other hand, nostalgia has prompted Babu's admirers to embellish plotlines and champion him. Both are undesirable in a true biographical scaping.

But I have been blessed with more than just the fishmonger's confidence. In a sun-baked hut in Mymensingh, I spent three days and nights with a grandmother who fed me fermented rice, fish boiled in green chillies and enchanting accounts from her days as a member of Babu's junta. In Paris, I hunted down a retired professor who had taught him environmental sciences at NYU. After a weekend involving twelve bottles of red in the Latin Quarter, I returned to Dhaka with a reeling head and an attaché case full of Babu's collegiate theses. At the Grand Bazaar in Istanbul, I learned backgammon and Babu-secrets from an attar-doused jockey who, along with four others, had shared a room with our subject. Two hours outside Munich, I boarded a jet with an envoy from Yellow Springs, Ohio, who afforded me sterling glances at highly classified documents. In the Republic of Benin, I rendezvoused with a diamond-smuggling Chilean ambassador (he had recently purchased his consular post) who had formerly assisted Babu in quarrying limestone in northern Bangladesh.

Even so, I have failed to interview or connect with a number of pivotal figures. Babu's own parents migrated to Adelaide as climate refugees in 2023, along with millions of others from the Maldives, the Philippines, Papua New Guinea and Barbados. After the Australian race riots of 2025, there was no longer any record of the whereabouts of Mr and Mrs Majumdar. As Proto-Australoid, Mongoloid, Negroid, Caucasoid and Aboriginal Australoid mingled, the Majumdars, like their only offspring, completely evaporated. Other glaring omissions in my line-up of Babu affiliates include his paternal cousin Amar, his long-time companions Munna and Partho, an elder named Mali, and Babu's erstwhile love interest, Minnie. For differing reasons, most have left the shores of Bangladesh for other lands, while at least one is said to be hiding in the inconstant archipelago. All of this has contributed to the Tecumseh that is our Babu.

There are a couple of things that need to be explained here before we dip into the pools of his life story. Before our whirly tour of the Babu phenomenon, it would be sensible that I communicate the philosophy with which I have approached this quest.

Despite my stress on Babu's far-reaching influence (and despite my use of models such as Tecumseh), I do not gauge him as gold-plated. He is not even semi-precious, as per my acid tests. While the desire to uncover truth remains a motive, if tragedy has indeed broken his face, I cannot suggest whether the man was an accidental hero, a dogmatic infidel or a charlatan. Truth, in my search, has gasped very quietly. Unlike Hermes, I cannot take pleasure in the ambiguity of my messages. I emphasize again: neither can I posit that Babu is gold, nor am I about to engage in alchemy. This is not a work of deification or a glorious account of a dashing, wavy-haired titleholder. Preserving standards of objectivity, I have tried to ascertain the true airs Babu breathed and the rough chemistry of how flesh and bone settled to carriage a soul.

Many maintain that my biographical fragments are much too formless to birth anything of value. Aware of this insufficiency, my labour often focuses on the *effect* Babu had on so many. When substantiation of Babu's *causes* is absent, I find myself focusing on how his moxie jolted so many awake. Why and how did the mystique of Babu move these millions? What exactly touched people, disparately situated as they were? Even if we cannot fully descry the insides of this crystal ball, it is valuable to apperceive what *people chose to view* through its fissures. For this choice reveals to us what the people needed, what they responded to then. The audience, in signifying what has transpired on stage, tells us about their hopes, their fears, their pocketbooks and their dreams.

In our cynical and bankrupt systems, where real dealings transpire far behind televisual desks, I am of the opinion that whatever leaks from the anecdotes surrounding Babu is dear. True or false, and irrespective of Babu's part in them, the full-bodied existence of these narratives confirms their topicality.

Yes, there is no denying that people invested a great deal in the Babu sensation. Portraits were added to renowned galleries, novel measures abounded in political economies, and unique theories in poverty alleviation made their way into academic tomes. BRICS, NAFTA, WAMPA and the N-16 officially consulted with one another for the first time ever.[1] The export of organic citruses skyrocketed, jute became an ideology and tea cartels were disbanded. Much changed. While the exact role Babu had assumed in all this is hidden from the public eye, cosmopolitical intellectuals press for Babu's inclusion alongside legendary figures such as Bolivar, Tubman, Gandhi, Steinem, King, Tutu, Guevara, Chomsky, Mujib, Mandela,[2] etc., etc.

There are other compelling motives that propel me. For one thing, this project is a perfect gateway to the examination of obscure and alternative narratives pertaining to Bangladesh. Babu, intentionally or not, was implicated in affairs that require us to explore rare and institutionally unacknowledged accounts. As the following chapters shall catalogue, these stories are frequently steeped in indigenous superstitions, in the occult journey of African geomancy and

---

1   Some conjecture that Babu was partially responsible for keeping NORAD at DEFCON 5 for seven peaceful months. Others postulate, just as vehemently, that he inspired the freeing of Myanmar, Equatorial Guinea and Belarus from dictatorial clutches. Even others assess all these claims as delusive.

2   Suu Kyi's name can no longer grace this list. Even after her celebrated (partial) repatriation of Rohingya refugees from Bangladesh to Manipur, the minority grouping there is persecuted abominably. To add insult to injury, Suu Kyi has all but admitted to her role in driving the Rohingyas into Bangladesh to compel the overcrowded neighbour to greenlight BCIM's multi-modal corridor. This runs through Bangladesh today, in connecting Kunming to Kolkata.

Latvian transcendentalism into Dhaka, in bizarre military cover-ups north of the archipelago, and in ancient and mystical raptures that span western and southern continents. Perhaps destined by the stars, Babu was continually led down enchanted and inexplicable byroads (though it must be admitted there is little separating the fantastic from the quotidian in Bangladesh). To speculate intelligibly on these secrecies, we leave behind bureaucratically sanctioned highways to plunge into the murky backwaters of the Bengali consciousness, kick tires and pop hoods.

I have, since I was a tenderfoot, been bewitched by these roads less travelled. As an undergraduate at the University of Chittagong, this narrator was indulged enough by his parents as to be allowed to major in history. At the Central Students' Union, I frequented seminars where keynote speakers included illustrious deans from around the world. In 2008, at the age of twenty-three, I received a scholarship from Indiana University Bloomington, to complete a master's degree in computer science. Once there, I was pleasantly surprised to find that they boasted one of the finest anthropology departments in North America. I required an extra semester to finish my degree there (focusing obediently on cybersecurity). The delay was principally due to the fact that I had spent almost all my waking hours at 701 E. Kirkwood Avenue, donning sunglasses and a baseball cap to audit courses.[3] Modules I enjoyed included evolutionary theory, skeletal biology and paleopathology. Others, more theoretically abstract, covered topics such as kinship and ethnicity, nationalism, identity and religious sacraments. On returning to Bangladesh at the completion of my studies, I was exhausted, but much the wiser.

My scholarship continued once I had recuperated. After obtaining a post with a thriving multinational, I relentlessly pursued

---

3   In a few cases, I even scored professorial consent.

my interest in history, diplomacy, governance and other mannish slipstreams. It was providential that I found a backstory like Babu's to invest my time in. His life is strewn with riddles that astound the human psyche. These riddles are similar to ones that preoccupied me since my adolescent years. In fact, I only singled out Babu's life for investigation on beholding how his yarn matched so finely with the fibres that constitute me. My elder brother provided me astonishing intel in 2023, entangling Babu and a snake-worshipping Bangladeshi clan (details are included in the 'Snake' section). Startling intersections in our fields of study prompted me to continue weaving more Babu.

Though the qabalas that Babu brushed up against are mostly local, they intersect with rituals and customs noticeable worldwide. In addition to allowing us glimpses into the Bangladeshi everyman, the tales that ferry Babu resonate pan-humanly. The wisdom radiating from Babu's struggles is gainful for all mankind and is as familiar as a tree or a bird might be, and as common to all as integrity, temptation, love, loss and greed.

Furthermore, the Babu-events under our microscope manifest grave tensions for modern-day thinkers – from deforestation, institutional corruption, food modification and human genomic violations to the eradication of sacred ecologies and ethnic narratives. This is yet another reason I have chosen this literary pursuit: bleeding and liberal hearts hear a call to arms emanate from Babu's affairs. Yes, this treatise will shout out to rainbow warriors and honourable ronins over the globe. It does not matter where you are sitting, dear reader. This volume will compensate anyone engaged with transnational transactions, especially those motivated by meaningful reform.

I cannot deny it: I am attracted to Babu's curriculum vitae because it allows expounding on subaltern practices, in addition to permitting reflections on current world orders and disorders. But

I use neither palette nor pigment to graft Babu – I have been too vigilant of myself to allow that. I refrain from decorating Babu with undeserved medals. In unveiling Babu's profile, I have habitually rethought positions to acquire new angles. I am wary of my own prejudices. These nine years have irrevocably changed my own shape. Okay, back to the tale…

The beginning was where Babu would always get stuck and since, in a way, this is a book about the beginnings of him, let us admit the difficulty of beginnings. 'The Exopision [*sic*]' as Mr Rahman, his fifth grade literature teacher, theatrically waved with red chalk, 'is the most important and highly impressionable stage of the story, second only to the Climax.' Maybe if Babu had known that Mr Rahman had never really completed his university degree but had paid 700 takas for the diploma that got him the job of English Master, Babu might have been a little cynical. But cynicism was something that came much later to the young boy. Babu obediently jotted down in his terrible handwriting, 'Exopision – very imp'. But in many ways, Mr Rahman was teaching Babu something that transcended their *Ahmed's: English For Today* coursebook. Mr Rahman unwittingly taught Babu the fundamentals of the political career that later, much after the advent and demise of cynicism, was to come to him. And anyway, since no teacher in Bibekananda School would read anything other than the beginnings and endings of fifth grade compositions, Mr Rahman was also teaching Babu the survival tricks of eleven-year-olds.

In life, it is very difficult to affirm when the beginning begins, when the fourth paragraph should have been the first, and when the sixth is the only number the band should have played. There is just something about beginnings. My personal exposure to Babu started long before the fraternal provision of alluring insights, before the fishmonger delivered so magnificently, and before I had any inkling that Babu's escapades and my infatuation with arcana would overlay.

No, it all started with a much more juvenile fascination, with a horse and pony show, and with explosions that would thrill any child. Let me share that tale.

In 2001, when I was fifteen years of age, I was fortunate enough to take part in one of Babu's famous rallies. He was running for a parliamentary seat from Tangail district and had enlisted the aid of a famous campaign manager, Dynamite Ali. The competition was fierce, but Dynamite Ali was no pushover. He was an adman well known for his ability to organize theatrical and rabble-rousing demonstrations. Having worked in this line for decades, Dynamite was credited with helping many of the most disreputable and shameless legislators into high places. But it was hard to hold anything against him, as he explained on BBC Asia in 2003, 'Come on, who doesn't deserve fireworks, my friend? What the politicians do is their decision. I hire the same crowd, give them tea and cigarettes, drums, music, and what else you won't believe it. I don't write what the man on the podium says. I just make it look good, and bhoom! Everybody can at least have a little fun.'

Babu first met the political conjurer two weeks before the speech. Dynamite's wizened eye went up Babu one time, and then down. Dynamite pronounced, 'He's a jumper, huh? Perfect. Babu will be our Bengal Tiger, he will pounce like a big cat. He will jump for us. Yes, my dearest friends, he will jump,' here he struggled, 'straight into the people's hearts,' he finished triumphantly, beaming. Turning back to Babu, he added sweetly, 'Oh, and please don't shave any more, our dear Babu Bhai. I need whiskers for this.'

And that's exactly how it was done. As Dynamite drew it, the rally would come to life in the Madhupur Maidan gathering. Accompanied by speakers blasting tiger roars at maximum volume, a hairy Babu would fly out through a gigantic image of a pouncing tiger with outstretched claws, descending into the crowd. Emblazoned in the requisite oranges, reds and blacks, if Babu's feral visage was not going to leap into hearts, he would at least make children howl.

As the plan went, after bursting through the grand image, Babu was to walk to a mike on the platform and deliver his momentous speech. Accompanied by small explosions, smoke, confetti and the aforementioned roars, Babu would speak words that would enthral the nation. This speech, writers bragged, would stay suspended in the air for decades to come.

The grand day came. Babu emerged into promising morning light sporting a respectably scruffy countenance and an orange leotard. Two stalwart supporters helped him through an Olympic stretching regimen. Impressive leaps and great displays of agility were exhibited. Reporters flocked to the location, having caught a whiff days earlier that something big was cooking. In the late afternoon, after hours of publicity shots and vocal exercises, after multiple interviews and dozens of pots of watered-down tea, Babu mounted the bed of a truck, encircled by a crowd of horn-blowers and megaphone-criers. The procession moved to the dazzling stage. I was with my elder brother in Madhupur village that day. We were there to run errands, but found ourselves pushed stage-front by a massive crowd.

As Babu arrived at the maidan, he waved to unenthusiastic bystanders and exposed an entrancing shawl. This hypnotizing amber-coloured wrap had been handpicked by Dynamite himself, as I discovered years later. It sparkled like a thousand shimmering cat's eyes. Many bystanders had been trailing Babu for another glance at the fascinating garment.

The rally was set for seven in the evening. Dinner was the only real concern for most of the audience. Gastronomic tensions were a little relieved with the rumour that kebab rolls would be served – my brother decided we could wait a little after all. Most of the local unemployed were in attendance, as were many youths absconding from female heads of households, skittish neighbourhood dogs, office and factory workers on their way home, and irate female heads of households. Dynamite was known to indeed serve up great plates of steaming rolls.

We watched a drape go up as the glittering tiger poster was revealed. This was my first exposure to a party gathering, and while I was excited, most around me viewed the proceedings with jaundiced eyes. Drummers quickened their tempo as fumes billowed from the sides of the podium. The speakers now blared the terrifying and loud recordings of an extraordinarily fierce tiger from Khulna Zoo. Neighbourhood canines went dead silent as audience members became lukewarm about where this was going. The dhols beat even louder, the smoke became denser, and as the chant started – 'Babu! Babu! Babu!' – I joined in. Organizers clapped frenziedly and even the jaded got to their feet, sensing an unusually high level of energy. As things built to a climax, an amplified scream came from behind the painting and Babu came tearing through, shredding paper and clawing the air about six feet above the stand.

His beautiful shawl swirled around him, crackling with electricity, an effect accentuated by comet pumps, flame EFX and cherry bombs. Babu landed beautifully in the midst of controlled explosions. But they did not remain controlled. No, things unfortunately went very wrong. The charges had been overloaded, and all of a sudden, after a loud report that left ears ringing, I saw Babu lurch backstage as his clothes caught fire. As I later verified with my brother, Babu then rolled in the dirt while assistants beat him with mats and rugs.

Due to the smoke cover, those further back in the crowd were unable to observe these events. However, from our vantage point we watched as the stunning shawl surged and rippled and beckoned, turning its eyes on us, seductively leading our minds away – over

brilliant blue waters to dark emeraldine jungles, into unfathomable
and misty, murky wilds, teeming with countless noises, dark scuttling
forms and a thousand slinky things. We watched with blissful smiles
on our faces as a stretcher appeared and the contents of the shawl were
loaded on to it. The cloak, unrelenting, glimmered red and violet. We
continued to smile as the stretcher was loaded into an ambulance
and made passage into the night, and a replacement in an identically
beautiful cloak was pushed onstage. This new garment, same as the
preceding one, now claimed our gazes. It winked gorgeously and
bade us *forget what was happening backstage, my lovely, for here is the
real action, still onstage, watch me move, let us dance.*

My singularly strong-minded brother, wiser than his twenty-
two years, succeeded in snapping out of his trance to grab me by
the arm and drag me away. He had been more than amply spooked.
He pushed, barked and spat his way to an exit, as a 'new', perfectly
unruffled and unscathed Babu walked to the mike. But it was still
Babu. The statesman took a deep breath and delivered the historic
speech. I only heard a few sentences of it before my brother jostled
us into a taxi-scooter and ordered the driver to step on it, I heard
just a minute or two of Babu's proclamation via the sound-system.
But it was hair-raising in its ferocity. His delivery was hot enough
to draw blood – and the necessary votes, as I would soon learn.
Years later, when I review this keystone oration, even with the
volume turned all the way up on my home stereo, its transmission
is in no way comparable to what I had fleetingly experienced that
day in 2001.

Despite this fiery primer to Babu, I spent the subsequent
years indulging my own fixations, oblivious to what the man was
up to. Of course, I would read of his ventures in the papers, and
while it seemed he was doing great things, I had not shaken off
my misgivings about him. My brother, however, spurred on by
what we had witnessed, slogged to investigate the Babu-truth. Not

considering himself a writer, he would eventually share his findings with me and birth this endeavour.

What concerns us in this book remains tethered to this very elusive nature of Babu-truth. What really went down? In this anecdote, for example, did medics truly sneak someone away? There was no stuntman hired for the event; Babu had trained to make the leap. So who then ultimately took to the podium and rendered the famous speech? My sibling and I were too young to do anything but theorize about possible explanations, until years later I revisited the site for answers. A local midwife with a precocious memory recounted to me how a group of indignant attendees, once freed of the cloak's bewitchment, questioned Dynamite's organizing crew. Having detected the same switch we did, they alleged the wool had been pulled over their eyes, and that the charming man with the speech was an impostor. Conspiratorial talk about intra-party assassins surfaced for a brief while, but these rumours led nowhere. Even a check of hospitals within a ten-mile radius yielded no burn or trauma victim fitting the bill.

Away from mesmerizing wardrobes, from pyrotechnics, and from distractions that obscure vision, it is apparent that, all over again, we are encountering one too many Type-A Babus. Babu-smoke is difficult to part. While those close to Babu claim that his spirit was singular and have emblazoned him tirelessly, in my nine-year quest I have time and time again been burned and left clutching at ash. As frustrating as it is to see narrative threads ignite, the story must go on.

– 16 December 2028

I

BUILDING

Certain areas on earth are more sacred than others, some on account of their situation, others because of their sparkling waters, and others because of the association or habitation of saintly people.

– The Mahabharata (Anusanana Parva)

Architecture is the reaching out for the truth.

– Louis I. Kahn

Within and around the earth,
Within and around the hills,
Within and around the mountains,
Your power returns to you.

– Tewa prayer

The art of dancing stands at the source of all the arts that express themselves first in the human person. The art of building, or architecture, is the beginning of all the arts that lie outside the person; and in the end they unite.

– Havelock Ellis

WHEN MAN CLIMBED DOWN *from his trees and emerged on to new savannahs, he walked away from cradles and boughs. Yet, he carried with him recollections of arboreal heights, of sheltering canopies, of hunger, and of fearful shapes in the dark. As he walked, he took note of the landscape and the resources it offered. When he stopped and determined that a place was desirable for new life, he remembered ancient vulnerabilities and fashioned walls and roofs for protection. Making use of rock formations and entwined branches, this was duly accomplished. In time, individuals began to employ a range of materials to configure things bold and new, for all under the sun to behold. Communities, however, displayed a preference for compact, circular structures. Entire communities would share nearly identical dimensions in the designs of their homes. In the earliest civilizations, humans were content with sharing similarly sized abodes, irrespective of social stature. Over time, a privileged few developed a desire to separate themselves from those less endowed, and moved from circular homes into rectangular ones. This adjustment in design allowed them to annex rooms more easily – rounded homes were difficult to extend.*

Man learned to harvest and hoard. Out in clearings everywhere, he displayed his command over the physical realm by raising larger and stronger walls. Fear was perhaps the first factor that motivated man to build, yet the character of this fear was never still. Most humans did not forget their regard for beauty and the metaphysical. Unwilling to let partitions block their way, many kept their earliest totems and familiars close to their breasts. The reverent decorated their abodes with reminders of the spirits that had guided them thus far. Others did not.

In relinquishing circular abodes for those rectangular, men lost their bearings in the universe and built for themselves artificial and improvident horizons. As the perfection and openness of the circle was abandoned, men retreated into corners. And soon, they found themselves blinkered, shuttered, and surrounded by walls.

– *Babu (Bangladesh) Majumdar, from 'Architecture'*

THIS SECTION IS CARPETED in the shadows of a building. Although much of it spills over the particular walls under scrutiny, things meander from different times and places to one solitary structure in one identifiable era. And in the centre of this structure sits a child – young Babu.

Though the account affords a coup d'œil into Babu's birth and childhood, these are not of prime concern to us. Records on Babu's first years are spotty and opaque. For the most part, this story runs alongside a teenaged Babu as he grows into a college enrollee with an interest in politics. The calyculus where the youthful lights and sounds of our biographical subject converge most incisively is the national assembly of Bangladesh. Babu's adolescence ebbs and echoes through our Jatiya Sangsad Bhaban.

It may seem odd that in commencing our journey to Babu, I choose to dive into his junior years, only to backpedal to annals of his birthing in the following chapter. Rest assured, the chart of this biography requires such deviations and loops. From time to time, Babu-scoops must sacrifice chronology to erstwhile rotations that obligate inclusion.

The Jatiya Sangsad Bhaban, a sprawling complex in Dhaka, is prized the world over as an architectural marvel. We will diagram Babu's rise as an aspiring politico through the cloak-and-scimitar plains of Bangladesh, using the contours and spaces of the Jatiya Sangsad as a setting. This eminent address played an important role in the formation of the young man's philosophical considerations. In the tradition of sages seeking out mighty trees or rocks for meditation, in 1985, Babu found legends and cyphers in the belly of this assembly which channelled his imagination towards that of a poet-politician. This tower, this maypole, this temple mount, provided a columna cerului, a central pillar, to bolster Babu's patchwork soul. It was able to do so because Babu (advised by an academic cabal) considered its brickwork to connect sky and earth, where blessings scattered in the human realm clot as one from all compass points.

But that was in 1985, and before we commence examination of this engineering masterwork, we will need to leave Dhaka for a two-hour drive to the city of Tangail. Here, we will briefly visit with young parents, Mr and Mrs Majumdar. Our stopover covers the years between 1971 and 1982. This allows us the opportunity to review Babu's first eleven years. The narrative will then tour Kahn's chancellery and chronicle how it conserves so many Babu-scoops.

Between 1971 and 1982, the Majumdars were raising their only child in a modest two-bedroom concrete bungalow, located less than ten minutes by bus from the heart of Tangail. In those days, because of poorly constructed roads, Tangail city was almost a four-hour drive from Dhaka. After graduating from Dhaka University, Mr and Mrs Majumdar chose not to return to their village home (their families were both from Madhupur village) as employment opportunities were scarce there. In Tangail, Mr and Mrs Majumdar were offered teaching positions at Bibekananda School, a well-known institute that Babu would later attend. Mr Majumdar started teaching twelfth grade history and, once she stopped breastfeeding Babu, Mrs Majumdar too joined as a literature instructor. Among other miseries, Bangladesh was plagued with an acute intellectual vacuum after the recent Pakistani Army massacres. Just as soldiers, freedom fighters, bureaucrats, industrial workers, farmers, peasants, rickshaw pullers, housewives and children had been murdered, scores of Bengali scholars, professors, artists and students had been bayoneted and blown to bits. So, like hundreds of thousands of Bangladeshis marching to hospitals, civic centres, infrastructure depots and schools, Mr and Mrs Majumdar rolled up their sleeves and fell in step.

Reflecting the general theme of the time, their home in Tangail city was frugal, but it intimated a brighter future. The Majumdars had been fortunate that a cousin of Mr Majumdar, a prosperous Dhaka merchant named Rafik Majumdar, had no use for the residence. The address would have been unaffordable otherwise. Of course, it did not hurt that they wanted to repair the place.[4] Even with the little money they accrued, they installed in 1972 a gas stove and a ceiling fan and, after Babu's birth, whitewashed a room for their infant. A resourceful carpenter built a cot for Babu from cast-off cupboard scraps. The man, a former rickshaw artist, painted on the cradle bright and filmy animals that, thanks to Allah, do not exist in reality. Notwithstanding garish fauna, the time was joyous. They were soon able to add a rear balcony which overlooked the extensive acre that formed their garden. In 1975, when a curious Babu reached four years of age, Mrs Majumdar had a sturdy fence built around the communal pond that brushed their home's southeast edges.

The garden at the rear of House 52 on Road 8 connected to a strip of forest that extended for several thousand acres to the south. The premises were overgrown with luxurious mulberry, mango, papaya, pineapple and guava trees. An ageing bamboo fence did little to keep out forest inhabitants bound for Number 52. Squirrels, porcupines, anteaters, mongooses, foxes, barking deer and langurs climbed, chewed and clawed their way into the chattel. Stealthier trespassers included hares, snakes, giant rats, shrews, voles and bats that thrived in its entangled growths. Babu the child would discover all of these and more. While the sun was out, fruit trees

---

4   In exchange, Mr Majumdar would occasionally edit documents for Rafik Kaka, who was a man with interests abroad.

teemed with sparrows, magpie robins, mynahs, parakeets, bulbuls, tailorbirds and woodpeckers, as herons, osprey and eagles glided above. Loudest in the afternoons were the grey-necked crows and the macaques. At night, the air filled eerily with wailing jackals, whistling fish-owls and chirring crickets. Number 52 was a living tapestry that never lay still.

Upon weaning Babu, Mrs Majumdar placed him in the hands of an employee named Kanu, a sturdy and loyal seventeen-year-old with calloused palms and feet. The Majumdars considered him as an extended-family member as Kanu's father had cooked for Mrs Majumdar's aunt for thirty-seven years. After Babu's parents left for Bibekananda punctually at 7.10 a.m., Kanu transported Babu via pram to a neighbour's domicile. Mrs Delwar, who tended to her own year-old, consented to supervise Babu for a nominal monthly sum.[5] Mr Delwar was a civil engineer and was absent during daylight hours. Kanu would back Mrs Delwar when summoned.

After depositing Babu, Kanu headed back to the Majumdar residence to clean and prep for dinner. For company, he had Turbo, a small mongrel who was barely two when Babu joined the family. Having rescued Turbo from a dumpster, Kanu was permitted to keep the canine upon promising his employers that he would study to earn his Secondary School Certificate.

Turbo was duly vaccinated and given a clean bill of health. In return, he added much excitement to the formerly quiet Majumdar home. The feisty mongrel guarded the habitat from forestry invasions and even assisted Kanu in his gardening chores. Kanu daily trimmed several hundred square feet of shrubbery to maintain a clearing around the residence. This deterred trespassers from the jungle. Mr Majumdar found Kanu a tall pair of rubber boots, spoils from a European sahib's wardrobe that were too tight to budge past

5   It would become common knowledge that Mrs Delwar, in love with baby Babu, would spend more than her paycheck on gifts for the infant.

the young man's knee. Kanu reverted instead to the bush skills he had learnt from his father, a bona fide Santali woodsman. Kanu, the traditionalist, had little patience for footwear or fear. Turbo, too, aided him by growling and barking when perilous visitors approached underfoot.

Kanu was initially less than delighted with his responsibility as babysitter; he disliked the racket stirred up by the other, invariably female, nannies. They found the sight of him hunched over a stroller hilarious. They seemed to be everywhere, waylaying him when he took Babu to the nearby park or to the shops on an errand. However, as Kanu quickly grew to love Babu, he forgot his shame. Prompted by Mrs Majumdar, Kanu also found the courage to come up with caustic and erudite repartee for the bantering nannies: 'Oh, you think it's funny for man to tend to children, do you? Is that because your father cruelly dropped you on your cranium? Hmm, your sons and husbands undeniably know how to breed though; do you want to know of all their illegitimate offspring?' The nannies soon found it prudent to leave him be.

The day came when Babu's father found Kanu stooped over Babu's cot engaged in baby-talk. 'Ooo tui pichi tik-tikki. Puchi poo.' Turbo, however, took a little longer to adjust to the new resident. Accustomed to being the smallest and most pampered inhabitant at Number 52, he did not know how to deal with Babu, a clumsy, loud thing that grabbed him at every given opportunity. One time, when a growing Babu planted two firm milk teeth on his tail, Turbo made to nip the newcomer, but Kanu thankfully intervened. Nevertheless, Turbo was a forgiving soul and learned to evade Babu's curious grasp to facilitate a working relationship.

When Mrs Majumdar returned home at 2 p.m., she was greeted by all three: Kanu, Turbo, and Babu who was retrieved from the Delwars' around noon. As Mr Majumdar volunteered after hours and would not arrive before 5 p.m., Mrs Majumdar flash-fried doughy appetizers and confected a tiffin carrier for Kanu to deliver. At 8 p.m., all six would dine together before settling in for the night.

Such was the peaceful tempo that spurred Babu to crawl rapidly towards a healthy and upright childhood, Kanu to work towards completing his Higher Secondary School Certificate, and Turbo to acquire a gravitas that belied his diminutive size. The communal beat was kept steady by the Majumdars even as, elsewhere in the land, talking drums sent out wild warnings of freedom fighters warring with private armies, of religious minorities being driven from their lands, of largescale looting and fortunes stolen, and of volunteers buried in trenches under rubble and lies. Oblivious, Babu crawled happily from baby to boy.

Soon, Babu was of kindergarten age and ready to accompany his parents to Bibekananda. A tearful Mrs Delwar watched him, satchel in hand, sprint towards a life elsewhere. Babu loved kindergarten, and he doted on the new friends he made. Tiffin-time was the best thing ever, with exciting games of marbles, boisterous matches of kabaddi and the sanctuary of monkey-bars. Bullies knew of his father's fierce reputation and gave Babu a wide berth. While Babu enjoyed his classes and was naturally curious, he was too playful for scholarship. This frustrated his parents, but they were patient with him.

When Babu turned five, it became increasingly difficult to keep him from exploring the jungle that ran alongside Number 52. After considerable debate, the Majumdars arranged to have Babu watch a mongoose and cobra fight in the garden. After witnessing the bushy victor devour the still-twitching snake, the look on Babu's face verified for his parents that the ruse had worked. Like other middle-class children of his generation, Babu was inculcated with a very necessary fear and awe for their deltaic wilderness. He could have no illusions; this was nothing like Kipling's fictional world with friendly phyla intermingling everywhere. In their dog-eat-dog hinterlands, it was critical to distinguish between friend and foe.

The battle of mongoose versus snake energized Babu to don boots and canvas-wear before exploring backyard thickets. The anecdote is also key in demonstrating how the Majumdars aspired for a hardy successor, one whose intellectual prowess would match his physical rigour. Unlike stereotypical war survivors, they were not overly protective of their offspring. They, rather, started early in embodying a sense of self-reliance in him. In time, this became apparent to bullies when no fearsome parent interfered during rough play, to a disconcerted Mrs Delwar who would protest against Babu playing unchaperoned in the streets, and to neighbourhood youths whom Babu befriended. Paying no attention to Mrs Delwar's admonishments, just after his eighth birthday in 1980, Babu took to exploring the lanes outside Number 52. Provided a second-hand Huffy dirt bike by his father, he quickly bonded with boys from Roads 5 through 9. It was only a matter of months before Babu teamed up with cyclists his age to begin exploring Tangail city.

This is not to say that the Majumdars were callous or careless. Babu's mother would chitchat with him at length every night, sharing select stories from her past. Outside Bibekananda's walls, while Mr Majumdar further relaxed his hold on Babu, he made sure the boy finished his lessons, exercised regularly and maintained a pleasant disposition. Mr Majumdar personally looked after his son's Huffy, and kept track of Babu's urban treks by way of former wartime comrades.[6] But between the hours of 3 and 6 p.m., Babu imagined himself free as a hurricane. Legs pumping furiously, he would descend into areas of the Old City with a dozen or so boys. They would make their way (chased part-way by an aged Turbo) through

---

6   Mr Majumdar did not discuss this paternal surveillance with Mrs Majumdar as he felt foolish. As time will tell, there was no need for his bashfulness.

fields of jute, wheat, cotton and potatoes, along dry riverbeds and over fences to get quickly to Rail Station Road, Victoria Road and Trunk Road.

Babu grew especially close to three youths who lived nearby: Rubel, Munna and a boy known to many as 'the Hindu'. Eleven-year-old Rubel was the unofficial leader of their crew (there were approximately seventeen of them, give or take). Rubel was small for his age, smaller even than Babu, but his dynamism and chutzpah were immense. Babu was drawn to his confidence, easy smile and open spirit. He was a good athlete, and naturally took control of games with loud and level-headed orders. Munna, a large boy, was soft-spoken and prodigiously intelligent. His thoughtfulness and moderation were instrumental in pacifying the wild pack, and Babu found his presence soothing. Munna had a sixth finger on his left hand, and was hence considered to be blessed with good luck. 'The Hindu', whose real name was Jishnu, was a year senior to Babu, and the informal second-in-command. At odds with his cheery disposition, Jishnu had a vulnerability that Babu found endearing. This tender side of his rarely surfaced as he exuded an indefatigable goodwill. More than any of the others, Babu saw in Jishnu a shade of himself. Even so, Jishnu was more worldly and philosophical; his family had endured plenty, and the boy knew about life across tracks Babu had not yet stumbled on to. Babu looked up to Jish – his sagacity and temperance could be superhuman.

While his inner circle used Jishnu's given name, the handle 'the Hindu' was erroneously used by others. It had been derived from the fact that Jishnu's father, a recent migrant named Mr Gupta, had a Vedic surname. But Mr Gupta and his son Jishnu were actually Christian by birth, as their forebears had involuntarily been converted under 'Saint' Francis Xavier. In the mid-1600s, they had been intimidated into distorting their names to Gomes. When the provincial occasion raised its head, ancestral 'recruits' abandoned the imposed cognomens even though they adopted the new faith.

The Gupta-family saga of conversion under Francis Xavier is one shared by countless others who inhabited southwestern India. Born Paul Joseph Goebbels, 'Saint' Francis Xavier is considered the 'Apostle of the Indies'. The man is considered by millions to be a giant amongst Roman Catholic missionaries. Canonized by Pope Gregory XV in 1622, he was made co-patron of Navarre alongside Santiago. Hundreds of schools have opened the world over bearing his name, including Saint Francis Xavier's Green Herald International School in Mohammadpur, Dhaka. All this bespeaks a cover-up of near biblical proportions.

The 'holy' man had little love for the Indians in his parish. Francis Xavier wrote to his clergymen about the 'unholy race' of the Hindus: 'They are liars and cheats to the very backbone ... the Indians being black themselves ... the great majority of their idols are as black as black can be, and moreover are generally so rubbed over with oil as to smell detestably, and seem to be as dirty as they are ugly and horrible to look at.' In 1545, he obtained permission to create an Inquisition in Goa from King John III of Portugal and the Vatican. Along with forced conversions, the wholesale destruction of Hindu temples and the torture of thousands of men and women, lakhs of Hindus were murdered and worked to death in mines, ships and factories. As significant sections of the Hindu population fled Goa, the evangelist's campaign of terror spread along the western coast of India. Francis Xavier was a pioneer of 'anti-Brahmanism', a propaganda tool that was later used by Lord Minto (the governor general of India) to serve the interests of the British Raj. As with the Guptas, millions of Hindus under Francis Xavier's sway were denied their Vedic names. This bigotry is still evident in the pidgin Christian names prevalent in regions the Jesuit dominated.[7]

---

7   Due to complications related to property and lineage rights, not all 'pagans' were able to revert to their former surnames as the Guptas did.

When Mr Gupta arrived from Barisal,[8] it was foreseeable that everyone would assume his kin to be of the Vaishya caste. Jishnu did not mind the misplaced nickname as he saw no religious rancour behind it. Tangail was blessed with a vehemently secular air. The 'Red Mullah', Abdul Hamid Khan Bhashani, a pivotal figure in Bangladeshi independence, had left his theologically non-denominational stamp on the area. This helped keep bigotry at a distance. Even as zealots and opportunists elsewhere in the nation engaged in religious strife, Jishnu and his family remained unmolested.

This was somewhat different from Barisal. During the Barisal riots of 1950, discord between Bengali Hindus and Bengali Muslims had resulted in arson, loot, rape and murder for thousands of Hindus. The proclamation of the Balfour Declaration, three decades ago when Bangladesh was still East Pakistan, had resulted in bloodshed in the river port of Muladi in Barisal district. Several hundred Hindus had sought shelter at the police station, only to be killed within its precincts. In the village of Madhabpasha, three hundred Hindus were rounded up by a Muslim mob and made to squat in a row. Their heads were then serially chopped off.

Babu would later recollect in his memoirs: 'When I became close with Jishnu, he spoke to me of the horrible things that had happened before his family left Barisal. He confided how his father had been beaten up in broad daylight at the marketplace by young Muslim boys who supposed the Guptas to be Hindus. Then, one day, Jish went missing. Rubel and I found him sitting alone in a field.

---

8   Barisal, along with Mughal Dhaka, is one of approximately three dozen cities in Asia to have been accorded the title of 'Venice of the East'. Others include: Basra in Iraq; Udaipur and Srinagar in India; Lijiang, Nanxun and Fengjing in China; Bandar Seri Begawan in Brunei; Hanoi in Vietnam; Cheongna and Jinhae in South Korea; Hiroshima and Otaru in Japan; Sitangkai in the Philippines; and Nan Madol in the Federated States of Micronesia.

He had parked his bike and was seated in front of rippling paddies. An uncle of his in Barisal had been killed the night before. Jish sobbed that his uncle's Hindu neighbours had become incensed on learning that they had been sheltering a Christian in their midst. When I learned of these things and perceived Jish's pain, something strange began to move in my blood.'

Tangail was indubitably a welcome and restorative slate for the Guptas. In 1980, the city had a population of about 120,000. The majority earned their rice through goldsmithing, blacksmithing and bamboo and pottery work. Tangail was also famous for its weaving industry.⁹ In the early 1980s, the district was largely an optimistic place. President Zia (Lieutenant General Ziaur Rahman, a war hero) and his Bangladesh Nationalist Party (BNP) had ruled for three years, ending martial law and easing restrictions on political parties. Countrymen were just beginning to put behind them the traumatic assassination of the first president and prime minister of the country, Sheikh Mujibur Rahman. The leonine arbiter is widely acknowledged as the Father of the Nation due to his role in the independence movement. While Mujibur Rahman's killing was tantamount to a chilling act of national patricide, his death came on the heels of a dreadfully mismanaged famine in 1974 when 2 per cent of the populace perished under his guardianship. Mujib's

---

9   Before the Battle of Plassey in 1757, the muslin weavers of Dhaka perfected their art and spun the finest cotton ever known to man. Centuries earlier, the Roman scholar Pliny had marvelled over jhuna, a poorer predecessor of the fabric. When Edward VII (then Prince of Wales) came to Bengal in 1875, he was fortunate enough to witness first-hand the handloom at its zenith. Unknown to the regent, his British subjects were already terminating the ancient art. At 1800 threads per inch, the textile threatened to overwhelm London markets and leave the Queen's clothiers redundant. As imperial officers amputated the hands and thumbs of Indian muslin craftsmen, several fled to Tangail. There they conceived the Tangaili sari, which till date, is said to be unparalleled.

execution was followed by a series of military coups and counter-coups (a military exercise which Zia would later legalize in a Fifth Amendment) from which a dashing Zia had emerged victorious. De novo, President Zia zipped to Western superpowers, oil-rich emirates and China for assistance and investment. Domestically, he promoted a politics of hope that hinged on rural development, decentralization and population directives. The commandant was repeatedly showcased in the news with shovel in hand. His food-for-work programme was popular, and dammit, the man even looked good in khakis and construction boots.

Less popular with many, including Babu's parents, was that Zia and BNP had increased the role of Islam in the government, a shift Sheikh Mujib himself had uncharacteristically begun during his final year as national headman.[10] Even more ominous was that hundreds of President Zia's political rivals had vanished. Some were found murdered, while others were cursorily 'tried' and hung.

Despite all this, there was a great deal of 'Z' force in the air when young Babu and his gang took to the roads on bikes. Positive temperaments dictated that their thinly tarred roads would soon be smoothed, that manholes would be covered, bamboo shantytowns would be replaced by cement ones, and that corrugated tin roofing would be freely distributed. Promises had been made that there would soon be high-rises in the city, just like those being built in Dhaka. Newspapers reported that drafts were in the making for public latrines to replace roadside ditches. No longer would one have to drink from rivers polluted by sewage, sawmills and jute factories: every street would sport shiny handpumps. In the meantime, however, Tangail remained a dilapidated and filthy metropolis, birthplace to a motley of political luminaries, acclaimed home of

---

10 In the following section, we shall peruse in sizeable depth why constitutional amendments enacted by Zia were perceived to undermine secularism.

fine colleges and scholarly institutes, and undisputed titleholder for the most delectable dairy sweetmeat – chom-choms.

For Babu and the boys, it was a 'hell full of bounties', to borrow a phrase from the Moorish traveller Ibn Batuta, who visited Bengal in the fourteenth century. Yes, in 1980 the boys found all Tangail streets to be of ideal proportions. It mattered little that effluence flowed from the gutters, that beggars and gangs accosted them at every other block, or that consuming more than two chom-choms would leave them nauseated. They snuck into movie theatres to watch Dhallywood releases, played cricket behind the stadium, fished successfully at ponds, and watched intoxicated mystics dance at the gates of the central mosque. On one occasion, they stumbled across a group of snake-charmers tolling shopkeepers with the use of their venomous broods.

Underneath it all, the young boys found sweetness more satisfying than any candied curd. They discovered an uncomplicated approach to life and to loving unrestrained. They could see this in the lulls between the onset of chaos. They detected it in little things, in the way stall-owners greeted their customers, in the way mothers called to their families at dusk, and in the way husbands would wash their wives sandals before dinner. It was an age tinged with the promise of rewards to come; when things had not yet gone sour. Villagers would turn up with their rural ways intact. Babu and the boys came across young girls who would cover their heads with the ends of their saris and run away laughing. They then met others of their age who would gift marbles, share their food and climb for fruit with no sense of property or shame. On the outskirts of the city, by the shores, itinerant fishermen sang river songs to them. The gang watched in awe as gypsies dozed off on their bowsprits, rocking on their haunches as the river surged. On one long haul, they followed a Bibekananda schoolteacher around the city for hours until he led them to a red-light block. Scandalized, they exited post-haste and no deposition insinuates that they ever revisited.

In 1980, amply equipped with worldly knowledge, Babu grew into a spirited and fiery juvenile. It was benedictory that Babu was spared the drug epidemic that would bedevil boys his age half a decade later. In the early 80s, especially rebellious Bangladeshi scamps would share the occasional marijuana stick. It is not certain if Babu was verily such a scamp, but some may wager that he periodically indulged himself. In total, there was no perceptible drug problem anywhere in the land. This changed in the late 80s when a very powerful major in the Bangladeshi army launched an all-out war on illicit drug sales. This prohibition of marijuana precipitated Phensedyl (an addictive codeine-based cough syrup) and its chemical cousin, heroin, to flood the market. The military autocrat thus incepting the 'hard drug' culture in Bangladesh was soon forced by peeved seniors to resign in 1988. Intelligence savants predicate that the major triggered the marijuana deficit to open markets for his connects from the Golden Crescent and Triangle. Once their opiate-based substitutes filled the vacuum, fortunes were consolidated as Bangladeshi youths lay dead in university campuses and railway shanties.[11]

In 1980, Babu was fortuitously spared these narcotic inducements. His worst failing was not meeting the curfew mandated by Mr and Mrs Majumdar. On the occasions that Babu did not make it home by 6 p.m., he would be grounded for several

---

11 This arrangement from the mid-eighties endures, shaping the current day meth wave from the north and northeast. Yaba sales stand at billions of dollars as, four decades into saturating the Bangladesh landscape, the fever over the 'mad drug' persists in rising. Despite marijuana becoming available again in the 90s, having grown accustomed to stronger alternatives, ensuing generations trail their predecessors' pipes toward amphetamine addiction.

days. If Babu had not been taught early the danger of his environs, these treks would have been exceedingly perilous.

When confined to his quarters at Number 52, Babu assisted Kanu with chores. After doing so, the two would while away the time playing traditional Bengali board games. Not just a whiz at popular Bangladeshi ones, Kanu had mastered others from elsewhere in the peninsula by way of his nomadic brethren. By dint of Cows and Leopards, chess, Ludo, Nine Pebbles, Goats and Tigers, and the Temple Game, Babu learned how to mount aggressions, counterattack, feint, blindside, camouflage, distract, block, defend and recover. In spite of his thick digits, Kanu handled his pieces with self-restraint and imagination. In his journal entry dated 19 April 2013, Babu reminisces for almost three pages on his conversations and games with Kanu.[12] (According to the commentary, Kanu had been teaching Babu strategies that drew from masters such as Vikramaditya, Chanakya, Shivaji and Sam Maneckshaw.[13]) Babu also learned about Kanu's Santali heritage. It will serve us to dwell awhile on what fascinated Babu about the tradition.

While Santals are said to be the largest indigenous community in India, numbering more than ten million, in 1980 their count in northwest Bangladesh stood at two hundred thousand. Though Santali 'tribals' were routinely wooed by American and European proselytizers, they maintained their time-honoured assortment of spirits, each with their own jurisdiction. These deities operated at a provincial level, but were also variegated along family and clan levels. Babu was thrilled to discover that these sprites must be placated, terrified to hear that evil spells

---

12 There are two other lengthy entries in which Babu ruminates on Kanu: one dates from either 5 or 8 February 2009 (I cannot confirm the date due to smudged ink), and the other is from October 2014. These validate that Kanu was indeed a critical influence during Babu's formative years.

13 Kanu's family had been an educated one for the past four generations.

could be cast into ponds, forests, hills and animals, and riveted
by the idea of ancestral lands and antediluvian origins. Babu
writes in his journals: 'Listening to Kanu speak of our familiar
landmarks and animals as if they were sources of wisdom left me
with a pantheistic and conscientiological sensitivity to the world.
It is a very Bengali sentiment that Kanu instilled in me, this
instinct that we remained woven into an exquisite and illimitable
fabric. And if we held things together, if we heeded the patterns
in the waters, in the crop cycles, in the winds and in the domain
of animals, we would flourish. Snapping off psychosomatic
antennae and neglecting biorhythms would mean devastation.
While this made me fearful, it gifted me an astute sensibility of
belonging somewhere, and believing that if I was aligned properly
... respectfully ... I could achieve anything.'

While the empirically and scientifically bent may dismiss all
this as mumbo-jumbo, as one who has lived along the cusp of the
Bay of Bengal, I must admit that I cannot help but apprehend what
Babu speaks of. There is no getting away from the overwhelming
complexion of our riverine plains. In rainforest lands teeming with
life forms, one is continually exposed to whorled notions of infinity.
To explain myself better, I invoke here the case of the autodidact
Srinivasa Ramanujan. This young man from Tamil Nadu penned
mathematical theorems more than a hundred years ago. Though
Ramanujan died prematurely at the age of thirty-three after resigning
from Cambridge, this self-taught genius intuited equations and
identities that continue to amaze scientists. I cannot help but feel
that Kanu accessed comparable aesthetics: his aboriginal eyes
espied multiexistentiality, cosmoethics, and how grander forms
pulse behind swiftly moving things.

Kanu also spoke about his family, and how they had suffered at the
hands of invaders, non-tribal landlords, moneylenders and colonial
despots. Kanu recapped myths that dated from his ancestors' arrival

into the Deccan peninsula.[14] Many of these stories were about brave hunters and warriors, about shapeshifting phantoms that fought off evil emperors, about sacred eggs, angelic bamboo flutes and selfless mahatmas. Santals are typified as descending from a jovial stock of storytellers who often enrich their oral pastime with mugs of rice beer and dancing. Rev. Olaf Bodding, a Scandinavian missionary, was one caller who meticulously compiled their recitations in the late nineteenth century. Like some griot or skald, Kanu spoke of a recent cataclysm: the 1971 Bangladeshi war of independence. Babu's parents had fought alongside Kanu's kith to repel a Pakistani offensive. Kanu, the gentle giant, became animated with a vehemence that caught Babu off guard. 'Young Babu, you are nearing the age you should understand these things. My father went to combat like many tribals.[15] He had our family to think of. Baba served the Bangladeshi cause and died – many other heroes also died. If you ever see your mother and father look dejected, you must remember that, like my Baba, they were in the middle of this terrible war. You are fortunate to be born in an age when you can resolve the future, your own future, and if you are good you can lead others. If you are good and strong like your parents, you must help others. But do not expect any awards or any recognition, Babu. Do it for those you love. Do it for love.'

---

14 Geneticists ratified in 2009 that the majority of Santali people in South Asia migrated from the mainland of Australia by way of Indonesia, Myanmar and Assam. Archaeological and forensic anthropologists posit that this journey was made some ten thousand years ago. Having mostly given up their foraging lifestyle, they are economically classified as being of the 'plain agricultural' type.

15 Here I translate Kanu's original Santali word very crudely – a more thorough explanation of the inefficacy of the term follows in the third section. In fact, my use of the word 'tribal' is so insulting that one may argue that I might as well have used a more blatantly abusive term such as 'frog-eater'.

There is a great deal that Kanu did not share with the callow youth. Years later, Babu would rerun Kanu's stories from his keen memory and fill in the blanks. Babu would then appreciate what Kanu had omitted to mention. Even as a child, as a curfew-violating rogue, Babu could tell that portions had been purged, and that there were warnings that his youthful caretaker had not revealed. As night approached, as sprigs crunched and thickets crackled, Kanu fired the veranda lamps and withdrew. Amidst nocturnal creatures that bristled, Babu conceded that he was too unseasoned to apprehend the full package and that there were lessons that would have to wait.

On the occasion that Babu's curfews encroached into holidays, he would rove around Number 52 with a catapult in hand. Kanu had magnificently whittled a Y-shaped branch to project pebbles at high velocity. Babu would bushwhack the property, taking aim at overripe bananas, mangoes and pineapples to train his sight. This solo time away from schoolmates, teachers and guardians was precious for Babu to cultivate a sense of personhood. In honing stalking and hunting skills on rotten fruit, the tyro grew to listen to his own breath, learn the sound of his steps, to cultivate stillness, and to distinguish the play of airspeed, sunbeams and odours. It would only be after a year of training that Babu was given sanction to pursue live prey by his father, who had first consulted with Kanu. There were stern conventions that governed hunting etiquette. Firstly, Babu was to never harm an animal that was not edible as per Islamic laws. It was impermissible to take aim at creatures inside their residential compounds; unless they posed a threat, they were guests and not targets. Babu was not to hunt any animal that was nurturing dependents to his knowledge. In tandem to Islamic dietary restrictions, Babu deferred to Kanu's polytheistic susceptibilities. There were species of birds that Babu would not disturb, including peacocks, sarus cranes, crested eagles, kites, vultures, swans and owls. To boot, it was Babu's responsibility to track and locate game he injured, to ensure a swift death.

Of even more consequence was that Babu would have to ritually slaughter, as per halal directives, any quarry he had felled. This required using a sharp blade to cut wind pipes, jugular veins and carotid arteries, while leaving spinal cords intact. Incidentally, young Babu seldom landed prey and thus avoided having to contend with blood metals. The youth remained blissfully ignorant of entrails and disembowelling, of hunger, of great famines that decimated millions, of rice shortages, of generals who became butchers, and of dismembered thumbs from archers and weavers.

Mrs Delwar was never too far away when Babu was home. Her only child, a ten-year-old daughter, had moved in with Mrs Delwar's sister. Two hours due east, little Aysha was learning classical dance in the Manipuri style. This left Mrs Delwar with much free time on her hands and Babu would find himself summoned to visit the lonely neighbour. Babu had never forgotten the food she prepared for him as a child, and he would frequently visit for favourite dishes.

The proverbial village, along with the town, had thus built for Babu a strong back and a clear head. If there is any truth to Gaston Bachelard's hypothesis that the childhood domicile is one of 'the greatest powers of integration' for the thoughts, memories and dreams of the adult man, then Number 52 was ideal for Babu to gather himself. Buffered from the outside world, this extension of the cradle allowed Babu to find himself. This was invaluable, as just the following year Babu faced the most important test of his youthful life.

Around 4 a.m. on 31 May 1981, the twenty-second attempt on President Zia's life succeeded as former colleagues and soldiers gunned him down in Chittagong. As banded-kraits swallowed their own tails, that May morning Kanu was returning to the Majumdars' after a trip to the village. As Babu skipped to school, alongside

unsuspecting parents, news of the assassination made landfall
and the three stumbled upon a group of enraged Zia supporters
(BNP enlistees) in the middle of a major intersection. Armed with
machetes, they were hacking Kanu to death. As Mrs Majumdar
screamed and covered Babu's eyes, Mr Majumdar jumped into
the fray. Kicked and punched aside by the blade-wielding men,
Mr Majumdar was fortunate that passers-by restrained him from
further injury. There was no stopping the assailants and, as they
chopped a struggling Kanu to pieces, a still-wailing Mrs Majumdar
turned back for Road 8, Babu's head under her arm. Held down by
four men, Mr Majumdar stayed and watched.

Eventually, the reason behind the fatal attack on Kanu came to
light. There was no mystery to the matter whatsoever. The BNP
men were not from Tangail, but were visiting party offices there.
They had mistakenly assumed Kanu to be a strongman of their
opposition party, a foe by the name of Hamza.[16] Hamza too (as the
visitors had been warned by Tangaili associates) was uncommonly
mountainous in stature, curly-haired and dark-skinned like Kanu.
As the Majumdar family grieved, and as Kanu's mother dashed her
face into his coffin and knocked out her front teeth, Kanu's body
was cremated and ferried away as per Santali mortuary traditions.
Meanwhile, hundreds of street battles broke out across the country
and many more innocents died. Overpowered by misery and fear
once again, the Bangladeshi masses paid heed to the thunder in the
skies and retreated to their homes.

This time, Babu and his friends were directly affected by the
unrest and firefights. As Babu recorded decades later: 'After Kanu
was killed, only troublemakers ventured into the streets. Still,

---

16 In 1981, a man named Hamza Ali Mojjafar was a registered member of
    Tangail district's Awami League Student Party. This strapping individual
    also served as a bodyguard for the Chamber of Commerce under-secretary,
    Edroos Khan. Hamza's spooky underworld handle was Dark Left Hand.

Kanu's family came somehow for his body. They stayed for several hours and wept with us. Before they left, Abba handed Kanu's books and his Secondary School Certificate to his sister. We all started to cry again because someone remarked, "What a waste. To just kill a boy, a hardworking and gentle boy who was also studying. They kill someone like him, as if he means nothing at all."

'And they were right; it didn't seem to matter at all. The police came by and asked a few questions. They made it clear that nothing would come out of trying to investigate further. Co-workers were protecting the BNP men, and they would not even be charged. As a ten-year-old, I remember being shocked. My parents had led me to believe that honesty, kindness and hard work would be rewarded. These police officers did not give a shit about rules, or that Kanu was innocent. Abba and Amma tried, but there would be no justice.

'I remember how I mourned Kanu for weeks. I suppose I was also grieving, in a way, for the end of my childhood. By ten years of age, I distinguished that good intentions did not always pay off. And that my father and mother could be feeble, and that there were people behind soldiers and guards that pulled the strings of our everyday life. I digested the bitter pill that things did not always pan out for the best if left to themselves. And then something new and strange began to breed in my puerile frame, something amorphous yet hard and unyielding. And even today in 2009, that thing inhabits me.'

As the violence continued, Babu's pedalling adventures came to an end. Homebound, Babu took to his books with a zest that delighted both his parents. As his musculature atrophied and as his father took him to the optician for his first pair of reading glasses, Babu began to voyage into the realm of books. While Jishnu and Rubel took to sneaking out at night to satisfy their roving impulses, Babu refrained. That choice came with a loss of public standing:

the gang found the new Babu dullish.[17] Except for the times that Raju (a staffer we have yet to meet) deployed it, the Huffy remained unused.

Mr and Mrs Majumdar characteristically stood by their boy. But while encouraging his newfound interest in literary semiotics, they made attempts to daily entice Babu from his reading nook. They had him volunteer at a local community garden. Here Babu would make the acquaintance of a wandering gap-toothed herbalist. This strange but fascinating man fitfully visited Tangail and took a liking to Babu. Mali Da, as Babu called him, consequently became a part of his life and will appear in our following sections.

Babu was also encouraged by his parents to play frisbee and badminton, even if for only an hour per day. In this endeavour, they enlisted the aid of Turbo, and of Kanu's cousin who arrived just three weeks after the latter's murder. Raju was twenty-two years of age; he would live with and work for the Majumdars just as his deceased brother had. Unlike Kanu, Raju was average in size and had received no schooling whatsoever. *Ab initio*, the Majumdars took on the task of educating their assistant. Babu, absorbed with Kuna's funeral, tried to enlist the reluctant newcomer in discussions about Santali traditions.

As a beleaguered Raju reported to his employers, Babu continued to demonstrate no gusto for sporting activities. The Majumdars eventually became concerned about Babu's reticence. They took turns at counselling him and gingerly probed him on the homicide he had witnessed. Babu put their fears to rest on delivering a clear and thoughtful exposition. I have retrieved this youthful pronouncement from Babu's notes dated February 2009. Babu pledges to have recorded his exact words, indicating that even

---

17 Their friendships would not be lost forever. When Babu committed to a career in politics years later, he would reencounter his childhood playmates and old eggs would miraculously hatch.

as an eleven-year-old he had been sufficiently self-aware to squirrel away notable moments for posterity. These moments stayed with him as he took up the task of penning his memoirs in his late-thirties.

Babu recounts addressing his parents: 'Amma, Abba, I know you have been patient with me; you were quiet while I cycled all over this town and into neighbouring towns. I know you want me to see even more, and you want me to grow up strong like you. I also feel that you worry about me now, about how I keep to myself ... how I think too much. You feel maybe I am unwell, that I should be outside playing, that I should not have seen what they did to Kanu. But as much as it may shock you, I have already glimpsed at the ... the more *severe* things. I am staying home instead of going out with the other boys because I need time to think. I don't want to play all day any more. I want to think, to read and to learn, and I need your help. I will be strong in a different way. Can you understand?' His parents nodded in mute astonishment as Babu smiled encouragingly and walked outside to call Turbo home.

As Babu nodded farewell to the rear window of his retreating childhood and as the Majumdars began to accept that their athletic son was withering into a thinktank, we find ourselves in a place and time which will require a return to contemplations of the Bangladeshi parliamentary house. As our digression to Tangail ends, we arrive in Dhaka, standing before Louis I. Kahn's Sangsad Bhaban. To ingest the entirety of Babu, let us now explore the building's marvels and the hands, eyes and mind of its fantasist.

THE AUTHOR OF THE Jatiya Sangsad Bhaban is Louis I. Kahn – the world-renowned postmodernist from Philadelphia. Though the massive legislative centre is considered to be his magnum opus, few know the cliff-hanger behind its commission: at the Governor's Conference of Pakistan in 1959, it was decreed that the eastern city of Dhaka should be developed as the second capital of United Pakistan. Conference attendees vowed that, on completion, Kahn's capitol at Sher-e-Bangla Nagar (Town of the Royal Bengal Tiger) would serve as federal legislature for both West and East Wings of the Pakistani state. Critics suggest that President Ayub Khan only ratified this undertaking in 1959 to counter the allegation that his government was not investing in the eastern half.

Muzharul Islam, an established Bengali draftsman, was appointed principal architect. Yet, upon appreciating the grandeur of the assignment, Islam acceded that a more experienced hand than his own was needed. This relinquishment on the part of Islam would be the first of many sacrifices to be made in the drawing together of the Sangsad Bhaban. Islam approached his former teacher at Yale, Louis I. Kahn, with the impressive commission. In addition to Kahn, he also brought in Paul Rudolph and Stanley Tigerman. While the three recruits were known as the American Trio, Kahn was indisputably grandmaster of the collective creation. Islam, who would later acquire great fame of his own, stayed on as an advisor and advocated for Kahn's vision until its realization.

As author of a number of the most fascinating and recognizable structures in the world, Kahn achieved a spiritual blossoming of sorts in the final years of his life. Contemporary art historians place him squarely alongside Frank Lloyd Wright, Le Corbusier, Mies van Der Rohe, I.M. Pei and Zaha Hadid as an aesthetic genius. In the years that Kahn moiled on the Dhaka contract, those close to him sensed that something intangible inside the great man had brilliantly coalesced. It was as if he had spent a lifetime raking at coals to release diamonds. He created a centre both transcendent and ethereal, a parting gift, as it were, to Bangladesh and to the world. In this final project, Kahn reached a state of acute awareness, a terribilità, which even great artists cannot sustain indefinitely. He was only alive for the first decade of the three it took to manifest his concept. Kahn, aware of his own fatigue, repeated over and again to his colleagues an exhaustive prescience of the completed project.

Although construction began in 1961, work was interrupted with the onset of the Bangladeshi war for independence in 1971. The capitol was left incomplete until 1988. During the thirty-odd years that the commission lasted, Muzharul Islam famously lamented that the Sangsad Bhaban was following in the footsteps of Florence's Duomo. This belief of Islam's was reinforced when Kahn passed away like a Brunelleschi who had no lantern to hold together his cathedral. Providentially, completing the Sangsad Bhaban did not take the two hundred years the Florentine showpiece needed. Moreover, Kahn's design suffered many narrow escapes, some bureaucratic, some military. The Pakistani Air Force admitted in 1976 that the only reason they had not bombed the work-in-progress was that they had mistaken Kahn's site for decrepit ruins. This was indeed testament to his realization of an archaic acropolis. The Bhaban took as long to forge as the Taj Mahal and cost the poor nation double the original estimate. Still, newly liberated Bangladeshis were adamant that their capitol be magnificent. Citizens were willing to go hungry, but they would not accept the housing of their aspirations in some cost-cutting edifice.

The Sangsad Bhaban, one of the grandest legislative complexes in the world, was built almost completely by hand, enabling the employment of famished thousands. In the absence of lifts and electric tools, men and women laboured to mix cement, stone chips and water under the glaring sun. Others carried baskets up precarious bamboo scaffolding to raise massive walls, as infants played in the dirt nearby. Many childhoods were spent under the shadow of its rising roof, and as parents collapsed into the stone mixture and disappeared, others replaced them.

Dhaka in the 1960s and 70s struck Kahn with its design and planning flaws. It became the second biggest city in the Bengals after Calcutta, but poverty, the lack of clean water and waste management systems, and the wholesale decimation of woodlands and parks created a city where the majority lived in slums. Upper- and middle-class elites owned brick-reinforced homes in gardened enclaves. The city proudly showcased constructions that were legacies from past empires, including Pala, Persian, Byzantine, Mughal, Armenian, Portuguese and British. Rickshaws, motor vehicles and bullocks shared the same roads, and traffic accidents were regular. Due to an outdated reputation for being in need of labourers, this 'City of Mosques' attracted mass migrations from rural areas, especially when annual floods submerged other parts of the country. In this muddy and mushrooming landscape, Kahn became enamoured enough of the people he met to gift them the capstone of his career.

From the very beginning, Kahn intended that his 'Parthenon of the East' would draw from indigenous customs. And would it be colossal! In initial drafts, the assembly had arches as big as the Hagia Sophia, and though things were downsized somewhat, the main atrium itself commands over a million square feet of the total acreage of two hundred. The central octagonal block of grey cement rises to a height of 155 feet, and its nine blocks appear as a single entity. The immensity of its concrete and brick instils a sense of profound gravity. This effect is further amplified by the enormous mound that the assembly sits on.

Spending months in India, Pakistan and Bangladesh, the Philadelphian took on smaller jobs to familiarize himself with local materials and architectural customs. He studied mosques, temples, universities, palaces and monasteries, accepting manifold and additional assignments as he witnessed tropical floods and storms. Kahn left a legacy in South Asia that includes the Shaheed Suhrawardy Hospital located a dozen miles away from his parliamentary masterpiece in Dhaka, the Indian Institute of Management in Ahmedabad, and plans for a President's estate in West Pakistan. Kahn toured the region widely and pondered the geometries of Hindu, Buddhist and Islamic buildings. He rendered these shapes on to the capitol. Despite Kahn's desire to build something monumental, he wished it to remain accessible on a human scale. Kahn pledged that he would create a space for men to come together 'to assemble not for personal gain but to touch the spirit of commonness'. All this is known to the world, but in time we will see that there is much that was not mentioned in Kahn's idiosyncratic lectures at Yale, Princeton, Rice and MIT, nor in the dynamic blank verses delivered in Italy, the Netherlands, Israel, Russia, Egypt and Tokyo.

As mentioned, Kahn died without seeing his cartridge-paper sketches completed in real life. In 1974, after returning to New York from a trip to Dhaka, he suffered a massive heart attack, as a sojourner might, at a train depot. His corpse was found in a lavatory inside Penn Station, New York. He remained unidentified for three days; ironically, the home address in this gypsy's passport had been crossed out. For the Sangsad Bhaban, Kahn had sacrificed a great deal more than his health: project costs had him indebted to the tune of hundreds of thousands of dollars and had resulted in alienating him from his family members. But he was by no means the last martyr the ziggurat would claim...

In observing and mining local customs, Kahn envisioned a huge, rectangular constellation of elevated grey basilicas floating on an artificially constructed lake. Because of complicated symmetries, layered juxtapositions, and the meeting of solemn stone and playful water, the immensity of the overwhelming grey blocks would be fragmented. And so was it realized. While the central stone-coloured blocks possess an air of immovability, the pool's clear surfaces boast a panorama of stairs, columns and patterns that ripple and flex infinitely. Onlookers feel disoriented near the reflecting waters. An abyss of illusory hallways suddenly appears to confound body and mind. And this, too, is exactly what Kahn intended; he publicly insisted that the interior be a 'world within a world'.

Kahn designed the capitol complex to incorporate a mosque in addition to guesthouses, dining halls and a hospital. While the initial allotment provided to him was only three thousand square feet, Kahn held out for a grander mosque. However, he approached inclusion of the mosque in a very peculiar fashion. He initially proposed raising the prayer hall a small distance away but aligned perfectly with the overall axis of the complex. When West Pakistani controllers objected, Kahn redesigned the mosque to be integrated as one of the four corners of the assembly, but shifted it off axis, purportedly to face towards Mecca to the west. Furthermore, he altered its shape into a pyramid and employed a baroque geometry that was entirely uncharacteristic of the southeast Asian idioms he had otherwise employed. In not allowing the national assembly to silently absorb a mosque, was Kahn perhaps, consciously or otherwise, expressing a personal bias for the separation of religion and state? Had he knowingly ensured in this design that the two remain perpetually locked in dialogue?

The Philadelphian had unmistakably absorbed how diverse religions had inhabited East Bengal. In a nation rife with the bequests of multiple denominations, it is almost inconceivable to me that Kahn had not picked up on the dynamics and tensions of plurality. Just a few years later, in 1972, the Four Founding Principles inaugurated in the first Bangladeshi Constitution included secularism alongside nationalism, socialism and democracy.

Hence the earlier mentioned protests to the insertion of Islam into legislative codes. This was a process that Sheikh Mujib himself had idiosyncratically inspired. The founder-president of the country publicly boasted that Bangladesh was the second most populous 'Muslim state' in the world. Mujib also abandoned usage of the secular Bangladeshi salutation *'Joy Bangla'* (Long Live Bengal) in favour of the Islamic *'Khoda Hafez'* (May God Protect You).[18] Reflecting the incorporation of Islamic expressions in his private vernacular, in his public appearances Mujib employed Islamic greetings, slogans and ideological allusions. The President even led prayers at a mosque on 4 November 1972. Mujib revived and then elevated the Islamic Academy (which had been banned in 1972 for suspected collusion with Pakistani forces) as a foundation to propagate Islamic ideals. His government outlawed the production and sale of alcohol. The 'un-Islamic' sport of horse-racing too met with the same kismet. Mujib sought Bangladesh's membership in the Organisation of the Islamic Conference as well as the Islamic Development Bank. Mujib's government also buckled to religious pressure and tripled the annual budgetary allocation for Islamic schools in 1973. While many reason that all this had to do with the need to woo the patronage of oil-rich Arab statesmen, there is little

---

18 In time, even the phrase *'Khoda Hafez'* would be seen as lacking in piety. Islamic scholars that favoured Arabic diction over others started a campaign to replace the salutation with *'Allah Hafez'* (May Allah Protect You).

doubt Bangladesh was not shaping out to be the secular nation it had initially declared itself to be.

Once General Zia assumed power in 1977, he amplified the prominence of Islam in Bangladesh and the founding principle of 'secularism' was removed altogether from the Constitution. (Two years later, General Zia would purge another of the founding principles: 'socialism' was replaced with 'economic and social justice'.) These trompe-l'œils were not accepted silently. In June 1988, when General Ershad mandated Islam as the Bangladeshi state religion, widespread discontentment was apparent. Politicians, intellectuals and students rejected the governmental imposition. Even though the nation was 85 per cent Muslim at the time, protests broke out on many college campuses. A cross-section of people from all spiritual walks spilled into the streets. Institutional might and a silence on the part of media moguls resulted in General Ershad's dictum being passed. As a result, traditions which were religiously ambiguous or devoid of faith-based content became 'Islamicized'. While the Bangladeshi supreme court would restore secularism as one of the basic tenets of the Constitution in 2010, the decades of religious conditioning had undeniably changed the character of the nation.

Even though Kahn could not have foreknown all of this, he was working in a country that was straddled between the poles of Quranic theocracy and secularism. In this, Bangladesh has not been unlike Malaysia, Turkey, Albania or the Maldives.

In his tours of the region and in his appraisals of its architectures, Kahn had come to develop a deep appreciation for the manner in which religions coexisted in the subcontinent's past. It is almost incontestable that he noticed how temples had been adapted into mosques, vice versa, and back and forth. In conversations with Muzharul Islam, Kahn gaped at how Byzantine hinges ended up in

Buddhist shrines, and how trabeated Hindu porticos merged with arch-and-dome.

On investigating Bengali ruins, Kahn surely detected, too, that resident carpenters had rejected labyrinthine and straight-line patterns imported from the Middle East, preferring stems and fronds from Pala temples. Had Kahn smiled to see how artisans and craftsmen, hardened over time against zealots and their new devotions, refused to abandon techniques when ordered to by transient lords? Any graphic scholar could expound on how the geometries typically ascribed to Islamic art were already extant in Hindu customs in the form of chequered squares, diamond crisscrossings, inter-segmenting circles and swastikas. Kahn was also struck by how homages stretched to the borrowing of mythological figures and constellations from other faiths. In his Bangladeshi journey, Kahn must have brushed up against a certain Nestorian grace, that of the genteel Bengali who refuses to be anything less than welcoming of everyone around him. Egalitarian to the bone, this learned creature championed an unceasing renaissance. This sort of Bengali treads softly, as if the ground beneath is sacred and as though the heavens may at any moment call him home.

The visiting American possibly perceived that those seated in Karachi, Islamabad and Rawalpindi were unaware that something quite different inhabited the air in the East Wing. This air, as Kahn must have gathered, was shared by a population that had thrived, for the most part, in harmony. In the late 1960s, East Bengal/East Pakistan was 4 per cent Christian, 9 per cent Buddhist and animist, 19 per cent Hindu and 68 per cent Muslim. Songs that united the nation boasted lyrics such as, 'Hindus, Buddhists, Christians and Muslims of Bengal – we are all Bengalis'. While we cannot be sure as to how much of the secular Bengali spirit Kahn had encountered in Dhaka, it is not insignificant that in the 'City of Mosques' affiliations between religious groups in the 1950s and 60s were binding enough for them to seamlessly join forces in 1971 to resist a Pakistani attack.

As the years shook out their wrinkles, this religious amity fell victim to greed, resentment and governmental dictates. The Vested Property Act of 1974 legitimized the seizing of properties from Bangladeshi Hindus and encouraged further their exodus, which had initially been spurred by Pakistan's mass exterminations. This exodus ultimately resulted in one of the largest displacements of a population based on ethnic or religious identity; approximately ten million Bengali Hindus (as well as a miscellany of indigenes) fled from Bangladesh to India.

But one cannot expect Kahn to have foreseen these schisms. Rather, he witnessed a passionate solidarity among the Bengalis he encountered. Touched by the spirit of harmony and partnership, Kahn had the secretariat extend its arms away from the parliament towards the city. This greeting is sustained through gardens and orchards that bestow respite to those seeking refuge from the humdrum of downtown Dhaka. Furthermore, as one approaches the main annex, one finds that the hulking grey walls are banded vertically with white strips of marble. Appearing every five feet, these bands reduce the Jatiya Sangsad's massive proportions to small blocks, as if to remind those who walk up and touch its sides that ordinary people, not giants, had stood on each other's backs, raised their hands into the ether, and pieced together this fairy-tale palace.

The gentle stairs and general openness of the floating structure pull in viewers with their softness and warmth. Conversely, in spaces reserved for those in service of the nation, and in the ambulatory where elected functionaries make contact, Kahn's design imparts a breath-taking grandeur. In the majesty of the vast interior, Kahn ensures that all are to be humbled by the mass of stone, steel, shadow and responsibility.

Babu was a child when first exposed to the grand arches of the Capitol. Children typically love its gardens, water troughs and mandalas. Babu was enthralled also by the elegant polygons and squares. The young boy was regaled by the level changes, facades and the numerous intimate recesses. The complex and its ornamentations struck Babu's youthful soul with its playfulness, and he felt invited to sport with others amidst wall, arch and waterway. All the while, parents lounged in cool tree groves, unpacked lunches and bargained with mobile vendors, while in the distance bigwigs in convoys were ushered away.

As a teenager, Babu regularly spent summers with his uncle Rafik Majumdar in Dhaka. Rafik Kaka lived in Dhanmondi on Road 27, about a ten-minute walk from the national assembly. The magnanimous man had seven children, but in his rambling two-storied dwelling he comfortably accommodated companions in need of lodging. Rafik Kaka was an industrialist and owned a readymade garments factory.[19] Long before Babu knew anything about state machinations, when he was just thirteen, he had a formative encounter in the shadows of the Sangsad Bhaban. In his memoirs there are assorted references to the summer of 1985, a pivotal time in the shaping of his weltanschauung. That summer, forces – cosmic and other – aligned in a manner that married Babu to the Sangsad Bhaban for life.

Accompanying two of his favourite cousins, Rafik Kaka's sons, Babu frequented the assembly gardens for games of cricket. Amar and Tanveer were eleven and fifteen respectively and were popular extroverts. Just the same, they had a soft spot for the bookish Babu. Following their lead, Babu had managed to keep his filial promise – he was a tolerably healthy teenager and was even a decent batsman.

---

19 Rafik Kaka expended considerable time and finances in befriending bureaucrats – these connections proved useful when Babu developed political aspirations.

Though prone to bouts of introspection, Babu exercised weekly with Raju and gave his parents little cause for concern.

Near the Reading Room in the Library, across from the Presidential Square, neighbourhood cricketers met to practise. That summer in 1985, when waiting for his turn to bat, a flash in the red brick of a vestibule caught Babu's eye. In an optical twist of fate, it seemed to Babu that an entity had split open the waters to enter the hyphen through a window. Babu could not pinpoint what had emerged from the artificial lake, he awkwardly describes it as a 'shimmering energy' and 'a spooky form that rippled dynamically'.[20] Walking towards the foyer in amazement, Babu claims that a series of images rushed through his mind, overwhelming him. A minute later, a drenched Babu found himself being revived by Tanveer. Babu had apparently slipped into the lake and passed out, terrifying the other boys.

On clearing his throat, Babu sputtered, 'Did you see that? Something jumped into the building, straight from the pool, into that window, that triangle window?' His playmates consoled him, 'Oh, you know Babu how this place is. It's just all the reflections and the light and water. Probably a person was looking out of the window and it looked like they were in the lake.' No matter how much they dismissed the apparition, Babu was convinced that the boys seemed on edge, as if they too had seen freakish things in the circus of the complex. The muted response of his mates convinced Babu that there was a tacit agreement between them to ignore some sorcery the premises sheltered. After all, admitting the validity of Babu's fantastical theory would oblige them to search for safer batting fields.

Babu returned to his uncle's home that day even more quiet and thoughtful than usual. Tanveer forbade Amar from sharing news of the playtime accident. Later that night, Babu would spend hours

---

20   Babu's Bengali version is even more awkward.

in his uncle's Road 27 study. Two publications captivated him: one on the Bangladeshi liberation war of 1971, and the second a pictography on famous Bengali buildings. Rafik Kaka, on seeing Babu's sudden interest in history, opened boxes and recovered catalogues of archaeological digs from the subcontinent. Having never really been bookish himself, he had originally collected the spines for display. Rafik Kaka was pleased that someone had at long last found them useful. The remainder of Babu's summer holiday was split between perusing his uncle's collection, making treks to libraries, and surveying the parliament from up close.

In studying the genealogy of the Sangsad Bhaban, Babu became enthralled with the collaborations and backhanded dealings that were necessary for its completion. He was also smitten by Kahn's personal spiel. While his peers unrelentingly swatted and chased after leather balls, Babu walked around the site with a rusty Polaroid given to him by his uncle. Most anyone who has found himself in proximity to Kahn's work of genius readily admits to being affected by its heady aura and overwhelming character. Caretakers and guards at the estate acquire an otherworldly air. Their detachment comes not from affluence (acquired via tourists seeking access to restricted areas) but, as colleagues maintain, from being awakened to transcendental wisdom and insight. Babu learned from acknowledged gossip masters that staff members, clicking in Solomon's language and scratching at their foreheads where a third eye might have diagrammatically fit, frequently abandon their posts after emotional meltdowns. It seems that only the strong-minded are able to reconcile the perplexing mandate of Kahn's legacy.

On returning to Tangail, Babu found that his parents were only too happy to supply him with a number of fascinating volumes, photos and newspaper articles, which sustained his newfound enthusiasm for all things related to the Sangsad Bhaban. When Babu returned to Dhaka the following summer, Tanveer and Amar greeted a solemn and pensive cousin. It became evident at dinner that night that Babu was obsessed with Kahn's work of genius, and that he had been reading a great deal.

But there was one adventure that Babu had shared with no one. In March 1986, Babu had chanced upon a clique that nourished his fascination with parliament 'fretwork'. Two men had approached him at a book festival where he was collecting materials on architects and their works. They exchanged pleasantries with Babu for a few minutes, long enough for brown eyes that glinted behind steely frames to appraise the teenager's substantial learnedness. When Babu babbled about being captivated by Kahn's tour de force above all other structures, they quickly exchanged glances and beheld the young scholar even more intensely. To Babu's curiosity, they recited in unison:

The child, in love with prints and maps,
Holds the whole world in his vast appetite.
How large the earth is under the lamplight!
But...

There they stopped, and smiled at Babu and each other. They informed Babu that they were members of a collective of folklorists, historians, ecologists, astrologers and anthropologists who studied endemic artistry. Entreating Babu to share his progress with them, they rattled off authors and digests he needed to deliberate over. Babu scrambled to jot these down, but the men chuckled that there was no rush and that, as long as he stayed in touch, they would aid him.

The men mesmerized Babu. He writes in an entry from April 2014 that they seemed to him 'wizards with gimlet eyes'. Babu rated them as privy to some 'obscure inner mana', to how gyres turned, and to where 'central gears pivoted'. As Babu traded his mailing information with them, his hands shook with excitement. Therein began a regular correspondence that would last years.

In 1986, blistering afternoons did not deter Babu as he canvassed the crowded mohalla for stories related to the Capitol. Though Rafik Kaka, Amar and Tanveer were all bewildered by Babu's odd fixation, Tanveer was noticeably testy. He was no fool and had not forgotten the previous year's fainting mishap. Worried that Babu might be dabbling in the 'black arts', Tanveer cross-examined him. On settling that there was nothing amiss[21] and that not a whiff of witchery could be disinterred, Tanveer pressed family members to support his cousin's passion for historical inquiry. Amar gladly obliged, he looked up to both brothers and never thought less of Babu for his horn-rimmed glasses.

Once a week or thereabouts, Babu would forward anything notable to the two scholars who remain unnamed in Babu's memoirs (it is likely that they never provided him with their details). They steered him through a parliamentary maze of stories in their letters. They also saw to it that Babu was suitably acquainted with the diverse stages and philosophies of world architecture. From Classicism to Brutalism, and from to Lu Ban's and Herod's manuscripts to singing rocks, they kept the novitiate reading.

In 1987 and 1988, Babu continued to uncover eerie legends that gummed the legislatorial grounds. There purportedly exist 'beauty' suites that are avoided by many. These assembly quarters are flooded with ethereal amber light that bounces off the walls and vaulted ceilings, lending the forms within an inexpressible joy. There are also lullaby-like murmurs that emanate due to the movement of air.[22] Many also claim that the rooms carry the mystifying and disarming fragrance of mango.

---

21 As proceedings shall reveal anon, perhaps Tanveer's qualms were not entirely without merit.

22 As Babu would identify in the years to come, highly esteemed scientists such as Nikola Tesla have found that, along their natural scales, smooth sinusoidal waveforms emit alpha brainwaves between 6 and 8 Hertz which induce a calm and meditative state in the human mind.

These compartments have, at more than one juncture, hosted the signing of inexplicably noble pacts and unexpected confessions. Those in the know avoid these chambers; office holders press-ganging fiats that are anything but noble steer away from them. Nonetheless, it is unfathomable to insiders how unscrupulous dealmakers (who know better) still end up inside these salons. Venal policymakers continue to fall prey to scheduling errors, missing signage and faulty lighting. In 1985, a contingent of foreign oil companies met with Bangladeshi energy agents in one of these rooms to sign irrationally unprofitable contracts. Multinational executives and local brokers jointly sacrificed compensations and commissions for clauses ensuring eco-friendly operations and massive investments in projects for the rural poor. A few years prior to this petrochemical windfall, a similar incident known to some as the '1979 Swedish Chartered Fiasco' had transpired in the same section of the Bhaban. Trustees of a multi-donor fund established by Sweden, Denmark and the United Kingdom had waived three hundred million pounds sterling in bad debt. In magnanimous reciprocity, Bangladeshi bureaucrats donated millions of their 'own' to launch microcredit institutions catering to the destitute. In some preposterous variety of a potlatch, four teary-eyed functionaries also admitted to having robbed ministerial accounts. This resulted in a front page scorcher of major proportions as magpie nests were torn asunder.

In the 1979 case, as in that of 1985, there were no embedded stipulations or 'catches' in implementing the miraculous grants. Beyond the vicinity of the hypnotizing and ecstatic 'beauty' rooms, confused directors frantically attempted to backpedal. However, they finalized treaties, blockchained smart-contracts and confessions so exhaustively that there was no scope to recover lost treasures and privileges.

Queer stories also allude to the exterior of the premises. Those sitting alongside its waters on winter evenings can descry how the compound periodically disappears into the mist. On steamy monsoon afternoons too, one may lose sight of its lichen-speckled walls. When festooned with lights for national celebrations, the grand lobby may appear to be ablaze as firefighters haplessly combat spectres and shifting flames.

Myths surrounding the ostensorium also include peculiar disappearances: on numerous instances, individuals and entire teams of administrators have gone missing for hours, reappearing with stories of having walked into a maze of deserted levels and rooms. On other occasions, diplomats complained of attacks by bats inside the main vestibule, or being deafened and terrified by the sound of pounding drums. According to some, a famous VIP vanished and, on resurfacing the next day, claimed that she had been held spellbound in a lonely corner by divine, birdlike singing. There was also a parable about a famous crime-lord who was strangled by a titanic constrictor in the garden. Still others point to its trees ... tall trees that twist and bend towards one another, always moving, watching and whispering. Babu writes of a delirious man, one sunset in August, running from the West Gardens shouting, 'The green, the green, the green.' As Babu inspected the tall and lonely palms, he too was carried away, and colourfully describes how they stood before him 'like fighting giants, like sentinels of some endangered race. With beards of down, these verdant tricksters had a grail to preserve, one that was ever growing and multiplying, shooting underground to spread green veins in the sky.'

And just as poor Babu had tripped, more than one unlucky leader has injuriously traversed the holding's snaky garden walkways. While broken long bones and dislocated shoulders are nothing new, in 1994 there was considerable hue and cry when a disreputable strongman, along with two bodyguards, was found dead in the shallow lake. By chance, a cameraman on the fourth floor of an adjacent hall vividly captured what transpired. His footage revealed how Boss Robin lost traction on the redbrick footpath to roll into the water unconscious. The two goons followed suit, though it is dubious whether they did so voluntarily. In the film, they wave their arms in an attempt to maintain balance, but slither into the water face forward. Of the two, one is knocked senseless and lays still. The other thrashes about in three feet of water for roughly twenty seconds before collapsing. In their investigations, detectives concluded that the subordinate had either experienced a seizure of some sort or been panic-stricken to the extent that he was unable to regain his wits. As indexed in his medical files, the tough did not suffer from any physical diseases – there were only logs of knife and gunshot injuries. In the recorded film, with the right eyes, one may espy ropes of writhing and whirling liquids envelop him.

There was also the disaster of 1988 that happened two months before Babu's June pilgrimage. A guesthouse wall at the Bhaban collapsed, killing three bank directors who were attendees at an exclusive conclave with seven financial luminaries. In the tradition of J.P. Morgan's Jekyll Island manoeuvring, they had taken phenomenal pains to keep their congress secret. In this instance, the objective was to manipulate the benchmark index of the Dhaka Stock Exchange. Capitalizing on the low central bank interest rate, they would have been able to create a financial crisis (à la the Wall Street crash of 1929). The plot was stymied in the inquiries that followed the peculiar disintegration of the guesthouse fortification. Had their scheme succeeded, they would have left millions of investors bankrupt. Of course, along with offspring and heirs, these men and their vile maxims would determinatively take their hindmost in 2002, and again in 2010 when the exchange astonishingly dropped 1,800 points in twenty-eight days. These heirs were likewise believed to have caused the Syndicated Bangladeshi Banking Collapse of 2021, when sixty of seventy-eight license-holders went belly up due to 'misdirected' capital reserves.

In the commotion of 1988, detectives flew in from around the world but failed to explain how the hefty panel had fallen. One conclusion postulated by sleuths was that, as the annex in question had been used in 1971 as an ammunitions depot, a quantity of overlooked explosives buried in its foundations had somehow fulminated. Stock Exchange potentates ensured that the intrigue received scant media coverage.

Babu gathered other stories from employees at the Secretariat; several custodians had worked there for decades. Babu, patient and humble, earned their trust. When Babu conveyed his discoveries to his two tight-lipped advisors, he was to find that they were already au courant. In the summer of 1986, and in the following five years, Babu collected more and more accounts. A particularly bizarre occurrence involved the entire 800 million ton (an estimated figure) Sangsad Bhaban disappearing for days. This had happened in a winter of national discontent, just before a military dictator was to relinquish his post. An abyss of fog and mist rolled in to shroud the entire complex. Roads and walkways were suddenly covered in carpets of algae and moss, conspiring to thwart attempts to approach the facility by car or foot.

A sexagenarian gardener disclosed to Babu: 'None of them could find the main hall, even with their expensive binoculars and fancy equipment. But I did not give up. I crawled on my knees to the East Wing, to an unused shed where I stored my belongings. Hai, hai, it was as if the whole damn place had decided no human was to enter. The shed doors couldn't be opened. The wooden framework had become waterlogged and warped. I gave up and crawled out covered in green filth, and on my way out I saw all manner of dark shapes moving around. It was terrifying. That place is still terrifying to me, with all its caves and holes. I cannot understand it.' News briefs affirm that after nine days the mists rolled away and, as totalitarians were imprisoned, heavy rains washed the Bhaban clean. Even though rotted wooden doors and lintels were replaced, the assembly has never been one to guarantee entryway to king, courtier or subject.

Towards the culmination of 1988, Babu's long-distance counsellors thought it apt to reveal details about their collective to the assiduous teenager. So far, they had divulged next to diddly about their work. Even the address they had provided Babu with was for a postal box in an obscure town. But in 1988, they agreed that the trainee had earned his stripes and could be trusted with specifics.

As Babu writes, on a summer day that year the two men met him in a shed near the capitol. The appointment was in the late afternoon and the sun shone down fiercely. When Babu faced them, as always, he could not tell them apart. They seemed gravitationally unbound to human precepts. Babu's head reeled as they explained that they were enlistees in a community that studied regional and international histories to better comprehend Kahn's gift. We will name this secretive coterie the Sangsad Bhaban Group (SBG) for purposes of narrative ease.

That day, the two SBG mystagogues also revealed their core tenets to Babu. They divulged that, after twenty years of investigations, their group had determined that the Sangsad Bhaban was located at a rare intersection of 'cosmic' influences. Lines were mentioned, those of spirits, dragons, mystics and dreams. Babu was alerted that, in order to understand these energies better, he would need to survey shamanic practices the world over. They were forceful in repudiating 'black sorcerers' of all varieties. They underlined how they only pursued wajib kifa'i and miracles spoken of by Muhammad Al-Ghazzali, Mulla Sadra and Murtada Mutahhari as obligatory for choice believers. They highlighted how their curriculum also followed in the sacred spirit of five-thousand-year-old Vedic astrology (jyotisha), in the divine notion of Hamsa and its chakras, and in the Buddhist tradition of mudras and mandalas.

Having assured him of the noblesse of the work, they then directed him to meditate on divination as applied variously in South America, Africa, Europe, Asia and Australia. Inchmeal, they directed him from prehistory, through the Middle Ages to the numerous renaissances and beyond. Though it would only be after three years of dredging that Babu would comprehend how Kahn's bequest and these métiers connected, he obediently took on the assignments. There is no indication to date that his parents knew anything about the mysterious swamis.

Even though Babu was disquieted by the avant garde bearing of his scholarship, the notion that Kahn's masterpiece derives an intelligence from natural forces was evidently not implausible to him. And as he kept studying, he mapped out SBG-endorsed threads to the dateless beginnings of men and their edifices. Engulfed by dusty volumes, he confirmed how man has universally been mystified by Noachian constructions and aesthetic projects. Babu increasingly developed a profound understanding of these matters. Years afterwards, he mused learnedly in his essays:

'As he came out of bogs and swung down sturdy branches, early man chose to rest near water, trees and, oftentimes, rock formations. In choosing what lands were best suited for habitation, man engaged in the first exercises of geomancy, deciding which side his entryway should face, and where rock, tree and stream should ideally lie. Very quickly, he learned to read the sky and follow stars in charting new homes, new civilizations and new empires. Man sprinted into the future, acquiring an astounding diversity of skills, and as he discarded weighty old tools, he developed elegant new ones. From the astronomical alignments of timeless megaliths, sepulchres, earthen mounds, and henges, to the geometries of the Great Pyramid of Giza; from the massive precision of the

stones of Peruvian Sacsayhuamán to the brooding silence of the
moai of Easter Island; and from the mirror at the Lighthouse of
Alexandria to the thousand-roomed Tibetan Potala Palace; our
technologies are yet to explain how the heavens reached down to
touch us so. As with the 'Tower of Brahma' puzzle at the temple in
Kashi Vishwanath, savants are compelled by echoed prophecies to
decode anagrams, even if they bring our world to an instantaneous
end.

'While select mavens accessed galactic orders to model earthly
maps and navels, others listened to reverberations within their
bodies and under the earth to manipulate sound with architectural
mass, texture and contour. Still others looked within their anima
and projected paintings and carvings on to caves and walls –
these surfaces are able to stir us deeply, as even today they impart
prophetic clarity and vision.'[23]

---

23 Babu (Bangladesh) Majumdar from 'Architecture'. He continues:
'Enchanted sites and habitats have forever blessed or cursed our destinies.
Greek and Druid oracles, like those of the prehistoric Americas, Chinas,
Indias and Africas, have shoved the barrows of time on to new trajectories and
courses unknown. The origin of many a holy site is shrouded in superstition
and mythos; while human hands are thought to have contributed, fantasts
assure us that the otherworldly has typically nudged beauty towards the
sublime. In many cases, stories abound regarding how angels and numinous
fingers assisted in the production of these wonders. Solomon was said to have
commandeered djinns to complete his First Temple at Jerusalem. Stonehenge
had the marvels of Merlin, and the dwarf magus Uxmal is thought to have
built his Mayan city in a single night. So did ghosts dig the Chand Baori wells
in Rajasthan. Nocturnal angels are popularly attributed the engineering feats
of the Ethiopian churches of Lalibela. Only high priests may access records of
this supernatural design. The Javanese Prambanan temples were also allegedly
built with the help of genies in a matter of hours. The Gayebi Masjid in Syhelt,
a three hour northeast drive from Dhaka, like other 'gayebi' mosques, is said
have just appeared one morning, free of human manufacture. And of course,
one cannot ignore the elephantine pyramids of ancient Egypt and tales of
their extra-terrestrial design. Hindu temple architecture is based on design

In the winter of 1988, the SBG turned Babu on to how he could travel to these foreign destinations himself and witness first hand their splendours. They brought to his attention travel grants for exceptional high school students. These grants were provided by Saudi, Asian and European foundations. With the help of the SBG, Babu obtained five such awards as a teenager. For a middle-class Bangladeshi youth, he was privileged to disembark at metropolises in four continents. Mr and Mrs Majumdar were only too delighted to help him fill out essays and applications – they had pronounced faith in Babu's good sense and, moreover, were hopeful that sightseeing might coax him out a little from his pedagogic shell. They kissed benedictions on to his forehead as he rushed to fill stand-by seats, soon to return with fascinating stories and pictures. Soon after kicking off on these jaunts, Babu began to himself acquire steel in his outlook.

It is poignant that, despite travelling to exotic milieus to seek inspiration, it was in Dhaka again that Babu was to experience his next startling revelation. This would take place in 1992. The breadcrumbs of this epiphany trailed all the way from Dhanmondi to Děčín and from Amman to Aarhus...

Babu had read about Kahn's mother, Bertha Mendelsohn, and her Delphian pursuits. Her influence was formative and ensured that a strong Germanic cultural presence informed Kahn's sensibilities. In addition, she had instructed her child on Jewish mysticism, including the Kabbalah and its adaptations. Latvian born, she had

---

principles and guidelines believed to have been laid by the universal architect Vishvakarma. The Quranic notion of paradise is that of a luxurious garden. Yet, as humans, we continue to give in to the impulse to raise walls around our orchards, denying ourselves of bounty and belonging to the unbound. In creating partitions and raising walls, man accelerates his ability to name things and separate himself from beasts and other men. He then increasingly shelters personal idols. As man distances and fears his tutelary spirits, men find themselves needing more walls.'

been extremely well educated. Besides being a gifted musician and a transcendentalist, she was an expert on Goethe and taught her son the metaphysical principles of the German Romantic genius. Babu, like most school-going Bengali teenagers, was vaguely familiar with Goethe's works. In 1974, in bustling Dhanmondi and a mere ten minutes from the Sangsad Bhaban, an institute was built to honour the author of *Faust*. A few years later, in 1983, the Humboldt Club in Bangladesh honoured another renowned Bavarian, the geographer and historian, Freiherr von Humboldt. But it was at the Goethe Institut in Dhaka that Babu unearthed an association that was to shock him.

Goethe, who had been fascinated with all things 'oriental' including Islamic and Sufi matters, brooded over Arabic grammar, travel-books, poetry, philo-anthologies and even biographies of Prophet Muhammad (PBUH). After the death of Frederick the Great in 1796, Goethe chanced upon an Egyptian obelisk in Rome and became enchanted with it. This beautiful granite specimen had symbols etched on it – indecipherable to most – but to Goethe there was something uncanny about the hieroglyphs. He had India rubber casts made of the obelisk, and grew so attached to them that he carried them with him on his travels.

One of these casts made its way to Dhaka in 1992, on loan from the Goethe Institut in Prague for a fundraiser in Dhanmondi. Upon coming across the cast in a cordoned-off display, it occurred to Babu that the hieroglyphs on it were virtually identical to North African geomantic symbols.[24]

---

24 These sixteen symbols were the very same ones that Jewish scholars believed to form the famous Sephirot Tree of Life in the Kabbalah. By the ninth century, there were numerous references in occult Judaic literature to this 'science of the sands'. According to Hermetic texts, the code has a mythological lineage descending from Prophet Idris, a man often identified with the Biblical Enoch. As legend has it, Idris was taught the system by Archangel Jibril, the Biblical Gabriel. In the European Renaissance,

And then, another sudden discernment left Babu clutching at table-tops and nearby patrons of the arts: Babu apprehended that *these alphabetic figures were present at the site of the Sangsad Bhaban itself.* Not being privy to the joys of bio-nano 3D printers and having only encountered the symbols in cheap prints, it was via a rubber mould of Goethe's obelisk that Babu came to affiliate Kahn's three-dimensional colossus with the African praxis of reading the future.

Babu rushed to the Bhaban. He circled and scrutinized the grounds and was able to identify most of the sixteen ciphers. Some were embedded within the geometric designs with which Kahn had embellished the Assembly. Even more figures were cast as shadows on the walls and, as the sun moved, old patterns disappeared to be replaced by new ones. Once darkness descended, Babu found that the arrangements created by electric lights were refreshed as tungsten bulbs flickered and as rippling waters reflected off the walls.

After a sleepless night, an excited Babu returned at daybreak to confirm that, due to altered atmospheric conditions, the cryptograms cast as shadows had again mutated overnight. The stonework was a true geomantic slate on which heliograms might deviate and transform hourly. In a twelve-page letter, Babu nervously explained his newfound theory to the SBG scholars. Babu cited umpteen examples, he referred to arcane Japanese concepts in which light may both obscure and reveal shapes and outlines. He wrote of the 1,100-year-old Temple of Kukulcan, where on spring and autumn equinoxes silhouettes appear on its pyramid as a serpent wriggling downward. Babu invoked the Great Mosque of Divrigi with its wondrous mirages of praying men and, of course, the play of lights and stars at the Rajput Jantar Mantars in Jaipur

---

geomancy was classified as one of the seven 'forbidden arts', along with necromancy, hydromancy, aeromancy, pyromancy, chiromancy (palmistry) and scapulimancy.

and Delhi. Babu alluded to the mysteries of the 'shadowless' Tamil
temple of Thanjavur, the effulgent weightlessness of Saint Chapelle,
the dancing floors at the Argentine Cathedral of Saltas, and the
ethereally glowing caves at Divje Babe in Slovenia. Babu pencil-
sketched several of the sixteen symbols to support his point. In spite
of the parallels, Babu fully expected his outlandish contention to be
dismissed.

But the surprises kept rolling in as the two gurus drafted and
signed a congratulatory response. It notified Babu that he was ready
to be formally introduced to other guild associates. An offer of
tier-2 membership was implied. The letter also underscored that,
although Kahn's interest in Egyptian hieroglyphics was known to a
scattering of bookworms, almost none had deduced that geomantic
symbols were enabled at the Dhaka site.

Babu's SBG friends did not trust this correspondence to postal
authorities. An uncommunicative boy of Babu's age hand-delivered
it. The dispatch explained to Babu the need for confidentiality.
It specified that, although the SBG was a scrupulous group
of 'watchers', privacy was vital in ensuring that the riddles of
the Capitol did not fall into the wrong hands. The 'SBG-ians'
proclaimed that there were colluders who wished to direct the
faculties of the Capitol towards purposes that were anything but
just and egalitarian. Learning from the fate of societies such as the
Knights Templar, the Bilderbergs and the International Order of St.
Hubertus, the SBG worked hard to remain a force for good. They
vouched this was imperative, notwithstanding how the Bhaban
itself rejected wrongdoing.

Babu was strictly mandated not to share his findings with others.
As the letter said: 'Young Babu, what you have to understand is that
the journey towards unlocking the tools within Kahn's composition
is a gradual one – it unfolds in steps. If you advertise your results,
the effects could be disastrous. True divination requires generations

to master, and initiates are chosen by forces we cannot command, by energies that lie in the skies, in the Earth and in the zinc of our blood. Your arrival at this particular cosmic kaleidoscope is most auspicious and has transpired far sooner than we expected. However, the spine of your *Puer* has barely hardened. It will take you years to fathom how to read occult signs in the national assembly, how to pose questions and how to elicit answers. You will have to find the Cup of Jamshid that Kahn left and drink from it. But to do this, you will have to be ruthless with yourself. You must always question your motives or you will never follow the truth, but rather what pleases you. Regarding our Sangsad Bhaban, the disclosures that you will find in its masonry are to be used for good only; mistakes are forbidden and punishments are severe. One day – years, maybe decades from now – when you are truly awakened, you may be blessed with your own disciples. And you will learn that there is no systematized manual with which to predict the future, but rather signposts that illuminate strong potentials. Rather than tell us what is going to happen, they recommend courses of action. You will come to learn this. But for now, this strange humming that surrounds you must be grasped in the pit of your stomach and concealed.' The message continued in this rather bizarre and unnerving spirit for several pages. Peppered with idioms and argots, it concluded with an order to burn after reading. Babu did not follow this final directive. Perhaps he saved the lengthy letter to better follow its elaborate instructions. I found it folded inside his ledgers. Nonetheless, the whole business frightened Babu sufficiently to ensure that he would indeed seal his lips and clutch his bowels tightly for years to come.

Over the next few years, Babu would direct tremendous efforts towards mastering the geomantic tradition in question. He meticulously analysed the workings of their four elements, their zodiacal correspondences, and their active and passive natures. He ruminated on their directions, types, elemental rulers and declinations. Then there was the translation of the figures into Boolean values or binary numbers with possible inversions and reversions.[25] Like Shakespeare, Dante,[26] and al-Buni, Babu was mesmerized by the veiled importance of the letter T and its calculation in tombs and temples. There were also Schumann resonances to chart and lightning discharges in the ionosphere to make sense of. He also found himself immersed in sub-continental schools of divination, including Islamic algorithms and intonations, the Vedic origins of Ramal, and the sorcery of bata and tea leaves. Much of this arcana is far too labyrinthine for me to perceive. To compensate for this, I shared excerpts from Babu's essay 'Divination' with pundits who heartily validated his logic and conclusions. At times, Babu wondered if he were truly ready for the curriculum he was exposed to.[27] But Babu had never forgotten Kanu's lessons on the need for balance, and was diligent in not straying from the blessed teachings of the angels Harut and Marut. He mentions praying regularly to ensure his dīn and his nafs stayed pure. Moreover, the two crackerjacks kept numerous eyes on him.

At this point, it will be necessary for our narrative to leap several years forward. In Babu's diary, almost a hundred pages covering these years are missing. Howbeit, our thriller will hold. When obliged, our timeline will be buttressed by first-hand testimonies and media reports. These missing years, while surely eventful, are

---

25 Much of this scholarship had developed when sub-Saharan traditions of *ifá* and sikidy travelled north and then into Europe, Arabia and India, meeting a mirror of themselves, and a likely partner in the trigrams and hexagrams of the Chinese I-Ching. Translators of these oracular traditions incorporated regional techniques in tailoring systems to their needs.

26 Dante's *Purgatoria* touches on the African 'sand science' in the first two stanzas of Canto 19.

27 There are veiled allusions in Babu's diary to new cognizance he had acquired and how he was worried he was too young 'to see so much'.

not vital to our understanding of where Babu was heading. The data I have accumulated indicates that his bearing as an apprentice never wavered.

We propel ourselves five years later to October 1994, when Babu was enrolled at Dhaka University. He was twenty-two, and in his third year of undergraduate pursuits. Insomuch as his tourism had provided contacts and coveted scholarships abroad, it is significant that he chose to remain in Bangladesh for his education. Mr and Mrs Majumdar, patriots that they were, had mixed emotions about this choice but deferred to Babu's judgement.

Tanveer had finagled a room for Babu to share with two others in Jagannath Hall. Even more, one of the new roommates was Babu's old friend Munna![28]

The youths wasted no time in renovating their past camaraderie. Munna had always been large, but in the years since they had parted ways, he had grown into a six-foot, 240-pound heavyweight. Some things were the same though: the gentle big-for-nothing still possessed an astute intellect as was evident from the full scholarship he had at the prestigious Department of Computer Science and Engineering.

As they roamed the city together, as they stood in line for 5 a.m. Haji Biryani, as they waited out the never-ending rains at tea stalls, and as they flipped through the latest albums at Rainbow and Geetali, the ingénues grew closer than ever before. The pair rifled through Bongo and College Gate shops for defective garments that were still wearable. Babu and Munna saved for weekend meals at Thatari Bazaar and Al-Razzaque, and then jointly suffered from stomach ulcers which were buried with tea. They spent Eids together, calling first on their favourite bloodstock, and then on the more affluent ones who would gift them crisp 100-taka notes. The

---

28 Amar had run across him on campus, and on recognizing the hulk, he
    collected Munna's details.

duo would then tuck in for Eid movie marathons; uninterrupted
by commercials, BTV featured old English favourites and the witty
Ityadi. The roommates would endeavour to flirt with women at
Madhu Canteen and at Chawk Bazaar hotspots, and engage in
'balcony flirting' from Rafik Kaka's Road 27 house. They were
customarily unsuccessful. The childhood buddies pooled finances
to haggle with fishermen from the Buriganga: in those days, the
unpolluted river yielded a selection of catches. Babu and Munna
whispered to each other in Balaka Cinema Hall while arguing over
directors. They would prank call women from their classes, but hang
up nervously without introducing themselves. Bi-weekly, the pair
would haunt Abahoni Matth to watch their favourite cricket team
practise. On holidays, they would go fishing at the very fashionable
Dhanmondi Lake.

Babu was moved to shed tears on his chicken cheese-burger at
Swiss Bakery when, out of the blue, Munna recounted Kanu's death
and how he too had been aggrieved. He said, 'Babu, I can never
understand how we do these things to each other, you know, how
Bangladeshis can hate so much, and for what? What they did to Kanu,
I can never forget. I also saw what had happened that morning, that
day I had been walking alone to Bibekananda, you see. After you left
the gang, I did the same. I was not interested in playing mindless
games. Like you, I became ... serious. And brother, I want to make
an impact, I want to fight for all the Kanus.' The lads stared at each
other, shuddering like infants, each drawing strength from the other
and, for the first time, Babu divulged confidences he had not even
allowed Tanveer and Amar.

College life was wonderful for the pair to reconnect. But life in the
dormitories was demanding – due to overcrowding, many students
had to sleep on verandas and sweltering rooftops. A majority
broke out in heat hives that mosaicked their body in jackfruit-like
spikes. Others succumbed to Neglected Tropical Diseases (NTDs)

including dengue, hookworm infection, lymphatic filariasis, chikungunya, rabies, amoebiasis, Japanese encephalitis and malaria. In emergencies, Babu would rush to Road 27, Dhanmondi, to use his cousins' dial-up internet and download medical notes.

Dhaka University in the mid-nineties emitted a bouquet of agitations. Protests against General Ershad had started in 1983 – soon after the administrator assumed power by means of a bloodless military coup and imposed martial law. An interesting aspect of the student rising was that a large portion of sophomoric Bangladeshis wanted to tear down the dictatorship and set up a leftist government.[29] Visions and reflections from 1971 had boomeranged into an uprising where political parties liaised. Granting that the military-head had resigned in December 1990, the march towards democratization was not yet extinct in Dhaka University. Anti-imperialist graffiti had only recently been washed off campus walls. A sprinkling of urban revolutionaries had yet to abandon their Star cigarettes, along with towering ideals.

While this was peripherally the case, there was a fever underway that was diametrically polar. Students from upper-middle and middle class backgrounds had become frantic to leave the motherland and resume their studies abroad. Concocting ruses to cheat on their TOEFL exams, the bulk applied to US universities. Guardians sold land, assets, jewellery, etc. to finance migration bids. The American Centre, called the USIS, became the focal point for students completing their high school. While Babu and Munna were not disposed to forsake the homeland, they empathized with Bangladeshis who despaired of democracy being attained. The

---

29   In 1987, the movement gathered fierce impetus when, at a rally, a pro-democracy activist named Nur Hossain, with the slogan 'Down with the autocrat, let democracy be free' written on his gaunt body, was shot and killed by the police. Bangladeshis have never taken well to gaunt students being assassinated by badge-wearers.

fever to quit their birthplace, along with the escalation of capital flight, still grips many a Bangladeshi presently...

This Bangladeshi hysteria to emigrate in the mid-nineties was quite justifiable. Despite paying lip service to principled and participatory jurisprudence, the truth is that Dhaka University was rotting from within. The decay became manifest during the anti-Ershad campaign, when student-elects from the Dhaka University Central Students Union (DUCSU) astounded peers with their duplicity and venality. DUCSU had traditionally contributed to civil reformation, but circumstances had declined en bloc. Bribery and the misuse of fiduciary clout were infused into enrolment processes, housing applications, examination panels, faculty recruitment and grounds management. It was dismaying to hear that male dormitories had become drug dens, that lecturers had to cede test-papers to brutal pupils before finals week, that departmental funds were confiscated by entrenched factions, and that attractive females were habitually abducted and raped by undergraduate captains. Although Babu and Munna were shielded from much of this due to Amar and Tanveer's connects (of course, Munna's girth was a factor too), both witnessed extreme acts of bullying.[30] The daily and public outrages they surveyed on the defenceless began to increasingly distress them.

By fall of 1994, due to 'session jams' and departmental closures, Babu's matriculation in Geographic Studies was deferred for an additional two years. It was at this pedagogic bottleneck that Babu first caught the student politics 'bug'. After years of exploring the

---

30 Amar was in high school at the time, and was shaping out to be sociable and intelligent. He was more philosophically inclined than Tanveer, whose rough neck sported impressive scars. Tanveer was thriving in their father's office, a mere ten minutes away. His repute kept troublemakers away. The four would regularly dine together and, as always, when the cousins swung by, Babu would find himself the centre of an admiring crowd.

globe, revising geomantic registers, and pondering men whose eyes were full of future, Babu was awestruck by those who grip the halters of nations. He reckoned it was time for him to do his share. As with Dhaka University, the country was in partisan shambles. There were almost daily curfews, strikes and street fights. Babu ranked himself as a good candidate for the governmental sphere as his convictions were genuine. By now, he was fully aware that student politics in Bangladesh was infected with violence and greed. Even so, Babu was positive: university politics had almost always been a mixed blessing ever since student movements had galvanized against both British and then Pakistani rule. All parties in the nation had active student wings; undergraduates have even been elected to the parliament, cheekily pushing aside seniors.

In Bangladesh version 1994, a mingle-mangle of titans competed for leverage. An apt classification of Bangladesh, then and now, would place it as a transnational and multi-level deep-state anarchy. Controllers and implementers included foreign intelligence and security apparatuses, transnational cartels, political and fiduciary heavyweights, oligarchs and dynasts, military and civilian bureaucrats, and the clergy. There was room for X-factors and rare birds but, for the thumping majority, every sphere had identifiable key players that vied to influence outcomes. Overall and in summation, the machinery of governance operated anarchically.

In 1994, the republic had an unofficial two-party system, with the Bangladeshi Nationalist Party (BNP) and the Awami League (AL) being the main contenders. They remained unrivalled as homegrown contestants in a struggle for organizational supremacy. Smaller fish (who usually allied with one of the two titans) included the Jamaat-i-Islami (Jamaat) and the Jatiya Party (JP). There was also a mélange of splintered leftist parties, some Marxist, some Leninist, some neither and some both. All of them grotesquely nibbled at the feet of either the BNP or the AL.

The party in command in 1994 was the Bangladeshi Nationalist
Party (BNP). Formed in 1978 in the bloody smithy of coups and
counter-coups, its creator was (the previously encountered and
already murdered) Lieutenant General Zia. Ideologically, BNP
differed little from the JP, which was incepted in 1986 by Lieutenant
General Hussain Muhammad Ershad. Both parties stressed the
importance of democracy, transparency, nationalism and free-
market economics, tempered with Islamic codes. While the AL had
originally included secularism as a founding principle, Jamaat, a far-
right Islamic party had 'theo-critically' opposed the creation of an
independent Bangladesh. Jamaat also faced condemnation for their
persecution of religious minorities and women, and their insistence
on Sharia law for the archipelago. Despite this, even cynical
Bangladeshi lawmakers acceded that many Jamaat joiners had
sacrificed personal fortunes to advance the interests of the Islamic
poor. Both the AL and Jamaat had historical roots that reached far
into the past. The Workers Party (WP) was yet another small fry
and had similarly evolved from disparate earlier consortiums. They
sought to implement socialist reforms through democratic means.

Despite their avowed principles and ideological charters, in
practice most Bangladeshi leaders operated with identical agendas
for personal advancement and self-enrichment. Partisan formations
would regularly sprout hydra-like heads to secure short-term goals.
Sworn enemies would ally to deal dirty and duplicitous hands
against mutual antagonists. Bribery, forgery, kidnapping and murder
were standard protocol, and student recruits were organized into
hit squads as needed.

In 1994, Babu gravitated towards a party much smaller than
any of these. The Jatiyo Samajtantrik Dal (JSD), translated into
English as the National Socialist Party, had sparked off in 1972
when socialist activists, military officers and student leaders
consolidated their organizations. Vehemently secular in nature,

they championed for a democratic redistribution of wealth and for governmental decentralization. Their command lay neither in stately appointments nor in weighty swords. Their potency rested firmly on the shoulders of picketers. They were staunch proponents for the mobilization of female workers, for regulation of big businesses, and for prosecuting war criminals. The JSD party manifesto also vowed to reinstate democracy, socialism, secularism and nationalism as the Four Founding Principles as per the 1972 Constitution.

The JSD was headed by retired freedom fighters and, though they were not perfect, they were the only band that Babu could typify as sympathetic and admirable. They retained the spirit of 1971 and the hope, idealism and desire to craft a golden motherland. In fact, an octogenarian 'founding father', affectionately known as Said Bhai, frequently broke down in official gatherings and asked those around him in distress, 'Is the war over? Have they left?' The party had sustained this innocence even as former comrades joined other factions, climbed aboard expensive cars and installed themselves in palaces. The poor masses looked on feebly, not knowing any longer what was true. And as the colours drained away from their dreams, hope fell clean off its bones.

In the economic and executive chaos that was dragging the country into a dubious new century, Babu was enthused by the example set by the JSD leaders. After attending meetings and workshops for months, he singled out their goals as pragmatic and desirable. The JSD was respected by the Bengali intelligentsia for having largely kept their hands clean of nepotism and corruption. Even their student wing was inclined to be a docile and pensive lot (yet tough enough to conduct the necessary street battles). Despite lucrative invitations, the JSD had tenaciously refused to surrender its autonomy to the larger parties. They refused even when guaranteed parliamentary seats by the AL coalition, opting instead for authentic *edificio de la nacion*. The Constitution did not mandate elections until early 1996, but Awami Leaguers had already taken to the streets demanding that BNP appointees step down. The AL called for the institution of a neutral caretaker government and for early elections. As mutually agreeable terms for 1996 were debated, violence escalated at hotspots nationwide, and universities adjourned sine die following armed clashes. With their commando-like posturing, face paint and automatic weapons (smuggled in via India), the undergraduates seemed a throwback to earlier times, resurrecting old fears of smoke and death. The climate was indeed grim; Bangladeshi citizens begged the BNP and the opposition to reconcile their grievances. Surveys showed that nearly 63 per cent felt that the country was facing an impending civil war.

This standoff had been decades in the making. Since independence in 1971, members in both parties had treated the country as a personal coffer. Sheikh Mujib's AL administration had been accused of misusing foreign aid, of nepotism, and of stamping out criticism and dissent. The subsequent leader, BNP's General Zia, had been reproached for allegedly vouchsafing a patronage system that offered sycophants ministerial and cabinet seats, trade concessions and bank loans. Both organizations also bickered over national patrimony, each deposing that its founder had been the true paterfamilias of the '71 war. The BNP platform had allegedly cost the country countless millions. They were faulted for refusing to cooperate with the Hindu-dominated Indian government to establish trade routes, negotiate water-sharing treaties and settle border disputes. The AL was conversely accused of endangering national sovereignty and security, as well as Islamic canons, by kowtowing to the dominant neighbour.

Scuffles between the two super-parties were occasionally interrupted by periods of martial law declared by disgruntled army despots as well as by the ostensibly 'independent' caretaker governments that oversaw election preparations. Neither type of regime was immune to profiteering and the trappings of authority. JP's prime mover, the General Ershad we have already crossed paths with, emerged supreme in 1982 as a martial law administrator. Shortly thereafter, he appointed himself president and dominated for seven years. Opposition aldermen, in the few historic cases where they actually took their official oaths, would anon boycott parliamentary sessions citing objections to electoral irregularities and unfavourable policies. In truth, this abstention from duty provided members from both sides the opportunity to tend to personal financial pursuits. The ethereal assembly chamber in the Sangsad Bhaban would remain vacant as sessions dissolved and as boycotts, protests and general strikes resumed. Nevertheless, the legislative grounds were still utilized because of their convenient location and commodious meeting facilities.

The misuse of provincial titles for self-promotion in Bangladesh has persistently been documented as highest in the world.[31] According to indexes prepared by Transparency International (TI), a Berlin-based ombudsman, Bangladesh was the world's most corrupt nation in 1992 and in 1993. According to this database, off-the-record payments to politicians by private firms in 1993 amounted to 14 per cent of the GDP. Academic provosts suggest, not altogether in jest, that resident business programmes start offering courses in the 'non-official components' of industry, including bribe-taking, lie-making, money laundering, and ass kissing.

---

31 In 2001, 2002, 2003, 2004 and 2005, Bangladesh was ranked the most corrupt country in the world according to the Corruption Perceptions Index (CPI). Things have somewhat improved in the last two decades, though the republic unfailingly stands among the 'Top Thirty Corrupt Nation-States'. After the Syndicated Bangladeshi Banking Collapse of 2021, the country found itself a top-tenner once again.

An urban myth from the time is that the Bangladesh government, mortified by the global scrutiny of topping TI's index two years in a row, sullied the following year's findings to prevent any repeats. To 'regulate' 1994 indexes, a team of diplomats was dispatched to Munich, Bern, Basel, Jakarta and Yaoundé. The outcome: Indonesia topped TI's 1994 list as number one in corruption (Bangladesh came in third, behind Chad). Government insiders boasted to confidants that they had arranged for this. One foreign affairs undersecretary claimed, 'We bribed our way out of number one; we did things that no one else thought of. Bonds shoved into pockets, thoroughbreds gifted to children, Bvlgari necklaces to mistresses... We're really still number one. We are the best at this bullshit. We made their damn transparency organization black as a crow's ass.' In a moment of humility, he added, 'Oyo, those Cameroonians are pretty good too.'

In 1994, the BNP government's failure to adhere to coherent programmes and policies, combined with public duplicity and a lack of accountability, frustrated the citizenry. In the mid-nineties, 67 per cent of Bangladeshis were illiterate and 48 per cent lived in poverty – leaving them impotent to effectively petition for an overhaul. Having seen how democracies flourished in so many parts of the world, young Babu could no longer sit idly by and watch Bangladesh flounder.

After weeks of deliberation, and after long talks with Munna, Rafik Kaka, Tanveer and his parents, Babu decided to pledge and run for a student post with the JSD. He also wrote letters to the SBG superiors to ask for their approval, and duly received it in the mail. Though there are no details as to whether Babu formally joined the SBG team or what exactly his status in their adhocracy was, Babu annotates in his journals that SBG pundits sanctioned his newfound ambition. One senior commented: 'Whereas it will not be easy to pilot our nation towards universal justice and prosperity, you have uncommon capabilities that will aid you in this quest. And

JSD is dear to us; we have worked together before and even share members. But never disremember, dear Babu, the moment you use your acumen for anything other than good, that hour will be your downfall. There is little forgiveness for swimming against currents you have already begun to identify for yourself. Anyway, politics will be good for growing hair on your chest.'

This administrative bid would not be Babu's first attempt in running for public office. At the age of nine, he had competed for the position of class prefect. The screening process required an academic standing in the top twentieth percentile, first standing in a 100-metre dash, and supremacy in a game of marbles. It goes without saying that favoured candidates needed a stature and spirit that would arouse respect in those they supervised.

In venturing into university government, Babu pinpointed that standards had evolved little. At twenty-two, though Babu was naturally timid, he was emboldened by an influential Rafik Kaka. While JSD neophytes were evaluated by standards that were more cerebral than those of the other political campus organizations, kingmakers knew that they needed hard-hitting leaders who could organize campaigns. Of course, there were always a few physically unimpressive youths who had something extra: a bravado that made their size irrelevant. As Babu was not prone to displays of daring, Tanveer twisted the arms and necks necessary to advance his younger cousin. In starting out, Babu was asked to meet JSD comrades at a university tea stall. There were about a dozen other hopefuls there. They postured, smoked cigarettes profusely, and laughed stridently as they walked into traffic.[32]

Swagger was crucial in the flashy world of civilian emissaries. The JSD scouts were unimpressed by Babu's soft manner of

---

32 When crossing roads, they preferred to walk into the middle of oncoming traffic, level curses at irate drivers, and demonstrate contempt for municipal codes.

speaking and his tendency to give way to others until one of them figured that he harboured an inner resolve that could be spotted in the gentle roll of his eyes and in the way his throbbing veins shifted their colours.

The head-hunter brought this to the attention of the others, 'That quiet one, he burns like a cigarette rope.[33] We can use him.' The scouts were unaware of Babu's agenda, but on their comrade's insistent prompting, they acceded that Babu must possess rare combustibles within. Thus, Babu passed this first assessment as his internals carried him forward.

The next stage of the JSD screening process required applicants to meet with senior and more erudite notaries. The rendezvous point was a Chinese restaurant, and this time, actual axioms and policies were on the table alongside fried rice, mixed vegetables and Szechuan chicken. The aspiring lads were questioned on the continuous boycott of parliament by opposition parties, campus violence, censorship and a rise in Islamic fundamentalism, the increasing role of NGOs as neoliberal Pied Pipers, foreign remittance, per capita income and the Rangpur famine, water-sharing and trade treaties with India, the repatriation of Rohingyas, and collusion between neo-imperialist outfits (namely GATT and the World Bank). There were five other student activists at the meeting but none approached Babu in his command of the topics. Having obtained notice beforehand from Tanveer that these topics would likely be reviewed, Munna and Rafik Kaka had drilled Babu for days.

Incalculable hours spent at Road 27 while his uncle assessed executive papers with peers had also versed Babu in civic procedures

---

33 A 'cigarette rope' is a stout, dense rope that hangs outside street cafés in shantytowns worldwide. Lit at their free end, these smouldering cords are used by smokers. These ropes are designed to ignite thickly and last entire days, withstanding winds and rain.

and their native calculus. All this, along with studies of Sangsad Bhaban sessions and special committee reports, had prepared him robustly for this round. He was congratulated, thumped jarringly and served shredded goat, a delicacy typically reserved for veteran members. He had made it to the third and final test.

Babu had initially hoped for a post as a student executive leader, but whispers now indicated that he would possibly find himself under archways even grander. Shrewd cohorts warned our dreamer that the final meeting was of prime importance. Babu was to sit with party founders, formidable men in every sense of the word. They were heralded as warriors and statesmen who over decades had sacrificed all fixings for the motherland. Extolled as ideologues, it was said they gazed into past, present and future states. Though the changing of guards and the forgetfulness of spotlights had left them unrewarded for their role in the independence movement, these men were said to possess immense shadows.

In his notes, Babu uses no recognizable names in relating the proceedings of this final assessment. The location, we do know for certain, was a hostel at the Sangsad Bhaban. Five men had met with Babu in the early evening. There was no competition; Babu was the only one on trial. And quite a trial it was. Although they were a kindly and parental lot, they were resolute in their inspection of Babu's innards. Like a pride of lions, they circled him.

Due to load-shedding, a need we have still not shed a quarter-century later, there was no electricity. In candle and kerosene dimness, they engaged. They argued over the secretive efforts by agri-chemical corporations and bifacial scientists to introduce terminator seeds and monoculture. They scrutinized energy policies that offered Bangladesh's entire oil and natural gas portfolios to foreign companies. One of the interrogators was passionate about the anomaly of deteriorating income distribution in a period of economic growth. He quizzed Babu on how to end the cycles of poverty and on the need for a deeper focus on education. Another lamented the disorder of student politics as well as unemployment and the lack of role models. And finally, after a critique of overcrowding in metropolitan areas and a lack of resources in rural Bangladesh, a man designated in Babu's journal as 'AC' vociferously grilled him on how to rekindle 'the fires of our revolution'.

By now, a sweaty Babu was bewildered as to whether all candidates were screened in this agonizing manner. He began to waver and his resolve flickered. But then, tired and frustrated as he was, Babu suddenly located within his sinew and framework the seer that crouches somewhere inside us all. His energies snapped into a point, and his mind cut like a blade through all the literature, gossip and opinions he had digested.

He answered AC: 'They will help you. There are many who never gave up the struggle. The momentum has been slowed; it is true, as you say – your movement is almost off the tracks. But there are people standing at the sides, looking on, sitting on the grass – they are watching you. Those sympathetic to you toil silently in publishing houses that issue lie after lie; they serve in the military but are filled with the same rebellion as their fathers; they are the fearless female professors who travel the world and talk about injustice and corruption … And they are ready to help lift you, to get things going again. The blood that has been spilled is still wet on the roads, in the very arches that surround us at this moment. Even here, most importantly *here*, you have many allies in the dark alcoves, behind the fallow walls. Look at the geometries they built in here. There are djinns everywhere that work for…'

Babu stopped abruptly as he snapped out of what had become a trance-like recitation. His voice had dropped to a deep, throaty drone in the last few lines, and he realized nervously that the elders were staring at him, transfixed. He had overwhelmed the room. His speech had carried a ringing, a shaking that made words sound as if they were coming from far away, from around hills and over vast open landscapes. His words had come by sea, skipping over waters and mounds, and from around corners that were totally foreign yet somehow remembered.

At the time, Babu was distressed by his own eerie vocalization. He wondered if he had taken advantage of their informal and open natures. Who was he, a mere twenty-two-year-old undergraduate, he asked himself, to tell them how the terrain outside lay? Then a man, unobtrusively seated in a niche the whole while, stood up. A wisp of white hair blew away from face and his eyes glowed brilliantly through the dark as he peered steadily into Babu. The man turned to a colleague and nodded firmly, exactly once. Babu surmised that this mute chieftain had passed the verdict; with unassuming authority, he had signalled his acceptance of Babu into the ranks of the JSD.

Later, Babu could not help wondering how his voice had transformed when he was responding to AC's question. There was also something thrilling in the manner that lights and shadows had moved in the room. Not having spent much time inside the Bhaban at night, Babu was amazed to spot geomantic figures inside the room. During the cross-examination, he had surreptitiously jotted down symbols, but lacked time to decode them. But what had happened during his impromptu oration was a mystery. It felt as if a phantom had travelled through him. It seemed that some peri from another time had used his body to make its presence audible.

Gradually, Babu recalled facts that seemed to explain things perfectly. In a discussion about the auditory capabilities of certain constructions, Kahn had brought up archaeo-acoustic evidence that many ancients had practised the art and science of manipulating sound with architecture to produce dreamlike effects. Examples cited by Kahn included the aesthetes who created the 3,000-year-old Andean Chavín de Huántar and the Temple of Kukulcan, where the echo of clapping hands reflects off the pyramid as the call of the sacred quetzal bird. A member of Kahn's firm in Chicago published a paper on the common resonance frequency that existed at stone monuments from England to East Timor. Ranging between 95 and 120 Hz, these frequencies are present in the human voice. Painstakingly arranged stones would sing back to those who gathered to chant under them. Rare stones also emit electromagnetic vibrations to which the *Homo sapiens'* temporal lobe responds orally. This was the case with the Whispering Knights dolmens in England. Childless females would pose questions of them and listen for answers emanating from the hollow of the stones.[34]

Babu had exhumed many a yarn mired in the soundscapes of the Bhaban. The assembly chamber where parliament met was known to be a distinctively bizarre space as speakers' voices rang jarringly off the concrete walls. There were very often fierce disagreements over what had been verbally expressed within its walls. Recording

---

34 Kahn has said that every forest, depending on its genus, has its own keynote. Some say the reverberations heard in the shaded aisles of evergreens, for instance, inspired the construction of Gothic cathedrals. Oracles spoke through breaking boughs, rustling leaves and the purling of sacred springs. Kahn planted a grove of trees in front of the Kimbell Art Museum in Texas, knowing that pyscho-acoustic filtration and forwarding systems could convert aural wavelengths to make the wind call out like a conch, distort footsteps into infantile laughter, or allow teenage chatter to resonate like high priests divining. When fundamental and 'sacred' geometries were incorporated into multi-dimensional soundscapes, transcendental effects could be achieved. The very same ratios were expressed in the transformative compositions of Bengali ragas, Tibetan overtone chants, Gregorian hymns and in African drumming. Goethe himself had famously surmised that architecture was only 'frozen music'.

devices, depending on their locations, would capture proceedings differently.[35]

One terrified journalist claimed in 1991 that, lost in the recesses of the south square, he found himself surrounded by a loud and unholy wailing. The tale went largely ignored due to the man's knack for sensationalism. Soon afterwards, he left the country and never wrote again. On another occasion, in 1989, a team of ornithologists from Copenhagen who were attending a climate symposium spent two days in the parliament complex chasing birds they identified from their songs as being the nearly extinct echo parakeet (*Psittacula echo*). Though they were unsuccessful in obtaining any video, their audio transcriptions were perfect and exist to this day. Still others claim that at night – when the boardrooms are supposedly deserted – voices from days past waft down and speeches that have been delivered years or hours thence inexplicably replay themselves, becoming ghostly reminders of broken promises and deceptions.

The transmogrification of Babu's voice during the JSD interrogation was not the only time that Babu would be confounded by the Bhaban's acoustic capabilities. Years later, in 2013, when Babu and several colleagues were absorbed in delicate political manoeuvres, they were stunned to find that they could hear their adversaries conversing hundreds of metres away. But these metres were not open parks, dear reader – the two groups were convened under separate roofs with tons of reinforced concrete, hardwood, clay and foam in between. Their rivals' exchanges had been redirected through dozens of rooms and open gardens, over water bodies and under trees by unknown means. Babu and his fellow collaborators nosed out that, if they positioned themselves in a specific spot in a specific room, they could distinctly hear every

---

35 Some have drawn parallels to another haunting, that of the United Nation's headquarters and its 'Avatar of Synthesis'. This presence is said to dwell in its General Assembly Hall in New York.

conspiratorial word uttered by their foes. The phenomenon might be scientifically explained as a case of whispering-gallery waves that can travel around the circumferences and ellipses of domes, caves and steps and be heard at staggering distances.[36]

After his acceptance by the JSD in 1994, Babu abandoned his studies for several months to devote time to courting influential municipal commissioners. It was no longer necessary to drop in at seminars or sit for exams – a golden GPA was guaranteed by JSD-sympathetic deans. Though our jejune crusader expected that deception would be integral to his work, he was astonished at the intrigues and treacheries that tied together this nebulous world. He had been given the position of national youth advisor, a post unprecedented for such a newcomer. Whereas his counterparts across the world negotiated for enhanced research facilities and improved library holdings, Babu had to prepare for paramilitary action. Instead of extending dormitory conveniences and inviting keynote speakers, his tasks comprised handling duffle bags full of cash and dealing with injured goons. He was expected to travel and recruit fresh blood. Typically accompanied by a cadre of students and JSD leaders, he was provided the muscle needed for safe politicking. Babu learned to hide his discomfort and devised ways to distance himself from the street fights, the buying of mandarins, and the sponsorship of hooliganism, hijacking, extortion and similar undertakings.

Though Babu has since vowed, time and again, to reporters, diplomats and legislators that he avoided wrongdoing and kept his hands clean of blood and blood money, his detractors claim otherwise. Babu argued that he was unable to stop more weathered

---

36 Famous instances of these sonic mirrors can of course be found in St. Paul's Cathedral in London, the Moorish Alhambra, the Temple of Heaven in Beijing, or in front of the legendary Oyster Bar & Restaurant at Grand Central Terminal in New York City.

comrades from abusing their authority, but that he did try to institute new rules to curb criminal activities within his ranks.

There is evidence that refutes these statements. In charge-sheet number 833, submitted in Paltan Police Station in Dhaka on 22 June 1995, Babu was 'the prime accused' in leading an attack on the news offices of *The Weekly Blitz*. The sheet indicated that the editor of the paper was physically assaulted and that attackers looted valuables from the premises, including a used tea set, a collection of maps and several illustrated reference books. *The Weekly Blitz* was known to be funded by the PBCP, another party that claimed to be left leaning but had sold out to the AL coalition. The animosity between the JSD and the PBCP was palpable. JSD hardliners felt betrayed by the encroachment of their former brothers-in-arms into their turf in the southwestern regions of the country, particularly Kushtia and Meherpur. Babu was named a culprit alongside others: Shintu, Shameem, Liton and Lisan. The ledger furthermore indicated that the man nicknamed Shintu was, in actuality, Monirul Amin, Director General of Forces Intelligence (DGFI), the primary intelligence agency of the Bangladeshi military. It was probably because of this bold claim that naught came of the case; after a nine-month investigation, no legal action was taken against Babu or the others. Mr Amin, outraged by the complaint that he had been spotted with looting teenagers, responded with all his institutional strength, and the *Blitz* staffers had to surrender all hope for the return of their reading materials and chipped chinaware.

In covering these years of Babu's speech-making and campaigning, I reference this case because, even decades after the alleged attack, I was able to unearth four credible witnesses. Two elderly journalists, a husband and wife that had worked at the *Blitz*, conveyed their memories of Babu's attack to me over lunch in an old Dhaka hotel. 'That bastard!' the husband remarked. 'There is no question in my mind that it was him. The way he slouched, those ugly glasses and those huge ears. It's all fresh in my mind.' The wife added, 'I cannot forget how they sat in editor sir's office, drinking his tea and scaring him. And yes, your Babu was definitely there. I was annoyed that he took at least four or five of our nicest leather-bound books.'

I was also able to find a middle-aged man who claimed to be the Liton mentioned in the case. He had since become a respectable headmaster in a madrasa three hours from Dhaka. 'We never attacked that office. The editor, I think his name was Jalal, was an old friend of Shameem's. After PBCP deserted us and joined the AL coalition, Jalal felt bad. He invited us to the office, and whatever we took, he gifted to us. He knew we had no supplies in our rec room. The case was false. Nobody hit anyone. I think a few of us arm-wrestled. Yes, Babu was with us.'

The final person to provide me with information about the *Blitz* episode was another JSD stalwart, but an individual much higher up in the organizational chain. The name of this personage is one well known to Bangladeshis, and I must keep his identity secret these days, as any ruminations on the topic of Babu are frowned upon. I will call him Mister J. He had first refused to speak to me, but after persistently dogging him, I persuaded him as to the value of my biographical handiwork. This esteemed gentleman remembers 22 June 1995 very well because it was the day he first met Babu. Mr J was Babu's superior at the time, and had driven to the Dhaka University campus to meet him. Having heard praises of the newcomer, he wished to discuss new plans for DU students.

'So I went to the JSD office at about eleven in the morning, and they told me Babu was under the bot tree. Sure enough, I smoked him out, curled up on a mat. He had a lapful of books with him, and we sat and talked for hours. I was impressed with his insights overall, and his specific proposals for the annual fundraiser. We lunched at the Sangsad Bhaban, and around 2 p.m. we met colleagues at the main square party-rooms. A few days later, I heard about the attack on the *Blitz* and how they had implicated Babu. It was a rubbish charge. The attack supposedly happened at five in the afternoon, but he was with us until almost eight in the evening. Someone told me that a couple of JSD rookies had been upset with that two-faced editor, and they got into a tussle. Who knows what happened, they were all old buddies. And yes, Monirul Amin, despite his title, was a friend. His mother and his grandfather had worked for us during the war, from Calcutta. Maybe he was there that day, but from what I know of him, he was always a wary chap. These cases you know are always orchestrated for one reason or the other. I don't know who told you he was at the *Blitz*. Who can tell why they lied? It was most likely set up by AL or BNP bigwigs.'

Mr J stopped here, looking uncomfortable, as if something were on his conscience. He continued, 'Look, I've thought about this a lot. And the truth is there was an odd moment that day. Maybe I should not mention this to you at all, but what's the harm? I mean, these are purely feelings of mine – the cold hard fact is that Babu was in a room with four of us when the incident allegedly took place … But what I want to say, though it is completely irrelevant, is that Babu seemed strange to me that day. I later came to love Babu like a son; he was always a hero to me. Maybe he slipped up here and there, but he was scrupulous in the main. But even once we became intimate, even then, Babu could surprise me with a face I had never seen before. That afternoon, he lay down around 4 p.m. for a nap. It was sweltering outside, but our ACs were running at full blast. So it was nice inside, very cold. We had four or five cots in our chamber and Babu went to sleep near the strongest AC, just out of our line of view. He was secluded in that freezing recess. I thought that perhaps he shouldn't be sleeping there like that, that it gets too cold there.

About two hours later, Babu woke up and came to my table. He was covered in sweat, and was very pale and panting heavily.

'And I recall staring at him. I thought he might have had a bad nightmare, so I asked him if everything was okay. And he said something like, "Yes, big brother, I am okay. Don't be worried, but there are times, you know ... At times I feel torn apart. Like my body is not mine. Like people are pulling me apart or untying me ... All loose parts ... I feel adrift ... It's the work and stress. I will rest more." This answer of his is burned into my head, because it was the first time I saw that side of him which I could not understand. His wild answer and the way he spoke in half sentences; I remember thinking, "Oh, there is something in this young man that is quite irregular, almost fearsome." It was as if there were things inside him that he could not share. And when he was talking, it was so eerie the way the light moved above his features – it looked like he was moulting colours or something. It was because of our office though. You know how it is with our beloved Sangsad Bhaban and its erratic hues. As I grew to love and know him better, I would come to trust him with anything, but that feeling never went away. That there was an untamed corner in Babu that was private; for no one else to see.

'So, if you ask me a hundred times, yes, I repeat he was with us. There is no door in the alcove where he had slept. We were seated in front of the only entrance and would have known if he had left. Unless he had flown out of a window like a bird, or climbed five floors of smooth walls, he could not have gone anywhere. So there you go. You have undoubtedly heard of other bad things people accused him of, but me, I know ... I am sure he would never hurt anyone.'

Mr J leaned forward and stressed, 'I refute that Babu would hurt anyone intentionally.' And as he said this, he flicked away a lock of stringy white hair and his face contorted in a manner that I thought was quite fearsome itself. I quickly ended the interview.

So, I do not know what to make of the *Blitz* case. Yet again, bilocation sits on its haunches and blocks my way. The witnesses I had consulted had naught to gain from deceiving me, so how can I tell which ones lied? I have even been tipped that a prominent JSD leader had personally called senior officers at Paltan Police Station to drop the case. But this call had been made on 19 June 1995, *three days before the attack actually took place.*

But I must continue. Like a locust that must march forward or be eaten by those to its rear, I lose the entirety if I stop. As my narrative speeds to the final part of this section, I must follow. If not, I will be cannibalized by indecision.

WE WILL NOW APPRAISE an incident from Babu's career that occupied him for most of 1999. Of course, it too is enmeshed in the Sangsad Bhaban's skein. To reinforce my avowal that these accounts of Babu's life are not to adulate or elevate him as an icon, we will immerse ourselves in another hugger-mugger in which Babu was accused of misconduct. And this case made a much bigger splash than the *Blitz* hearsay. This is no simple Punch-and-Babu show, but rather a complex and multifaceted affair. This yarn will require us to peer into that which is most rotten yet most green in the body politic of Bangladesh. This anecdote is entangled in ministerial assassinations, brothel bargains, real estate collusions and religious extremism, in addition to foreign aid misappropriations and CIA operations. In it, we will also review how a faction of JSD devotees betrayed party ideologies to conspire against Babu. This puzzle also reveals cracks in JSD's hitherto unassailable façade, which would eventually widen and result in Babu's separation from the central committee.

By March 1999, Babu had been promoted to secretary, Dhaka city, an appreciable step up. Having received his master's degree the previous year, at age twenty-seven Babu was well equipped to stride into plusher partisan arenas. He and Munna had stumbled upon an apartment in Indira Road. Though a scholar in history and anthropology, Babu followed in the footsteps of Mrs Majumdar and tutored teenagers in English literature. Munna, obsessed with advances in telecommunications, had sniffed out work in a nearby electronics store. As expected, Munna had graduated with honours – professors unravelled his technical instincts to border on genius. His reading interests now included science fiction, and the apartment was littered with garish covers. Pooling their salaries and their learning, Munna and Babu had become inseparable friends. Amar too could be spotted there most evenings, and spent many a night at the bachelor pad. Amar followed Babu and Munna in developing a taste for advanced studies – he had become enamoured of Bengali literature. And while Tanveer was increasingly busy, as a geriatric Rafik Kaka had forsaken his businesses and handed over management to his eldest, the four were still as thick as ever.

The BNP government had fallen years earlier, and as treasures spilled out of Trojan steeds, Awami Leaguers had swooped in to pluck at the entrails. In the four years since the *Blitz* outrage, the AL was entrenched as the new boss, but an accelerating dissidence heralded the end of their supremacy. The BNP, now the opposition, had taken to the streets, agitating against inadequate provision of basic utilities, recent price hikes, food shortages and the detention of political prisoners. It is ironic that, just when the nation found reason to celebrate its February qualification for the Cricket World Cup for the very first time, a fiasco of international proportions erupted.

Since the beginning of the year, an AL representative from Narayanganj, whom we will rename Mr Aman, had been coordinating meetings and rallies to eliminate two red-light precincts from his jurisdiction. He formed a fifty-one-member Citizen's Action Committee and fixed his sights on the brothels located in Tanbazar and Nimtoli. This historic purlieu, ten miles south of Dhaka, had housed nearly 30 per cent of all sex workers in Bangladesh for more than two centuries. Founded during the British colonial era, they originally catered to traders inside a cluster of moss-stained brick shanties and tin sheds. For three years, the businesswomen had been paying Aman hefty sums, as they had with law-enforcement administrators and local thugs. But Aman was acutely aware that the AL government was entering a lame

duck period and that pendulums would soon swing back in favour
of the BNP. He knew that, once he lost his clout, he would be forced
to relinquish management of the bordellos and would no longer
collect the kickbacks. His rivals from BNP had already started
muscling in, winning over the twelve-member female committee
that represented the parlour owners.

An account of Aman discussing strategy with his subordinates
was provided to me by one of his toughs. Predictably, he has
asked to remain nameless in my book – Mr Aman is still a man
to reckon with. He recalls Aman to have said something to the
effect of: 'Okay, so we strike quick and throw them out. In the early
morning, we raid them, swoop in, shove them on to lorries, take
them to rehab centres at least forty miles away. Before the press
gets there, we can flatten the place like a chapatti. Then, within two
or three weeks, Rajuk will be able to sell the land. I will ask for 35
per cent of the market price. If I come out with barely 20 per cent,
that will still be hundreds of crores. That land they're shitting on,
it's gold ... The ministry of social welfare has five million dollars
from UNDP to help these bitches ... We can dive into most of
that money, keep it for ourselves. We have to make a show as if
we're giving it to the hookers. We'll set up handicraft classes, some
bullshit small businesses for them to run, throw them some goats
and geese to sell. We won't have to spend much; the rest will go in
our pockets.' When warned by edgy underlings that these women
were not to be pushed around easily, Aman allegedly responded
with 'poohs' and 'pahs'.

Aman's impudence would cost him dearly. Irrespective of his
fancy aquiline metaphors, the ladies of Tanbazar and Nimtoli
were very resourceful. Dumb luck alone had not sustained them
through centuries of persecution by government officials, mohalla
gangs and religious hardliners. There were 'sardarnis' (madams)
who had inherited their positions from their grandmothers and

had established over time a community of supporters and patrons that extended, warren-like, throughout the nation. The businesses enlisted as many as 20,000 sex workers, pimps, musclemen and shopkeepers. They were said to take in approximately 15,000 USD a night. This was a hefty sum of money in 1999, when the per capita annual income was only 300 USD. The women were shrewd entrepreneurs – most invested their earnings in endeavours run by their relatives, making it next to impossible to estimate the true extent of their economic worth.

A union comprised of matriarchs from both Tanbazar and Nimtoli supervised the everyday workings of both locations. Called Uronto – Bengali for 'flight' or 'airborne' – the entity spread out its wings to shelter women on both sides. This is not to say that everyone working in Tanbazar and Nimtoli was free from abuse. The truth was far from that. Many had been sold into cathouses as young as seven years of age and serviced up to fifteen customers a day in order to purchase their freedom.[37]

Although prostitution was tolerated by the authorities, it was not constitutionally legal, and so there were no fixed standards to govern its practices. However, victims of the flesh trade insisted that any resolutions affecting their futures should be theirs to make. Though forced into slavery by their own families, they were hunted down like witches outside of their new homes. Many of them had the choice to leave after paying off their brothel debts, yet chose to remain. They disliked the cruelties and hypocrisies of the outside world. The girls found life with the sardarnis to be at times nearly unbearable, but due to Uronto's campaign for

---

37 Even more troubling was that Bangladeshi brothels, which operated outside the protection of unions, executed uncooperative workers periodically. This practice, also employed in Indian counterparts, has never been as widespread in Vietnam, Cambodia or Thailand, making Bangladeshi and Indian sexhouses the most brutal in the world.

improved living and working conditions, they were optimistic for a better future. Women's rights advocates also nurtured this hope. In the 1980s, international commentators anticipated that the newly emerging Bangladeshi women's rights movement would mirror Western counterparts. Despite these predictions, in a matter of months, hundreds of corps sprouted to deliver social services and skills training. They pressed for right of access to credit and to the means of production. Contrary to expectations, the movement did not entrench itself in neo-equalitarian debates: it wasted no time in equipping itself to combat urgent and indigenous vices including rape, dowry- and fatwa-murders, and acid-throwing.

Female underworld bosses paid bribes and provided girls to top dogs in the police force and at public administration offices. Those on the inside knew how the women also had personal access to the most eminent of domestic leaders. A ring of working girls resided at the hostels located inside the Sangsad Bhaban and openly entertained state elites. These damsels were the cream of the crop, possessing the charms and wiles needed to bring chancellors, generals and despots to their knees. In the late 1980s, a belle named Sadia had become the beloved of a military man we will dub General K, reputed to be the third most powerful man in the country. In time, buxom Sadia herself was rumoured to be the fourth most powerful person in Bangladesh. In the tradition of Pakistan's Yahya Khan and his concubine Aqleem Akhtar, Sadia became indispensable for the running of domestic clockworks. Politicians, foreign diplomats, bank directors and CIA chiefs vied for her attentions.[38]

---

38 Though Sadia had had no official post in the republic, she was given 'full protocol'. Sadia did not forget her former sisters-in-arms and introduced no-cost healthcare for sex workers at clinics countrywide. She convinced foreign donors to invest in microcredit enterprises, schooling for destitute offspring and health education. Sadia also pushed for the Bangladesh Election Commission to recognize prostitution as a profession on new voter ID cards. Before she succeeded in this, General K was ousted in the 1990 coup, and

Thus lay the land when, on 24 February 1999, some 500 police officers entered the targeted properties in a pre-dawn raid. They began beating inhabitants and dragging them towards lines of waiting buses. With armed men on board, these vehicles were to transport the madams and their aides to 'vagrant homes' run by the Department of Social Services. The compound they were to be boarded in resembled a penal complex and was located at Kashimpur, thirty miles outside of Dhaka.

Yet, from the very onset of Aman's ambitious heist, no chips fell easily. In fact, many police officers were the first to fall. Aman's minions had failed to bring to his attention the fact that the females in the area were unusually swarthy and muscular. Though providing an advantage to the women on the night the police attacked, their large size was the result of a tragic addiction. Many Bangladeshis favour robust and plump women as more desirable. This attitude stems from an ancient poverty in which well-fed women signified wealth. The working girls of Tanbazar and Nimtoli took the potent corticosteroid dexamethasone to achieve the desired grand proportions. Incidentally, it also served to numb them from the traumas inflicted by rough clients.

At the time of the 1999 raid, it was estimated that a third of the parlour-women were hooked on the steroid. As a result, the blows that the constables levelled at them were largely ineffective. The women became livid and, as the heftiest of them took on three to four officers each, their smaller sisters slipped through cordons and fled. The escapees, in short course, contacted reporters and friends and, within a half hour, photojournalists lined up to snap pictures

---

our Sadia was placed under house arrest without means of communicating with the outside world. Her crime, in the words of an eminent lawyer, was that she 'understood too much'. Today, Sadia is believed to live in a palatial residence in downtown Kuala Lumpur and, like the most discreet of her profession, maintains a strict silence about her years as 'The Madam'.

of screaming 'Corporals Struggling with Oversized Prostitutes'.[39] The buses were slowly and painstakingly filled with a total of only 400 women. The operation was a disaster. Aman was incensed by the chaos and ordered the area to be closed off, but due to media presence, he halted the bulldozers from their razing mission.

While the 400 captives were taken to holding facilities outside Dhaka, the remaining women got to work. Within two hours, Uronto commandeered the lawns in front of the Sangsad Bhaban. Their demands, amplified through portable speakers and microphones, rang throughout the hallways, disrupting meetings and briefings. By mid-afternoon, Uronto cardholders were joined by an assortment of non-governmental rigs, including the Women's Health Coalition, CARE Bangladesh, Human Rights Journalists Forum, and the Urban Poor Trust. The list of organizations that would board their solidarity action initiative would total sixty-two in the following days.

The Dhaka offices of the United Nations Development Programme were corralled and picketed, as word had gotten out that they had partnered with the Department of Social Welfare. Sex workers argued stridently that the evictions diverged from stated project-goals. The debates escalated when international health-experts opined that dismantling the bordellos would make it difficult to control AIDS and other venereal diseases. BNP officials extended their support as well, due in part to their role as the opposition, and because they had no desire to lose a source of guaranteed income. A prominent admiral was heard to grumble that Aman had gotten 'much too big for his Batas'.

The incarcerated, no-longer 'of the streets' women further embarrassed the government by going on a hunger strike. Having being threatened and abused, they announced that they would

---

39 *Morning Star* headline, 25 February 1999.

rather commit suicide than be treated like vagrants. After five raucous days, the 400 women were released. Aman had to provide each of them with 5,000 takas in cash, three egg-laying hens and one sewing machine. Even so, in a press conference following their discharge, the women petitioned the authorities for the return of their impounded workplaces.

Meanwhile, at a peaceful rally in Tanbazar, notorious gang-lords Machine Gun Mishal and Kidney Ali dispersed demonstrators by firing blanks at them. Although this incident befell in broad daylight only fifty yards from Sadar Police Station, the authorities took no action. It was obvious that Aman had not yet given up his real estate aspirations. After all, scarcity of land in the capital had, in the preceding years, resulted in prices per square foot soaring in Narayanganj. Dhaka followed Mumbai, Taipei and Hong Kong in being the priciest realty market in the continent.

All through these developments, Babu had been working fulltime behind the scenes. He had arrived bright and early that morning when Aman's officers had first descended on the infamous sex quarters. He was there before the first of the journalists had arrived, a detail that Babu critics have used as an accusation of sorts. As one retiree recounts, 'A single fella, of course he was right in the middle of that mayhem. I heard he was half undressed and reeking of booze when the cops got there. Oh, those girls and their nautch and cooch. Yes, he must have been a regular. You know how baby-faced thugs are – Babu, Habu or Shabu.'

As his biographer, I have developed the habit of taking innuendo pertaining to Babu's amorous affiliations with a pinch of salt. After years of toiling, I have been unable to confirm whether Babu had relations with any woman other than the 'love of his life'. Whatever his faults were, he could hardly be accused of being a Lothario or a Genghis Khan. It is more likely that, as a representative of JSD, Babu had chanced to be in the area and had immediately joined

proletarian groups in protesting the police action. This generous
reading will be tested again in the telling of the brothel scandal.

JSD maintained a firm stance through the whole affair and
issued a statement that, apart from minors that were employed in
the sex trade, inhabitants of Tanbazar and Nimtoli should only be
relocated if and when they wished. The JSD held that Aman had no
right to force adults into anything. They called for a constitutional
amendment to protect the disadvantaged women and their children.
Babu was proud of this and lead a group of JSD aficionados in a
peaceful picket outside the National Press Club and again, later,
outside the high court.

But there is more to Babu's role than pokes the eye. In fact,
there are planks that must be removed for us to see clearly. Five
and a half partially faded pages from his personal diary helped me
to render coherent a complex and otherworldly affair – one that
harkens to Solomon and the imperium of the Barakah. Alongside
Kahn's fantastic bequest, we will now observe Babu become firmly
entrenched in the heart of Bengali politics. His involvement went
from parade-leading to deep political intrigue when religious
fundamentalists entered the fray. Babu, like many Bangladeshis,
was wary of Islamic disciplinarians and their aggressive programme
to impose Sharia law in the country.[40] The right-wingers entered

---

40 Sharia (Islamic law) deals with many topics addressed by secular law,
    including crime, politics, economics, contract law, as well as personal
    matters such as sexual intercourse, physical hygiene, diet and fasting,
    the observance of prayers, as well as everyday societal etiquette. While
    there is no codified and uniform set of laws that can be called Sharia, in a
    handful of Muslim countries – including Saudi Arabia, Sudan, Iran, Brunei,
    Mauritania, United Arab Emirates and Qatar – flogging and stoning are
    legally recognized as acceptable sentences. It is, thus, no surprise that the
    majority of Bangladeshis regard Sharia law less than welcomingly. In some
    areas, however, Islamic law has been legislated in Bangladesh. For example,
    inheritance laws dictate that properties must be divided as per a person's
    religion. For a Bangladeshi Muslim family, men invariably inherit more than

the fray when parlour-workers took to hiding themselves in burqas. Covered from head to toe, they were able to watch over their confiscated acreage. Sergeants caught whiff of this, and there soon followed incidents of burqa-clad women being harassed and stripped wrongly.

These incidents delightfully provoked the more religiously bent, who had been itching for a share of the spotlight. They demanded an apology on behalf of the affronted ladies. Aman took it on himself to personally express remorse for the errors, rebuke law enforcement commandants, and enlist the Islamic disciplinarians in his campaign to demolish red-door locations. Though the Awami League officially distanced itself from Islamic politics, Aman knew that he could use hardliner help. After some backroom meetings, a Jihadist group named Harkat-ul-Jihad-al-Islami (HUJI) joined his campaign. In 1999, this group was still legal in Bangladesh and boasted about 15,000 dedicated minions. Though this number may seem negligible in a population of some 120 million, they were organized and feared. Drawing supporters from the Jamaat, they began to intensify pressure on the prime minister to proceed with the removal of the ill-reputed neighbourhoods.

Nobody, it seems, had advised the prime minister as to the true activity on the ground. She was inclined to accept Aman's effort as socially progressive and admirable. The PM assessed the rehabilitation of 'the working girls' as communally desirable and, while she mistrusted the religious extremists, she respected the United Nations Development Programme and its financial sway. Nevertheless, she was unfamiliar with the autonomy these women had held for centuries. The PM announced that there would be

women do. Reception of Sharia law has not been uniform the world over. Several countries in Asia, Africa and Europe recognize Sharia and use it as the basis for divorce, inheritance, and for other personal affairs involving their Islamic populations.

a televised debate on 5 March focusing on the 'helpless women's plight'. This grand meeting was to be held at the national assembly itself. Foreign and domestic NGOs would first present their arguments in favour of safeguarding the brothels, after which the PM would take the microphone to introduce government officials who would then articulate their rationale for clearing the dwellings of ill repute. Many insiders reasoned that the debate was basically a variety show and only served to direct media attention away from an emerging scandal connected to the purchase of overpriced Indian jetfighters. The bulldozers were to be given the all clear to proceed on 6 or 7 March, irrespective of the outcome of the discussion. Other insiders even claimed that the PM's son had been promised a significant portion of the revenues expected from the sale of the Tanbazar lands. Consequently, it was almost positive that Aman's demolition campaign would be given the green light.

In preparation for this convocation, it appears that half the nation's politicians were engrossed in some form of subterfuge or the other. The most daring plot, however, was concocted by Aman and the HUJI. Their idea was to set off incendiaries when sex-worker lobbyists took the stage. Their intention was not to kill, but to rather strike terror into the hearts of their foes and disrupt the televised deliveries. There is no logical explanation as to why they wished to do this when the match was already fixed in their favour. One can surmise that the decision was a spiteful one. Aman's frightening explosions were probably intended to heap assault upon ignominy and, in his words, to scare 'those damn foreign do-gooders back to their own damn countries'. His jingoistic rationality hardly made sense as most of the women's advocates were homegrown champions. But the HUJI and Jamaat hated all left-leaning social activists, domestic or foreign. For years, their attempts to institute regressive policies had been routinely tested. Aman met with his new 'allies' multiple times to approve a watertight plan; one of these clandestine trysts was held at an MP hostel at the Sangsad Bhaban.

What they came up with was a rather complex arrangement. A trusted team of three, referred to as Unit A, would position themselves at the presidential square during the debate. They would trigger a remote device once the human rights defenders had taken the podium. Upon activation, this device would send an alert to Unit B – another team of three parked a few minutes away (Dhaka mobile phone reception was notoriously unreliable in 1999). Unit B would then drive their vehicle to the assembly carrying forged paperwork that would allow access to the inner pandal. Once inside, Unit B would activate the dynamite. The delay they set would give them four minutes before the charges fired, giving both units ample time to relocate to a safe distance. There would be no urgent need to leave the compound, as the detonation was to be theatrical and not life-threatening. The vehicle and forged papers would be set afire in the explosion; no trace of the plot would lead back to Aman and his associates.

While Aman and HUJI wanted noise and smoke in impressive quantities, they ordered that the explosion be contained within a reinforced carriage. They had no desire to rack up a death toll. Political assassinations that were not first cleared by the Americans (represented domestically by CIA men) and the Indian Research and Analysis Wing (RAW) could result in serious repercussions. US operatives in Bangladesh were currently preoccupied with the scandal over the new aircraft, as were Indian RAW agents. Both agencies had been in meetings with military chiefs to discuss whether BNP deserved to 'win' the next round of elections. In addition and as expected, RAW refused to liaison with Jamaat and other Islamic hardliners. Aman and his co-conspirators knew this mission would have to stay under the radar. They would ensure that no VIPs were hurt, that injuries were kept minimal, and that the units left no evidence at the scene.

Babu's journal indicates that two Uronto members, who were entertaining clients at an MP hostel, observed a tryst that took place between Aman and his HUJI partners on the capitol estate. On a cigarette break, the two females were alarmed at the sight of religiously garbed elders skulking about in the middle of the night. Men who frequented these scandalous residences were typically discreet and solitary; the presence of a large group of bearded and kurta-clad men was therefore suspicious. The clever ladies slipped into a neighbouring chamber and lifted tiles to listen in. They had worked in the hostels for years and knew every brick and stone in the corral. Due to security precautions taken by Aman's men, it was only safe for the two nervous women to stay a few minutes, but that was time enough.

Babu does not indicate how he came across the information about this eavesdropping. After combing through Babu's contacts, I eventually found myself seated across from Boro Ma, a dowager in her seventies whom I was told could help clarify the matter. She was an NGO worker, mayor of a small city, and a materfamilias from the oldest systems of the subcontinent. I had been told that she cherished Babu as a son and had been a mentor to him from his twenties on. Boro Ma was also said to be intimate with the mysterious but famous Babli Ma.[41]

It had been almost impossible to get Boro Ma to speak to me. Un bel di, she asked to read my manuscript first before agreeing to meet. In violation of my general policy never to let anyone read more than a few pages, I gave her a hundred. Fiercely protective of Babu's

---

41 Babli Ma, who had gone into hiding in the late 1990s, will visit us in the following chapter. While Babu's journals make frequent mention of Boro Ma, there are none whatsoever of Babli Ma.

memory, she had mourned him for years since his disappearance. Finally, she agreed to allow me an hour for a tête-à-tête.

We met at a restaurant in Mohammadpur. Wearing a plain green cotton sari, she looked strong but could not fairly be described as heavy-set. Seated in a corner, she was on her mobile when I arrived. The air was rather solemn, and I sat quietly. An order of aromatic chicken soup arrived and, without asking, she served me a bowl. She called to two female associates in the foyer and served them as well. They returned to their lobby seats with generous portions. Boro Ma was in her fifties in 1999, but within minutes she was sifting back in in time, like a poet hunting lost verses.

'First thing I want to say,' she told me, 'is that I approve of what you're doing. I like your book, and that you're trying to help others understand Babu. Otherwise, I would not be here. Okay, let me start … In 1999 I was an assistant, working with Babli Ma. We had been hiding in a small hotel. We were afraid because the police were searching for us. Babli Ma received this call on her mobile around four o'clock in the morning. It was still dark. These girls, I don't know their names, but they were experienced, both were in their thirties. Anyway, one of them was Babli Ma's relative. They were terrified and relayed scores from the HUJI meeting at the Sangsad Bhaban. We immediately had the ladies transported from Dhaka to one of our hideouts. They told us the whole caboodle, the sum of what they had heard. We were even able to identify three of the four HUJI men from the names they canted. And of course, that MP rat, Aman, was there.

'So Babli Ma and I both contacted people we knew who could help stop HUJI. And Babu came to see me the next morning, so I told him too. We were all worried. You know a little about my relationship with Babu already, but maybe you don't know how much I loved that dear boy. I watched him grow up – his mother was my junior in college. I also knew his two cousins, Amar and Tanveer, but Babu was special to me. I would trust Babu with my life – with anything. Whatever happened afterwards, whatever they say Babu did, I know he did it with true principles. I don't know what else you want to know.'

After this exposition, she sat with pursed lips. I felt there was a great deal buffeting about in her. I had agitated winds in the vast expanse of her interior, winds that were now shaking her branches to the core. I pushed.

'Boro Ma, thank you so much. You have done so much for us already. By the way, this soup is really first-rate. I am going to have to come back here. But I have to ask you, what do you think Babu's relationship with the JSD was? Do you think they helped him during the 5 March crisis? Or not?'

'We respect many in the JSD. They were our comrades in 1971. And they didn't become corrupt, unlike the others. But in 1999, JSD had a lot of internal problems. They were not able to help Babu with the 5 March disaster. But it did not matter; we were there. We assumed control.'

Still not satisfied, I continued, 'But the HUJI and Jamaat were formidable then. How could Babu have hoped to take them on in addition to Aman and all the other rivals? I mean, when I look at all these influential names, what hope did Babu have? He was but a newcomer.'

Boro Ma sighed and fixed her gaze on me. The air about us stilled. Her green eyes became whorls of rustling leaves and vines with foliage layered, interlaced and limitless. 'Young man, you have much good in you. I like what you are trying to do. But listen to me: do not *ever* give up hope. Yes, a lot of bad things have happened. In merely a few decades, we have had to salvage a shipwrecked country, pull it out of the water, out of blood, and fashion a home for everyone. After '71, many people were terrified and did things to protect themselves, to ensure that those things would not happen again. But inside countless people, inside us still, there is a wall you will hit time and time again. Time and time again you will come across Bangladeshis who have inside them a line that no wrongdoing shall pass through. We will fight those bastard HUJI and Jamaat types, and we will fight prime ministers and their thieving sons, any man who mistreats our daughters, or our Hindu and Jumma friends, and watch as our children starve. I can see you want to cry, na? In your pages and in your words, I can see you are also drowning in what you have uncovered. I cannot disclose the whole enchilada, but you should know that *we* are the many, not them. We linked our arms centuries ago, and they cannot break us. We will fight and we will win, like we did in 1999. And when we lose, we go back and teach others to continue. Those tender ladies you see outside, they are the future. You are also the future. They will protect you like we did with Babu. If you are doing good, you will never be alone. Even if you think yourself helpless and weak, *we are here*. Do not doubt us for a second.'

And indeed I did start to cry, I found myself in her embrace, I fell against her and held her as if she were a tree. I suppose the evidence I had been uncovering had made me feel dirty, as if I were writing a shameful book and washing national laundry in public. And if I was dismayed by my biographical struggles, once Boro Ma kissed me on the forehead, she replaced my fears with a jewel. She embedded in my skull the beginnings of a wild pearl, one that would sustain me and enable me to proceed with this work. The two girls came in from the foyer, had my soup packed to go, and led me away from Boro Ma.

I am sorry, dear reader, for burdening you with my woes, but it feels important to minute the concord I reached with Boro Ma after I bared my spiritual tangles to her. Now, as I wipe away tears and fears, I return to business.

There is another version of how Babu acquired knowledge of the overheard conference. Less charitably, cynics collar a once again half-dressed Babu inside an MP hostel, as two girls by the names of Hena and Khushi shared their report of the eavesdropping. Either way, it is definite that on 2 March, Babu took it upon himself to foil Aman's plot. Babu's actions during the first week of March 1999 are not wholly attributable to his JSD membership. Rather, an analysis of Babu's life indicates that his mother had indelibly shaped his feminist inclinations. As we shall discover in the following chapter, as a student activist in 1971, she had lost a congregation of female relatives to Pakistani army sex camps.[42]

Babu's mother, after his birth at the end of the war, had worked to rehabilitate many women rescued from the army sex camps. She continued in this engagement even after moving to Tangail and gaining employment as an educator. The rapes and mass killings of 1971 had permeated into Babu's dreams as a young man. His mother's obscure fury when it came to autonomy for Bengali women had firmly taken root in her only child. As a youth, Babu was made familiar with the struggles that Bangladeshi women faced. Mrs Majumdar made sure her singleton was aware of Fakir Lalon Shah's famous verses (a line that Babu loved quoting was: *Only worshipping your mother will lead you to the address of your father*) and the divine notions of Shakti and Rahmah. In his life, Babu demonstrated time and time again a sense of compassion and respect for female compatriots that makes it difficult to accept rumours of his lolling around half naked in the presence of paid consorts. Moreover, virtually every prominent male figure associated with the brothel

---

42 These camps had been formed with the help of pro-Pakistani Bengalis who did not support Bangladeshi independence and collaborated with invading soldiers, providing them with tactical assistance and sex slaves. In a cruel and incredible twist of fate, once Bangladesh was independent, many of these traitors were to head the Jamaat Party. Although legally exculpated, their betrayals and wartime crimes were not forgotten – these men were disliked by millions.

intrigues of 1999, including Aman and Jamaat leaders, had been accused of dallying with harlots.

An added ingredient to the Aman and HUJI plot was a name that the girls heard mentioned at the overheard deliberations. In excited and high-pitched voices, the male connivers had discussed how Shah Ilyas, an internationally notorious terrorist, had contacted them. He had sent word that he was sailing to Dhaka to function as lodestar for the mission. Ilyas was an Islamic hardliner and a global ideologue in the tradition of Carlos the Jackal. Ilyas supervised cells in settings as diverse as Denmark, Turkey, Kashmir and Indonesia. Ilyas's whereabouts were never known, but his presence in Asia had been ubiquitous. He often went by the sobriquet The Dark Blade. Ilyas had vanished in 1997, and many thought him captured or dead. His Saudi backers had been mute for two years and there was no meaningful chatter. When word arrived that Ilyas would be in Dhaka to end the irreverent chaos of overweight 'bimbos', HUJI stalwarts were both thrilled and petrified. They had not expected such a distinguished Islamic warrior to be interested in their backyard squabbles.

Beards trembled and prayer caps dripped sweat with the fear that Ilyas might find fault with their life choices or their handling of domestic affairs. The majority of them would have secretly preferred it if Ilyas had just stayed missing or remained busy with real manoeuvres like blowing up imperialist vessels, holiday resorts and nightclubs. HUJI and Jamaat were content with alarming officials with spooky threats directed at railway stations and airports than with actual destruction. There was no telling what Ilyas's intentions might be; he might order their bombing to be more ambitious and leave thousands dead. What if he desired to blow up the entire Sangsad Bhaban with a fleet of inconspicuous vans? He might presumably find the idea of a Bangladeshi Capitol built by a Jewish architect of synagogues to be an affront to the Islamic populace. Men like him were scary and almost unstoppable.

It is feasible that news of this man's arrival had made Babu steadfast in foiling the inter-organizational conspiracy. From what can be salvaged of the waterlogged pages of his journals, it appears that Babu elicited the aid of a mole on 4 March to penetrate the HUJI. From this informant, Babu obtained the lowdown as to where Unit A would meet and where Unit B would likely park. No specifics on Ilyas could be elicited, however. To everyone's relief, it appears that apart from his initial correspondence, the enigmatic man was heard from no more.

Babu also noted that he had contacted his mentors in the SBG to run ideas by them. He then studied books, consulted his divinatory charts, and meditated in the shade of the presidential square. In all fairness, he was not the only foot soldier drafted by Uronto; their network, dark and centuries old, reached out to tap awake allies in National Security Intelligence and the Special Branch. On that fateful day, a throng of forces were to collide in the presidential square. From articles published in glossy gazettes, from Babu's faded pages, and from titbits I painstakingly solicited from working girls and embittered old men, the following is what I have on 5 March 1999.

At about 4 p.m., the gates to the plaza opened, and thousands of attendees started filling its premises. As was standard, governmental crews had ushered in rent-a-crowd layabouts and professional space-fillers. Apart from them, many hundreds there were genuinely piqued by the debate. They included young college students, aid workers, community leaders, the religiously inclined, and residents from Aman's constituency. Also present were hundreds of wives from local constabularies – many still irate about the injuries the 'bitches' had dealt to their husbands in the early morning raid. In their midst, our heroic Babu was accompanied by two young armed assistants and a panting Munna. They were stalking Unit A. One may venture that somewhere in the crowd was a shadowy Shah Ilyas, or one may not. No definite accounts corroborate his presence or participation.

According to his own records, Babu entered the Bhaban just a few dozen feet behind three bearded men comprising Unit A. He had followed them from their rendezvous point at Kamalapur train station, acting on a tip provided by his spy. The three men moved away from the main area to a corner that stood about two hundred feet high, tapering into a nook small enough for a cat to sleep in. The three men waited in front of this recess while a crowd of eight thousand gathered before them. In Babu's opinion, they had chosen a singularly potent vantage point. Hovering just behind the men was a dominating tallness. It blocked out the firmament and took the men wordlessly into its fold. By Babu's estimation, they had chosen a spot in the Bhaban where its forces are most dynamic. Unit A had doomed themselves to failure.

The remainder of the square is a gentle area with sweeping and decorative elevations both exhilarating and soothing. White steps rise on the north and south side and spill over on to redbrick platforms. The VIPs were to deliver their speeches from the north platform. Other executives of consequence seated themselves on the south platform, while less extraordinary citizens filled remaining areas. By 4.40 p.m. the place was almost fully occupied, and Babu stood scarcely a few feet away from Unit A. He sported a video camera with which he filmed the proceedings, and which served as a perfect cover for his sweeping surveillance of the packed complex and its crowded balconies. Although this recording has been lost to the vagaries of time, I have obtained footage captured by others. Moreover, before Babu's recording disappeared, several in his inner circle had scrutinized its contents and, to this day, they reminisce about its puzzling fifty-seven minutes.

At around 4.45 p.m., it appears that Unit A experienced an inexplicable confusion. They turned to silently stare at the walls behind them for ample minutes, ignoring the activities taking place in the heart of the square. While gripped by this bizarre exercise, a Unit A fellow puzzlingly placed their signalling mechanism on the floor. They then proceeded to stare at the south platform, completely ignoring the north platform where the activists were readying to deliver their arguments. The Unit A henchmen then gesticulated wildly to one another and appeared to find something hilarious about the south end. From video recordings and from Babu's notes, we know that bystanders noticed their erratic behaviour and gave them a wide berth.

The two youths with Babu were SSF (Special Security Force) officers in plainclothes. They had already taken the remote device into their possession, but were carefully observing Unit A to prevent any attempt to contact Unit B via mobiles. Two other teams had been positioned near the two gates to watch out for automobiles that appeared to be weighed down, as this would intimate the presence of a VBIED (Vehicle Borne Improvised Explosive Device). Any automobile stopping for more than a few seconds was immediately approached. Babu had enlisted the services of a dozen close friends gathered from army and intelligence agencies. Though they officially worked for the government, on that day they were independent of any authority. Most of them had no faith in their superiors.

At exactly 5.19 p.m., sex-worker spokespersons were well into their deliveries, and Babu and his agents were standing just a few feet away from Unit A. Suddenly, the distinct ringing of a Motorola phone could be heard coming from the pocket of one of the suspects. Babu's men reached for their guns and prepared to take the three terrorists into custody when, in some strange way, *time came to a standstill*. Unit A scouts had been standing motionless for quite a while now, not responding to shrill phones or to the loud cheers or to people who pushed by. They had been staring at the flooring expressionlessly, and as Babu and his deputies approached, they too felt a sense of lethargy and confusion. An overwhelming listlessness overcame them, and before Babu dropped his camera on to the deck, it captured an image of an enormous figure hovering overhead. This winged form glided majestically above, cloaking them in a grey silence. Those who examined the tape later explained the illusion as possibly being caused by clouds and shades moving over concrete-coloured walls. Others argue that the avian phenomenon closely resembled low-altitude chemtrails.

The muting of the sounds on the tape remained unexplained but, once again, almost anyone would admit that Kahn's geometric constructions were susceptible to perplexing auditory impressions. Atmospheric temperatures, ground cover, wavelength refraction and acoustic shadows can meet to create silence. Echoes might have conceivably collided in that architectural cleft to negate each other, like identical wheels turning in opposite directions with a net effect of zero. The sheer rise in the Bhaban's walls, the dark gloom of the blind corner, and the heavy air of colliding sounds might well have induced a sense of torpidity, disabling all seven men.

Babu's sturdy camera continued to film from the parquet. Through its limited aperture it captured splendidly the stationary feet and trousers of the group. In the footage, there is also, unmistakably, a section of Munna's heaving chest. For twenty-seven minutes, the seven men stood silent and immobile like chastised youngsters. The SSF boys had walkie-talkies, and Babu's camera picked up the muffled bleeps of attempts made to contact them. Midway through the twenty-seven minutes, two women in pretty saris could be heard whispering and laughing before they left the scene. Babu and the others remained unresponsive the whole while, as if communing with some absent genie, as if intoxicated atop some flying carpet.

According to the camera and the documents I have gathered, at 5.46 p.m., after the aid workers had exited and the PM had taken the stage, a loud report jolted the seven out of their semi-comatose states. Eight gunshots fired from close by could be heard immediately afterwards. Awakening from their stupor, Babu's SSF supporters had drawn their guns and shot the three men of Unit A dead. They then scrambled towards the gates where the eruption had originated. Before abandoning the still forms of Unit A, Babu paused and collected his digital recorder. In the commotion, nobody in the frenzied crowd had noticed the assassination of Unit A. As Babu and his men made their way to the gates, they passed the north platform, which had sustained some damage. Once in the parking area, which had borne the brunt of the discharge, they estimated at least thirty dead amongst the smoke and the hundreds of screaming and wounded. The VIPs were being evacuated and Babu and his companions helped to clear debris and load ambulances. After four hours of picking through survivors and corpses, they found that all eight of their comrades entrusted with bomb detection and disposal had been killed. And the biggest shock of all was when Babu discovered that Tanveer had been with them. Tanveer, an unexpected last-minute volunteer, was the ninth of Babu's team to die.

A great deal happened over the following days. The enraged PM had the FBI, Scotland Yard and a selection of joint taskforces investigate the attack. Aman and leaders from the HUJI and Jamaat were imprisoned. Brothel owners ripped aside police cordons and made their way home. Hundreds of theocrats trimmed their beards, and underworld figures fled the country or went into hiding. On 14 March, the Dhaka high court concluded that there was no legal justification to evict the brothel occupants because prostitution, when it formed the basis for a woman's livelihood, was not illegal under the Constitution. The AL government was no longer interested in the matter anyhow; it was out for right-wing blood. As the 'women of the street' danced in them, returned to their children, held galas and organized fashion shows, citizens throughout the country attacked neighbourhood Islamic hardliners. Kahn's blueprints were retrieved from archives to conduct repairs, and the HUJI conspirators were put under torture. The gravity of the matter far exceeded anything Aman had estimated. Forty-three people had died from the car bomb, including two top-tier Awami Leaguers who were arriving late.

The strength of the detonation had been sufficient to send rubble flying towards the PM. She was lucky to have escaped unscathed except for a severe headache she later complained of. Experts in explosives pinned down Unit B's actions in the ignition of a rigged vehicle. Chemical traces on their clothing indicated that all three in Unit B had perished in the explosion, but the trail ended there.

However, detectives soon discovered that HUJI militants had purchased ninety grams of RDX from reluctant Ramna Market traders. This quantity could barely blow a hole in a wall, so it was impossible that it had been responsible for the presidential square bombing. The principal compound recovered from ground zero was based on PETN. This particular nitrate-based explosive, a favourite of the former Irish Republican Army, was rare and next to impossible to purchase.

In spite of first responders having contaminated the crime scene, forensic scientists meticulously collected enough tics and petrochemical signatures to make a sensational claim. They declared the 5 March blast as the work of a talent known as Ibrahim al-Anwari, a Yemen-based bomb wizard better known by his nom de guerre, The Engineer. He was confirmed as the mastermind behind major attacks in the Netherlands, Israel, Somalia and Thailand. And no more than a little poking, a little Oogling and a little dot-joining will uncover, dear reader, his connection to a certain Shah Ilyas.

Babu and his partners were taken in for questioning, but were released after a week due to lack of evidence. When grilled by investigators, Babu and his team admitted that they had received info regarding a sinister collaboration and had been conducting surveillance. They admitted nothing more. They argued that their initial fear was that the three men had been strapped with explosives but, on hearing the blast from the other side of the plaza, they abandoned the idea. One SSF officer told his superiors, 'Sir, we followed them lockstep from the front gate. They proceeded to a corner far away from direct action. We thought our intel must have been bad because these guys were doing zilch. But we continued to watch them in case they moved towards the platforms. But they never did. When we heard the explosion at the gate, we left to help. That is the whole truth.' Detectives could not use ballistic evidence to trace the bullets from the Unit A corpses to Babu and his men, as the firearms used had been quickly dispatched to riverbeds by cohorts. In any case, they were unregistered and untraceable. The clothes worn by Babu's team on 5 March were tested for gunshot residue, but results were inconclusive as the items were saturated with lead, barium and antimony collected during their relief efforts after the blast. Furthermore, there was no apparent motive for these level-headed patriots to open fire on the three unarmed loafers.

Babu and his team had competently covered their tracks. They disposed of Unit A's remote device, severing any links between the three dead men and the blast. The SSF operatives were reprimanded for failing to inform their captains before partaking in their well-intentioned but misguided reconnaissance, and Babu was sternly warned to stay out of official matters. National and international intelligence personnel reached the shared conclusion that the affair had been masterminded by non-Bangladeshi hardliners. Nonetheless, they still suspected the HUJI of some complicity, including the deaths of the three strangers. Two years after the attack, the organization was permanently banned by the government. Of course, HUJI leaders simply retyped letterheads to resume operations, but that is another twister.

Aman was released by the military after a few days for the sake of party solidarity and to deflect public attention towards 'Islamists'. After he protested, begged and apologized at the PM's feet for his foolish stunt, she allowed him to return to his constituency. Due to her displeasure, it would take him more than a decade to reconstitute his political base. The Tanbazar and Nimtoli areas came under the patronage of BNP toughs. The joke about town was that Aman and his goons had taken to wearing burqas and kitten heels when travelling away from home. The CIA had concluded that AL was not to win the upcoming elections: BNP had allegedly promised natural gas and telecom contracts to US interests, and to stave off Chinese efforts to construct a deep-sea port in Bangladesh. This trumped anything the AL was said to have offered. JSD chiefs severely reprimanded Babu for his participation in the disastrous proceedings. SBG ollams were upset about the loss of life and the damage done to the Bhaban. But repairs were started, and the wheels of the state resumed their customary erratic revolutions.

Babu and his friends studied his Sony tape in seclusion. They scrutinized the twenty-seven minutes that they could not account for in their memories. They theorized that they had been drugged, and attempted to recall the shebang of what they had ingested. They speculated on incapacitating agents which could be administered in the form of a vapour. The lethargy and incoherence they remembered from 5.19 p.m. to 5.46 p.m. could easily have been caused by diphenylacetate poisoning, they surmised. Had some stealthy figure brushed by and contaminated them? Had some airplane passed overhead and sprayed their section?[43] There must have been more to the Aman-and-HUJI plan than they knew of.

Munna, a firm believer of mind control (à la *The Manchurian Candidate*) and of conspiracy fantasies in general, was adamant that they had been the victims of military psy-ops. He swore that a lieutenant general in Afghanistan was training homegrown operatives in the use of 'human behavioural engineering'. Had they somehow been triggered to become disjointed at the sound of the Motorola ringtone? Nothing had come up on their RADINT (Radar Intelligence) that could explain the deaths of Unit B and their own eight brothers, or the fact that a deadly PETN bomb had been used. And what could explain Unit A's peculiar behaviour? Had they discerned that they were being followed? Was Unit A just for a decoy for sciamachy? Or were Shah Ilyas and his cronies possibly behind some of this?

Babu and the others explained the strange muteness in the recording, the muffling that lasted exactly twenty-seven minutes, as possibly due to a ground object that had obstructed the microphone. Of course, they did not really attempt to explain what had hovered up above, how the breezes seemed to stop blowing, why their trousers looked so stiff and unmoving, or how two women walked into their midst and exited as if in slow motion. At the 5.46 p.m. mark, when Babu picked up the machine and rushed to help survivors, the frames per second revert to normal. Babu pretended to agree with his colleagues that the recorder must have been damaged on falling. They declared that some inner electric component must have been

---

43 We must remember that these events took place in 1999, when MAMS (Miniature Aerial Munition Systems, aka mini-drones) were not in production. While, nowadays, anyone with access to a 3D printer can fashion their own taka-sized Unmanned Combat Aerial Vehicle from home, the technology was not available then.

jarred out of alignment with the impact, but had dropped back into place once the recorder was picked off the floor.

In private consultations with the SBG however, Babu attempted to understand what the Bhaban had done to him on 5 March. After taking meticulous measurements from the Presidential Square, he made Buni-esque calculations invoking squares and the intrinsic harmony of numbers that they demonstrate.[44]

Babu collected tapes from miscellaneous debate enthusiasts and archivists to decode the geomantic shadows cast at the Assembly that fateful afternoon. He recalled that, prior to the twenty-seven-minute blackout, he had made various attempts to pair symbols for assistance but had only drawn blanks. There was only the recursion of the Cauda Draconis – a menacing omen in most situations.[45] Other than this dramatic caution, Babu felt as if Kahn's casements had drawn their blinds shut and were determined to obscure the facts of the attack. Babu was disappointed, but accepted that the assembly had made him no promises. He was nothing but a single vibrating fibre in a grand concerto of thousands.

In sifting and resifting through debris, I finally found an entrypoint into tents to behold the fantastic circus of 5 March. This hidden and inconstant pathway is provided by two of Babu's old partners. Both are wary steppers and were initially reluctant to

---

44 Babu writes in his essays of the seminaries that originate from ancient Africa, India and China, and how the tradition of squaring the circle is a mathematical proposition that captures an infinite architectural imagination, in addition to geomantic projections from the divine. It is even said to provide patterns upon which the sigils of djinns, angels and demons can be charted.

45 Cauda Dracon is Latin for 'the tail of the dragon' and the figure of the south node of the moon. It is dreaded as a bad omen in most situations. Its inner and outer elements are both fire. Associated with Saturn and Mars, it is only good in circumstances for ending or completing things, such as breaking up a relationship. It brings good with evil, and evil with good. In traditions of yore, if this was the first figure drawn, the geomantic reading was stopped.

share their memories with me. Once convinced of the fair-minded nature of my work, the two men revealed previously inaccessible panoramas. I learned that in the passing years, although their affiliations with Babu had dwindled, they had maintained their loyalty. Mutual friends had brought us together. My contacts assured me that while the two men would remain unidentified, they had truly been members of Babu's inner circle.

From all my studies, I was convinced that one of them was Rubel, Babu's childhood friend who had returned to jump aboard the Babu political cruiser. The Rubel-like confidant informed me that after the presidential plaza incident, Babu was hunted by a fifth column of HUJI soldiers and that this had been the primary reason he left the JSD and Dhaka. He told me, 'We too were JSD cadets, but after fifth March, things began to fall apart. It was as if the explosion had knocked something out of whack with the central committee; they started to team with the Awami League for the upcoming elections. After all those years, they gave up being independent. It was as if the bomb had scared them and made them apprehend that if the AL could be attacked in such a manner, the JSD's survival as a small party was hopeless. But we did not agree with this. They did not protect Babu. Journalists and the SSF and the CIA punished Babu for his involvement. He was tortured. We were all beaten. Instead of helping us, the JSD higher-ups were busy connecting with old-time crooks. You know who got us out? I think it was that Babli Ma and Rafik Kaka, they pushed for our release. Babu also mentioned some group of professors, some society he was connected with, but he wouldn't tell us more.'

The other anonymous source spoke after glancing at 'Rubel': 'There were some strange things though. We were close to Babu and knew everything, inside and out. After being released, yes, he spent several days in the Sangsad Bhaban, going over what had happened. But our enemies were moving in fast and there was no way we could figure everything out. There were many loose ends. Everyone thought that the remote device from Unit A had been destroyed. But we actually kept it and had some guys open it up.

'They said the timer in the electronic box registered activation at exactly 5.33 p.m., thirteen minutes before the blast, just when the PM took the stage. So, had someone recalibrated the arrangements so that the explosion would hit the PM, not the Tanbazar supporters? Babu and the guys with him said they were drugged during the operation. So who pressed the remote? Don't get me wrong, we saw the video, we trusted Babu. But this whole thing was ridiculous. Where did the PETN come from? We had no access to anything of that grade. Neither did the HUJI. And why did Unit B stay with the bomb? They had five minutes to clear out. And the video, if you could just see it. Hai Allah, the hairs on my arms stand up when I think of it. It was like al-qamrah, the way they stood there. That video, the colours were funny, the air looked like something from another world. There is a chicanery of the eye, some kind of a spell, and then the qamrah wears off and things return to their normal states.'

In facing yet again a blind arch which allows no passage, I took to sitting in the square myself to ruminate and let loose my doubts. I found few answers but plenty of new questions. There are some who point to Babu's travels as a youth to places Saudi donors sent him, where a man named Shah Ilyas had been seen. Could Babu conceivably have been in cahoots with The Dark Blade? Were the mysterious explosives and their detonation during the PM's delivery arranged by Babu in conjunction with others? Did Babu already know where the JSD was heading? Was this attempted assassination a last-ditch ploy to shake things up? Was Babu, at twenty-seven, ambitious and ruthless? Had he left the country to lament the role his own hand played in the inadvertent killing of Tanveer?

My instincts tell me not, but how can I be sure? As with any illusion, in examining Babu's political life, all it takes is a scant play with angles and corners to confound the senses. A little trimming, texturing and repositioning can unravel a false world where things had earlier merged seamlessly.

So much surrounding our Sangsad Bhaban appears arbitrary. So much gives the impression of having fallen into place by sheer chance. When I deliberate over how much Bangladeshis love this edifice and how many acted selflessly, I am reminded how the damage done to the square was repaired in only weeks. Furthermore, I came across a writ petition filed by the Institute of Architects demanding announcement of the parliament building as part of national heritage. It was soon followed by a high court judgment that declared any new additions that might 'distort the original design of architect Louis I. Kahn's 1973 masterpiece' to be illegal.[46] I appreciate that the legalization of prostitution in 2000 helped alleviate many municipal hindrances.

My spirits are lifted until my mind wanders to 2005, when Tanbazar and Nimtoli were indeed demolished by a different government with the same motives, reminding me that the women's rights movement in Bangladesh has only intermittently flourished in a male-dominated political system. I also inventory how journalists, professors and activists are kidnapped and killed while protesting social injustices; how the police fire on crowds that gather to protest mining operations in the north; how Minsky ministers conspire to take over banks; and how a forward-thinking Nobel laureate becomes an enemy of the state.

I weep for our lost forests and our lost tribes. I watch a boom in the export of tiger-shrimp drive out Royal Bengal tigers from salty

---

46 In 2010, there was much dissension when the AL licensed the erection of an iron fence around the Capitol for security purposes. Many contend that Kahn's vision would have never allowed for this.

marshes. I mourn the forty-three dead from 5 March. In the calm of the Sangsad Bhaban, in its grand presence, I cannot help but muse over why some beloved traditions and points in our ley lines are wiped out while others are enhaloed. In the groves of the Capitol, I endeavour to imagine the nature of the balance on which martyrs are weighed. And to what end? What victory will give compensation to those who have gone under and for that which has been irrevocably lost? But the Bhaban does not yield this to me. Like a child, like some Ulysses or Hafez, I too must drink from its cup.

I backtrack to Muzharul Islam and how he fought with all his influence to ensure that Kahn had the receipts needed to complete the assignment. I watch Kahn's son crying on video, trying to understand the mind of a father who looks past the faces of his own offspring into abstracts beyond. But then I read about how Islam had initially approached Alvar Aalto and Le Corbusier with the commission for the Sangsad Bhaban. What hands had twisted fate so that the task was Kahn's instead? Did those that wielded these hands know that Kahn's genius included identifying potential in others and orchestrating teams towards a vision? Could these nameless marionettes have discerned the purity of Kahn's soul and determined that his process was the most appropriate for the diagramming of a nation's heart?

The Indian subcontinent has a tradition in which yogis and Sufis, Hindu, Buddhist and Islamic, choose a place to meditate, often by riverbanks, at mountain edges or before caves. On assuming a position, perhaps the lotus, perhaps not, they draw a circle about themselves to mark a sacred sphere, establishing a horizon that loops the infinite cosmos outside, keeping their human body as the centre point. Thus fixed, the sky over and under holds them in a bubble of compassion and learning. In much the same manner had Kahn seated himself amidst acres of grass, mud and stone and swung into place around himself the mammoth of annexes, parks and waterways. But while Kahn did not allow himself repose or rest, others arrived and seated themselves. Kahn left the newcomers to fill themselves with thoughtful light, and to recognize their own commission in building beauty.

The assembly stands there today as ponderous and majestic as need be and as light and airy as allowed. As the face of the main complex peers over the citizens that gaze into it, it ushers them into its folds and shelters them under its many wings. It does so while surveying the ether and knowing that more are to die, that there is both triumph and disaster ahead, and that the need for martyrdom has not yet ceased. All the while, it spreads into the national landscape, like a spider or a fungus, like some strange machine descended from the sky.

Babu, with a bindle on his back, fled Dhaka sometime after the debacle of 5 March. Before leaving Dhaka and its politics, Babu visited the Capitol once more to ponder its silhouette and pay his respect. As he turned to walk away, he abruptly stopped and glanced back. He was overcome with a feeling of gratitude. It then occurred to him that he would frequently have to look back and remind himself of the good intentions and profound sacrifices the construction embodied. He would need to return when he was the most unsure and weak in his resolve. Like all Bangladeshis or imprisoned kings, Babu knew that in times of uncertainty he would gain much from considering closely the waters of the Sangsad Bhaban, to catch its diamond-like reflection of a clearer Bangladesh, one even more lovely and blessed.

II
TREE

The ancient tea mountains bathed in the setting sunshine.
The old tea trees stretching out their ancient branches
As if turning their nose to the human world and recalling
antiquity.

– Yang Jiang Ming

Trees are sanctuaries. Whoever knows how to speak to them,
whoever knows how to listen to them, can learn the truth. They
do not preach learning and precepts, they preach, undeterred by
particulars, the ancient law of life.

– Hermann Hesse

Exhalation of moss, mycelium, black mould; wafted savour of
a thousand earthly growths, damp, clinging, redolent; aroma of
mighty roots, of invisible spawn and seed – all the vast stirring
of the earth's desire.

– Virginia Garland

NOT UNLIKE MANY AN epic, or a moral lesson, our Babu-teaser should have probably begun somewhere under a tree. So, with absolute disregard for chronology, we will backtrack now. We will visit the days before Babu's conception, to a time when his young mother and father were still finding themselves. In the centre of this digression, and in the centre of Babu's creation, stands a tree.

The tree in question is no ordinary growth, however. The banyan we are concerned with is located in the heart of Dhaka University (DU). Babu himself was particularly fascinated with this tree after he overheard an intimate conversation between his parents which led him to surmise that he was conceived under the noble fig. Mr and Mrs Majumdar had both attended Dhaka University. The recently married couple had been on campus during the upheavals of the war for Bangladeshi independence in 1971. As we shall see, both the university and the tree were crucial to the Bangladeshi resistance ... and to Babu's entrance on to our screens. The young couple was to devote all its energies to the independence struggle. Well, almost all their energies, if one accounts for their engaging in the behaviours necessary for Babu's birth towards the end of 1971.

Mr and Mrs Majumdar's political endeavours at the university took place in the neighbourhood of this banyan. In the months before and after March, they worked with the Independent Bangladesh Students Movement and participated in its 'non-tolerance' of the West. This tree, because of its involvement in reformation struggles, is an apposite elemental symbol for Babu's later life.

In the shade of this tree in 1971, thousands of young students rallied for the liberation of Bangladesh (then East Pakistan) from

Pakistan (then West Pakistan). Decades earlier, others had convened under a similar tree located hardly a few hundred yards away. The West Wing of Pakistan in 1952, separated from the East Wing by 1,600 kilometres of Indian territory, dictated that Urdu was to be the national tongue. Bengali students gathered in indignation under the banyan's predecessor. They did so to protest the governmental ruling that Bengali, like Punjabi, Sindhi, Pashto and Baluchi, was not to be recognized officially. This was decreed even though Urdu was only spoken by 7 per cent of the winged nation.

When protests broke out in the Bengali-speaking Dhaka University on 21 February 1952, students were fired upon by security forces. The Language Movement thus sprung. After four years of civil unrest, legislators reluctantly inducted Bengali into the Constitution. Triumphant commemoration and memorial acts ensued in East Pakistan as Bengali arts flourished, giving cause to some claims that a virtually extinct Bengali Renaissance was exhibiting signs of life. Almost fifty years later, in tribute to that 21 February, the day was to be designated as International Mother Language Day by the United Nations.

However, what transpired in Bangladesh under and near that tree in 1971 is of a far graver nature. A category-three cyclone had hit the country not quite five months ago in November 1970. With wind speeds reaching hundreds of kilometres per hour, it is considered one of the deadliest natural disasters since antiquity. The cyclone left between three hundred thousand to one million Bengalis dead, and millions without food or shelter. West Pakistan was uninterested in aiding these countrymen. While rows of gleaming helicopters sat idle in Islamabad, hundreds of thousands of Bengalis starved as relief crept in from India via train and truck.[47]

---

47 The Bengalis in East Pakistan did not forgive the Punjabi dominated military-bureaucratic elite in West Pakistan for their refusal to send aid during this time of crisis. This sentiment of neglect was exacerbated by the fact that,

In the national elections held in January 1971, the Bengali Awami League won 167 out of 169 seats in East Pakistan. This show of unity in the East Wing resulted in it now holding the majority of seats in the national assembly. In effect, it now governed its Urdu counterpart, and not vice versa. This sudden swing in longitudinal power-poles was not accepted by rulers in Islamabad. As a famous officer put it, there was no intention of letting Bengali 'black bastards' assume control of the government. This declaration also serves to reflect how West Pakistanis prided their Aryan heritage and held in contempt the Dravidian roots the East Wingers possessed. General Peerzada, a key player in West Pakistan's ruling junta, asserted before TV cameras that the 'non-martial' Bengali race should never have the chance to rule the nation. President Yahya Khan, on seemingly grasping that his Bengali subjects were insistent that the ballot count be honoured, finally commanded his generals: 'Kill three million of them; the rest will eat out of our hands.'

And this they did. While misleadingly maintaining a dialogue on the exchange of seats with Bengali representatives, the West Wing surreptitiously sent over thousands of undercover army personnel. The East Wingers did not see what was coming. They were blinded by a somewhat naïve belief that their electorate had remained peaceable and had, even more, offered to relinquish their control over affairs that pertained to the West. When the alarm was raised, Sheikh Mujibur Rahman, who spearheaded the Bengalis in their quest for autonomy, allowed himself to be imprisoned, thinking that this would prevent a massacre. He was wrong. On 25 March,

---

for decades, Bengalis in the East Wing had been financially exploited by their western counterparts. The substantial foreign exchange earned from the export of Bengali jute had been routinely appropriated for economic development in the western half. The bulk of this money went to generals and the armed forces, for toys such as tanks, ships and the aforementioned helicopters.

a genocide commenced, and Mujib's people, still reeling from the disastrous cyclone, faced the most unnatural agent on earth – the human being.

With Operation Searchlight, the Pakistani army fixed its glare on four main targets. These included Bengali police forces, Bengali regiments, the slums of old Dhaka where insurgents could hide, and Dhaka University. The university was selected due to its heritage of anti-West-Wing activism. In the months before Operation Searchlight, students had drilled and conditioned themselves in case the West turned a violent fist towards them. Black-and-white photographs famously captured hundreds of tender-footed men and women carrying dummy weapons and marching.[48] There were, however, fully functional arms stored on campus grounds. Five students that had received advanced combat instruction, including Babu's father, will join us in this account.

Operation Searchlight projected taking control of major cities within a few days, followed by an elimination of all opposition, political and military, within a month. This did not turn out to be the case. While approximately seven thousand were murdered in Dhaka the first night, within a week, half the population of the Bengali capital had fled. By April, almost thirty million had walked to Indian borders. Major General Farman Ali let loose all assets at his disposal, killing civilians on sight as part of a scorched earth policy. The mass exterminations of 1971 vie with the annihilation of the Soviet POWs, Chairman Mao's Cultural Revolution, the Jewish holocaust and the Rwandan genocide as the most concentrated act of civilian-murder. The Guinness Book of World Records lists the Bangladeshi genocide among the deadliest five of the twentieth century. As with those who had perished in the recent hurricane, it is difficult to know the exact number of dead. Bengalis in 1971 were

---

48 Of these trainees, most were not on university grounds on 25 March, but subsequently joined with the ranks Bengali guerrillas elsewhere.

a poor people with no birth records, no accurate census reports and no functional system that accounted for human life. Citizens then, as now, were annually scattered by the winds and the waters to seek a livelihood. They simply vanished, glyphless, when they failed. Until today, how many of the 75 million Bengalis in 1971 were killed remains unconfirmed. Academic estimates place it anywhere from 300,000 to three million. In the meanest twist of fate, Yahya Khan's outrageous quota might actually have been reached. But he was wrong on one count – the rest did not feed from his hands.

As Zulfikar Ali Bhutto, the prime minister of Pakistan, wagged his finger and tore resolutions to throw in the face of the UN Security Council, his troopers slew every Bengali male they found between the ages of twelve and sixty. As rallies were held in Hyde Park, London, and in the United States in New York and DC, Bengali Hindus were hunted down and professors and students were decapitated. As Japanese children saved their tiffin money to donate to the struggling Bangladesh, and George Harrison and Ravi Shankar organized relief-raising concerts, military death camps were built to match the refugee camps that were springing up along the Bangladesh-India border. As representatives of Guyana, New Zealand, Sierra Leone, the Netherlands and the Soviet Union spoke out about the pogrom, the Bengalis trained themselves to repel the assault.

As this grand blurring occurred over the surface of the earth, and as cardinal points collapsed in dark and nebulous holes, the Indian military assisted Bangladeshi freedom fighters to defeat the Pakistani forces. What was to happen afterwards, the looting of Bangladeshi factories and supplies by Indian forces, the water-sharing and border agreements subsequently violated by India to the detriment of its tiny neighbour, is not of concern to us at this juncture. We are not concerned with the lack of spoils, or that there were no true victors. The events of 1971 are of a nature so horrific that no memorial service, no international conference, nor any number of commemorative statues, songs, books, paintings or movies have been able to undo what had been done.

But we must backpedal a little from the midst of this great massacre to the Dhaka University campus before Operation Searchlight commenced, to that particular cherished tree. That is where this story will take place; in this epic, everything centres about that banyan tree. While this may seem an allegory about betrayal and the atrocities that humankind can inflict upon itself, this is also a story about perseverance and triumphs, small though they appear in our green and red tapestry. There is love in this most horrific of stories. There is amity and sacrifice between sworn enemies; there is the unflinching devotion of a citizen for his homeland, and there is the passion of a newlywed couple that braves death at its most unmasked. And lastly, this is an apologue about birth – the birth of a nation, and of our Babu.

First, we must contemplate awhile the institution that is Dhaka University. Since its inception in 1921, the institution had been lauded as a stellar multi-disciplinary research institute, eventually winning the patronage of many noteworthy pundits, artists and scholars. Among them were Albert Einstein and his co-worker Satyendranath Bose (the namesake of the boson), the Islamic modernist Sir Ahmad F. Rahman, the British educationalist Sir Philip Hartog, and the anti-establishment scholar Humayun Azad. Still others included poets Allen Ginsberg, Jasimuddin and Kazi Nazrul Islam. Poet-seer and Nobel laureate Rabindranath Tagore visited the campus and greeted students in their residential halls. The university was also recognized as the principal breeding ground for political and intellectual pursuits involving the region. It became known as the Oxford of the East. Celebrating its hundredth anniversary just a few years ago, the school today is the alma mater of 60 per cent of university-educated Bangladeshis.

The campus is an eclectic blend of Vedic, Turco-Persian, Mughal and European architectures. Of course its Asian influences can be seen in its numerous lotus ponds, in its stone sculptures, and in the use of trees. Much of the campus was built in the style of a garden home, with green zones everywhere, large open verandas, lattices, perforated screens and inner courtyards. Our beat will pause within this architecture; we will peer betwixt its myriad pockets to piece together our account.

Centrally located in the republic's capital, the campus's southern boundary straddles the city's Zero Point, an omphalos of sorts from which all directions and distances are measured. This poignantly captures how the institution connects the earlier parts of Dhaka with its more modern facets, establishing a zone that harmonizes centuries of traditions. Regarding the university in this light, it becomes clear why the area was chosen again and again as a meeting place – it was a space which reacted both physically and psychologically to the pulse of its occupants. Even the wisest sages would become infantile in its rainforest of colours; shedding age was easy in this most verdant of agoras.

An especially favourite spot on campus was the area about the enormous banyan our saga focuses on. The local name of this tree and its canopy was 'bot tola', literally translating as 'the banyan's shade'. This cultural icon grew in front of the renowned Arts Building. Students took refuge from the heat under this centuries-old fig. It served as a social hub where study sessions transpired, political speeches combusted and suitors wooed their beloveds. Mr and Mrs Majumdar had, in fact, first met under this tree. They had discussed their aspirations under its broad and soothing shoulders. Amidst the rustling of birds and small animals, thousands of Bengalis spent hours exploring poetry, civil society, differences and dreams. Professors brought their children and grandchildren here, as did busy employees from the university and from the neighbourhood – in this safest of places, infants would be looked after by familiar and kind faces.

Things were not always tranquil, however. In the build-up to the events of 1971, this banyan played a vital role as a gathering point for students and intellectuals agitating for an independent Bangladesh. Many rousing disquisitions had been heard under its shade, as had many an impassioned rally shot out from its tremendous trunks. In fact, Babu's parents had cheered the hoisting of the first Bangladeshi flag in front of this perennial, on 2 March. At that time, locals had finally accepted that those in Islamabad were not going to honour electoral results. Rumours had made it to the West that the bot cast supernatural spells amongst the Bengali populace, inciting defiance in the men and women who mingled underneath it.

This celebrated banyan had become so pivotal that when invading soldiers charged Dhaka on 25 March, they had a score to settle with the old tree. Due to the considerable entanglements of 1969 and 1970, university authorities had been too busy to see to the trimming of the bot, and its elephantine branches and trunks had spread unchecked. High-ranking Pakistani officers regarded the felling of the giant tree as a chief objective. After dormitories and campus blocks were torched, after female scholars had been carted off to military outposts, after professors, students, laboratory and staff members had been shot and buried in mass graves, the occupying gunmen turned their attentions to the sprawling banyan. By official reports, they chopped down the infamous flora in the early morning hours of 26 March.

Our current recreation of the time hinges on a little known myth about the bot tola. We will focus on one particular version of what happened with the tree in those tumultuous times. There is an alternative version, both military and civilian, which states that the tree was not actually felled on 26 March. There are those who claim that it took the Pakistani forces almost five days to destroy the particular hardwood. Proponents of this theory argue that numerous acts of sabotage and misdirection had kept a clowder of soldiers from the West busy with the *Ficus benghalensis* for a number of days. This rendering, from fringes forgotten, highlights how certain volunteers clandestinely manoeuvred to protect the tree. We will also concentrate on the tree's eventual destruction, and of its role as both a symbol and a blueprint for Bangladesh's military efforts to fend off the invasion from the West.

Babu's diary addresses this discrepant account. His was the first mention I had ever heard made of the officially discounted military fiasco. He spends several pages exploring the possibility that the area around the famous landmark had been cordoned off between 25 March and 1 April by a Pakistani regiment to conceal their remarkable failure to demolish the bot. He alludes to unconfirmed intelligence that explosives had failed to ignite, and how tanks, bulldozers, mortars, rocket-launchers and all manner of electrical equipment had malfunctioned. My own inquiries have substantiated much of this, and additionally exposed indications that four Pakistani officers had had emotional meltdowns and were sent back to Karachi from their university stations. These officers received counselling for years. In 1988, there was an attempt by one of them to publish chronicles that validate Babu's alternative narrative concerning the tree, but Ghulam Ishaq Khan's government immediately banned the book. Moreover, after needling numerous former freedom fighters in Bangladesh, I found that many had heard rumours of a miraculous five-day resistance organized by DU students. I also began to quickly discriminate that word of the five-day miracle had been suppressed by those who wished for national spotlights to remain on their own martial contributions. Also in the aftermath of the 1971 horrors, few Bangladeshis cared for an astonishing anecdote in which valiant Pakistani conscripts cooperated with Bengali students to save a national icon.

When Operation Searchlight was launched, Pakistani squads first silenced all communication channels in Dhaka, including radio and TV stations. However, those with their ears closest to the ground discerned army units encircling the university from the east, south and north. Teenagers arrived on motorcycles with the terrifying update that battalions were shooting everyone on sight. By the time contingents had established themselves in the British Council library, using it as a firebase to shell dormitories, Babu's mother and father joined a core of student council volunteers to rouse a covey of their compatriots. Once the bombing commenced, these lucky survivors rushed to hiding spots on campus. Some made their way into the dark inner-rooms of the teachers–students canteen, the library and the Greek mausoleum, while others jumped into dark olive pools and hid in shrubbery. Still others took refuge inside the three temples built on campus for Hindus and Sikhs. These were destroyed sometime over the next two days, but are said to have sheltered a passel that black night in Bangladesh. A handful of students thus survived the initial massacres of 25 March. In the days following, as our chiller will reveal, many remained on campus to protect the tree and stoke the spirit of the independence movement. Though Mr and Mrs Majumdar never went on record regarding their involvement in the resistance operation I will refer to as the Five-Day Mission, two of their comrades were interviewed for this account.

It was difficult to remain in hiding once the carnage started. As approximately 200 were killed in Jahrul Hoque Hall, and a similar number at Iqbal Hall, Jagannath was mortared before rooms were individually cleared of survivors. Rokeya was set ablaze with female students still inside. Friends held on to friends, not allowing them to rush out into the wailing night, not allowing them to give their lives to the tanks and jeeps and bayonets. Babu's mother firmly held on to her husband as he writhed and punched her like a demon, striking her for the first and last time in his life. He tried to leave the gurdwara to go search for a cousin and for his wife's sister, but Mrs Majumdar did not release her hold. They all held on to one another on that darkest of nights, as the green grasses and the spirits of the university went silent in disbelief.

Step by silent step, they made their way to the Dhaka Medical College Hospital, which was located on university grounds, about a mile's distance from the epicentre of the destruction. The hospital had been visited already; there were signs of damage outside and, inside, the immobile figures of medical staff. The students took shelter in the emergency ward due to the fact that several of them had sustained minor injuries and needed first aid. At one point, a convoy of vehicles drove past to cursorily scout the place. When the gunshots began to peter out at around 1 a.m., in a reversal of their usual role, the deepest shadows suddenly produced light. More specifically, the eleven activists hiding inside the hospital ward heard quiet voices speaking in Punjabi. The eavesdropping Bengali students were astonished to observe three soldiers from the West express their horror over what was happening. These men, seated on the lawns, had slipped away from their regiments. They were stunned at what their comrades were doing. One declared, 'I cannot go back to my wife and let her know I let them kill these children.' Another private cried quietly, while the third contended, 'We can do something about this. I know those five by the pond; they have not expended a single bullet. I think they helped some students get away over the railway lines. They are also talking to others who don't want to kill any more civilians.'

After listening breathlessly for an hour, to everyone's horror, Babu's mother bolted out of the medical facility into the garden, and stood before the three Punjabis. Her husband fainted, while the soldiers yelled in terror at the dishevelled apparition that had emerged from cupola and cornice. Fear, after all, had been master of the night so far. But this is when things began to change; almost about to open fire, the Punjabis realized that they were staring at an unarmed woman in the dark. They lowered their weapons to ask her in Urdu, 'Who are you? What do you want?' as if it was she who had entered their homes and taken them by surprise.

'I am a Bengali woman ... a student here,' she replied in her mother tongue. 'I want your help. My sister is in Rokeya Hall.'

The three looked at each other, their eyes reflecting fear, disbelief and shame. 'Gentle lady,' said the one that had been crying earlier, 'I can give you water, clean water, but you have to leave here, they are busy now. After they cut the tree, they may come here again.'

'How can I leave? My sister ... the others?' she responded.

The servicemen whispered amongst themselves and then said, 'We cannot save anyone inside the dormitories; they have them surrounded. But we can help you escape from the west side, there are hardly any guards there. If you had your sister here, we could help...' Once again, the shadows moved as shame threw a heavy cloak over them. 'But there are no other survivors.'

'You are wrong.' She had barely said this aloud when those from inside the hospital stepped out, young men and women, pale and shaking, but each as tall as a monument. Prepared to be fired upon, they held their heads high, as if to shoot heavenwards. Once again, the startled enlistees prepared to fire, but on observing that these were unarmed, ragtag youngsters, they softened.

'How many of you are there? We can help you get out of here, but it will not be easy. They are setting up checkpoints outside Dhaka for those who try to escape.'

'We do not wish to escape. We want to die here ... We cannot leave. If you don't like that, kill us now.'

What ensued was vigorous and passionate bargaining, in both Punjabi and Bengali, between soldiers and students, students and students, and plebes and soldiers. Their tangled exchanges conveyed grief, hope and determination, as well as entreaties, endearments and frustrations. All this was done with the awareness that death could advance from any direction during the night, but as students and disillusioned troopers conspired, they could sense the architecture around them, including trees, ponds, shrubs and vines, begin to take new life. They could hear stones rasp and pavilions creak in their fulcrums to break free of their mould and act as guardians. As night-birds collected, and as the foliage stretched its arms, the environment that had formerly terrified the three men now began to embrace them, as the collaborators collaborated, the protectors became protected, and both victim and aggressor could not be discriminated from one another.

But something is getting overlooked here. None of them had realized that only just a few hundred yards away from their negotiations was a large mango tree. This tree was the very same aam tola ('the shade of the mango') that had been the former social hub of the university. Two decades earlier, the hospital used to be the old Arts Building, and this aam had been the bot's predecessor.[49] So in 1952, on the infamous day that Bengali protestors agitating for language independence were shot dead, this tree had been a rallying point, not the bot as some mistakenly believe. They had gathered here and, hours later, on approaching the East Bengal legislative assembly located a stone's throw away, had been shot dead. For decades, this tree had nurtured those with dreams, fears and struggles very similar to those of the Bengalis and Punjabis arguing under it that dreadful night in 1971.

Perhaps this tree played a part in bringing out the best in these noble spirits. Perhaps in the midst of war, the achingly sweet scent of mangoes touched the child inside them and worked its wizardry. The students and jawans decided on the following: they would first

---

49 Only once had a departmental shift been made to the current Arts Building, did intellectuals and political activists shift their patronage to the bot.

search for the others hiding in nearby cloisters and, after a quick and silent survey of the halls, they would be secreted over the railway tracks or via the neighbouring slums into parts of the city that were safer. All this would have to be done in less than three hours as, once the sun had risen, there would be no chance of escape. This, at least, was the initial idea. However, on retrieving more fellow activists from ponds and dark storerooms, the Bengalis began to argue amongst themselves all over again. The exasperated Punjabis watched and listened while the youth talked to each other. Mr Majumdar then spoke in Punjabi, 'We will not all leave. Can you help a few of us stay back for a few days? We want to defend the tree. If they plan on cutting it down tonight as you say, they will destroy something crucial to our independence. We have a few guns and dynamite that we have hidden away. Will you help us? They cannot cut our bot like this. *It will not happen.*'

Once filled in by Mr Majumdar that five of the Bengalis were familiar with basic combat, the foreign soldiers were easier to convince. In fact, it seemed that the spirit of resistance was overtaking them as well. They claimed they had colleagues from three regiments who would help. Their next objective now became to lead the students in retrieving weapons that had been stored in room 1052 in the Students Union. The idea of launching an overt attack on the troops was quickly dismissed as impractical. All involved accepted that the only way to protect the tree would be by sabotage. Then, it was time to search for survivors.

As the group stealthily made their way from one end of the campus to the other, they discussed possible tactics in whispers, but conversation was difficult when feet would slip into pools of blood or when agonized cries rang around them. Death squads could be heard from the apartment adjoining the campus where faculty members resided. The troupe trekked through the corridors of slaughter and the fields of carcasses as they measured how piles of bodies had been hastily dumped together for later disposal. Of the two former students I was fortunate enough to interview, one said, 'It is so strange that we humans, when intact, do not smell the way we do when taken apart – as if all the smell lies just beneath our skins.' Both soldiers and students were barely able to keep their wits about them and often forgot to crouch or breathe. The former guerrilla described how she felt that the spirits of Dhaka University had concentrated their energies on sheltering them through the ordeal.

By 3 a.m. on the first day of the five-day counter-manoeuvre, the little group had grown to a total of approximately thirty students; the Punjabis also enlisted three additional uniformed friends. Maintaining an appropriate demeanour inside killing zones, these men helped the Bengali students out of campus grounds. They also approached intimate colleagues and established a small network of brothers-in-arms. They were careful and gave a wide berth to those that would not be sympathetic to their defection. After having participated in several hours of the ghastly campaign, the men they cautiously selected to approach were willing to help in one capacity or another. No one was told everything; the original three were not taking unnecessary risks. There were others that might have agreed to join, but on closer inspection their glazed eyes betrayed the incapacitating signs of trauma; essentially, hours into the war, they could barely function any more.

By 4 a.m., the soldiers had shepherded about thirty-nine Bengali students to the railway lines. Except for twelve students, the remainder were sent outside Dhaka under the aegis of four newly recruited jawans. These draftees were able to use the darkness, their official uniforms, and weapons to safely usher the men and women on to buses leaving the city. Babu's father and mother were the first of the twelve to be equipped with goggles and waterproof materials by the soldiers. These would enable them to lie concealed in the numerous ponds on campus properties (after a swift appraisal of prospective hiding places, they had all realized that the ponds, full of still silhouettes, were the safest place to hide). The events of the next few days bear out the wisdom of this decision. While they sheltered in these macabre hiding places during daylight hours, they would spend their nights together at the hospital, grooming and caring for each other after completing tasks allocated to them to save the banyan. However, the five days that they did manage to safeguard the tree took a psychological toll on them that was immeasurable. Without their night-time rendezvous and without faith in the nobility of their mission, it was unlikely that these youths would have survived the gruesome ordeal.

Apart from extracts from Babu's diaries, the interviews with the two former students and information obtained from former Pakistani combatants, I have received corroboration from eyewitness accounts and from photographs that were taken over those days. These were mostly taken by citizens who found cameras to eternalize the extraordinary era they found themselves in. Even more had been taken by Nikon-sporting Pakistani officers and stolen by local photo-technicians and media assistants. They would replace used cartridges with blank film whenever they were able to access equipment. People took grave risks to observe and document the conflict. There is also a series of 9.5 mm movies shot by a professor of engineering whose flat provided a vantage point over several of the residential halls. He remain hidden for three days while his neighbours were dragged out into the stairwells. His six hours of film were crucial in weaving together this account. Around that same time, a professor at the Atomic Energy Centre was engrossed in his own project: recording wireless transmissions between Pakistani army units. The spool of radio traffic was converted to audio cassettes and circulated widely.

After devoting myself to the task for months, I painstakingly re-transcribed the seventy-odd hours recorded by the professor. In doing so, I was able to identify brief exchanges that uphold the hypothesis that the banyan did indeed survive for several days into Operation Searchlight. I will introduce snippets from these a little later in the narrative. Why these passages have escaped the attention of other scholars is explained partially by the fact that a substantial portion of the radio chatter was conducted utilizing coded terms and phrases, as well by the simple reason that no one prior to me had combed through the hundreds of pages seeking information pertaining to the tree's survival. This myth is a little known one, and my exclusive access to Babu's insights has allowed me to piece together an outline of events known to very, very few. A former West Pakistani officer who had been psychologically scarred by the senseless killing met with me over several weeks to crack military cyphers and to share memories. Since our collaboration, the retired rifleman has gone into hiding.

These sources will appear over and again in my ensuing framework of the Five-Day Mission. However, before we plunge ourselves into the ghastly and triumphant five days of which the axis mundi is the DU banyan, we must shift gears and double back once again, this time to the birth of ante-historic man. We will leave our narrative – leave both our bot and our aam – to gaze awhile into the thickets of earliest men. We must wander like pilgrims in considering our Ogygian fascination with trees. As evident from an essay, Babu pledged himself to charting man's purposeful stride, both towards and away from trees. Essential to much of what composes this episode, and our comprehension of war, human attachments, sacrifice, rebirth and forgiveness, are the metaphors that trees embody. There is something about the gnarly silhouette of a tree against the bare sky, its arms waving against the azure;

something remotely uncanny and beloved about it that keeps drawing us in.

Let us turn to an extract from one of Babu's eight undated essays. For working purposes, I have unofficially titled it 'Dendranthropology':

'Modern man, like his earliest predecessors in the grasslands, has an indelible kinship with trees. On valuing fruit, certain forebears of ours climbed on to boughs and made themselves at home. In growing longer arms and fingers, they became expert in finding the steps and ladders between branches. In vegetal abundance, without the need to compete for food, it was possible to coexist amiably with others, including different hominids. This harmony was seldom found in open plains, at perilous watering holes, or inside foreboding caves. Straddled securely on bounteous trees, they could observe and peer into one another's minds, and espy the familiar. Under swaying branches, in the presence of singing birds, anthropoids became deeply ingratiated to the sturdy and warm stems that nourished them. It became difficult to tell where the body of these rudimentary apes ended and where that of the tree began. They ate of its foliage, gave birth in its shade and died at its foot, limb inside limb, trunk against trunk, while the trees grew and grew.

'When the weather changed and fertile savannahs started to wither, starving hominids descended from the trees and departed. Their hefty arms grew shorter as they marched, and as their legs grew longer and straighter, broader hips made for a more efficient bipedal gait. Their skulls shifted, their faces flattened, and their eyes moved closer together in order to allow them to look forward. But even as they continued to walk, on the journey away from hunger and towards fresh sources of nutrition, shelter and companionship, early men found hitherto unknown timberlands and, once again, took comfort in them. Even in places where meat and fish were added to man's diet, when available, he would still seek an orchard to retire to. Forests could conceal him from predators, boughs could serve as lookout points, and saplings could bend to form walls. When man began to first walk upright, he identified with trees in a new fashion, especially with those that shot up into the sky with trunks straight and true. Man gradually learned to hold his chin up and keep his back straight, as he became an expert biped and warrior. His first classroom was defined by the branches of trees. As elders and their students crouched under their leafy shade, man's knowledge burgeoned in circles about trees. Later, as communities twisted more intimate knots, man felt his backbone extend a peculiar strength to his arms. Soon, like trees extending their branches, men reached to draw others in ... protecting, loving and promising.

'When we happened to evolve into sapient humans and took leave of our fundamental origins, in looking back to remember wherefrom we had come, all we discerned was a familiar arboretum, or the silhouette of a beloved perennial. And in identifying these first markers of birth and community, and in being unable to separate our existence from the groves under which our primordial consciousness had developed, we often saw the tree as creator. We located their timelessly nurturing features within ourselves. Hence lies an ancient motivation in dendrolatry and the worship of flora.

'So, much like lakes and ponds, and land and animals, trees were the first godlings of nature to branch the space between totems and fetishes. They incarnated a supreme vitality, yet unlike the sun and the wind, they were individually accessible. As human mental faculties grew, we adopted a variety of mystical traditions, yet in most every brain-twister recounted, we accommodated our favourite plantlets. Particular seedlings came to signify our cosmic origins, as others were designated as guardians and foes. Even others were said to herald our biological demises. While every community chose particular specimens to assign these roles to, in moving away from tree, water, element and animal to more abstract gods, man has quite never descended from his archetypal tree.'

I must insert here that though much of Babu's conclusions are validated by scientific evidence, there is scant surety that his observations are empirically verifiable. The following is condensed from Babu's notes, though with additions and edits made by me:

Amongst the oldest examples of tree worship are seals discovered in Mohenjo-daro, Pakistan, not so far from our bot tola. These date back to the third or fourth millennium BC. Terracotta figurines of naked females with their legs spread wide birthing plants also affirm the human affiliation with the verdancy of flora. Further west, in many African countries, the baobab was decorated and revered. The Herero in the Kalahari chart their origins from a tree. Majhwars of the Dumar or 'fig sect' believe that their first ancestor was born under this holy perennial. And in ancient Egypt, several types of trees appear in mythology and art, as they do in neolithic Greece and Japan. When man moved from a horizontal animal world to the world of erect beings, his mind rapidly developed an appreciation and mystical awe of the vertical dimension. Spiritual and material progress became for man an upward progress, and an extension of his upright spine. Trees, like mountains, and the largest animals, were the first recognized masters of these vertical axes. Celtic imaginations later associated vegetal species with wisdom.[50] Just as Etz Chayim (the Tree of Life) stands in the centre of Paradise in the Torah, in Islam there is a Lotus Tree (in Paradise), a Tree of Knowledge, as well as an Infernal Tree in Hell. From the mossy women of Tyrol in Germany to the Norse Yggdrasil, from the forest-spirits of Russia to the Chaldean tree of fertility, from the wood-demons of Peru and Brazil to the green

---

50   The Celtic word 'druid' derives in part from the root 'dru', meaning 'oak'.

footprints of the mysterious figure of Al-Khidr, the human animal has continued climbing his woods.

As we shall see, botanic bounties played a central role in sustaining the Five-Day Mission. This following selection from Babu's essay touches upon some of the uses to which plant extracts were applied:

'In unlocking the secret chemicals of certain shrubs and herbs, man further stimulated his mind into stepping without the landscape he inhabits. Drugs transported humans from mundane to divine spheres, transforming reality and revealing veiled dimensions. Archaeological evidence specifies the use of psychoactive substances dating back at least 10,000 years, ranging from a variety of fungi, and plant parts including seeds, roots, bark, leaves, fruits and beans.'

As we move closer geographically to the feature at hand, in antediluvian and Vedic traditions, a pantheistic outlook ensured the role of tree idolatry. In various festivals, forest, tree and garden deities were celebrated with superlative pomp, as were gods of fields and lotus ponds. Followers of Buddhism, Jainism and Brahminism later adopted with zeal this notion of heavenly trees. The Chinese tiangou is a fierce demon that has been adopted by other cultures as a protective spirit of forests. The King Willow of Tibetan mythology has its roots in the underworld, its trunk in this world, and its branches in heaven. The old angiosperm under which Buddha attained enlightenment is venerated, and from the four boughs of the Buddhist Tree of Wisdom flow the rivers of life.[51]

With the arrival of Islam in the eleventh century, new stories were set down. Similar to the Hebrew condemnation of pagan tree cults, Islam fundamentally opposes the sanctification of physical

---

51 The five sacred trees in Indra's paradise eerily echo the allegory of 'Five Trees in Paradise' in the famous Coptic Gospel of Thomas.

objects.[52] All the same, olive branches and grape leaves surround
luscious paradisiacal gardens on prayer rugs from the Indo-Asiatic
region. In the Islamic architecture that followed the Sufi saints, trees
abound. As with the Dome of the Rock in Jerusalem, the Sehzade
Mosque in Istanbul, and the Shajarat al-Tuba referred to by Prophet
Mohammed (PBUH) and the inimitable Sufi Ibn al-Arabi, the
enclosed mosque at the Taj Mahal features an inverted Tree of Bliss.
Rooted at the heavens, the archetype fills the main sanctuary.[53]

While local arboreal specimens are cherished for varying reasons,
a hierarchy of sorts usually develops and one can most certainly
identify this in the vicinity of Bangladesh. These preferences,
carried by traditions, tribes and cults have travelled all over the
subcontinent: there is a diaspora in most dendrolatrous societies.
Much of this was already known to Mr and Mrs Majumdar. All
these backstories had filtered through time and circumstance to
spur an adoration of the bot. Long before Babu would begin his
studies regarding flora, he would encounter the reverence of trees
via the free spirit that was Mali.

---

52 Babu, in his forties, would become preoccupied with the Islamic Lote
    Tree, the Tree of Knowledge and the Tree of Immortality and how, on the
    Day of Judgment, Allah uses them to provide shade to those worthy of his
    benediction.
53 When Muslim conquerors and poets arrived from Persia, Central Asia, they
    brought with them a passion for orchards. It is widely established that ancient
    Indo-Aryans worshipped oaks. The Naqshbandi Sufi order, which played a
    crucial role in the introduction of Islam across Asia, has a holy mulberry at
    their shrine in Bukhara, Uzbekistan. On the banks of the Narmada, stands a
    revered banyan. It is thought to have grown from a twig used as a toothpick
    by the Sufi poet Kabir. On the side of Delhi's Qutub Minar, a UNESCO
    World Heritage Site with the tallest brick minaret in the world, a tenacious
    little peepul grows. This climber has made its home inside a crack in the
    Minar's walls. It is honoured as a divine benediction, invoking the adage that
    the only thing that separates a weed from a flower is human judgement.

In the five hellish days that the attack on the bot lasted, our heroic protestors relied on botanical aids to sustain themselves. After emerging from the pool of dead at night, they groomed themselves using neem twigs for their teeth, coconut-palm oil for their hair, turmeric as a disinfectant, as well as sandalwood soap, jute loofahs and local medicines made of root, stem, leaf, fruit, flower and bark extracts. While most of these were obtained from campus gardens, some provisions were found at Dhaka Medical College. This facility would continue to nurture freedom fighters in the following months. Though the medical institute had been looted earlier that day, a thorough search by the students yielded a trove of vegetal and ayurvedic supplies. There are a number of growths that are especially meaningful to those that dwell in Bangladesh and neighbouring lands. We will later encounter some of these.

It is time to return to the Five-Day Mission. Emerging from these antiquated woods, we must make our way to that special tree in that extraordinary time. That first night of the military crackdown, after seventeen students were assisted in fleeing the university campus, the remaining twelve activists, Babu's mother and father included, collaborated with a network of about eleven Pakistani officers and yard-birds. Let us now return to that night of March. To facilitate matters, let us designate the tree saviours as the TT (Tree Team), Bengali students and locals as Bs, the patriotic Pakistanis as PPs, and the Pakistanis who helped the TT as the PSs (the S standing for 'sympathizers').

Day One – 26 March

A little after 0400 hours on the first day of the rebuttal galvanized by the students, the soldiers collected clothing to waterproof all twelve of them. The Bs would have to remain submerged in university ponds during daylight hours. In truth, no amount of moisture-repelling polyvinyl, rubber or polyurethane could insulate our Bs from the effects of the decaying bodies that littered the ponds. In fact, these corpses ensured the survival of the remaining students: the stench and gore kept army personnel away. The sun was expected to rise around 0600 hours; on the first night of the operation, our makeshift taskforce had less than two hours to formulate a plan to save the tree. The first night was the easiest night for the TT – intelligence had it that the army intended to use explosives and bulldozers to topple the large growth. Most PPs had already left the university

164

premises – General Farman Ali had ordered them to move on to Dhaka's old town and the neighbouring Hindu-populated areas. The local police at Rajarbag, aided by volunteers, were putting up a spirited resistance, and Central Command did not see the need to leave an excess of Pakistani contingents at DU. Approximately 200 infantrymen from various battalions remained to demolish the tree and designated structures, and to patrol the digs. General Tikka Khan, the governor general and the chief martial law administrator of Bangladesh, planned to have classes back in session within a month to normalize the image of the country in the eyes of the international community.

Of the soldiers on campus, a total of nine were now assisting the Bs in their banyan crusade. Four of them had had to deceive superiors and peers to remain at the university barracks. The officer left in charge of the now quiet campus was a forty-three-year-old major named Tareq Saud. Major Saud's performance thus far in Operation Searchlight had been rather disappointing; he displayed no particular zeal or drive in the operation to subdue East Pakistan. As his seniors reckoned that the campus posed no further threat, they decided to post him there. Major Saud was in charge of personnel that were mainly Punjabi, Baluchi, Pathan and Sindhi.

Major Saud himself was from Gujrat, but had served most of his military career in the Kashmir wars. He had then earned a reputation for being a brave volunteer. The gruff major had had a happy childhood – having come from a large household, he had been sociable and outgoing. None of his men could possibly guess that under his starched and abrasive exterior was a man who was remembered fondly by most in his town. It was impossible to tell that as a boy Major Saud had been inseparable from his beloved canine Brandy, or that he had been popular in cadet college. After two decades of artillery duty, those close to the major knew how he had lost his desire for a military career, and seemed disinterested as juniors superseded him in rank. Few knew this listlessness stemmed from having witnessed one too many governmentally orchestrated bloodbaths. By the time Major Saud was assigned to Operation Searchlight, the boots on this soldier were definitely not as dedicated as higher-ups wanted them to be. He was thus given charge of demolishing the bot and securing the deserted zone, as the army initiative pushed determinedly into more contested areas.

As Major Saud was not especially vigilant over his ranks, the PSs succeeded in dodging inquiries regarding their contra-directive presence by keeping a low profile. These PSs damaged the batteries of the two army bulldozers on campus grounds, and stole a number of fuses and cords that would be needed for detonations. Rocket-launchers and grenades were likewise incapacitated. All this went very smoothly, with no suspicions being aroused. By 0530 hours, the twelve Bs were immersed in nearby ponds and, shortly afterwards, the major ordered his platoon sergeant to prep the bot tola for a blast. After an hour, feedback from engineers and blasters indicated that essential equipment was missing, and that the dynamite and combustibles were damp. After the bulldozers failed to start, Major Saud contacted High Command and requisitioned parts and supplies from the Central Ordnance Depot. These were estimated to reach DU by 1200 hours, and he was told to sit tight.

Around 1300 hours, when the major was readying to resume the bot assignment with fresh cordite, heavy rainfall postponed further incendiary gambles. Some marksmen were assigned to safeguard that the nitro-glycerine compounds stayed dry, while others were allotted dormitories and nearby apartments to collect dead bodies from. They commandeered a group of captive Bengalis to carry these bodies to the open fields in front of the residential halls. After digging a large pit, the prisoners were told to throw the dead bodies in. Movie footage recorded by a Professor Nurul-Ullah shows one such burial site in front of Jagannath Hall, and how diggers were themselves forced into the pits and shot dead. However, what the film could not record was that there was inevitably a body or two with skin unscathed: a few would faint, overcome by stench, labour and terror, to awaken later. One of these fortunate souls later plays a small part in our tree campaign.

Around 1700 hours, the Bs exited the ponds to meet in the hospital as planned. On reuniting, they were barely able to speak. One of them was able to start boiling water, collect soap and start an hour-long cleansing process that gradually restored their sense of humanity. In interviews with the two former student-activists, I was struck by something they both expressed to me separately. They both referred to a sense of disconnect from their bodies. After lying still amidst the piles of corpses and silently witnessing the actions of man against man, it was as if they did not want to return to being alive, or to being human.

A little after 2000 hours, they were joined at the aam tola by two of the PSs and were informed that the major had decided it should be dry enough at 2300 hours to complete the tree mission. Saud was not a particularly creative galvanizer, and there was no change in the tactics employed: dynamite and demolition tractors it still was. But as the provisions were guarded this time, the PSs were unable to access the ordnance. The PPs guarding the explosives had been chosen personally by the major's second-in-command and were not suitable for treasonous proposals.

After a forty-minute discussion, the TT fixed on the following proposal: when everything was in place for the gunpowder to be ignited, the students would start the bulldozers and drive them away from the campus. As the area surrounding the bot would have been cleared for the blast, this peripheral diversion would allow the PSs an opportunity to disable the charges. In the confusion, they would then access the remaining arsenal; appointed guards would surely have left their posts in anticipation of a pyrotechnic spectacle. They could hardly be expected to remain vigilant over spare consignments after what was needed for the tree had been used. The PSs had already drugged transport operators with sedatives from the hospital to facilitate their removal. The Bs would have to, however, infiltrate the area where the vehicles were parked, and for this it was decided that Pakistani army uniforms were needed once again, enemy and friend became confused as boots and uniforms were borrowed, and courageous revolutionaries transgressed identity lines.

Babu's mother was an expert mechanic, and was chosen to be one of the three drivers. The three Bs who were to commandeer the bulldozers apprehended that their part in the undertaking was key, as well as most perilous. The three Bs would also have to escape to safety after hijacking the vehicles. The heavy machines were slow moving – they would only have about two to three minutes before losing the element of surprise and before confused PP forces would reach them. The daring Bs knew their campus so well they were confident that they could escape if given a few hundred yards head-start. Their PS counterparts were also at significant risk as they would have to hide quite close to the tree. If the detonation was not thwarted, they would suffer injuries. Timing was of the essence.

Fortunately, everything went according to plan. As the major and his PPs gathered around demolitionists and readied themselves for the blast, the students started the machines and drove them away, horns blaring. The PP operators had indeed been fast asleep and had been pushed aside. Once the troops realized that the loud automobiles were suspiciously heading in the wrong direction, they turned as one and gave chase. The PSs then snatched the explosives from the fig, discarded them into ponds, and headed for the remaining supplies. On reaching the storage tent, they found an unconscious officer: Babu's father and another B, dressed in black, had penetrated the secured compound. It only took a few seconds to confiscate the leftover stockpile, after which the Bs fled to their hiding places and the PSs to their official ranks. In the meanwhile, the PPs had reacquired their tractors, sleeping drivers and all, but had been unable to catch the swift youths before they melted back into the night. They did however report to the major that the hijackers had been men of their own cloth – a disclosure that caused significant agitation.

The troops returned to the blasting site and recommenced their operation. However, when nothing happened, not a crack or fizzle, perplexed engineers discovered the missing charges. Major Saud, now irate, stormed to the ammunitions tent and proceeded to slap the guards after realizing that his reserves were stolen as well. He then continued to the slap the drowsy drivers and everyone else around him. Screaming, he told his men, 'Cocksuckers, we are going to see this darn sapling go down even if we have to cut it by hand!' Years later, when attempting to publish his memoirs, the major confided to an editor that he had become obsessed with destroying that bot.

With that, our day ends. The Bs gradually made their way to the hospital again to prepare for another day of immersion in the pools. Mrs Majumdar returned from the base to a crying husband; no one was certain if the drivers were safe. The Bs shared their experiences and discussed further schemes that could be implemented. But as there was no info concerning the major's exact programme, they had to be satisfied for the night. A conspicuous event from day one is that a particular B felt poorly and asked to leave. He was joined by a young woman that had been found alive in a pond earlier that day. That left eleven Bs and eleven bold PSs to continue in the effort.

Day Two – 27 March

While millions were tuning into the thirty-third NCAA Men's Basketball Championship, few remembered how on that very day in 922 CE, the Persian mystic Al-Hallaj was sentenced to death at the age of sixty-four. The alleged rabble-rouser was flogged, mutilated and beheaded for advocating reform of the Caliphate. Many had also forgotten how on that day in 1942, Japanese-Americans residing in California were ordered to evacuate within twenty-four hours, shortly thereafter being interred. Two years later, on the same date, two thousand Jews were murdered in Kaunas, Lithuania. But on 27 March 1971, as chance would have it, a Japanese ship in the Bay of Bengal providentially picked up a radio transmission from Commander Ziaur Rahman in which he officially declared the independence of Bangladesh on behalf of Mujibur Rahman. This was then retransmitted by Radio Australia and by the British Broadcasting Corporation to the world.

But all this mattered little to the major that morning. On the second day of the campaign, Major Saud lined all his men up so as to examine papers, uniforms and characters. This prompted the three PSs that were at DU in violation of orders to quickly depart. Now, only nine PS members remained. After lunch, the major sent his men to flatten the three un-Islamic temples on campus, while he remained at the bot with nearly a dozen guns. The major acquired a motorized chainsaw and cut down several aerial roots with his own hands before collapsing in a sweaty pile. While most trees can be tipped to fall in a particular direction with notches cut into their trunks, this was impossible with a large banyan due to the vertical roots that burrowed into the dirt. When standing near the broad bot, one felt as if they were in a forest rather than under an individual plant. Major Saud, tired with blasters and engineers, requested a tank from Central Command. Radio transcripts indicate that he had remarked, 'Let's see how this damn thing stands up to a nice fat 105 mm round from one of our M24s.'

The major's spirits rose when his men returned from destroying the temples successfully and again when it was verified that an M24 would soon be arriving, 'Get ready for a bonfire, boys.' Sure enough, the armoured car reported to him before dusk. The major immediately ushered it treeward. The driver parked appropriately, the gunner saluted smartly, and the first shell was sent off, right past the bot into the flower gardens in the west. The major yelled through a mike-set, 'Fool. Where are you looking?' The second shot delivered was even wider off the mark but, to the gunner's credit, the men at the site contended that his aim had been true and that the missile had bizarrely turned southward. In fact, Professor Nurul-Ullah had captured this on tape. Despite its grainy resolution, experts can trace the fire-signature of the missile to affirm that it did veer away randomly. This second shell demolished part of Jagannath Hall, which was definitely not part of army plans.

After a pause, the major started screaming, 'Get out, get out you cross-eyed monkeys!' and approached the tank as if to climb into it. Tanker and gunner fled the scene post-haste. They returned to headquarters swearing that things were very peculiar at DU. In fact, this particular gunner was known as a good shot, and his unnerving claims that demons had swatted his shots away resonated amongst the bleary eyed gunslingers who had been working overtime in death-squads.

After recovering from a prolonged and vehement outburst, Major Saud radioed Central Command. He was questioned directly by Major General Farman Ali who, too, was not happily encamped. Their transcribed exchange follows.

Major Saud: 84 for 89. Thank you for the tank, sir. Everything is going fine. Three Hindu and Buddhist temples destroyed, all elements extinguished. Over.

Control: 84, roger. Everything is okay how? Regarding the escape routes west of the railway line, that is in your area, hope that necessary blocks have come into position so that elements that are facing 26 and 79 in the campus do not pull out westwards. But Big Bird [Sheikh Mujibur Rahman] is out of the picture, so what can these snipper-snappers do anyway? Over.

Major Saud: 84 for 89. Sir. We are very extensively patrolling the area. Every minute we are passing through and we are on the watch. We have blocked all the roads and secured the Second Capital Exchange, and have also set up blocks for any people trying to escape from the campus towards the west. Over.

Control: 41, roger. That is good then. But what about Mission Root Removal? I have heard from Cheetah [Infantry Unit] and Big Brother [Tank Unit] that you have not yet completed it. It's been almost three days, what is going on? From our position in the commissioner's office, we can see the dozers. Are they in working order? Over.

Major Saud: 84 for 89. Sir, Big Brother attempted two shots, but both missed. I had to call it off. We have also been having problems with defective equipment, but rest assured I will have the mission settled very soon. Over.

Control: Do not waste any more time. Have the tree removed, or I will have you relieved. This is critical, hearsay is that you have treasonous elements in your ranks. Let's not even discuss how absurd that sounds. Just take care of Root Removal. That's all for now. Out.

Major Saud: 84 for 89. Sir. Yes, sir … Affirmative. Out.

A disconcerted major returned to his duties. He dedicated part of his forces to clearing debris from Jagannath, and others to requisition local masons and carpenters to repair damaged dormitories. Some of these Bengalis noticed that the bot had been cordoned off. The major and three of his best men employed handsaws to cut several more aerial root branches. After spending several hours under the growth, Major Saud declared that this *Ficus benghalensis* was no normal tree. With its numerous roots that formed accessory trunks, there was no central axis to isolate. It was rather like having to cut down several dozen interconnected hardwoods. The larger trunks were so firmly entrenched that it seemed one would have to tear up the entire area to remove them. With shoots connected to each other both over and under the soil, the knotted thing was a complex structure.

Be that as it may, the major had dozers move in and fix steel cables around its girth. They aligned to face the same direction and synchronously revved. After spinning wheels for several minutes, temperature gauges and the smell of burning oil indicated that the machines could do no more. The fig had not budged. Earlier rains had softened the earth, and the vehicles were unable to gain sufficient traction. This can be seen on Professor Nurul-Ullah's 9.5 mm film; it even shows smoke billowing out from engines. The major tried having stones placed under the tires, but these sank instantly. The tapes also capture the image of an agitated officer unholster his weapon and discharge it at the bot several times before marching into a tent. Later that night, more branches were sawed, but no substantial headway was made.

After sunset, the Bs exited the ponds and cautiously trickled into
the hospital once again. The daylong immersions were taking their
toll, and yet another B tearfully asked to leave. While they gently
rubbed coconut oil, sandalwood paste and rosewater on to one
another, a number of ideas were discussed. One childlike B, leaning
against the mango growth, looked into its sinuous branches and
exclaimed, 'Snakes! Let us get a bunch of snakes and let them loose
in the barracks.' The others agreed that gypsy bedeys and ojhas –
mystic healers – could help fill the area with deadly vipers. These
traditional snake-charmers had probably taken to the waters on
hearing of the invasion, but could likely be located by someone who
knew their migratory patterns.

Another B had the idea of using hallucinogenic growths to doctor
the PP food supply; mild toxins would not kill (in event of which
new soldiers would arrive), but would rather leave victims deluded
and confused. One proponent referred to the Bacon Rebellion
of 1676 in Virginia Colony, when British ensigns had mistakenly
consumed datura in a salad and were left disabled for two weeks.
Other Bs wished to camouflage themselves and launch minor
sorties on the PPs. Five of the TT youths had trained for months
before Operation Searchlight had gone the extra cardiovascular
mile. The five included Babu's father.

In the long days they spent in the ponds, these youths quickly
remembered the hours they had spent watching various gurus,
yogis and fakirs exercise riverside.[54] After days of controlling
breath, stature, reflex and thought, these Bs became proficient in

---

54 For centuries, Indians have employed a variety of calisthenics to acquire
    corporeal and corporal skills. Many posit that these later contributed
    majorly to the development of Asian martial arts. A legendary figure in the
    origins of Kung Fu, Bodhidharma was an Indian monk who authored tomes
    on muscle, tendon and mind programming.

mastering time and space, and in cloaking their chakras. To spy on their enemy and traverse across the breadth of DU, they remained motionless, often submersing themselves amidst corpses. In the evenings, just a foot away from the adversaries, they vanished into nooks and crevices, using animal calls and pebbles to misdirect attention. Like primordial green-men, in the tradition of al-Khidr, they shed bones from their thumbs and became like leaf. These five also possessed the faculties that enabled the conversion of trauma into technique; they converted the currencies of horror and rage into a lizard like stop-motion. These skillsets were vital as it was becoming less apparent what stratagems the major might employ next.

Several PSs joined the Bs around 0700 hours, bringing food and hope. They had identified weaknesses in the army roadblocks and patrol arrangements, and had solicited even more supporters. They had also found two more Bengalis alive in the ditches, and had fed them and concealed them nearby. Both were strong and wished to join the TT. The PSs claimed that their network was now capable of moving Bs in and out of the university holdings rapidly. Furthermore, on being briefed on the latest schemes that the Bs had brainstormed, the PSs assured they could easily access PP food supplies.

Four Bs left shortly afterwards, under the protection of several PSs, to search for the bedeys and their snakes, as well as for edible narcotics. The TT that remained at DU would endure with what they had at hand. And that very night, they demonstrated their abilities: dressed in black clothing, five of them applied burnt cork to their faces and speared into the enemy camps, climbing into vegetation and painstakingly moving forward, inch by inch, via gutters and drains. They gathered data and tactical particulars before returning to the ponds.

Day Three – 28 March

Perhaps the ghostly cork-faced Bs had been spotted the previous night as, first thing in the morning, the major sequestered a no-entry zone of 500 feet around the bot. The munitions engineer, who had come with the delivery, surveyed the tree and made suggestions regarding how dynamite could be successfully used to eradicate the tenacious plant. The engineer promised he would bring the necessary supplies the following day – it would take a while to obtain the exact payload needed. The major bade him to make speed, and proceeded with several PPs to the bot to hew the branches and roots that anchored the ponderous trunks. However, just barely a few minutes into their exertions, a loud buzzing descended from the solid canopy overhead. To the horror of Major Saud and his troops, dark clouds of wasps descended from the rustling foliage to sting them. Everyone within a quarter-mile radius had to take shelter. The troops were bitten terribly, but most had to make do without painkillers. There were temporarily no further attempts to tackle the bot. The major scratched at his neck and arms, and swore profusely as ice packs were applied. After a couple of hours, he grabbed a rocket-launcher and fired at the tree from a distance. Although injury to the banyan was minimal, irater Apocrita appeared.

We will step back here for a moment, on this 28 March 1971, to contemplate the age-old notion that there is nothing new under the sun. As winged creatures buzz about our reveries, as rafters fall from collapsing skies perfectly into place creating something afresh, we need to look higher into the ether to briefly cogitate the mathematics of infinity, of recurrence, and how men and women betray their own.

The number twenty-eight has an important role in the Julian calendar, since it corresponds to the solar cycle of twenty-eight years, at the end of which the days of the week return to the same days of the month. The world famous numerologist, Cheiro, professes that 'the number twenty-eight combines cyclic times: four, and the evolutionary times: seven.' Cherio unfathomably claims that twenty-eight is the 'spiral of the evolution unfolding among the perpetual cycles of nature'. Twenty-eight is the number of chapters in the Gospel of Matthew and the number of days that the Buddha meditated under the Bodhi Tree. The Chinese have a zodiac of twenty-eight animals. 28 March, according to heavenly whims, is about a week after the spring equinox, which is considered the beginning of the new zodiacal year and a time of new commencements. Ecclesiastes, in chapter 3, verses 2 to 8, enumerates that there are twenty-eight different kinds of time: 'There is a time for giving birth and a time for dying, for planting and for uprooting what has been planted, to kill and heal, to destroy and build, to cry and laugh, to mourn and dance, to throw stones away and to gather them, to embrace and to refrain from embracing, to search and lose, to keep and discard, to tear and sew, for keeping silent and to speak, to love and to hate, and finally a time for war and a time for peace.'

If there is but only twenty-eight times under the sun, if everything in the universe has been recurring, and will continue to recur, in a self-similar form an infinite number of times, the question begs itself as to why man has not yet identified the rounded ocean he rows within. The concept of eternal returns is found in Indian philosophy, in antediluvian Egypt and, later, in the Pythagorean Stoics. If every human is but a Sisyphus, forever rolling a boulder uphill only for it to roll back down, why can we not spare some love from our amor fati to extend to others around us, each of whom rolls their own boulder?

The major most likely had none of this on his mind that morning, just as he was probably unaware how on 28 March 1933, the German Reichstag had conferred dictatorial mandates on Hitler, or how on

28 March 1969, the Greek poet and Nobel Prize laureate Giorgos Seferis opposed the Regime of the Colonels that was to last seven years. Major Saud was absolutely not expected to know how, on that very day exactly a decade later, Viv Richards would score a century in the first Test match in Antigua, or how on 28 March 1994, African National Congress snipers would fire upon Zulu nationalists in a confrontation that would claim tens of thousands.

The Latin month Martius was named for Mars, most commonly known as the Roman god of war. Mars, however, was also regarded as a guardian of agriculture and March was the beginning of the season for both farming and warfare. For the major, that March morning was decidedly a time for uprooting, discarding, destroying and killing. After the bout with the wasps, the major forwarded his beleaguered men into the city to track down pest-exterminators along with the requisite poisons and gear. This proved easier than thought: by the early evening, the wasps were gone. Unknown to him, however, was that substitutions were already being procured. Two of the Bs who had left the night before in search of supplies returned Mackandal-like after sunset with large sacks of miscellaneous fungi, datura and nutmeg powder.[55]

While a portion of the hallucinogenic compounds were dispensed to PSs to contaminate the PP encampment, the bulk of it was given to the five Bs who broke away the moment the packages were placed in their hands. Within an hour, they had edged and joggled their way into the PP mess to poison rations. Having accomplished this, they attempted to access the PP

---

55 They also brought stories with them, litanies of bereavement and sickening violations – tales of a devastated city. All was not lost though; they conveyed how an underground resistance had already set into place, and how they even knew of the initiative to thwart Mission Root Removal. The returning Bs expressed their confidence that, with the backing of the emerging resistance, the bedeys and ojhas would soon be found.

chainsaws, but this is when things went wrong ... at least for three of them. A coterie of PPs distinguished themselves as exceptionally vigilant: working together in small bands, they had studied the landscape and had acquired the skills needed to detect the fluid Bs. At around 0800 hours, these PPs spotted Bs near their base and successfully captured three. Babu's father was fortunate enough to escape with one other B. After the major had looked these prisoners over, he stated, 'These are no normal Bengalis. These ones are special; look at them.' The major rubbed their black visages clean, looked into their impenetrable eyes, listened to their almost imperceptible breaths, and the night turned towards tragedy. The Bengalis were tortured for hours. Perhaps the hours of screaming, gasping, swearing, bleeding, cutting and beating, finally began to take their toll on the bot tola. Both my former student informants concurred that the tree's will finally began break on this long night.

Dinner was consumed while the torture was underway and, as the drugs set in, a kind of frenzy descended on the PPs. The tree was forgotten, while attention shifted to the captives. Major Saud behaved like a man possessed, venting dark furies upon the three, surgically removing ears, fingers, toes and limbs. The PSs watched helplessly, in silence. The misery of that night did not only affect the TT (who listened from farther away). The PPs, too, spent a sleepless night. They later recounted how they had muttered and shuddered in dread. The narcotics heightened the senses of the other soldiers, as the Bengalis reappeared in their dreams, crawling with the scaly skins of motionless turtles ... intertwined in brushwood ... as snakes began to swallow staffs and their own tails ... circling around tightly, choking...

The remaining Bs huddled together that night and soothed one another through the harrowing and audible deaths of their peers. Babu's mother and father were inseparable that night: one of the captured Bs was a dear friend. But the night and its sacrifices ended as a lightening sky warned that it was time to return to the waters.

Day Four – 29 March

On day four, as Lieutenant William Calley was found guilty in Fort Benning, Georgia, of twenty-two murders out of the hundreds of civilians killed in My Lai, Vietnam, and sentenced to life imprisonment (only to be later pardoned), as Chilean President Salvador Allende nationalized banks and copper mines, and as the MMR hepatitis vaccine for infants was announced, Major Saud was awoken by a radio operator. A furious General Farman was demanding an update on the status of Mission Root Removal. The major was still very much under the influence of psychoactive substances during the conversation:

Control: 84, hello. What is going on over there? Major are you asleep at 1027? I have been hearing the oddest things about your camp. Listen, Major, we're here to secure a whole bleeding country, why is that you're still stuck with Root Removal? And I hear you've destroyed about half the university. We're supposed to restart classes ASAP. Do I have to fight this whole damn war by myself? Over.

Major Saud: 84 for 89. Good morning, ahh, good morning. Sir. Do not think I have not tried. Sir, I have tried everything ... This tree, I swear every morning it gets bigger ... Last night I saw it with my own eyes, it was growing more branches while we were cutting others ... My Cheetahs saw it too. But I will get it, bastard strangling fig. I will send its corpse to India. Over.

Control: Major Saud ... you sound ... are you drunk, you fool? We're facing pot-shots from these bloody Bengalis and you're doing what ... drinking? Even without Big Bird, they're still fighting back. Listen, this is it, I am personally coming over tonight, I have a feeling a good thrashing might help your elements. Over.

Major Saud: 84 for 89. Please, sir, can you bring some more electric arm lamps, sir, the powerful ones. Night here is very bad, sir, things are moving always. Over.

Control: I have nothing more to say to you, you filthy madman. Out.

Major Saud: 84 for 89. Thank you so much, sir. Out.

This brief exchange is the closest thing I have found to an official admission of what was happening with the bot. Even if all the evidence and testimonies I have acquired are to be dismissed, this short clip validates the telling of this tale.

After the dialogue with General Farman, a rather befuddled major returned to his operations at DU. He was having disturbing flashes from the previous night and began to remember his wrathful antics. He looked over his men and realized they looked rundown. A transistor somewhere was tuned into Voice of America, and he could hear a presenter debating the Los Angeles jury recommendation that Charles Manson and three female followers be given the death sentence. Acting on orders, another operator was tuned into All India Radio's broadcasts from Calcutta, where the day's coverage focused on the 114th anniversary of the Sepoy Mutiny of 29 March 1857, when a Bengali named Mangal Pandey had rebelled against his British commanders. When Sepoy Pandey of the 34th Regiment was court-martialled and hung, he inspired India's first War of Independence. The major's superiors could have gained much from heeding events such as these from Bengal's history before the launch of a 1971 onslaught. But it was too late now and, for the moment, there were commissions to requite.

Major Saud learned that the munitions engineer had arrived at 0800 hours and had procured the incendiaries as promised. The major was visibly relieved as he looked over the goods and the fresh cordite. He immediately had the engineer prepare a charge for the bot. Now, there are differing accounts of what transpired on day four, and our investigations will attempt to cover most of them.

Those privy to what was going on with the bot report that several attempts to demolish the tree failed that afternoon. The keen ballistics technologist circled it with gunpowder, only to knock away bits of bark and a few branches. He then painstakingly inserted charges in between limbs and on stems at strategic points, before once again igniting to no avail. Those familiar with the effects of dynamite on trees will attest that it is no simple matter to fell a large growth. There is one sure way to take out sturdy trunks like those of the banyan, but neither Major Saud nor his men knew it. One of the TT participants who contributed to this narrative claimed that the PSs had managed to turn the engineer and had persuaded him to spare the bot. Another account had it that the plebe had lunched at the DU base and was thereby rendered incompetent by narcotic agents. Irrespective of the exact details, the major badgered an increasingly ineffective and reticent demolitions novice into the late hours of the afternoon when Major General Farman arrived with his men.

A string of vehicles raised a cloud of dust as they rolled in and, on disembarking from his vehicle, the infamous Major General continued to raise hell. Farman was regarded by privates on the ground as more callous than President Yahya Khan. His meticulous and thorough blueprint for Operation Searchlight surprised even the bloodthirsty General Tikka Khan, who was not immodestly nicknamed the Butcher of Bengal. Farman immediately dismissed the major. He filed a report alleging that he found Major Saud weeping in public, with a pistol in his hand. Furthermore, the major's Cheetahs lacked morale, exhibited signs of fatigue and did not look fit enough to tackle neighbourhood ravens, let alone a potential counter-insurgence.

Farman had three other officers – two colonels and a lieutenant-colonel – removed from active duty and airlifted back to Karachi with the major. Having been in the war business for decades, Farman correctly suspected that many of the men were experiencing narco-induced side-effects. He had all food rations destroyed, dishes and uniforms soaked in boiling water, and the encampment sterilized, disinfected and treated for contamination. This was done in a matter of hours and, through it all, Farman's eye was fixed on the obstinate bot.

Around 2000 hours, two men from his ammunitions corps befittingly suggested that deep holes be drilled into the main trunks to create mortises which could be filled with dynamite (this was the trick that the major had missed). They explained that if the holes were sealed with clay and allowed to harden for hours, the effects of the charge would be greatly magnified. Farman's men asserted that a brisance of this nature would fracture the tree from within; it would be an easy matter to knock the bot down afterwards. Farman liked the idea and cleared them to proceed.

The men worked until close to 0000 hours, and left the clay to dry. Farman returned to the cantonment garrison and was met by intelligence, surveillance and reconnaissance agents. Reports were filtering in that Bengalis all over the nation were fleeing towards India to drill at border camps. This was not remarkable, but what was particularly unexpected was that word had somehow made it to several high-ranking Pakistani officers, as well as to the Bengali

militia, that the bot at Dhaka University was somehow trumping
the potential of Pakistani regiments. There was even talk about a
bot Bahini ('bahini' meaning 'army' in Bengali) and its fight to save
the perennial.

Farman vented these frustrations to a certain Dutch-Australian,
William Ouderland. The foreigner had dropped in to chat and
share anecdotes about local events. Ouderland, new to the region,
had been posted as director of a shoe factory shortly before
the war broke out. Having been a sergeant in World War II, the
Dutchman quickly befriended Farman, Tikka and General A.A.K.
Niazi, commander of the Eastern Military High Command.
Ouderland was issued a security pass, allowing free access to the
headquarters of Eastern Command. But what his new friends did
not know was that Ouderland (who had formerly worked with
the Dutch Underground Resistance Movement) had joined the
Bengali uprising on commencement of Operation Searchlight. On
infiltrating Dhaka cantonment, Ouderland not only provided vital
information to the growing insurgency, but also personally organized
and directed a number of guerrilla operations. Unrecognized and
unexpected heroes such as he toiled to ensure that the Bengali
victories continued rolling in.

General Tikka arrived at the cantonment a little later, and
on being apprised of the tree situation, volunteered to take over
campus operations. Farman assented. As Tikka received notice that
a snake infestation had overwhelmed their men at the university,
he scheduled his visit for the next morning. The two Bs had indeed
returned with several bedeys carrying sacks of poisonous snakes.
With the help of Mr Majumdar and a few others, these serpents
were released into the barracks at the heart of DU. The area would
have to be cleared of underbrush and gear, and rations would need
to be meticulously inspected before being pronounced safe. Thus
ended day four.

Day Five – 30 March

By 0900 hours, Tikka was alerted that the area had been cleared of reptiles and other offenders. A quiet general, clad in knee-high boots, arrived at DU at 1100 hours. Almost two hundred kraits, cobras, sea-snakes and vipers had been exterminated, along with iridescent poison-dart frogs and outlandish cone snails. The atmosphere at DU was sombre. It is terrifying to share a dark night on three square kilometres with scores of snakes, each carrying enough venom to kill multiple men. Circa a dozen conscripts had received bites and were rushed to the military hospital – three had perished.

Swishing a rattan, Tikka walked to within a quarter mile of the bot and seated himself for a clear view of the blasts. Apart from the main trunk, several others had been drilled, filled with nitro-glycerine compounds, and mortised. There was a call of 'fire in the hole' followed by earth-shattering reports. The smoke cleared as Tikka and his men approached the banyan. All the aerial roots lay splintered and prostrate, but the central trunk remained upright. It had a gaping hole in its side. The fig seemed to move, favouring one side and then the other.

The PPs stood well away from its branchy reach, but later commented that there was something extraordinary about the noises the huge banyan had made. It heaved and emitted a songlike lament, and as huge birds silently flew overhead, the sky went dark. With its burnt foliage and ashen bark, the tree wore a huge charcoal beard. Having been stripped of all its branches and roots, the banyan was naked of the life that had huddled about it. For the first time in hundreds of years, all that remained was the dead of its ringed centre. As a wisp of smoke poured out of its side and parted into the breeze, a sudden hush descended. All noises receded as birds withdrew. The soldiers found their own heads pounding as the environs shrank away, and when bulldozers fluently knocked the bot over, they were left in a landscape where the affiliation between man and tree was suspended.

The TT, Bs and PSs, whether a mile or a few hundred yards away, inexplicably knew that the bot had fallen and that this mission was over. Most of the Bs were at the hospital; they felt no need to hide in ponds, as patrols no longer visited the area. Furthermore, two Bs and one PS had been bitten while handling snakes the night before, and despite receiving first aid at the emergency room, had died in the early morning. Their comrades buried them at the foot of the expansive mango. As the rebels sat near the fresh graves and consoled one another, there was an abrupt and violent trembling in the aam tree. They recount the evergreen to have poured away green leaves and young fruit rather bizarrely. This was not quite a few minutes after Tikka had the bot ripped apart. One may hazard a guess that the *Mangifera indica* was grieving.

The young and not-so-young members looked each other in the eye – there was no need to embrace or join hands in superficial farewells. Over the previous days, they had become connected in some strange and prehistoric order of things; the bodies they occupied were now shared habitats. Over the five days, they had returned to the most organic of their natures. This resulted from having died every morning, and from being nocturnally reborn in one another's arms. The team disassembled and, like pollen, fragmented into the breeze; there was no sense of loss or parting, but rather continuity and the promise of unremitting progress. Of the six remaining Bs, four left immediately. The PSs helped them in this egress, their last mission. Mr and Mrs Majumdar wished to stay on until nightfall. They insisted they would be able to make their way out without aid.

Babu's parents had only been married a year now, but the trials and tests of these five days had bequeathed them a rare affiliation.

The bot experience had allowed them, *required them*, to peer into the depths of one another's anima, into the green and orange and black that burns behind our innermost workings, into forges far below the surface. In addition to this great intimacy, in the following hours, the two would share the interpersonal union of creating life.

Neither spouse was ready to sever ties to the bot and, in the cover of darkness, the couple found their way to its massive trunk. It had been dragged to the Ramna Race Course a mile to the east. The young lovers sat against its wood, remembering what had been. Looking into each other, they discerned in the lines of their brows, in the set of their jaws and in the expanse of their eyes, an uncanny prescience of what was to be. Nothing would be the same, yet there were echoes rising from an old void, from the deep black pit of war a clarion sounded. Shaking like animals emerging from dust, like leaves after the rain, the young couple held each other, and as they listened to faraway canons and to the cries of the mortally wounded, they pressed their chests and faces together. Sobbing in desperation, they pressed together a new life, one that would be delivered nine months later in the body of our Babu Bangladesh.

Before daybreak, the two trekked through the city into the countryside. Neither had stepped outside the university properties for the past five days, and neither was ready for what they were to witness. Amongst the still smoking buildings, they detected obese dogs nibbling livers from corpses. The streets were overrun with jackals, monitors, mongooses and buzzards. Radios could be heard playing music from inside mass graves. They saw a cow stumble by wildly, the naked corpse of a woman spread-eagled on its back. The cow had been shot in its right front leg. They walked past buses full of passengers that had been burned alive, past bodies of rickshaw-pullers strewn over their rickshaws, and vagrants who been pushed into drains, along with day labourers and street children. As they walked, they were challenged by crows everywhere, crows that stood waist-high with red-flecked beaks, with round eyes rolling like orange and black tigers. They observed how bookshops had been torched and temples mortared, and as they walked on, they saw pink rivers outside the city bellyful with bodies. They trailed cadavers that had crawled into the fields on all fours, like lesser apes. After being bayoneted, these lay open like jackfruit among the stalks and plants. And everywhere there were buzzing flies, flies too sated to take to the air.

In their passage through all this, the young couple watched and listened cautiously. They did not enter into open spaces. They scuttled between columns and saplings to slowly journey to the rice sheaves and the water-lilies of the countryside. Finally, when they had reached the limits of their sanity, they found themselves in the arms of bristling freedom fighters. Many had heard about the insurgent operation at Dhaka University and the two were whisked like champions to Bengali camps.

Over the next few days, as Babu's mother and father related their thriller, they found themselves being questioned by Bengali officers who were directing a national resistance. An instructive audio cassette was prepared for military leaders (who were soon to consolidate the ranks of the Mukti Bahini fighters) detailing all intel gathered by them over the five days. The battle over the tree would serve both as a rallying cry for the rebellion and as a case study for campaigns of sabotage and attrition. Bengali fighters appraised the strategic potential offered in their local geography: canals, banks, rivers and forests could be used for lethal ambushes. Mines were to be scattered like serpents, rivers and water bodies would be used for transport and concealment, and select perennials would serve as roadblocks for tanks and heavy vehicles, while others would screen sharpshooters.

The Mukti Bahini, which was in place by mid-April, also drew from the works of Che Guevara, the French Maquis and the Viet

Cong. Headed by Colonel Ghani Osmani, they planned full-out frontal assaults, but followed TT-like stratagems in disrupting power and supply chains, in collecting intelligence within enemy ranks, and in conducting psychological warfare. They relied on weather, flora and fauna when needed. The anopheles mosquito was a great Bengali ally; scorpions, the monsoon rains, snakes, wild boars, crocodiles, elephants and the Royal Bengal Tiger were similarly enlisted in the cause. Paratroopers in one outfit recounted how they had been fighting off bees when mountain bandits, plastered in mud from head to toe, descended on them with swords.

From May onwards, Pakistanis were exhausted with surprise attacks. Every man, animal, mineral and tree became suspect. Bridges caved in once driven on to, villages and towns exploded when entered, and women transporting cactus lilies suddenly brandished automatic weapons. Invading battalions fought one another in the dark as radio frequencies were hijacked. Smattered with fruit, vehicles lay abandoned as their operators were drenched in agonizing chilli powders. As in numerous jackpot operations, a 50,000-strong Kaderia Bahini captured a Pakistani ship at Bhuapur and found onboard large quantities of arms and ammunitions. It was a period when wolves were kicked away by nursing cows, and when enormous toads broke into song, unmistakably warbling Nazrul Islam's '*Chol, chol, chol*'[56] to the horror of Baluchi pistoleers.

An article published in the *Daily Tribune* (a little-known Pakistani gazette) in September 1976 features the stumper that when troopers from the Western Wing attempted to communicate wirelessly, their channels were periodically jammed with repetitive declarations of Bangladeshi independence. These recitations not only included Commander Ziaur Rahman's 27 March delivery, but also showcased the voices of unidentified Bengalis, random militia members and

---

56 'March on, march on, march on.'

nondescript civilians, all of whom joyously declared their homeland free. In a night-time onslaught on Barrapind, a 13th Lancers squadron expended significant arsenal upon its own company as inexplicably delirious riflemen fell back on their own support.[57]

Bengali breakthroughs were witnessed throughout the country: in violation of curfews, mobs of civilians would fall upon Pakistani positions, allowing suicide bombers to breach through. Once courses resumed at Dhaka University, attendance rose to an unprecedented high as students lobbed grenades at occupying forces before vanishing into packed classrooms. One faction of student guerrillas used the unfinished national Capitol, Louis I. Kahn's Jatiya Sangsad Bhaban, as a meeting point. Its hulking walls and concrete heart threw an impermeable canopy over them: enemy combatants refused to enter the parliamentary premises, sensing in its mass something primal and something very Bengali, something that moved deceptively and menacingly before their very eyes. The college hospital likewise treated mutineers secretly, as university sprites shielded them. Babu's parents continued to work closely with the resistance for the next several months, even once it had been confirmed that Babu's mother was pregnant. Only in her third trimester did she rest, while her husband laboured for a different kind of birth – that of their country.

---

57 These uncanny manoeuvres echo centuries old campaigns from the domain. The *Alamgirnama* (penned during Emperor Aurangzeb's reign) records how in 1337 AD, a massive force of 1,00,000 horsemen sent by Mohammed Shah to invade Assam and Bengal 'perished in that land of witchcraft and not a trace of it was left'. Another army was despatched by the Shah, but when it reached Bengal, it was likewise consumed. Shihabuddin, a historian left an account in 1662 in which he says, 'the Bengals, like Assam, is a wild and dreadful country, abounding in danger ... And as no one who entered this country ever came back, and the manners of its natives were never made known to the outsiders, the people of Hindustan used to call its inhabitants sorcerers and magicians and considered them as standing outside the pale of human species.'

WHILE THIS FIVE-DAY VERSION of the bot's demise is denied by both Bangladeshi and Pakistani officials, its influence during the war was not inconsiderable. On the Pakistani side, when the bot legend made it rounds, it caused panic and depression. Officers had begun to question the feasibility of subduing the East Wing. The 'non-martial' Bengalis were proving deadly in jungle and forest combat. Many Pakistani soldiers demonstrated symptoms of nyctophobia and experienced incapacitating night terrors. It was quietly admitted that their servicemen had been checked in the south by a contingent of female warriors from aboriginal tribes. Even more demoralizing for the foreign troops was the realization that the hill-dwelling women had stopped their jawans with bows and arrows.

Some knew how Major Saud, along with two others, had been hospitalized in a psychiatric ward in the Western Wing. PPs from the bot mission shared their bizarre five-day trial, adding to the dejection and paranoia of their armed compatriots. Alarmed by the influx of Bengali refugees, and emboldened by Soviet support, India joined the war on the Bangladeshi side. As worldwide opinion turned against the Bhutto and Yahya regime, President Nixon ordered the aircraft carrier, USS Enterprise, to the Bay of Bengal as a show of support for careworn West Pakistani forces. There was little point in doing so: it would be only weeks before the campaign to crush Bangladesh collapsed.

Once Islamabad appraised that their forces could not prevail against the India–Bangladesh alliance, a final push was made on 13 and 14 December to hunt down and slaughter any remaining Bengali professionals. Hundreds of scholars, lawyers, journalists, politicians, scientists and businessmen were killed in this final purge. This baffling act can only be interpreted as an expression of malice toward the Bengali people; it was a parting shot into the neural cortex of an infant nation. On 16 December 1971, almost nine months after the commencement of Operation Searchlight, Pakistan officially admitted defeat as their commander signed an Instrument of Surrender to his Indian counterpart. This unforgettable moment transpired at the race course, almost exactly where the ashes of the bot had been crushed into the soil.

Two months later, US Senator Ted Kennedy would visit the liberated nation and plant a banyan sapling to replace the toppled bot. He had been campaigning for Bangladesh for months, and had been pivotal in passing a bill in the US Congress that banned arms sales to Pakistan. During the war, Kennedy had visited Bengali refugee camps in order to gather evidence that would help end US support for Bhutto. He accomplished this despite obstruction from President Nixon's White House. At the time of the genocide in 1971, Islamabad was regarded as a close ally by the US as it provided an effective counterbalance to the growing India–USSR partnership. Nixon was reluctant to estrange the Pakistani military junta, but Kennedy tenacity is never to be underestimated.

Ted was greeted as a hero by a fledgling Bangladesh, one that was honoured to have him plant a fresh banyan that could grow anew with the country. The plantlet he presented was affectionately nicknamed 'Kennedy' by locals, in homage to a man who spoke out for them when so many had turned their backs. The grafting of a tree, in this industrial world, can be a revolutionary statement of sorts and a restitution of all that is hopeful. When people link their arms to protect a forest or vegetal habitat, it is an attestation that hegemonies can be opposed, and that news conglomerates and multinational corporations are not invincible. When a Catholic senator, a Dutch-Australian legionnaire and thousands of world citizens raise their voices to protect the weak, they drown out the white noise that fills our airwaves. The Kennedy bot brought with it the hope that perhaps there are things we cannot cut down, root out or bleach away; that perhaps there are places under the sun that will be nourished and occupied by what is just and virtuous.

The world continues to turn without a pause, even in moments when millions jump to their feet in joy; the mighty earth continues its spin as the human ape cuts down trees and betrays his promises. If I had earlier indicated that modern man often finds himself in clearings, bereft of branches and leaves, let me establish here a vital and contradictory notion. This oppositional truth draws from a certain tenacity – that of bacteria and archaea, and eventually of algae, moss and fern. These are the dogged heralds of plantdom, awaiting an opportune moment to generate life. If man departs this planet, after terrestrial continents and governments fall, whether to rising waters or to industrial and unstoppable fires, the emeralds and sapphires of life will return. It may take a million years, or tens of millions of years, but tendrils will snake their way back and miraculous collaborations will recommence. We can observe this is in regions that have been subjected to civilization's fiercest atomic fires: we have been astonished at how new clades nettle back in extraordinary and *unearthly* ways.[58] We cannot know

---

58 In 1991, three melanin-containing fungi were discovered growing inside and around the Chernobyl Nuclear Power Plant. These radiotrophic fungi appear to use melanin to convert gamma radiation into chemical energy for growth. Research at the Albert Einstein College of Medicine showed that these new strains were not simply radiation resistant, but actually thrived with radiation levels 500 times higher than normal. Studies have shown that these eukaryotes produce 'special biological molecules' that can fight illnesses including depression and cancer. In 2016, eight species of fungi gathered from Chernobyl were launched by NASA to dock at its International Space Station (ISS). Scientists sent the microorganisms to the ISS to reconnoitre if they would form new compounds in microgravity. The fungi were returned to Earth after fourteen days by personnel at the ISS, but for the past twelve years NASA has withheld any information regarding additional mutations the organisms may have experienced.

what will come after us, but what is indubitable is that after our tracks have eroded, long after our mortal coils have spun out, out there in clearings everywhere, new trees will eventually straighten their backs.

In the meanwhile, man continues in his betrayals ... After the Pakistani surrender, the Indian government compelled the then-revolutionary government of Bangladesh, exiled in India, to sign uneven agreements that paved the way for decades of exploitation. Indian forces then placed curfews on Bangladeshi towns, industrial bases, ports, cantonments, commercial, and even residential areas, to facilitate an unprecedented looting. They lifted everything from military machines to ceiling fans, from jute, textile and steel mills, to water taps and utensils. After plundering banks, markets, schools, colleges and private homes, Indian soldiers seized thousands of vehicles to exit the impoverished nation and return home.

Pakistan, in turn, did not return to Bangladesh the hundreds of millions of dollars it had hijacked from international donors, money that had been sent to help the Bangladeshi victims of the 1970 cyclone. Furthermore, Pakistan refused to divide pre-independence assets, going so far as to deny individual Bengalis rights to their private holdings. The government of Pakistan has never apologized for or even acknowledged its actions in 1971. This denial continues to offend Bangladeshis. But they are by no means the only disappointed ones – embarrassed leaders in Islamabad refused to repatriate their own stranded 'Biharis' from Bangladesh, leaving them suspended for decades with no official nationality in still-hostile 'enemy' territory.

The abundant treacheries that followed were not limited to any one party; as chronicles from the war surfaced, it became evident that duplicity had abounded even within Bengali files. Testimonials flooded in regarding torture and systematic murder that Bangladeshi collaborators had helped the enemy perpetrate. Biharis (some had helped the troops from the West) attested to how they too had been slaughtered and abused by Bengali freedom fighters, in perfect emulation of the enemy. But the horrors did not stop there as Bangladeshi women came forward and pointed fingers at their own Mukti Bahini; with the breakdown of law and order, armed men had raped their own helpless nationals. This phenomenon is not uncommon during wartime.

The duplicities did not quite end there. Over the next few years, freedom fighters found themselves marginalized by a Bangladeshi government that was vulnerable to cronyism, and many war stories, including that of our bot, were covered with plush carpets of state rhetoric. (As Babu's parents found, no one dared to recount or discuss the Five-Day Mission; resistance reports were censored to champion select individuals as the Bangladeshi campaigns of 1971 were converted into hard currency.) Enemy collaborators were invited back from Pakistan to assume prominent roles in the government, and non-Bengali and non-Muslim indigenous communities that had fought selflessly alongside the Bangladeshis were hunted out of their lands as the looting continued. They are now almost hunted out of existence. Shortly after a terrifying famine that claimed 2 per cent of the population, the father of the Bangladeshi nation, Sheikh Mujib, was assassinated in 1975 by his children, and as some of the conspirators became national leaders, innocents were made villains and executed.

The defeated Pakistani forces continued their own intrigues. Prime Minister Bhutto (who would be hanged in 1979) had General Yahya Khan overthrown. After the soldier's military decorations were withdrawn, he was placed under house arrest for the remainder of his life. General Niazi too became a domestic scapegoat for signing the capitulation. The major and other rankers attempted to publish apologies for the atrocities they had committed: some were silenced, while others went on the lam. Several generals turned on one other and published titles such as *The Betrayal of East Pakistan* and *The Unending Conflict*, portraying brothers-in-arms as opportunists, swindlers and butchers. Once again, numbers were doomed to repeat themselves, antique mammoths rose wearily, and the integers of time danced deafly to old tunes. For many, this was a time when no secret bark or root could nurture back to life what had been lost.

The state emblem adopted by Bangladesh includes a water lily bordered on two sides by rice sheaves. Above the water lily are four stars and three connected jute leaves. The water lily is the country's national flower, and represents the many rivers that run through Bangladesh. The sheaves acknowledge the distinction of rice being the staple food, while jute was included as the golden fibre, a major national export at the time. The four stars represent the four founding principles that were originally enshrined in the first Constitution of Bangladesh in 1972: nationalism, secularism, socialism and democracy.

Yet, from the very start, the young republic was straddled between irreconcilable poles: Islamic religiosity versus secularism, rampant corruption and economic oppression versus socialist principles, and a one-party system versus democracy. In the flag chosen by the grateful country, a green backdrop symbolizes the trees and fields of the countryside, while a red circle in its middle represents both a rising sun as well as the bloodshed of the liberation war. The national anthem was adapted from a poem by Tagore and connects a love for the natural realm with the national identity. Bangladesh, once the world's largest delta and a native rainforest has now less than 4 per cent tree coverage – it is now one of the least forested lands in the world, facing a host of problems including soil erosion, plummeting biodiversity, as well as air pollution. All has become timber and taka as the stars are belied. In 2010, the mango evergreen was declared the Bangladeshi national tree, but the once-famous aam tola, the vegetation under which so much of Bengal budded, and under which the bodies of fallen heroes lie, is now untended, forgotten and barely standing.[59]

It is not the intention of this account of Babu's birth to vilify or exalt Pakistan, India, the US or Bangladesh. Neither is it to declare the Bangladeshi conquest as pyrrhic. The objective of this account is, rather, to direct a beacon into the darkness of the times, and reveal how so many of different races, nationalities and languages sacrificed so much. While probing the tragedy of our human ways, this rendition is motivated by a desire to acknowledge those who birthed a nation in which Bangladeshis could determine their own futures. But it is heart-breaking, this brave little story of ours.

One particular case that received some international attention will be briefly treated here. It is estimated between 2,00,000 and 4,00,000 Bengali women were raped over the nine-month war, many of them housed in military brothels. Scholars of this arrangement describe the incarcerations and violations of these women as acts of sustained torture. In December, when Bangladeshi soldiers searched deserted Pakistani barracks for these missing women, they were stunned to find them fully naked inside their quarters. They had been living like this for months, to discourage escape. Some

---

59 These behaviours are not exclusive to Bangladesh, or to any one nation. Rather, these are hallmark of all mankind. As Babu poignantly put it: 'Since when man became a biped and straightened his carriage, he became aware of a vertical dimension, one that is not fully appreciated by a creature for which the horizon lies in the ground in front of its feet. Bipedal man was challenged by the realization of the cosmic axis, and his newly stimulated imagination leaped into the ether to perceive the harmony of divine spheres. But man who could stand upright also responded to the vertical challenge by conquering heights – he began to climb trees and mountains, hunt large animals and, eventually, took to the skies. Man thus asserted his mastery over celestial latitudes … In decimating tree populations around the world, men abandoned their earliest godlings: it was, then, inevitable that men would turn on one another and abandon their own kind.'

women clutched their hair to their faces (many had become bald as a result of what had been done to them[60]) as they privately retreated to distant and inaccessible places.

As shocked rescuers averted their eyes and took off their shirts to drape the women, they were attacked by females who could no longer distinguish between uniforms; in their state of near madness, they could not tolerate any male presence. Many of these victims committed suicide afterwards – poison and drowning were most common. The majority of those who did not kill themselves were abandoned by husbands, families and society in general. Extensive socioeconomic attempts were made to integrate them into Bangladeshi communities. Even today, a beautiful statue in Mijibnagar depicts a birongina[61] in a sari being pulled away by a soldier. Prime minister Sheikh Mujibur Rahman had pronounced them national heroines. There is a sombre account of the day that Mujib visited a small village called Sohagpur. Its population was composed solely of tormented female 'survivors' who could no longer bear to live alongside men. On meeting them and apprehending their desolation, Sheikh Mujib fell to his knees and cried, 'Mother, what have they done to you?' All the same, few Bangladeshis were willing to tolerate the presence of these 'dishonoured' souls. Soldiers demanded incentives from the government for taking these women as wives; these men requested gifts ranging from the latest model of Japanese motorbikes to housing materials, from new refrigerators to the publication of unpublished poems.

Of the 25,000 women who became pregnant as a result of the assaults, half obtained crude abortions and suffered from

---

60 Telogen effluvium is a scalp disorder where hair loss is experienced after major trauma or shock.

61 Bengali for 'heroine'. This was the official title Mujib conferred on the rape camp survivors.

complications for the duration of their remaining days. But, as Babu's mother gave birth to a screaming boy at Dhaka Medical College – near the shelter of the mango tree, more than 10,000 Bangladeshi women carried to full term their rape pregnancies. As bedeys cleared the campus of remaining snakes, as shovels uncovered mass graves, as blood washed off branches, as statues were built and eternal fires lit, as birds descended to their nesting places, and as prophets, rousing themselves from under trees, resumed their travels, these women brooded into their arms brand-new babies.

So at the end of everything, after all lines were crossed and riddled and everyone and everything had been loved, fought for, fought over, forgiven and betrayed, at the end of all this and in its middle, stood a mother and a triumphant baby, and the trees bowed and rustled.

III

SNAKE

Man's heart is never satisfied; the snake would swallow the elephant.

– Chinese proverb

Politics encircles us today like the coil of a snake from which one cannot get out, no matter how much one tries. I wish therefore to wrestle with the snake.

– Mahatma Gandhi

The world of men is dreaming, it has gone mad in its sleep, and a snake is strangling it, but it can't wake up.

– D. H. Lawrence

If you see a snake, just kill it – don't appoint a committee on snakes.

– Ross Perot

IN THIS SECTION, WE wind along the coils of a still young and somewhat downcast Babu, for the five long years of 2001 through 2006. We accompany him from the age of twenty-nine through thirty-five as rainforests vanish, as indigenes are driven from the last of their Bangladeshi lands, as avenging deities are summoned from the underworld, and as Babu's life is nearly ended. Yet, in this time too, inexistent species rise from the dead like some al-Eizariya, thousands forgo unethical quick bucks, natives retrieve ancient regimes. After decades of disarray and despair, after the genocide of snakes and cousins, people anticipate once again a fecund and plentiful Bangladesh. This Bangladesh confounds algebras and predictions of its going under. It staunchly defends itself from sinister gyres that come swirling in from the Bay. In this Bangladesh, children are newly promised buoyant futures, and as grace falls from the skies like soma, men and women learn themselves afresh. In locating under his feet his own origins, many a countryman becomes authentic and organic. Babu, too, meets formidable challenges, stains his lungi, and almost loses his dignity. Almost. To survive, he must shed skin and earn new stripes.

This particular account tails Babu as he resumes his ascent through the political landscape of Bangladesh. In these pages, he is inducted into parliament, after which a cosmopolitical courtship for his favours intensifies. However, the innermost eye of this narrative rests unflinchingly on events that transpired in Madhupur village in the winter of 2003. Everything that leads up to and follows after is intended to assist the reader in comprehending the sweeping reach and roll of what happened to Babu in that deep, green year.

After fleeing Dhaka in 1999, following the HUJI and Sangsad Bhaban bombing debacle, Babu emigrated to Dubai to work in a shipyard. He was miserable there and spent his life's savings to purchase a visa to the USA, where he spent almost two years in New York City. Amar and Munna joined Babu for several months in the Big Apple and accompanied him on his return in mid-2001. For the most part, we only concentrate on the time Babu spent abroad in order to gauge how it rehabilitated his political stratagem and ideologies.

When Babu returned to Bangladesh after the new millennium, national tempers had cooled towards him and the fatwas had been lifted. Babu, too, had changed significantly. He had shed the depression experienced while living in exile. Like an emperor returned, Babu had big plans. He was determined to reimmerse himself in the political scenery and immediately set about canvassing for a parliamentary seat, using his parents' home in Madhupur upazila as his campaign base. The next elections were scheduled for late 2002, but as it was definite that the opposition would press for an earlier date, there was no time to waste.

Though I have employed the metaphor of regality, let it be clear that in 2001, Babu was by no means pompous or haughty. The pages of his diaries, as well as the testimonies of those he encountered, sketch the portrait of a man who, while expansive and dynamic, was deeply thoughtful and humble. And he had good cause to be; his stately ambitions had been enabled by the generosity of others. Munna, who had acquired wealth after helping to design and sell a prototype for the Braille Glove, had gifted him almost a million dollars. Amar, too, had pledged revenues from his share of the family holdings.

The time abroad had also encouraged Babu to explore his identity and examine the mechanism of his being. Like countless other expatriates, he had faced an identity loss while residing in NYC. At the Curry Palace in Astoria, Queens, Babu had been promoted to sous-chef. Many a night, he would ritually prep condiments for his grandmother's boti kebab, Kanu's biryani and his mother's saag-aloo, only to find in the morning a strange fusion of spices that seemed derived from Greek, Dominican and Egyptian influences. Convinced that someone was sabotaging his dishes, Babu started taking home his work (much to the objection of his flatmates). Nonetheless, when Babu leapt out of bed at the crack of dawn to inspect his seasonings, he would inevitably find mixtures very false. This eventually resulted in Babu fearing himself schizophrenic and quitting the restaurant. He went cold for more than a month and, as I have confirmed with his fellow boarders in Queens, the self-imposed sequestration ended with the arrival of Amar and Munna from Bangladesh. On forcing his door open, they tripped over rotting vegetables, magazines and water bottles. Once inside the dark and rank room, they finally uncovered Babu, rolled up bearlike on the floor and staring suspiciously. It took nearly two months to cajole him out of his émigré funk. Babu made the most progress when reminded of things native to his birthplace: Tangail, Bangladeshi movies and Bengali songs. Amar read out choice poems from Ramprasad Sen, Michael Madhusudan, Nazrul Islam and Tagore – all long-time favourites of the recovering refugee. On discovering that Babu had turned vegetarian, Munna cooked up a few Bengali favourites: eggplant with fried tomatoes, onions and cumin; bottle gourd with green chillies and ginger; and okra with poppy and mustard seeds. He filled the former hermitage with delicious smells. Amar also shared stories from Babu's childhood, and while Babu delighted greatly in these nostalgic accounts, Munna found his friendship with Babu deepening as he learned about the years he and Babu had spent apart. Like a mountain moved, Munna sat quietly and listened, providing Babu a sense of security and comfort.

Over the subsequent months, Amar worked for his father and won business contracts for garments production in Bangladesh, and Munna joined an IT start-up. Babu spent most of his time reading, and pondering the role he wished to play in the future of his country. Munna was earning enough for Babu to indulge his political stratagems. During that time, Babu was drawn to the fundamentals that most inspired him. He wished to fight for the simple things about Bangladesh that made him most happy: its vegetal abundance, its colourful animal kingdom, and the diversity of religions, cultures and peoples – all of which were quickly vanishing. Babu enrolled in classes in environmental studies at NYU and spent every free hour in its Greenwich Village departments (as I did in Bloomington's counterparts). As he had not worked at the Queens eatery for almost eight months, it was only a matter of time before immigration authorities informed him that his visa had been revoked. This did not vex the trio. Babu's informed and passionate ideas about reform in Bangladesh had spurred Munna and Amar to raise the funds necessary for Babu to return and re-engage in the political realm. In August 2001, the three boarded a Biman flight for the motherland.

On arrival, Babu initially sought the blessings of Rafik Kaka, Boro Ma, the shadowy SBG, and sympathizers both influential and nominal, some of whom were remarkably still JCD members. Babu decided to run as an independent candidate from the Tangail-3 constituency, situated near the heart of the once grand Madhupur forest. This was a bold move. Even though Madhupur was not a highly contested area due to its relative poverty, there were very few public servants in Bangladesh who could successfully run as independents and not be overwhelmed by larger political coalitions. But Babu was adamant, and eventually his admirers acquiesced.

According to guidelines set by the Legislative Information Centre, any citizen over the age of twenty-five is eligible to run for elected office in Bangladesh. Those disqualified are the 'certified insane, undischarged bankrupts, persons who on conviction for a criminal offence involving moral turpitude have been sentenced to imprisonment for not less than two years unless five years have elapsed since their release [sic], persons owing allegiance to a foreign state, and persons holding an office of profit in the service of the Republic'. Of course, in reality, this list could be read as a good rubric in predicting who would likely contend and triumph in regional realpolitik.

There were certain advantages to Babu's circumvention of the larger parties. It was common knowledge that all nominations in the Awami League, in the Bangladeshi Nationalist Party and in the Jatiya Party were processed by a handful of elites. These patriarchs and matriarchs, having established their own bases at the birth of the nation, gave first preference to blood relatives, then to relatives through marriage, then to friends, then friends of friends, etc. Unless one fit into one of these categories, the only other way to gain entry was to make sizeable financial contributions to the organization in question. In spite of Munna and Amar's enabling generosity, Babu found this corrupt practice most distasteful. Moreover, as Jamaat was out of the question (even after reshuffling and repositioning, the party still despised him) and as the JCD was divided on his candidacy, there really was no alternative to his seeking office as a lone wolf.

For electioneering purposes, he was advised by all to come up with a catchy campaign handle – a simple and universal moniker that would appeal to the masses. One day, as Munna and he were sitting at his parents' Tangail residence on Road 8, his friend quietly advised him, 'There are too many Babus already; every division has some Babu politician. You have to add something more to your name. Think of something easy but with style, you know, something with a little flair.' Babu sat for a while, thinking. And then suddenly

a memory from Curry Palace flashed into his mind. The owner's
stepdaughter, a fiery redhead of Irish origins, ran the establishment
and served as hostess. Babu was infatuated with her, but was much
too shy to demonstrate his feelings. The vivacious woman (Babu
never mentions her name in his journals), oblivious of Babu's
infatuation, routinely forgot who he was and found it curious that
the man was always tongue-tied. One busy Friday night, when the
restaurant was bustling with patrons, she needed a table cleared
quickly and, spying Babu in the dining area, called to him, 'You
there, come here. What's your name, again? Yes, you. I forget, what's
your name, wherryafrom?'

Babu swooned and stuttered, 'Me, I'm Babu, Babu ... Bangladesh.'

'Babu Bangladesh?' She shrieked with laughter, and from that
day he had a new name at the eatery.

'Munna,' said Babu, 'what do you think of Babu Bangladesh?'

Munna was quiet for a minute but then smiled. 'Perfect. Almost
stupid in its simplicity, but very direct and easy. No one important
is using the name now. There was that one guy in the sixties ...
but nobody remembers him now. Yes, you can be our new Babu
Bangladesh.'

So began Babu Bangladesh's adventures as legislative candidate
from Madhupur upazila. The region was named after the high-
quality honey ('madhu' in Bengali) obtained from its bees. It had
been famous for its Deccan rainforests that were at least 22,000 years
old. Records from six decades ago indicated that they teemed with a
deciduous biodiversity rivalling that of their cousins in the Amazon
basin. In the dense biome, shimmering kingfishers, woodpeckers,
gibbons and lorises had seated themselves on the knotted limbs
of giant sals, as rivers carried past their load of deadly snakes and
crocodiles as well as dolphins, ducks and fish of a thousand colours,
including hilsas, giant catfish, knife fish, sharks, stingrays and
snake eels. On the banks, thirsty wild buffalo had congregated, as

had bantengs, rhinoceroses and various species of deer. They had their time at the water, as did the elephants, wolves, bears, tigers and leopards. Mangoes, bananas, coconuts, sugarcane and berries were trampled underfoot as the inhabitants of the forest made their way through its tangled and vibrant maze. This was the topography Babu remembered from his childhood.

But this was all in the past. By 2001, 85 per cent of the forest had been cut down. Despite treaties and accords, the Bangladeshi military continued to drive helpless citizens from their lands and had sold the rights to timber and mining interests. The native residents of the Madhupur tracts were not part of the nation's Bengali-speaking majority but consisted of clans that could linguistically trace their roots to Austric influences. These were the people who established agricultural precedents on which the earliest Indic civilizations were founded. While experts in biogenetic and forensic anthropology have yet to reach consensus on the identity of the first humans to occupy the area (there is evidence of a Negrito population similar to the Andamanese arriving between 30,000 and 65,000 years ago), Austroasiatic families quickly became prominent. For thousands of years, masterful alliances governed the local kingdoms and a distinct culture developed. These indigenous populations were very conservative and practised ecologically sustainable and 'primitive' farming methods which allowed their woodlands to thrive. Diego de Astor, a Portuguese visitor, published maps of the region in 1615 in which he delineated their kingdoms. Though these Tibeto-Burmese and Mon-Khmer groups distinguished forty-five 'tribes' among themselves, they later became collectively known as 'Jumma' (a term stemming from their 'jum', which reflects their agricultural habit of 'slash and burn') or as 'Adivasis' (from the Sanskrit 'adi' meaning 'original' and 'vasi' meaning 'inhabitant'). The necessity for these homogenizing terms was simultaneously accepted and renounced by the forty-five discrete groups, but in time they found themselves compelled to huddle as one in voicing their humanity.

Threats to Jumma autonomy inevitably arrived in the form of new waves of Dravidians, Indo-Aryans, Africans, Alpines, Mughals, Turks and Pashtuns. Though many of them succeeded in intermarrying with the existing Austro-Asiatic and Austric tribes, the established communities refused to abandon their age-old sacraments, ceremonies and divine trees. Newcomers either assimilated or stayed out altogether. The Jummas refused to abandon their teachings on karma, transmigration, animism and yoga, which had formed the bedrock of the Vedic tradition (of Shiva, Devi and Vishnu) and of Buddhism. They were unperturbed by the arrival of Islam in the thirteenth century CE. Their refusal to convert was tolerated by benevolent Mughal rulers. One group known as the 'Mandis' (a term that derives from 'Achik Mandi', literally 'hill people') even retained their matriarchal communal structure. In their custom, husbands lived in the houses of wives and engaged in household work. New arrivals to the region observed that in Mandi societies, mothers owned all household properties, and after their death a nominated daughter became heir.

However, not all newcomers were benevolent. Warriors found justifications, if not in the legal framework then at least in the eyes of their personal gods, to force peaceful farmers off their lands and confiscate their property. This land-grabbing has continued for two centuries now, and while the aboriginals of Bengal have rebelled, been granted amnesty and promised rehabilitation, their forests have continued to crumble. Even the Jumma who fought for Bangladeshi independence from Pakistan found that after the war was won, the Bangladeshi government refused to recognize them as equal comrades. Of the estimated four to seven million ethnic minorities in Bangladesh in 2001, there were approximately

1,70,000 in Tangail, of which 70,000 resided in Madhupur upazila. Bureaucratic persecution extended not only to the seizing of their lands, but to denying them rights to their languages, religions and traditions. This remains one of the most tragic betrayals the Bangladeshi nation has inflicted upon itself. As a result of this policy, Bangladeshis severed arteries to their birth cord, a link that stretches into antediluvian times, connecting them to the first humans to inhabit their lands.

Of course, the plight of the Jumma was shared by the Hindus in Bangladesh. A litany of communal horrors pockmarking the years between 1947 through 1971 had ensured that the Bangladeshi Hindu family had been all but destroyed. Since 1971, whenever there was any type of discontent in the small country, Hindus were commonly delegated as scapegoats and executed. Over the decades of persecution, millions of Hindus sought refuge in India. Those with deeper pockets and better luck left for Europe, Australia, Canada, the USA and the Middle East, weeping as they departed. On looking back towards their receding homeland, they saw bearded men in crisp white hats, baring their teeth and flashing sabres to hasten them away. But behind these ominous figures, further inland, there were millions that looked on in silent disbelief. Former friends, neighbours, and lovers too, wept. They wept that brothers and sisters were being evicted in this most un-Bengali of ways, and they wept at their own negligence and fear and at their failure to halt the oppression that drove this great hegira.

By 2001, the protohuman and mighty trunks of Madhupur were shedding the last of their leaves. Only 7,000 acres remained of the original 46,000 acres of forest in Tangail. Approximately a thousand acres were cleared for use as an air force firing range, and even more for military encampments, training centres and infrastructural enhancements. Bureaucrats pocketed kickbacks and turned a blind eye as medicinal plants and tubers were pushed to extinction. An influx of settlers, many of whom received government incentives to occupy these newly cleared lands, found work in sawmills, brick kilns, furniture shops, and in pesticide and hormone factories. Other newcomers were employed in weaving, in blacksmith and goldsmith workshops, in pottery production and as tailors. What was remained of the forests was rapidly reconstituted with commercially planted pineapples, bananas, rubber plants, and silk and cotton growths of alien species. Since 1984, the forest department had variously implemented 'tree plantation projects', which in reality encouraged the decimation of native trees to make way for fast-growing, saline-resistant and foreign acacias and eucalyptuses. As the biodiverse tracts gradually became wastelands, Bangladesh became indebted to the tune of millions of dollars in soft loans from the Asian Development Bank for these ill-conceived reforestation initiatives.

Because of the dire situation in Madhupur upazila, Babu was adamant that it be the constituency he would contest. Political conventions also dictate that aspirants run for a seat from the area that their father was born in, and as both parents were from Madhupur, this bound Babu's aspirations to the ravaged region. Babu was extremely eager to take on the challenges that plagued Madhupur, so he had trained himself perfectly to address its deficiencies. While émigré despair had prompted Babu to identify exactly what moved him, those intimate with him found nothing novel or unexpected in his avowed direction. Anyone familiar with Babu knew that even as a teenager he had strongly supported the indigenous rights movement. While he was with the JCD, Babu had made it a point to recruit Mandi, Kochi and Khasa volunteers who were mindful of their longevous heritages. JCD higher-ups were well aware of this and had encouraged him. His proclivity to safeguard Bangladeshi ethnic minorities had been nurtured from childhood by Mr and Mrs Majumdar, who were active campaigners for racial and cultural rights, and also by Babu's childhood playmate and mentor, Kanu. The vagabond herbalist Mali Da, who had taken a liking to young Babu, was also a proud member of the Hajong peoples.

From New York, Babu had kept up with their struggles and operations across the nation. He was very familiar with how their land papers dating from the colonial era had been rejected as bogus. He knew how former residents had been moved to police and army camps that dotted the highway route. Babu was well versed in how the Forest Acts had been used to remove thousands from their homesteads into inhumane 'cluster villages'. Babu was aware that they were not only prohibited from cultivation, but were unable to collect firewood, honey, wax, herbs, or any other Madhupur bounties which had sustained them from time immemorial.

The parallels between these legislative acts and the policies of the lumbering and mining companies that had driven millions from India's Red Corridor (an area encompassing almost all eastern areas of the country and extending north towards the Bengals) were evident. The only difference is that under the cloak of Maoism and Naxalism, Indian subalterns have been successful in uniting to resist governmental and corporate domination. In Bangladesh however, Jumma guerrillas had finally signed peace accords after decades of armed resistance. Once the Jumma rebels surrendered their weapons, the Bangladeshi army proceeded to 'strategically hamlet' villages (i.e. burn and raze, sometimes with inhabitants inside), and rape or kill those who resisted – and even many who did not. As activists watched in horror, indigenous Bangladeshis dematerialized en masse as they changed their religions, traditions and languages in order to assimilate and avoid persecution. A small minority vanished into the darkness of the remaining trees, with some crossing into India.

Babu had studied similar situations around the world, including those of the Rakhines in Myanmar, the Muslim Uighurs in China, and the Igorots of the Philippines (who had been visited by T.S. Eliot, inspiring the story 'The Man Who Was King'), aided by NYU instructors and the university libraries. Enthused by Bangladeshi champions such as Sher Doulat, Santu Larma and Sultana Kamal, Babu hit the ground running upon landing in the midst of the explosive upazila.

As already evidenced in Babu's essays on dendrology and on the importance of trees in the evolution of human customs, Babu had a deeply engrained respect for the natural environment. On returning from New York, Babu took merely a few days to appraise the gravity of the situation, and after zipping between his parents' Madhupur estate, Tangail city and Dhaka, our Shaka Zulu quickly acquired a clear picture of the terrain he was to grapple for. The next step was to approach comrades in the Workers' Party of Bangladesh (who had historically been very supportive of wronged minorities) and various national and multinational human-rights committees, and to meet with influential university professors, legal advocates and civilians who worked to safeguard territorial biospheres. Much of this happened in the environs of the Sangsad Bhaban, whose structures Babu believed could still be used as an ally.

The principled strategists whom Babu approached were acquainted with his idealism, and they quickly pledged themselves to his undertaking. Others who were less versed with Babu were inevitably impressed by his mastery over environmental research debates, soil sciences, geological and marine biology, and ethno-geographic mediations. They were left speechless by his spiffy verbiage and by the vigour and depth of his convictions. Babu made evident his familiarity with autochthonic and globally imported farming practices, revolving crop cycles, agroforestry technologies, livestock and biodiversity management, as well as green innovations in industry and engineering. He spoke forcefully of the value of phyto-remediation in mitigating pollution and purifying water. He proposed that funding be raised for greater research into natural attenuation, broke into tears when speaking of freshwater dolphins and blue whales, and posed incisive questions about de-sedimentation in the Sundarban mangroves. Babu did all of this while keeping the interests of the Jummas smack in the centre. He breathlessly gushed study after study affirming their unique, inherited expertise, their rituals regarding tree-pathology, and the ethno-botanical wonders they were capable of attaining.

Though a large portion of Babu's chatter went over his audience's heads, on subsequently visiting forests with him, most perceived the organic ingenuity of the centuries-old practices that Babu endeavoured to revive. Ultimately, a sizeable number agreed that Jumma wisdom, used in conjunction with emerging technologies, might just save the remaining trees of Madhupur. Even more, allowing forest-dwellers to return (albeit 'afresh') to ancient ways would end a contentious and ugly chapter in Bangladeshi minutes.

Having closely considered parallels from India, Egypt and Granada to the Swiss Alps, the Americas, the Fijian Islands and Australia, Babu was confident that Bangladesh had unlimited potential for becoming a coveted hotspot for leisure travellers. He outlined how the borders of the Madhupur National Park should be further extended to accommodate outdoor recreational facilities for eco-tourists, including solar-fuelled rest-houses and zero carbon camping grounds. Babu pointed to the Indian Kanha Tiger Reserve, to ventures in the Maldives, to the Sun Ranch in Montana, the Siwa Oasis in the Libyan Desert, the eco-lodges of Queensland and the coral gardens in Tanzania. He argued convincingly that Tangail was ideal for stocked lakes and fly fishing, for bee-farm resorts, for forest trails and bicycle tracks, for a five-star vegetarian restaurant, and perhaps even for a golfing range or two. He indicated how funds already forthcoming from foreign banks could jumpstart these endeavours. Babu brilliantly used pie charts and multimedia presentations (made by Munna) to show how fraudulent deforestation policies would leave nothing but wastelands within a decade, whereas his investment schemes would generate revenues that could very possibly snowball. Furthermore, he demonstrated that they would offer better opportunities, even in the short run, to Bengali migrants who found themselves bonded to the owners of the factories they worked in.

In spite of significant commendations from well-intentioned intellectuals and future-looking bureaucrats, Babu had next to no support at the grassroots level. He was virtually unknown to voters. In most parts of Bangladesh, this would only pose a fiscal problem: votes were shamelessly purchased by those who had the biggest backers. But in the Madhupur and Ghatail upalizas, there was an X-factor – the Jummas would not sell their votes. For Babu, this was provident. If he were able to make contact with the 'tribal' (they vigorously resisted such denominations) leaders and reveal his operational tactics, Babu was confident he could broker a genuine alliance. Not having to buy their endorsement would also mean that Babu could make do with a more modest campaign budget, which would be a relief as the coffers of Amar, Munna and the intellectuals and progressives who were backing Babu were already strained. The competitors Babu faced for the parliamentary seat were Muslim Bengalis who displayed little interest in securing the Jumma constituency. They would rather throw money at newer Bengali settlers, election officers, army colonels and caretaker-government commissioners. Babu would unavoidably have to enter these bidding frays, so every taka saved would help.

It is likely, dear reader, that if you are not from the 'third world' or an economically challenged and morally teetering legislature, you may find the next few pages distasteful. You may find repugnant the backdoor dealings, the underhanded duplicity and the artful winks and nods exchanged in Babu's pursuit of his ambitions. This is the side of Babu that I, too, find the least pleasing; it is in these wheelings and dealings that I find Babu's departure from moral conduct most unbecoming. However, after careful study and consideration of accounts most unfavourable (some of which will be included in the following narrative), I find myself throwing my hands in the air. Once again, it is difficult to ascertain whether Babu crossed lines that are absolutely unpardonable. While often resembling an Iago, a Bolivar diGriz or a Rasputin, in playing the role of trickster, Babu seems to have been primarily guided by honourable objectives. In my reckoning, he did attempt to remain a noble caudillo, but by no means should this be interpreted as a categorical assessment.

As we have already seen in the 'Building' section, the major powers in Bangladeshi politics at the time were the ideologically fluid parties, their student communities, trade unions and workers' federations, wealthy businessmen (in rural areas this was typically comprised of landowners), and military and civilian apparatuses. Of course, farther away and just out of sight were strings pulled by non-native authorities such as the USA and India, who used the CIA and the RAW respectively, on a ground level. Both countries had backdoor channels into the Bangladeshi armed forces; higher-up generals were allegedly paid well to stand at beck and call. Despite this, elections in Bangladesh were never wholly predictable. Until the very last minute, negotiations and investments were made in order to procure supremacy.

Another benefit of his independent candidature was that Babu could free himself from much inter- and intra-party intrigues and avoid being liable to foreign kingmakers. This proved to be especially provident in 2002 when the AL and the BNP were separately implicated in scandals involving receipts and disbursals of unaccounted millions. They were caught up in these along with three brigadiers, the Jamaat (who had joined forces with the BNP), a US senator, a certain Madam Commission, and the head of Directorate General of Forces Intelligence (DFGI), who was a vocal RAW sympathizer. Babu would profit from titanic clashes, slipping into an unwatched parliamentary seat while others battled for golden heartlands. We will now peruse the details of how exactly this transpired.

In 2001, the 70,000 forest acres of Madhupur and Ghatail upazilas were managed under the Tangail Forest Division. As most of the acreage was officially reserved as a protected range, there were no formal landowners for Babu to meet with. Army personnel and bureaucrats divided the spoils amongst themselves. They initially proved quite immune to Babu's circles of influence, as did the black-market moneylenders (provincially called 'mohazon'). At the start of his ballot seeking efforts, Babu focused his energies elsewhere, knowing he would eventually have to return to their camps to guarantee a win. So Babu decided to focus on the common denizens of Madhupur and Ghatail instead.

To ensure street popularity, Babu hired the services of Dynamite Ali, the campaign conjuror we have already encountered in the preface to this book. Dynamite wasted no time in getting the buzz about Babu started. Rickshaws, scooters and taxis took to the streets with megaphones and loudspeakers. Though they communicated no meaningful talking points, they were quite effective in acoustically drilling 'Babu Bangladesh' into both right and left temporal lobes. Garishly coloured images of Babu gazing philosophically into emerald skies were quickly plastered by graffiti crews and signage teams on to public and private properties. In violation of the law, no lamp post, appurtenance, kerbstone, sidewalk, tree, hydrant or bridge was spared from their efforts. However, Dynamite gave in to Babu's objections and had images removed from trees and asked his workers to refrain from littering with Babu signage, handbills or placards. Though Dynamite was typically loath to follow instructions from political clients – having been in the business for decades, he had nothing but disdain for their kind – Babu's advisors communicated to the maestro that he should handle Babu as a unique client. They explained to the firebrand that polluting neighbourhoods to promote Babu would be antithetical to his eco-platform.

Dynamite first guffawed incredulously, 'What, your Babu wants to save the trees and the homeless tribals? What kind of an idea is Save-the-Park? How's he going to buy the votes with damn fool notions like that?' After realizing that they were sincere in their quest to preserve the disintegrating woodlands, and upon catching whiff of their plans for fiscally gainful bioreserves, Dynamite acquiesced. 'Well, I'll bloody well still say it sounds like a fool's dream, but that's fine with me. Just don't think you can boss me around or anything. I'll have them clean up the mess they made in the streets, but I'll run the show as I see fit. I have been doing this since before you could even find your mouth with your thumb.' Munna and Raju (sent by the Majumdars to safeguard Babu) swallowed their objections, knowing full well they would need his virtuosity to succeed.

Babu, on his end, appeared at just about every fete, soirée, birthday bash, fundraiser, musical evening and mela in town. Expansive and garrulous, this Babu was nothing like the timid university student originally conscripted by the JCD. He cut a rather striking figure – pedantic, world travelled and cosmopolitical. Garbed in local organic cottons, Babu presented an admixture few Bangladeshis had encountered before. While he was inevitably surrounded by a throng of curious men and women who had questions about his radical platform, there were many who were uneasy in his presence. At every social gathering, there was a silent coterie who eyed him with mistrust. To them, the notion of a man who possessed monied supporters but chose to wear beggarly wraps made no sense. They could not understand how a waiter from New York could sound so educated or run his campaign from a tin-roofed property in Madhupur village.

Since his awakening in America, Babu had not only become vegetarian, but had taken to growing his own natural foods, thus returning to the flower gardens of his youth and the plants he had raised as a child. He shunned colognes and toiletries that were not organic and cruelty free. He refused to sit on chairs as well – he always carried with him a jute mat which he insisted was better for circulation, bowel movements and his back pain. In his disconcerting presence, many people apologetically hid meaty aperitifs and rare leather accessories and looked around vaguely as if for recycling bins before exiting. Gossip had already started regarding his affiliation with indigenous forest folk, in particular a female-headed clan that worshipped giant snakes. We shall soon delve into this association more closely.

In the preface, I have already mentioned the theatrical pronunciations at a Madhupur Union Maidan for which I was partially present. At the time, I was only thirteen and was under the charge of my twenty-two-year-old brother. Though he had hurried me away from the explosions on stage and the terrifying spectacle of a burning man who was replaced seconds later by a surrogate, I could never quite shake the memory of those moments. My brother, too, was never able to forget. In fact, my project on Babu commenced in 2023 when my brother shared the bounty of his own fieldwork implicating Manasa-revering matriarchs in the fantastic onstage resurrection.

But I insist that I must hold off on discussing serpent votaries, no matter how badly I want to. It will confuse you, dear reader, if I do so. At this juncture, we will attend to how Babu won the attention of Tangail's masses.

I have expended great efforts in attempting to recapture and decipher the dreamlike quality of those moments. Despite the fraternal collaboration in this, I have been unable to apprehend what exactly ensued at that rally and how our diffident Babu had transformed into such a virile orator. Nonetheless, I will include here a full translation of that November 2001 delivery. This English rendition of Babu's original pronunciation is not my sole creation. I have consulted with newspapers and professional journals in effectively capturing the roar issued that day, the clarion that rang far outside the provinces he was attempting to court. But first, a few lines from his memoirs in which Babu recollects the interval before the monologue:

'Before leaping out through the poster, I stood there listening to the speakers and the crowd. The drums had a dizzying effect, as did the smell of gunpowder in the air when the discharges started. Dynamite had not allowed anyone to accompany me backstage – not my father, Rafik Kaka, Amar or Munna – nobody. He said it would interfere with things. So the only ones there were some of his guys. I had a handkerchief pressed to my mouth. The smoke was making me sick and I could barely see what was happening. I almost fainted, but two guys held me up. And then, as the explosions continued, I was pushed forward, and suddenly there I was before the mike. I do not even remember jumping through the poster – others later congratulated me on my impressive theatrical dive, but I recall none of it. All I know is that I was backstage, barely conscious, and then I was in front. The ridiculous shawl that Dynamite had made me wear was still wrapped around my torso. It was hot and stifling, and it took a minute or two for my eyes to clear. My throat was still stinging when I saw the sea of faces that was waiting for me. There was a commotion in the wings behind me, but I paid no attention. I was entranced by the thousands of glittering eyes around me. Again,

I became worried that I would faint. The smoke and rush made my head light, and the countless eyes and flashing lights became blurry. After a few deep breaths though, I regained my strength.

'As I looked into the crowd and into individual faces, I saw deep cynicism and anger. Their frustrations had nothing to do with the fact that they had been forced to attend another rally. It had nothing to do with hunger or having to wait in the sun for hours. Their exasperation was rooted in scepticism; they had watched countless of my predecessors strut and fret before the cameras. But little had changed afterwards. The murmuration was a mixture of Jummas and Bengalis, but in all of their faces I read the same account of despair. In their bodies, I read the same history of centuries of deprival, of wasting away. With just enough to eat, they weren't dying of starvation. They died of diseases like TB, measles and malaria, because their immune systems had shut down in a condition dubbed "nutritional AIDS" by experts. In the trees that dotted the maidan, I saw the bearers of our yesteryears, and our only hope for a future. But they saw me as a common picaro. Their wretched understanding, reached from extensive experience, was that everything I was doing was rehearsed. I was a bullroarer for hire, a mercenary leader. They expected me to return afterwards to an air-conditioned home aboard an air-conditioned car, to betray all that I had said. They watched, waiting for that customary blink or that stutter that would validate their disbelief and let them return to their conversations and card games, to their cheap cigarettes and their hunger. And I felt their desperation begin to fill me as the earth began to rise under our feet.'

These lines will prove valuable later when we deliberate how scores of us present at the rally had witnessed the man who jumped through the poster catch fire and leave in an ambulance. But for now, the speech itself:

'Brothers. Sisters. Look at us. Look around; look at one another. Look at the dirt on our hands. Yes, I too know of crop raising. You may find it hard to believe, but it is the same dirt we come from. Every single one of us. But every single one of us is separated by differences that they tell us are more important. You are from this village, I am from that one. You speak this dialect, and maybe I speak a different language. Your family follows this pir, and maybe mine believes in a god with a wholly new name. Even if we are both from the same tradition, there are things that we are told should separate us. My house has three rooms, yours has but one. But look at our hands. Yes, it is the same dirt. For how many centuries have we shared this same dirt? We died in this. We lived in this. For centuries, we were able to live together, to respect and value each other.

'But what is happening now? We are all being pitted against each other. There is little land, but we fight for it. There are very few wells, and we all need to draw from the same ones. So we are taught to treat each other as enemies and as competitors. I know. I grew up here like you did. Maybe my house had three rooms, *but I know*. Should I let the fact that I was more fortunate than some stop me from speaking the truth? Should I be disqualified from objecting to what is wrong, when every fibre of my being screams out that this should stop? *This should stop and this is wrong*. There is no need for you to fight each other. I have to come here and speak because when you kill each other, you kill me. I am nothing without you. Some of you know already – I was able to leave and live abroad. But I don't belong there. I belong here, with you. And I cannot sit back and let this happen to you.

'Who is making all this happen? Who is pitting you against each other? I will answer this out loud and, if you disagree, you should shout at me. All of you should shout together. Drown out my voice if I speak lies. Do not trust me. Watch me now and ask yourself if I am lying.

'We are all from the same dirt, but each one of us is like a well. You are all wells here, just simple wells. And there are people who have been drawing from you. They take and take and take. They drink you calmly. If you work for them, they give you just enough to walk back the next morning. When you possessed land, they didn't let you buy seed. They stopped the rivers, and they forbade others to buy your crop. All this I have experienced myself. I know this. If you work on their land, they pay you so little that you must borrow. And the interest they charge you, why, soon they own your skin. It is the same for all of you who work in their factories, in their shops and mills. You work like slaves, and you still owe them. Nothing has changed for hundreds of years. There are no zamindars here, but the cane still strikes your backs. It is the same system, the one they had before the British arrived, a system thousands of years old. They now have guns and words and their laws to help them. All the forests, all the lands are theirs now.

'I know how many of you die of poor health and from the lack of medicines and treatment. You die because there are no vaccinations, no one to teach your children hygiene. They leave you without crops, a strip of soil or a future. They leave your children sick and hungry. And more than that, they leave us without faces and without names. An empty well is the world's shame.

'And who is doing this to you? They are the government workers who are bribed to plant their water pumps where the rich want them. They are the soldiers who beat you. We are betrayed by maulvis who tell us to pray and not to disturb the local council. The politicians know what is happening but are too busy collecting their own money. These people kill you and then complain of the smell. It is dangerous for me to speak these words out loud. They are here too, hidden and listening. I may die for speaking these truths, but at least you have heard these words. Please … do not forget them.

'Inside our wells, it is a dark and small world. There are no stars in our sky. They show us pictures, count numbers and make promises, but we are sick of waiting. I want light here now, down here in the bottom of the well where we lie. *Now*. So our children can play, so they can eat and learn. They make us fight each other, Jummas and Bengalis. Muslims and amussulmen. Are we to attack each other for their scraps? Yes, we learned to make shahi tukra from the bread crusts that shahs flung at us.[62] But now, there is no milk, no sugar. Why must the lowest two rungs on a ladder fight each other? In doing so we have stopped each other from climbing out of our wells.

'The foreign NGOs have helped us. It is true that they do some good. But we must hold our dictate in our own hands. Our streets are mined by our killers and our oppressors. They stare at us every day, every hour, to remind us that we live because they choose to let us. But if we join together, *these roads can be ours again*. It is time we all raise our voices and lend our backs to each other so that we can climb out of our holes. I say it is time to raise our fists if need be. And the next time they come to draw from us, the next time our masters try to take away from our hands, *I say it is time we pull them into the well with us!*'

This is where the public address ended, and here I will include another passage from Babu's own notes to best explain his emotions at the time:

---

62 Shahi tukra, a bread pudding of sorts, literally means 'royal scraps'. A legend roots the name of the desert in an Awadh shah who was not known for charity. The shah had a habit of tossing stale bread to the poor when he surveyed his properties. A discontented chef in the shah's culinary stables, perhaps in an act of rebellion, thought of a way to reconstitute the unappetizing scraps. He fried the bread, soaked it in syrup, spices and sweetened milk. Thus may have been born the blessing we know today as the shahi tukra.

'By the end of my speech, I was screaming. My hands were shaking, and I sensed things fall from the podium. The shawl had come off. There was no way I was speaking coherently – I had almost immediately abandoned the script I had written earlier. The silence and the stillness of the crowd assured me of their attention. The silence and stillness of a mammoth crowd, especially on such a hot day, is a very big thing. I looked into their faces and I realized that they had heard.'

And they had indeed heard. Within hours, radio stations across the country were replaying the oratorical triumph. Private TV channels aired clips of his eerie howls, and Babu's name immediately came up in NGO briefs. It is distressingly clear to me that the expressions I have translated, and the speech that I have provided, cannot remotely compare to the presentation made by Babu. My lyrics sit flat on a page; his rose up as a mountain before the people. His exclamations hung in the air, their glyphs taking shape – rounded, fervid and glorious. It filled their bellies with fire, and their frames, too, started to shake. I know – I was there. My resurrection of the speech fails utterly.

Over the following weeks, Babu was invited to talk shows, think tanks and public debates and was given opportunities to expound on his plans for a revamped national park and global tourism. Babu was thorough in his outlines and captivated everyone with the feasibility and practicability of his economic proposals.

It was inevitable that Babu's brave and resounding call to arms on the part of the downtrodden would infuriate brigadiers, captains, politicians and entrepreneurial highfliers. But while the public eye was so diligently fixed on Babu, there was little they could do to silence him. The general verdict was that, as soon as the masses lost interest in Babu, he would be brought down to size for his dramatic klaxon and bravado.

For the moment, however, there was no touching him. Even Dynamite Ali had been astonished by Babu's bombastic rhetoric. Convening with Babu's team shortly afterwards, Dynamite declared: 'I swear by God, this guy looks like the real deal, huh? He's not just talking shit, he really means it. It's either that or he's a fool. They will kill him if he's not prepared to go all the way. But if he is genuine, I'll tell you what, and this is not about money any more, if your Babu means what he's saying, I'm on your side. I never take sides, ask anyone. But I'm tired of these bull-shitters and bastards. If Babu Bangladesh is truly going to do all this, let me tell you, no one will be able to touch him. I will make sure he wins.'

Notwithstanding Dynamite's generous assurances, Babu and his crew knew there was much work to be done. In fact, days after the speech, at the foot of the Road-8 residence front door, someone carefully laid a large, broken mirror. Amar insisted this was a threat and hurried off to consult with some friends. Many new recruits joined Babu's side. Noteworthy swayers who nodded their approval of the fiery tiger included Rashed Khan Menon, Dr Kamal Hossain, Colonel Oli Ahmed, Kanu Jalil and Sadeq Hossain Khoka. As amici degli amici made no concrete pledges, they indicated that a victory for Babu might not be unacceptable. Boro Ma, Rafik Kaka's clan and Dynamite joined ranks to help steer Babu through dangerous day-to-day waters. The SBG kept spin-doctors busy with Babu-titbits and galvanized scholars to join his advisory body. Several local pirs and imams were brought on board and helped assure the non-Jumma populace that Babu was rightfully their brother.

His team had decided that the next step in Babu's manoeuvrings should be to placate CIA authorities. If CIA chiefs could be made to regard Babu's candidacy as desirable, half the battle would be over. An appointment was set up for Babu with the wealthy Dhaka-based journalist Manzoor Iqbal, who was one of the most important CIA

negotiators in Bangladesh. The following text is based off a clip I
obtained from a man in Colorado Springs. I cannot share any more
than that the recording was made without permission. Nonetheless,
I have very good reason to have confidence in its authenticity – the
voice matches Babu's almost perfectly.

File No. 6178

12-01-01
Audio Attachment to US Rep. William Nelson
Interview of Babu Majumdar by Manzoor Iqbal

Manzoor Iqbal: Good evening. I am Manzoor Iqbal, editor of
Midday Star.

Babu Majumdar: Oh, thank you, sir. May I sit here? Thank you. I am
so glad I could meet you. I believe you already have questions for
me? By all means, I am at your disposal. However long it takes. Go
ahead, shoot now rather than later. Ha ha.

MI: Thank you. I have a few questions about your parliamentary
candidature and your platform. Answer briefly and directly, and
we can be done with this quickly. In your election promises, there
seems to be a strong element of regulated markets. Are the new
measures you wish to put in place going to stifle good business?
Are you going to shut down holdings that have proved to work
for decades and try new experiments on us? I have also heard talk
about taxing multinationals and allowing no more free-trade zones?

BM: By no means, sir, no. All I meant was that currently, for
example, the way some local retailers are monopolizing the loans
from the IMF, the World Bank or the ADB, or even someone like

Peregrine. You know how many of them act funny with repaying loans. I want better access for multinationals and domestics to compete for these concessions. I'm not trying to stop anyone from trading. Those who have already built their empires, I know they will still play a part in the competition. I cannot control whether they pay you back or not. All I am saying is that some of the funds are not managed with maximum efficiency. In some cases, you know, someone slips in from the shadows – a cousin or a wife – and takes money and contracts but never pays back or delivers. The finances that are my chief worry are those monies that slip through cracks and do not particularly benefit anyone – not the banks, not the American or European companies, and none of the big players. If I can channel these towards a few young entrepreneurs who really have the knowledge and desire to get things started, this could be a super success story. Just think what the effect will be if even an iota of the money is used to rescue a tropical mangrove and to open nice eco-hotels. It will be a tremendous accomplishment. People all over the world are looking at saving the Brazilian and Costa Rican rainforests. We too have signed the Convention of Biological Diversity and are annually taken to task for failing to conserve our natural resources. If we flip that and create some buzz over saving the woodlands and give jobs to the Jumma in some environmentally friendly green district, everybody will gain. The high-up guys can keep their money or, if they decide, they can invest and be part of this momentous leap forward.

MI: Yes, but what about free-trade zones? And taxes? And what do you get out of all this? Are you going to control who sets up these new businesses and everything?

BM: Not at all, sir. There will be independent committees set up by our university professors from various parties. No one party will be favoured. They can all decide on whether the bids that come in from contractors are legitimate, if prices are fair and if standards are good. Processes must remain transparent and democratic. Just like in the US, you know? No new construction will be made without careful review. I know some of the old-timers normally get these contracts, and sure, they will be able to compete, but whoever does a good job gets a tax write-off. If they build badly and their dams and bridges start falling apart, then sure, they will be accountable for repairs and remunerations. You know how disgraceful it is when celebrities and VVIPs come to visit and the air-conditioning doesn't work or the toilets don't flush. We want top-notch work, and those who deliver will prosper along with the park.

Sir, with EPZ zones, it just doesn't make sense here. If we can get the army to move their firing ranges somewhere else, then of course the land will open up and we can definitely start something. But they will have to maintain environmental standards, you understand, or the park will be affected. If foreign visitors like the eco-hotels, maybe they will want to come back and invest in more domestic enterprises. They hardly like visiting Dhaka. Dhaka, as you know, is so congested and dangerous. Can you imagine these top executives sipping their cool drinks on a safari, on beautiful and peaceful golfing dunes? This could be great in attracting new venture capitalists. So yes, there will be some attention on good regulation and keeping operations clean, but everyone will gain from it. I know most of you enjoy taking your families abroad for holidays. Just think if we could cater to non-Bangladeshis in the same manner. Sri Lanka still has not stepped in to organize whale tours and cruisers; that stretch of ocean is wide open and ready for us to make use of. The Jummas have such interesting traditions, you know, they can share some of their stories and put on plays and musical shows.

Yes, and to answer your question: what do I get out of it? After all, I will be putting everything I have into preparing this, so just like anyone else, maybe I will make some money from a new restaurant or lodge. I will have to repay my election debts. But do not worry – I am not interested in making a fortune. I will be happy if we are able to develop the area and reverse the massive geophysical damage. You see, sir, I grew up here and was happiest with all the animals and trees. I don't need millions for myself; as long as the air and water is clean and I have a small and comfortable home, I will be fine.

MI: Yes, all this is good. I have heard you like living simply. But your plans all sound long term. Where's the capital to jumpstart this? Otherwise you will need years to get this running.

BM: Sir, I assure you, I have plenty of people who are interested in getting this new park built. Just see how excited all the people who live there are about this, and how all the newspapers and university professors are promoting our message. But the only problem – and here I need help from the Americans – is to get the army to allow us access to the forest lands. If we can reclaim even a portion of the protected lands, we can show how much money everyone can make from a wildlife preserve. We're not trying to kick the army out. Many of them now live here. They will all find opportunities when tourism brings money in. This will guarantee a healthy and prosperous future for their own children. Sir, over the next few days you will be visited by some of my supporters. Many of them are already your colleagues and friends. Please listen to them to confirm the details I am citing. I know Madhupur is not of much interest to you, but please help me in bringing this dream to life. It will be great for the image of the Western banks that have lent us money and for foreign NGOs who do so much to help. We will not upset anyone. All we ask for is a portion of the lands that are lying there barren and access to the minimum of funds, and then we'll be out of your hair.

MI: Well, I'll see who comes to me on your behalf, but I'll warn you now, be artful in not shaking things up too much. You stay on your toes, keep out of our way, and we'll let you be.

BM: Thank you, sir. With your blessings, I am sure we will succeed. Thank you. I leave you to more important work now. Thank you.

It seems that a number of notable persons did meet with Iqbal over the following weeks to convince him that Babu would indeed be good news for multilateral lenders and foreign brokers. Even more, they contended he would very likely become a media sweetheart and placate environmentalists. Iqbal was eventually persuaded; he intimated to Virginia that he was going to do interesting things with an overlooked forest in Bangladesh. In fact, rumour is that an influential US Second Lady phoned his bosses in the agency to advise them to lend Babu any support he might need. It seems Babu had gone viral – largely due to Munna's mastery of social media. George Clooney, Gayatri Chakravorty Spivak and His Holiness the Dalai Lama had each made mention of Babu. Arundhati Roy had spent an entire interview expounding on the genius of his agenda. After a particular undersea cable link call was terminated, Iqbal was irrevocably assured of Babu's far-reaching fame. He immediately updated his stooges in the Bangladeshi armed forces, apprising them to stay clear of Babu. Iqbal made it clear that if the army were to interfere with Babu's securing a victory, heads would roll and promotions, along with contracts, would be withheld. He impressed this upon them in no uncertain terms. Iqbal also sent a polite missive notifying Babu that he had obtained approval for Babu's seat and that Babu should solicit his services if there was ever a need.

IT WOULD NOW BE useful for us to spotlight Babu's encounters with the Manasa-worshipping cult. Before delving any deeper into Babu's clandestine negotiations with policy-setting barons, we must acquaint ourselves with the unnerving dynamics that can be traced to these Jumma matriarchs.

In front of public cameras, Babu first approached Jumma torchbearers around January 2002. He oversaw numerous round-table talks, conducted one-on-one interviews using semi-structured questionnaires, met with refugees at IPAC and WorldFish sites, and invited disputants to FD beat offices to dialogue with rangers. Shortly thereafter, Babu involved various non-governmental organizations that offered credit to dispossessed individuals. He negotiated loans that would be tied to programmes in livestock and poultry rearing, bee farming, aquaculture and aquaponics, and in growing Ayurvedic and Unani herbs for health providers in Nepal, Bhutan, the Maldives, Indonesia, Korea, the USA and Thailand.

Before any of this was done under the media spotlight, compelling evidence reveals that he had surreptitiously extended olive branches to non-Bengali elders as far back as September 2001 – long before he had commenced mediations with Bengali dons. Away from civic scrutiny, Babu had felt compelled to consult with Jumma leaders.

In private discussions, he vowed to chairmen, presiding heads and priests that he would eject the army and their encampments from 'tribal' lands. He also swore to bring an end to the influx of Bangladeshis from other regions and to find new homes for those who had been allowed to annex Jumma lands. Babu reasoned that, while extending boundaries for an eco-park would deliver employment for a number of Bengalis (in addition to the Jummas), others would be provided the basic training needed by construction companies contracted to complete the bridge and other infrastructural projects. Babu maintained that after attending technical workshops, the Madhupur and Ghatail Bengalis would be welcomed by EPZ factories. Their salaries and lifestyle would be drastically improved – even a few weeks of instruction would allow Bengalis to break out of the vicious fiscal cycles they were entrenched in. Once again, Babu explained how the bulk of the funds needed for these prep centres could be obtained from multinationals and domestic corporations that badly needed semi-skilled personnel.

Babu reassured the Jumma chieftains that their kin would be sustained not only by salaried prospects in the resorts, but also by being put in charge of salvaging and replanting indigenous vegetal specimens. He meticulously listed names that would have to be brought to the table to leverage these pacts. Jumma bellwethers were famously wary of Bengali technocrats, and they initially regarded Babu with mistrust. Having said that, they knew full well that the incumbent Awami League seat-holder had no incentive to change the status quo. If Babu were to follow through with just a serving of his assurances, it would still beat anything others might assent to. This prompted them to hold court with the green revolutionary, and in time, he earned their troth.

There are clues aplenty which indicate that soon after endearing himself to Madhupur and Ghatail Jummas, Babu took to spending days and even weeks at their ramshackle shelters, huts and hamlets. In the decrepit park (as it existed then), Babu spent time at mosques, Hindu temples, and churches that had been constructed by foreign missionaries. Many local Mandis, Bormons and Kochis had pretended to convert from animism, Hinduism, Buddhism and their countless syncretic beliefs to Christianity at the behest of visiting Baptist, Catholic, Seventh Day Adventist and Anglican organizations. They did so to avail themselves of educational, medicinal, residential and sanitation facilities. The foreign clergymen also had the bureaucratic clout to protect new Christian recruits from Muslim violence. However, it soon became apparent that the Jummas had no intention of abandoning their traditions, which they continued to scandalously practise when not under evangelical observation.

As per multiple sources, it was sometime in October 2001 that Babu made the acquaintance of certain Mandi mother-heads. Though Bangladeshi Mrus and Khumis are popularly believed to be the original carriers of animist traditions (idols include the elephant, peacock, monkey and tiger), this sect of Mandi women have quite naturally woven worship of the serpent goddess Manasa into their ancient matrilineal fabrics. Also revered by the Hindus, the anthropomorphic Manasa has multiple names and is sacred in Bengal and other parts of northeast India. In addition to preventing and curing snakebites, it is held that she bestows fertility, prosperity and justice. Manasa is the sister of Vasuki, the King of Nagas. These Jumma women thus traced their immediate lineage to inhabitants of the remote Indian state, Nagaland. Similar to their kinfolk across the border, Bangladeshi Mandis worship snakes as the weather gods of the hills, the gods and spirits of the springs, the creators of the streams and lakes. Manasa, to the contrary, is not always looked upon with affection and admiration. Myths emphasize her bad temper and unhappiness due to unfair treatment at the hands of her father (Lord Shiva), her husband (the erudite Jagatkaru) and her stepmother (Chandni or Parvati). Manasa is depicted as kind and protective towards her devotees, but harsh to people who oppose her. Even with her distinguished pedigree, Manasa was denied full godhead due to her mixed parentage (her mother was said to be a statue). Her worldly obsession became to fully establish her authority as a goddess and to acquire steadfast human votaries. The Mandi women befriended by Babu duly paid their obeisance to this rather vengeful goddess and performed various pujas and rituals to appease her. In time, they allowed Babu to attend prayers with them. He was privileged to watch their sacrificial ceremonies, admire their intricate sculptures, and marvel at their enmity with the eagle king Garuda. While chanting mantras, an alarmed Babu witnessed bacchants pierce their bodies with needles and display poisonous snakes on altar-tops while performing episodes from Manasa's life and legends.

Babu was astounded by the strength of the priestesses he came across. They could carry a tree on their shoulders, give birth and return to work the next day, drink most men under the table, and then skin and roast a wild boar for the village feast. Their hybrid Madhupur sorority kept to itself in the shade of the tropical broadleaf, protected from visitors by their fierce reputation and by the deadly malaria carried by Anopheles mosquitoes that their haemoglobin E blood type was immune to. Their matriarchs had evolved an elaborate naturopathic culture that is based on natural energies and phytotherapy.[63] However, when extremely distressed, they turned to Manasa. As a female naga (a nagini), not only is she esteemed as a provider, but a guardian as well. Manasa is said to be capable of bringing floods and droughts. She is thought to possess the ability to shapeshift into a giant viper, a Medusa-like figure with a snaky torso, a mermaid with a reptilian tail, or a Hydra-headed ophidian. Manasa may also manifest herself as an ordinary man or woman.

Why the normally cautious sisterhood had allowed Babu into their midst can be explained by the fact that both goddess Manasa

---

63 This form of medicine is based on a belief in 'vitalism', which posits that a special vital energy guides human processes such as metabolism, reproduction, growth and adaptation.

and her adherents are particularly incensed by acts destructive to the environment. On hearing of Babu's goal to restore ecological harmonies, the women had sought him out. There are ample leads to certify that the materfamilias had committed to smoothen the road to victory for Babu on the condition that he stay faithful to his election oaths. Most Bangladeshis, whatever religion they may be, regard Jumma shamans with dread. Nagas from time immemorial have been depicted in Vedic texts, epic poems, puranas and Buddhist sutras as being fearsome and potent. Manasa and her kind boasted command over fire, rain, the wind and other elemental wheels. Bangladeshi Muslims could not just forget centuries of stories entangled in naga spells. They were also infamous for their fatal hypnotic gaze, a lightning-borne venom that incinerated anything alive, and the ability to revive the dead. Legends abound about them penetrating hard walls and appearing and disappearing at will. The partnership extended to Babu was not optional. It was decidedly imperative.

Dear reader, I inject the narrative with paranormal potions here as it is only fair to keep this covenant of Babu's in mind while we leaf through his overture for the Tangail-3 seat. Even if one is to dismiss this mystical Mandi ring as outdated and irrelevant, there is no getting away from the fact that they inextricably insinuated themselves into Babu's affairs. As these pages turn, the subtleties of this relationship will serve up sizeable food for thought. I must consequently petition that you allow these queer spices to remain on your plate and season your reading. Only then can we return to Babu and his bargains with Bengali patrons.

After the conference with Manzoor Iqbal, the next important address Babu would deliver was just a couple of months later. On 4 February 2002, he was invited to give the opening talk at the annual gala dinner of the Youthful Entrepreneur Association of Bangladesh (YEAB). Though members of the guild were mostly Dhaka-based and the ball was being held at a hotel in Tongi (almost forty-five miles away from Tangail), the influence and wealth of this coterie extended into all domestic mechanisms. If wooed by Babu's notion of a zero-carbon biosphere reserve catering to the discerning tourist, it would be a trifle for them to hoist Babu into the Sangsad Bhaban. This group of young money-makers had lived or studied abroad at some point in their lives and were quite the cosmopolitan audience. Unlike their forebears, this new breed of financiers travelled constantly and had their eyes opened to world markets. They vacationed in the Alps, the Himalayas and the Pyrenees. They booked rooms across from the Blue Mosque and the Hagia Sophia Cathedral and shopped in the Gold Souk, at the Berjaya Times Square and at Av Las Heras. This second generation of petit moguls was moreover sympathetic to the idea of being environmentally friendly. Although most encouraged their children to migrate to fairer climes, they were somewhat intrigued and refreshed by the idea of saving Bangladeshi forests and wildlife. Many of the men loved fishing and playing golf, so they were personally excited by the proposal for five-star sporting facilities.

The transcript from Babu's Regency Hotel & Resort exposition was enthusiastically broadcast at the time, and a translation (edited by me) follows:

'Dearly gathered, I am delighted that you have asked me to speak at this auspicious event. A number of you already know me. I have had the honour of talking to you about the future of our country and, in some cases, I have shared with you my vision for Tangail and the Madhupur tracts. Every person here is already a party to great changes, new ventures and projects that are helping to develop the country. I come to share with you a small story – the potential for a small and forgotten upazila to flourish and become a jewel in Bangladesh's crown. But we will talk about that shortly. Let me first address many of the concerns you face as pioneers in these challenging times.

'When I say change, I do not mean starting all over again. Many of you have worked hard for what you have. We have spent years devoting blood and sweat to create where there was nothing. Some of you were not there to watch your children begin to walk and utter their first word. You were not there to help when your mother had a stroke, or when your uncle was kidnapped and executed. As a result of those sacrifices, your standing is now strong. However, few of you want to stop. You deserve rest, yet you do not allow yourselves the luxury. You travel abroad and bring back new ideas to implement here. Let me explain how I can help you succeed better if I am able to arrange affairs in my Tangail corporations and municipalities.

'I will drastically improve the infrastructure of the region. Jamuna Bridge 2 has already been budgeted for. I will finish the job. For many of you, easier transportation will mean an increase in turnover of seven hundred lakhs. New underwater fibre-optic cables are to be installed with bandwidths that are ten times speedier than now. A German company is to build two gas power plants which can generate G-gas from CO_2 and renewable electricity. This will be less toxic than any fuel station in Asia at the moment. If I am given the authority to oversee these assignments, I can use MOAs to bring in the Filipinos and the Japanese.

'The water treatment plant in Basail upazila, as you all know, has been ready for sixteen months. It cost us forty million dollars, but it has not delivered a single drop of water. And why? Because certain bosses are at loggerheads with the Building Workers Association. The facility has been lying there unused because they don't want to pay labourers who were injured at that accident. Better quality water can easily solve the problems you are facing with scaling and corrosion and mechanical breakdowns in the Ishwardi, Adamjee and Dhaka zones. I know how your assembly lines keep failing in your garments and weaving shops and in electrical equipment and component manufacture. Your medical and pharmaceutical sector is especially hurting, as are your leather tanneries. With your support, I can end this entire mess. Waste water and sewage is also doing great damage to surrounding areas, and your children and their children's children will pay the penalty for this if we do nothing.

'On a different matter, I know how many corporations outside the EPZs are experiencing a shortage of skilled workers. Though Tangail is blessed with an abundance of fine schools and universities, Madhupur and Ghatail students do not possess the finances to obtain diplomas or enrol in courses that will ready them for your production floors. If I can assure that educational funds are used correctly, Bangabandhu Textile College, Mawlana Bhashani Science and Technology University can offer free certification programmes. I will also ensure that primary education is up to the mark, otherwise the whole system will collapse. With the possibility that jute is going to come back in a big way, we must prepare to meet the demand for our golden fibre.

'Actually, jute is a perfect example of how the world markets and perspectives are evolving. Just as the demand for biodegradable products and the desirability of green lifestyles is growing, tourists want to holiday in solar-powered bungalows in exotic surroundings. Graced by our Brobdingnagian rivers, Tangail's biome has the potential to compete with Thailand, Malaysia, Indonesia and India for these hard currencies. And what a magnificent success story it can be! The world will want to celebrate with us the saving of ancient rainforests and the restoring of a beautiful indigenous culture. Foreign direct investment will be attracted when they see the region is stable and prosperous. But I will need just a little help from you to build this dream. I will need your assistance in convincing the army that the tracts that have been closed off for firing ranges are currently being wasted. If we can salvage just a portion of these lands and restore them to their former glory, we can start a financial entertainment juggernaut that will result in the planting of trees, not in the decimation of our once golden land.

'In conclusion, I want to bring to your attention some ethical and moral issues. I know, who cares for them in these cut-throat times? But just bear with me for a minute.

'Even if life does not run as smoothly as we would wish, something that we have forgotten is how much we had to struggle at the beginning, how difficult it was to achieve anything. We watched our parents fight tooth and nail to leave us something. And how strong their opponents were, even if we only wanted scraps from them. We were denied our rights. We worked twice as hard but were given nothing of the opportunities we deserved. We knew in our hearts how unfair they were to us. How someone with a neighbour, a friend, a distant relative or a school connection, would take our due from our hands. How we felt that we had no chance with things the way they were.

'What most of us do not realize though is that we are doing the same thing. Now that we're the bosses, we crush anyone, no matter how small, who stands in our way. I am not rich like you, but the habit is the same. Politics can be a dirty calling. To justify our behaviour, we say, "Well, that's the way things have always been. The big eats the little. It is the food chain." But think for a minute, does the tiger normally hunt the mouse? It is only the maimed or starving predator that picks on the smallest. And are we either? Inshallah, I look around this room and see faces shining with health. But we are at this minute sending people to the doctor, victims to the hospital, skeletons to the masjid, and refusing to pay for their burial.

'I will stop now. I am not here to fill you with sad stories or to make you feel guilty. I am here to ask for your help in fixing things in just one little forest. And it will not cost you a penny. You will be able to invest in the rest-houses and entertainment facilities. You can make your fortunes. But help me convince the armed forces to relocate their camps elsewhere. There are incentives we can propose to induce them to move to other places. If you can back me in this, I will work doubly hard to finish all the infrastructural work in Tangail, in my jurisdiction, so that your current operations can thrive at a capacity you would not believe. My district can provide the utilities you desperately require. So, in closing, I ask you, deal or no deal?'

Before any deals were forthcoming, a consortium of capitalist heavyweights asked to meet with Babu (post-Regency gala) for a lengthy caucus at a conference room in the massive Bangladesh–China Friendship Conference Centre just across from the Sangsad Bhaban. I was able to obtain intel pertaining to this closed-door gathering with assistance from Boro Ma. After our collaboration on the brothel scandals of the 'Building' section, she had permitted me to stay in close touch. She had read my 'Building' section and was pleased with the narrative. (NB: I left out the bit about her gripping me like an enormous tree in case she felt the comparison was less than flattering.) Even when swamped with work – she had amazing stamina for a seventy-three-year-old – she made time for me to consult with her. One evening, I complained to her over tea in Dhanmondi that I lacked credible intelligence about the conference centre talks. Boro Ma went silent for a long while, longer than usual. Finally, she indicated that she might be able to locate someone who had been in attendance at the summit. Sure enough, just four days after I had started pestering her about the corporate consortium, Boro Ma telephoned. She sounded breathless and excited and made a strange request of me. She told me to take a rush-hour train from my flat in Dhaka to a quiet suburb of Khulna. She explicitly instructed that I was to tell no one of the rendezvous. She could hear the bewilderment in my voice and added, 'There is someone I want you to meet. A very special someone, but no one must know.

You must make sure you're not followed. Someone will meet you at the station. That's all I can say for now.'

As ordered, I followed her directives and deposited myself at a certain Khulna booking point at approximately 1 a.m. The train had been congested and stifling for the first few hours, and while I made a mental note to write an op-ed about the poor service, I was much too curious to let diesel fumes and sweat dampen my spirits. Two women in their early twenties were waiting for me. They accompanied me to a scooter van, and though the station and streets were now deserted, they took pains to check that we were not being tailed. After a twenty-minute ride, we waited a while under a solitary streetlight. Eventually, we boarded a rickshaw cart that dropped us in the middle of a slum. The whole time, one of the girls consulted with others on a rather hi-tech mobile phone. We entered a tea shop and, after a few minutes, Boro Ma joined us. All smiles, she embraced me and explained, 'You must be wondering why all this secrecy. Well, let me tell you exactly why. Today, inshallah, in just a few minutes you will meet with Babli Ma.'

As my jaw unhinged and descended on to my chest, a whirlwind of thoughts rushed through my head. By all accounts I had heard thus far, the enigmatic Babli Ma was very dead. When she had been active in Bangladesh in the 1990s, she was said to have been in her sixties. If she were somehow miraculously alive – and I had no reason to doubt Boro Ma on this – she would be in her nineties. Very little was known of the 'shero' Babli Ma. I had never come across a picture or recording of her. She was believed by some people to actually be the philanthropic 'madam' that formerly went by the name of Sadia (we have already discussed her in a previous episode). This made absolutely no logical sense as Sadia was supposedly a good thirty years younger, but such was the nature of the mystery surrounding Babli Ma. Others upheld that Babli Ma was no brothel-worker but a royal descendant of the gracious and valiant Rani Bhabani, who

had governed her husband's kingdom for forty years when he died
in 1775.[64] I suppose in many ways Babli Ma's legacy resembled
Babu's – both were variously loved and censured. But unlike Babu,
Dorothy O'Grady or Anna Vasilyevna Chapman, no biographer
had attempted to unravel the layers behind Babli Ma's exceedingly
complex and obscure existence.

Once I was able to control my jaw and had finished swallowing
the absurdly large egg, I blurted out at Boro Ma, 'Huh? How can it
be? How old is she? I mean, what's really the truth about her?'

Boro Ma, smiling a little less now, replied, 'Listen, we are not
here to discuss her life with you. She is a very private person, I must
ask you to respect that. Trust me, she was there at the China Centre
discussion. She is very aged now, but still remembers quite a lot.
Anyway, she has heard nothing but good things about you from
me, and wants to meet you. But I warn you again, do not ask any
questions. Let her do the questioning.'

Just as Boro Ma was done voicing the caution, mobile phones
began ringing as two large men escorted a tiny woman inside the
kerosene-lit hut. Once the sari-draped figure had settled comfortably
on a mat, the others left Boro Ma and me with her. Peering in
the darkness, I was able to make out her face to some extent. The
human being before me was indeed old. With hardly any hair on her
head, she had reached that stage in life where it was difficult to tell
whether she was male or female, and whether she was still with us or
had already departed. Somewhere between human and sprite, she
appeared cracked open to time. She was an abyss that I dared not

---

64 Still others claimed that Babli Ma was the celebrated spy, Noor Inayat Khan,
    who had worked for the French Resistance during World War II. This too
    was preposterous: Khan had been born in 1914 (which would make her over
    a hundred now) and had been publicly executed by the Gestapo in 1944. All
    the same, there are those who are convinced that Babli Ma was the decorated
    spy and had been working for India in the mid-1990s.

look into for long. As I paid great attention to my muddied shoes, I heard a voice address me, 'So you're writing about Babu?'

I was surprised to hear that her voice was rather playful, almost mischievous in its lilt. I looked up in relief and responded affirmatively.

'Good,' she said. 'I like you already. But if I didn't, you wouldn't be here.' Boro Ma maintained her smile through our exchange, but for the first time since I had met her, she seemed somewhat skittish. It was almost as if she were a teenager in the presence of a crush.

I smiled, and Babli Ma continued, 'Okay, let's get down to business. Give me a minute to think. Ah yes, the China Centre conference. Well, I was there. So was Babu. But he didn't come alone. That wily boy, he came in with four Jumma women. They didn't expect that. These women were obviously from the forest. Those stiff-shirted kingpins were appalled. But I understood what Babu was doing.'

Here Babli Ma stopped and drifted off. Both Boro Ma and I were silent. We watched as years flashed before us. You could almost feel drafts of air, as if some star-traveller were flipping through the pages of days gone by.

On returning, Babli Ma continued, 'But these were not ordinary women, you see. The moment they entered, I could tell that they were touched. They didn't have to say anything, and I don't recall them piping or squeaking the entire three hours. I know Babu had people like Dynamite and Rafik working for him, but these women, they worked in a different way. Most of the people in that room had never met womenfolk like that. Yes, these czars had jumped on jet planes and had enjoyed champagne and caviar the world over, but they had never visited our remote jungles. They had never spent hours or days looking into the trees to watch the shapes that move behind them. These Jummas brought to that assembly room centuries of Bengali history – a presence, or absence if you may, that those barons, those Khans, and those Chaudhuries were unacquainted with.

'But you, I see you have been studying, huh? You're not such a fool; I can tell you're beginning to understand. But even you, have you visited the jungles?'

I nodded. 'There is so much I don't know. But thank you, I will keep trying. I will go and see as much as I can.' I kept my answers short in fear of Boro Ma's disapproval.

'Good,' the amiable figure uttered and then added, 'I'll have my eyes on you ... But let me wrap up. Over the three hours, the dialogues did not go so smoothly. Babu did a good job of pitching his ideas to them, but several of them found the whole park thing outlandish. They just couldn't believe that such a bold, idealistic move could work in a corrupt country like ours. The four women could see this, and I think they kept things in check. All they had to do was cough and scratch their heads or spit into their hands, and everybody would calm down and resume listening. On that China Centre trading floor, I think most of them were quite scared of the Jummas. Even so, I was initially of the opinion that Babu had lost this round. The bigwigs weren't convinced enough to support him. And that would mean no seat. No seat for Babu. All the money he had paid people, all of it would be in vain.

'But there was a surprise waiting. We broke for lunch to give the industrialists time to talk amongst themselves. But when the food was served, things really turned around. The Madhupur women did not eat from the buffet, but opened tin carriers. God knows what they had in there, but the fragrance was divine. I think it must have filled the complete building. It was like we had just smelled amrit. I remember people in the room crowded about them – everyone forgot their fear and wanted to see what they had. I went too, and when I looked into their tin bowls, my hunch that these Jummas were not ordinary was reinforced. They were sorceresses. Inside their bowls, there was this green and red broth, and it looked like the oils and vegetables were stirring and bubbling. There was definitely golden honey in there. Perhaps you already know how Jummas and Mrus use honey in their spells and potions, hmm? I could also smell apricots, ginger, jaggery, basil, and then the mixture parted and you could see through it into amazing rainforests, and I swear you could hear animals calling. Not that anyone wanted to eat the stuff. I don't even remember if the women ate it, but it was thrilling all the same. It felt like we were all a little drunk, and that boring aluminium-and-plastic room was filled with bright and exotic visions. We were all really euphoric for no good reason.

'I guess that pretty much sealed the pact. After lunch, the businessmen were on a high of sorts. They had become elated about saving Madhupur, and a rumpus of them wanted to return with the women for sightseeing. They gave Babu the green light for his replanting projects and guaranteed their cooperation.

'And there you have it. That's all I can remember. A long, boring meeting, and then those hypnotizing spices and smells. I've tried to find out more about what they had in their tin carriers, but even I cannot open all doors. Babu was quite the lucky man. But I suppose he had the right intentions. Okay, I am tired now; I must go. Keep doing our good work and, who knows, maybe we will meet again one day, maybe in another thirty years?'

She laughed after finishing with that, and then Babli Ma left me. I had not been able to pose a single question but was still overcome with gratitude that the mythic woman had visited with me. And when she said thirty years, I did not doubt it. I bowed low as she left the hut. I returned to Dhaka the next morning. Our narrative must also move onward now.

THE VERY LAST TÊTE-À-TÊTE Babu was to have with acknowledged bigwigs was held at the Ghatail cantonment. Located alongside the Tangail–Jamalpur–Mymensingh highway, it was the regional headquarters of the Bangladeshi army, navy and air force. Babu had to wrangle considerable influence to arrange this rendezvous with admirals, captains and brigadiers.

Irrespective of directives issued by their paymasters in Washington and the wishes of Bangladeshi market magnates, the fact remains that the army was wont to dismiss Babu's application for a bureaucratic post. For decades they had the Ghatail and Madhupur areas under their sole dominion, and the notion that some pesky civilian was to order them about and shake things up was most unwelcome. Still, they grudgingly set aside some time to gauge first-hand the young man who had been making waves that battered their frigates. These gunmen prided themselves on being some of the most experienced combatants in the world. In their lucrative employment as UN peacekeepers, they were valued as among the best in skirmishes. This ironically was the result of Bangladeshi enlistees, in the 1980s, being routinely selected to first enter warzones – it was cheaper to deal with a dead Bangladeshi than it was with a European or American counterpart. After decades of deaths, Bangladeshi units hardened and became unsurpassed in fighting styles and in the artifices of bomb-disposal. As a result, the UN hires more recruits from Bangladeshi forces than any other country in the world (Pakistan, Rwanda and Uruguay customarily follow) to deploy them in forty-five conflict zones.

Bengal tigers in blue hats were also ranked as the most efficient night-strike force due to years of drilling in the dark during the inescapable Bangladeshi electricity outages. They easily trumped Western counterparts, even those equipped with high-fidelity night scopes and eighth-generation thermal imagers. Trained and outfitted in a manner akin to US Navy SEALs and the UDT of Korea, they were truly elite in the world of professional warriors. This military supremacy had resulted in a palpable sense of arrogance. In times of domestic unrest, special battalions dressed in all-black uniforms with black bandanas and wraparound sunglasses cut an imposing presence on the streets of the republic. These units soon began to take the law into their own hands and cursorily executed thousands of 'troublemakers', professing little faith in the Bangladeshi criminal justice system. Each a self-appointed Hammurabi, their arrogance was stunningly apparent in June 2004 when the US secretary of defence Donald Rumsfeld arrived in Dhaka. He magnanimously offered soldiers a role in the invasion of Iraq but found his bids rebuked by the Islamic generals.

So, despite the fact that Babu was widely applauded by so many (Dynamite had done an outstanding job) and had been given the go-ahead by American honchos and provincial magnates, there was no surety about how receptive the brass would be to him. Their personal estimation of him would be vital. It was rather like returning to the days at Dhaka University as a JSD aspirant – swagger and confidence were decisive in engaging these high-rankers.

The subsequent version of the encounter was patched together by me from testimony obtained from a certain navy officer who had been present at the talk, and from a brief note scribbled by Babu. The naval commander was eager to recount what he had witnessed at the negotiations that day. They had terminated in a manner that had profoundly shaken him. He said it had been rather like a dream, but terrifying and murky.

Babu appeared before the soldiers on 8 March 2002, at 2 p.m. in Conference Chamber 6. He was made to wait for almost an hour outside before being ushered into the large and striking room that ambitiously incorporates two magnificent trees which rise right through its high ceilings and extend into the sky above. Large circular glass portholes (lined with cork) allow observers to view the branches as they spread their large canopy overhead and filter out the bright sunlight. The architect of this building had obviously been inspired to integrate the jungles that had surrounded the cantonment at the time of design in the early eighties. A cement wall runs the length of the huge chamber and has steps layered from the roof to the flooring. In 2002, these terraces were planted with a number of rare specimens of local plants and flowers. Over the years, due to lack of tending, the foliage had overflowed its banks and had taken over part of the chamber's floor. It was and still is a remarkable room, and Babu wrote of it in his brief note.

In the centre of the room, lounging about an enormous and priceless Burma teak table were various notables, who hardly glanced at Babu as he was escorted to a chair. After a few minutes, a lieutenant general turned to Babu without waiting for a formal introduction, and asked:

'So, you're the new kid on the block, huh? Our Royal Bengal Babu Bangladesh?'

There were sniggers around the table while Babu's head bobbed about ingratiatingly. The conversation continued in this vein for over ninety minutes – the defence bosses made light of Babu's objectives, cast aspersions on his lifestyle, and accused him of being a charlatan. Babu, on his part, was expansive and gregarious, explaining in minute detail every aspect of his eco-park and how he would leave their principal holdings untouched. He humbly clarified how he would also focus on completing the infrastructural missions and how he would be sure to include them in all stages of development.

Babu practically prostrated himself to their superiority, ignoring their taunts and innuendoes. After he had spent himself thoroughly and bared his dreams and hopes before their 20/20 vision, he appealed to them, saying, 'Please, please, you must understand, this is … this is a good way. All our old trees, animals and plants, the things we grew up with, we can save them. The tourists will bring in the necessary funds. If you authorize just a small portion of the budget allocated by the ministry of environment and forest, I can jumpstart roadwork and replantation. Private investors have already pledged to build the rest. And we will finish the projects carefully, with minimal damage to the environment. We will fashion a haven for the world to come and marvel at. And more and more money will arrive. Please understand … this is the only practical way in the long run.'

The highest-ranking officer rose from his seat and, swishing his rattan about slowly, asked, 'And what if we respond in the negative? Even if everything you say is true, what do we care? What if I don't like your stupid face and decide to ruin your career?' There were smiles around the table as the lot turned towards Babu menacingly.

While the following is missing from Babu's note, my naval informant impressed on me that some incredible changes took place in that chamber after the officer's challenge. The man became visibly agitated as he tried to articulate himself.

'Be advised, after that idiot four-star general threatened Babu like that, many of us felt bad. It was obvious your poor Babu was sincere. It was very unusual for us to find a statesman who genuinely wanted to make outstanding improvements. But they didn't care. Even though they had been told by the Americans, Indians, Japanese and all these businessmen to support Babu, they wanted to give him a hard time. But at that moment, something crazy happened. Your Babu stood up straight like a missile. He did not look so small any more. He was holding a cup of tea in his hand, and there was a loud snap as the cup crumbled into his closed fist. Babu opened his hand and flicked away pieces of china.

'The room was suddenly drenched in darkness. It was like clouds had completely covered the afternoon sun. Through those glass holes at the top, we could see the trees spread over us like giants. Inside the chamber, plants suddenly started to rustle like there was a wind blowing through. But there was no air moving in that boardroom – it had become stifling and heavy. And then started the low hissing. All of us turned to the wall behind Babu where the shrubs and vines were. It was horrible, but it appeared as if there was something huge moving inside. Something was behind there, and your Babu suddenly started smiling as we yelled and scrambled back in fear. A shiver of my comrades unholstered their sidearms but we were all stricken, nobody could hold a weapon. It felt as if there were eyes glowing from the foliage, watching and contemplating our souls.

'There was no breath left in my body when Babu suddenly spoke to us, "If you try to stop me, I will thrash you to within an inch of your lives."'

My naval confidant stopped and wiped his eyes. 'All of us were standing at attention now. I think two or three were even saluting him. It felt like the chamber had been suddenly filled with this awesome and foreboding terror. The wooden table was still shaking from Babu's blow, but it was shuddering as if a bahamut had awoken.

'Babu had changed. Now, in his face was the desperation of a terrorist. His voice – it was heavy and sounded like a thousand other voices echoed in it. It made me think of mutineers within our ranks. Everyone knew of garrisons that favoured Babu. And his silhouette, it seemed like it kept changing shape. He was huffing and puffing and became huge. In him, you could sense the strength of the masses and the thousands he had on his side. That day, Babu won the unconditional respect and loyalty of everyone in that room, and more importantly as we are soldiers after all, he earned our fear. Your Babu scared us badly. I'm still fearful of him. He helped many, and I hold no grudges against him. But I wish he had spared me that.'

Visibly overcome, he sat without speaking for minutes.

As a result of these painstaking speeches, threats, endearments and bribes, Babu won Tangail-3 in 2002. Notwithstanding the fact that he won by just a narrow margin, his camp was ecstatic. So was he. In a celebration that overflowed the small tin-roofed shack in Madhupur village, Babu tearfully thanked all those who had helped. Surrounding him were his parents, his cousins and uncle, Munna, Kanu, Dynamite, Mandi women and a miscellany of factory owners, NGO leaders and army personnel who had involved themselves in the campaign. They patted him on the back and warned him that the real challenges were yet to come.

We are not to go into extensive detail here, but over the following year, Babu dashed about the country to jumpstart his initiatives. All and sundry demonstrated a disposition to contribute and progress was slow but steady. The army cleared out of several sectors. Funds were made available to students for manual and skilled preparative modules, and land, seed and salaries were allocated to Jummas for reforestation. Topsoil levelling had started three miles outside the park with governmentally allocated monies, and soon Babu saw the blueprints of his resorts start to take shape. NGOs moved in and initiated microcredit programmes for indigent Bengalis. For all appearances, things seemed to be heading in the right direction.

This lasted from June 2002 until May 2003. Though Babu was disappointed with the pace at which advancements were being made, he was reassured by friend and foe that bureaucratic wheels could not reverse any faster. His outline had stipulated two years of preparation before yields could be expected from the revamped park and from the unfinished grid of roads, bridges and telecom services.

However, after a year of lacklustre efforts, things started to collapse. Commercial enthusiasm for the Madhupur reclamation dwindled. Financiers were waking up from earlier euphoric stupors, bewildered as to why they had supported the curious scheme. Furthermore, just before elections, the AL government had presaged a loss of authority by purportedly auctioning off seven gas fields after stealthy arbitrations. They sold the resources at extremely unfavourable terms to foreign energy refineries. Soon enough, exploratory drilling and processing personnel landed in Bangladesh. National mercantilists became frantic to lock in a piece of this malodorous but profitable pie for themselves.

Once brass-hats surmised that Babu had lost the favour of the moneyed men, military camps reappeared in the exact same lands vacated months earlier. Washington, too, was preoccupied with a huge uprising of residents in Rangpur over proposals by an energy conglomerate for an open-cast coal mine that would destroy the homes, lands and water sources of approximately 3,80,000. Demonstrators had been fired upon by paramilitary troops, and the movement had become a media circus. Consequently, construction at the park lodges came to a halt as bureaucratic moneymen no longer felt compelled to provide for Babu's upazilas. Scholarships dried up and were 're-appropriated' by venal deans.

To top all this, NGOs found themselves in the crosshairs of vengeful bureaucrats. The BNP government was persecuting NGOs for a scandal involving a Nobel Prize recipient from Bangladesh. This ascetic educator had attained fame from the success of his NGO in helping millions of rural poor. Babu greatly admired the man, and they had had numerous private meetings. When the Nobel laureate attempted to form an independent political party in

2002, established power-players plucked at his gauntlet mid-air and tore it to bits. AL and BNP forces swiftly broke the humanitarian's back. Not literally, as that would have resulted in worldwide outrage, but they sent him scurrying back to his professorial station. Once finished with him, they took aim at other NGO deans.

A few of Babu's friends, including navy officers who were not easily swayed, attempted to turn things around, but there simply was not enough support for Babu. Even Babli Ma, the SBG and other significant well-wishers were busy with the coal mine fiasco and the complications arising from the post-haste sale of gas sectors. The half-finished roads, bridges and telecom services remained unattended to, and no opportunities were flowing Tangail-ward.

During 2002 and 2003, Babu became quite frantic and attempted to appeal to administrative headliners. He found himself seated in waiting rooms for hours. Soon, Babu took to pounding on their heavy teak doors in desperation and was roughly escorted out despite Munna's best efforts. MP or not, he lacked the weight of an affluent constituency, and even undersecretaries had the gall to admonish him for his persistence. Amar and Raju were explicitly threatened by construction companies and warned to stay away from Jamuna 2. In Madhupur, the Bengali populace found itself back in squares that can only be described as 'one'. As indentured servants, they returned to combatting the Jummas for whatever grain lay scattered. Army chiefs morosely ordered Babu to return to his home district and to allow the lumbering to continue. They warranted that after they had received their cut, they would consent to Babu stashing away a few million for himself. To Babu, it was as if a beautiful dream had been hijacked overnight. This is when both friends and foes say something in Babu snapped.

In September 2003, Babu vacated his humble Madhupur shack for a much grander municipal compound. This property, 22 Kalabari Road, was a grand estate of twenty-two square acres, which had recently been overhauled and renovated. When Babu moved in that September, it had been equipped with state-of-the-available-art facilities, including a private swimming pool, teak-accented hallways, and bathrooms equipped with lavish footbaths. Babu moved in without any fanfare. A tax lawyer I cannot name has authenticated for me that the title to the holding was in Babu's name.

The neighbourhood was swept for agitators by a small contingent of security officers. Barbed walls kept the forest out and trees were chopped down for surveillance purposes. For the first time in his career, Babu was sequestered from commoners and from civilian traffic. He made no contact with anyone – Munna had to rush back to New York for work, and Amar and Raju found Babu increasingly distant and evasive. Babli Ma and even his parents found him invariably 'in a meeting' when attempting to make contact, and their messages were left unanswered. I know of one occasion on which Babu sent lavish presents to the Majumdar residence on Road 8, but his enraged mother had them returned immediately. As new woodcutters moved in, Babu did not emerge from his digs for weeks on end.

It became obvious to locals that nothing had changed from the past, and that sufferance was still their badge. Babu's standing with the Jumma had really soured. He was not the first king who had illuded the aboriginals. It was widely acknowledged that Babu had indeed lined his own pockets, thus feeding off their misery. One winter morning in 2003, a team of Babu's former Mandi companions turned up at his Madhupur sanctuary. They were adamant in seeking his audience and refused to leave without an interview. Bengali guards scrutinized the red-faced women distrustfully and fearfully.

When Babu was informed about their demand, he behaved most peculiarly, first running into his room, then locking the door and making choking noises for a half hour. He then emerged, bold and clear-eyed. He was carrying a large urn-shaped burner with at least four glowing sticks. He commanded his men to escort his constituents into the grand foyer.

When they were ushered into Babu's presence, it was obvious from their retracted brows, heaving chests and flushed faces, that this was a band of angry women. The women totalled eight, and it was evident that a middle-aged female was their chosen spokesperson. 'Dear Babu … Sir,' she said thoughtfully. 'You have failed in all your promises to us. There are no lands left for us, no chicken, no cattle. Militias and outsiders loot from us at will. They burn our temples and then rape our daughters. Before the election, you spent weeks in our villages. You witnessed the tragedy yourself. We supported you with all our strength. You could not have been triumphant without us. How can you now let things continue as before? It might not be easy to accomplish the things you promised, but instead, you have invited foreign companies to take our precious groves. You have left us refugees again with no earth to settle on. We have become driftwood, Babu … Sir.'

The woman was strong and her voice rang out through the compound, right through the steamy kitchen into the back gardens. But it was clear that there was voluminous sorrow in her – and a devastating fury. Little wonder that Babu squirmed around in his chair, painfully glancing first at the door and then at his bodyguards with a pleading expression. They cleared their throats and swished their batons around nervously. The confident Babu who had agreed to the meeting just fifteen minutes before was now gone. And these women were quite intimidating – even the quiet ones watched limply as if from behind tall grasses.

Babu finally jumped out of his seat and paced around. 'I know,' he exclaimed, 'that you think I'm doing bad things. But this is the only way … the only way. I do not see any other way, trust me, in time everything will be better. I will make sure everything works out for the best.' Babu almost seemed to believe himself, but it was apparent the women did not share his confidence. Our irresolute Babu rather felt like a plump frog thrown into a bed of ravenous snakes.

'Sir, you speak of time, but we do not have the luxury of waiting. We have nothing, certainly not time. Work out for the best? Whose best? Are you Jaratkaru?' The elderly lady became positively feral; the guards drew back in fear as the women banded together around their elder. Two of them started to mutter below their breaths, their expressions writhed together like an incantation, and Babu went white. He tried to speak but could barely even stammer, and then the soldiers realized it was time to act. Moving together in formation, they raised their sticks and warned, 'Hey, okay, this meeting is over. Sir is tired. He has heard you and answered you. Leave now.' The women started to withdraw, but three were audibly chanting under their breaths. A terrified guard I interviewed years afterwards distinctly reported how their words scuttled throughout the room like a thousand teeming bodies, words they shed like scales, wet words that were sodden with poison, dry words that rubbed together as if to catch fire. The elder said, 'Babu, you have betrayed us in the most abominable way. *A thousand curses upon you.*'

The women were forced out of the front gates and left staring at a steel gate that had 'MGT – All India Franchise' stamped on the side. For days after, Babu remained in a stupor of paranoia and various physical discomforts. He wandered around the compound listlessly, his appetite lost. He kept pointing to a tree in the back gardens, a particularly large acacia imported from Australia. Babu grumbled that there was something large in the tree that twisted and turned menacingly, but after exhaustive searches his staff affirmed that his fears were unwarranted.

Things continued as the women had charged. Babu entertained local businessmen and corrupt politicians who were very grateful for being allowed to continue with their old operations. They entertained Babu in turn with lavish gifts, threw luau-like dinners for him, imported diamond-encrusted mooncakes, and kept slipping large brown envelopes into expensive bags that were left under Babu's teak chair. The intimidating Mandi women were nowhere to be seen: true to their nature, they fragmented back into the landscape. Babu forgot his earlier trepidations and took to napping in the back gardens, often under the large acacia that provided ample shade from the afternoon sun. One such day, everything changed.

Orderlies and aides were shocked by a loud screaming. Babu was in the garden, and something was very wrong. They rushed to find him bleeding from the mouth and barely able to move. As they quickly carried him indoors, he whispered about a snake that had tried to suffocate him. Bangladesh is home to various large constrictors (the giant Burmese python is one such creature), and soldiers immediately explored the compound for an offending reptile. Nothing was found.

Over the next few days, doctors rushed to Babu's mansion, and details were established. Babu remonstrated that he woke up under the tree to find an extremely large snake draped around his neck. After Babu had wrestled and pummelled at the beast for an eternity of minutes, the giant serpent finally released its hold and slithered away. Babu then fell unconscious from his exertions and, on awakening, released the aforementioned bloodcurdling yells. When asked to describe the creature, Babu appeared confused and kept insisting it was of a species he had never seen before. Though he was febrile and badly bruised, he insisted that local herpetologists bring their books and sit by his bed. Hundreds of pictures and drawings of rare constrictors were shown to an ashen and ailing Babu, but he waved them away.

About a week into his search, Babu's eyes went very round and he grabbed the wrist of a poor graduate student from Bandarka Ecology Research Institute. The talented young man had already humoured Babu for three long nights, and was praying that the arduous commission would end as he wished to return to his studies. The particular image that had excited Babu's interest was of a snake of the *Liasis* species. It was a distinct looking animal with teeth on the premaxilla bone at the front of the snout, large symmetrical scutes on the head, and unique pits in scales alongside its face. Babu shrieked hoarsely, 'This is the one that tried to kill me! I remember this monster, that nose with that horn. Dark brown above and light brown below. This is the one!' The student shifted uncomfortably in his seat before politely offering, 'Sir, err, this painting is of the snake ... *Liasis takshaka* ... Sir ... it has been extinct for over forty thousand years. I believe ... I beg your pardon, you may please possibly be mistaken, Sir...' Babu, sick and withering as he was, had the student sent home. 'I know what I saw. There's no use telling me that what was wrapped around my neck trying to swallow my head is forty thousand years dead.' Babu remained unconvinced that he was mistaken, and no one wished to aggravate him further. More physicians arrived as Babu's condition worsened by the day.

It soon became necessary for Babu to leave the country to seek treatment. Resting on the sturdy shoulders of his bodyguards, he toured three different continents. These travels were hard on his employees – Babu was delusional and convinced that something was hiding behind every curtain, door and room-service trolley. He insisted on sleeping with the lights on, fully clothed and wearing running shoes. Two lookouts were always standing watch. He was examined in distant lands by a prattle of knowledgeable herbalists, biomedical engineers and quacks. Volcano ash and decapitated pigeons were rubbed on him, followed by immersions in hot sands.

Ant stings, cactus powder and fish facials were applied, and camel faeces, gecko tails and spiderwebs were consumed. He was bathed with ivory soaps, made to stand with lemons under his armpits and onions under his feet, shocked by eels and agonized with cauterizing irons. No remedy worked, and so a ragged Babu returned to the village, his condition still an enigma, with diagnoses ranging from Anarchic Hand, Lilliput Sight, Exploding Head Syndrome and Jumping Frenchman Disorder. It had now been three months since the mysterious reptilian assault.

A gloom pervaded the governmental chambers, and even swarthy henchmen were reduced to petulant sighs. Governmental officials signalled that this would be the end of Babu's career if things did not improve quickly. Staff personnel became careless in their responsibilities, and as many sought careers elsewhere, Babu was left to himself. Despondent and hopeless, Babu did not protest. He mumbled the names of famous statesmen who had been murdered (including King Jaja of Opobo, Emperor Hui of Jin, Imam Ali, Dmitriy Yurievich Shemyaka, Timoji, etc.) as he feverishly wandered the halls of the building in a wheelchair. Family members and comrades were barred from visiting. With a pallid visage, and a dingy towel draped around his neck, Babu was spotted sleeping in the pantry, under a recreation table in the servants' quarters, and in the gardeners' bathroom.

At this critical juncture, Mali Da appeared in front of the compound gates. The sentinels took one look at the scraggy, barefoot and toothless man with his shawl of hemp and untreated leather, and raised their guns. Mali Da was unperturbed. He continued to chew on something out of a little bag. His face, pockmarked from a childhood infection of measles, spat juices out unceremoniously. He stepped back a few paces and seated himself cross-legged across from the property gate. For two days he did not budge, and one could not even tell if he was breathing.

Babu's sentries were at a loss as to what they should do, but there was something eerie about Mali, something disarming in the way he had looked into their depths that had scared them. It was as if he was familiar with the very matter that had birthed them. And anyway, it was not as if they really had any boss to answer to. After two days, this uncanny individual suddenly rose and demanded, 'Tell Babu that the Mali is here, I come to treat him.'

The sepoys looked at him uncomfortably, itching to use their canes. But they could not muster the courage. The young men stared at him flabbergasted as his Methuselian eyes swivelled. As they strained their necks to trail the trajectory of his gaze, sparrow-hawks screamed in the sky, and a high-pitched voice rang out from somewhere under their feet. 'Go!' it commanded. The conscript from whom this exact account was obtained years later gave a barely coherent account of experiencing, at that moment, a 'sentiment of the psyche finding its place in the natural world' and of a 'tapping into infinite energies.'

The gatemen scrambled inside to convey the news. A cyclopean commotion was heard from the residential quarters, and two caretakers hurried to usher the frail man inside. Mali Da spent three days in Babu's room, sitting on the floor in a corner, refusing food and water. He chewed on twigs, meditated and hummed, bewildering curious staff-members. Unknown to them, Mali Da was an herbalist belonging to the Hajong people. They were uniquely famous in the South Asian archipelago as secretive experts in the healing arts. The Hajong had a number of primeval therapies including 'gun ban' which was the negating of a poison with another poison. This wizened man, a childhood mentor of Babu's, had walked from the east of the country on hearing of his acolyte's illness.

After three days of sitting, while Babu thrashed and tussled about in bed, Mali Da rose and said to Babu, 'My child, you proceed in direction against the scales of the great serpent. I go search for plants we need. I also visit Jor Bangla Temple at Pabna and call on blessings of the mighty bird. If fortunate, Babu, I manage this. But they cannot heal you full. You have to pay the Snake Spirit.'

He left, and returned eight days later. The hoary man seemed exhausted but satisfied. With tinctures of leaves, shoots, tree bark, roots, herbs, seeds and ash, he compressed little balls that were fed to Babu. Within the week, Babu started to recover. Mali Da stayed with him during this time, and the two could be heard having subdued conversations late into the night.

And then, just as mysteriously as he had appeared, Mali Da left. Babu, fully healed, bounded out of bed and called for staff meetings. He meticulously reviewed all activities of the past three months and fired a respectable number of aberrant employees. He then had all lumbering executives assemble for a grand dinner. If one was to suppose that perhaps now would be a good time for a reenergized Babu to end unscrupulous economic activities, one would be wrong. Babu seemed to have learned nothing. He congratulated the timbering giants and assured them that he would open up even more lands for the harvest of precious woods. And this he did.

But, as history attests, things took a most ironic turn. As more land surveyors flew in from overseas to catalogue sylvan estates, somehow everything changed. The details are rather odd, but a particular group of botanists brought in by a Norwegian logging conglomerate stumbled across a particular species of snake that was believed to be extinct. Inside the faintly beating heart of Madhupur, these scientists discovered a small red-and-yellow viper whose binomial nomenclature was *Tricecatus domeli.* The last living member of this deadly species had been found in Cambodia almost forty years ago. This particular family of reptile was priceless in the pharmaceutical industry as tests of its venom (obtained from vials in Singapore) had isolated two peptides that activated enzymes to kill carcinogens in 30 per cent of cancerous growths. The molecular structure of this venom had been studied in tumour formation and mutagenesis and possessed an active agent with the ability to bind with cancerous cells, encouraging them to die.

One of the Norwegians happened to be a proficient herpetologist and immediately recognized the prized red-and-yellow treasure. The Scandinavian, paying no heed to her survey contracts with clear-cutting bosses, snapped a few hasty pictures of the captured specimen and forwarded them to oncologists conducting research at Stanford. They immediately classified the images to be of a *Tricecatus domeli*, and within hours the game-changing news started to spread in the medical world. State phones started ringing shortly afterwards, and on the historic night of 21 April 2004, ministers, prime and otherwise, along with directors, ambassadors, generals, chancellors, COOs, CFOs and CEOs would obtain little sleep. The next morning, as ordered by the prime minister himself, the Bangladesh army withdrew every single one of its camps from the Madhupur tracts and secured a perimeter of roughly eighty square miles, sealing off about 32,000 acres of the threatened floodplains. Bengalis and Jummas were gathered and gently rehabilitated to temporary camps set up by the army. Babu had woken up famous and now assumed a visible role. Along with Dynamite and a bevy of reporters, he superintended the population relocation. While not a soul was to be allowed into the arbours, it was tacitly known that there were still a number of shadowy Jummas concealed within the deciduous radius.

As teams of scientists arrived from the US, Canada, Argentina, Laos, Botswana, India, Switzerland, Qatar and Hong Kong, airports struggled to cope. Experts paid exorbitant prices for chartered flights to Dhaka and Chittagong, whizzing in from the universities of Glasgow, Washington, Adelaide, Texas, Sheffield and Dartmouth. Under the gruelling scrutiny of the medical world and environmental organizations, woodcutting companies cut their losses and beat a hasty retreat. The Bangladeshi government, terrified at the intensity of the attention, scrambled to appease superpowers.

On 29 April, the Madhupur National Park was proclaimed a protected area by the United Nations Environment Programme and the World Conservation Monitoring Centre (UNEP-WCMC). Professionals were sent in to carefully dismantle illegal kilns, shops and buildings. They terminated sources of contamination and pin-picked away refuse and waste materials. While this effort was conducted by soft-treading researchers in full bodysuits, others compiled flora and fauna databases. Many of these specialists noticed human shapes flitting amongst the trees. After a month, Jumma leaders from various denominations were asked to enter the park to make contact with those that were still in hiding. Babu was centre-stage in these parleys and was entrusted with ensuring that the building of bridges, roads, telecom cables, research laboratories and hotels was efficiently brought to completion. Bengalis and Jummas had moved from temporary camps to comfortable single-storeyed homes which had been constructed for them about three miles from the park and boasted running water, electricity and subterranean drains. The foreign missionaries had been transplanted here but found their popularity waning as the Jummas were increasingly able to fend for themselves economically. Money, in sums unfathomable to the poor republic, was wired from miscellaneous accounts to endow domestic research institutes and to procure state-of-the-art amenities for academic institutions and biomedical organizations.

Within six months, foreign observers in tandem with Mandis, Hajongs, Khasas, Kochis, Santals and Marmas, had collected seedlings from 142 endangered species for grafting and planting an additional 22,000 acres. The Jumma people had an uncanny ability to navigate the Pleistocene terraces and floodplains to locate yellowish sand-clay containing just the right concentration of magniferous iron where uncommon herbs thrived.

Outside the park, as Babu had projected, eco-friendly resorts mushroomed. Incorporating rest-houses, picnic facilities, campsites, flower gardens, orchid houses, butterfly enclosures, aviaries and a five-metre high and 400-metre long canopy walk, they were an instant success. This was all done by October 2004. Even the area outside official park boundaries became a biosphere reserve, a refugium for relict species. Both Jummas and Bengalis were delighted with the modulations and with the participatory approaches that developers had adopted.

It took two years for ethno-veterinarians to locate, collect and breed various infraspecific taxa that were on the verge of dying out in Madhupur. These animals were cupped into human palms, and life was breathed back into them. They included rhesus macaques, golden langurs, spotted eagle owls, four-toed terrapins, red-crowned turtles, flying squirrels, Bengal tigers, Sumatran rhinoceroses, fish-eating crocodiles, pygmy hogs, clouded leopards, and a new species of peacock that was named *Pavo madhupuri*. Between 2007 and 2024, sightings were reported of the Himalayan wolf, the Moschid fanged deer, and the white-rumped vulture, but these claims have remained unconfirmed.

The wonders generated from the venom of the *Tricecatus domeli* still enthuse bio-geneticists today, but Madhupur never stops in newly rewarding its caretakers. Most recently, a multi-billion-dollar drug was derived from a previously unknown fungus harvested from its recesses. With spores that rely on insect hosts, it rapidly accelerates organ splicing and transplantation procedures. In 2005, the World Health Organization held an international meeting in Canberra, Australia, to promote the use of traditional medicines from Bangladesh. Import of pharmaceutical raw materials from Bangladesh that year hit a high of thirty-four billion dollars (an astounding 30 per cent of total GNP). The Madhupur example has made it into environmental and economic databanks the world over as one of the most rewarding participatory eco-projects ever. Its 'village forest model' has been replicated in over forty countries and has even been applied in small cities in the Americas and Europe.

All of this propelled Babu into the international spotlight and, to be fair to the man, he shone under its heady glare. He made amends with the Mandi women, moved out of the main hall at 22 Kalabari Road to a barebones cabin, and reverted to his rudimentary lifestyle. He fell at his parents' feet, apologized profusely to formerly snubbed relatives and friends, and encouraged rigorous audits of his finances as an example for other state heads. He chaired arboreal committees and land-partnership summits in Nepal, Bolivia, Mozambique, Tajikistan and New Zealand, to name a few places. Fish populations made a comeback in the Hakaluki Haor. Fishermen, and fisheries department officials as well, attributed this comeback to Babu declaring several permanent fish sanctuaries in this northwest wetland area. In 2006, he was awarded the Goldman Prize for 'excellence in protecting the environment' as well as the Rachel Carson Prize. National Geographic, Green TV and Animal Planet filmed award-winning features on Madhupur National Park. Babu was chosen as narrator in several of these documentaries. Despite honorific wreaths being extended to him worldwide, a thorn that plagued Babu bitterly was the rejection of his offers to partner with trustees at the Bangladeshi Sundarbans. Custodians at the Tiger Reserve had summarily dismissed his well-intentioned proposals, but that is another story altogether.

In piecing together what happened in those eventful years, in reassembling rubble back into former edifices, we have once again gone into the business of mucking about in the dirt. We have had to scoop up handfuls of filth, lies, rumours and dreams to powder back into place a notion of what-happened-back-there. But surfaces crack and fall apart as we are left with a thousand unrequited riddles. Where should we start?

I am especially perplexed by the omission in Babu's memoirs of affiliations with the Mandi women. I know the relationship is not invented. Numerous sepoys attest to their having confronted Babu at the Madhupur compound and, acting on Babli Ma's suggestion, I have indeed 'stared at the jungles'. I befriended two talkative members of the Madhupur Upazila Women's Committee who were not afraid of spilling the beans. These matriarchs intuited that I was harmless and confided in me. There was also a graduate from Bandarka Ecology Research Institute who was rather irate at Babu and did not hesitate to inform me why.

If Babu selectively scripted away his campaign trail, was he perchance ashamed of certain actions? Were the omissions meant to conceal his transgressions? We have his commentaries from Ali's park gathering, but the rest seems to be missing. What he chronicled regarding the cantonment meeting could essentially be boiled down to 'met with guys at cantonment – they are on board' (in addition to a meandering architectural evaluation of the premises). It is conceivable that Babu may have written of Manasa interactions and benedictions. These may well be amongst the pages that are missing from my fishmonger's shoebox.

Another related puzzle that troubles me pertains to the Scandinavian scientists who identified the invaluable red-and-yellow. Was it sheer dumb luck that they stumbled across the rare ophidian, or had it been prearranged that they make footfall there? Had someone, perhaps a toothless curandero, guided cherry-picked herpetologists to a promising spot in the woods? What had Babu and Mali Da avidly discussed before the Hajong departed? Babu wrote nothing regarding his illness and recovery.

The flag that Babu had the foresight and desire to surreptitiously plot a green revolution flaps annoyingly in our faces. Is it improbable that, knowing the institutional odds he was up against, Babu asked Mali Da's furtive help in the rusty ophidian's discovery? It is old hat how environmental types are routinely crushed by industrial wheels. Even our mythical Khona, the Bengali astrologer, naturalist and arch-poetess of agriculture, lost her tongue to enemies. According to the watchdog group Glocal Witness, 180 conservational activists, eco-warriors and land-protectors were killed in 2005. Over thirty years, we have seen grassroots celebrities clear-felled (the kidnapping of Julia 'Butterfly' Hill in 2004 comes to mind) alongside green icons (Babu was mindful of the tribulations Gifford Pinchot and Winona LaDuke faced). More recently, there is the 2016 murder of Isidro Baldenegro López, a Mexican indigenous guardian and foe to prohibited logging. And barely a year thereupon, we saw another Lopez crash: the Filipino environment minister, Regina Lopez. Invoking the ire of business-overseers with environmental compliance audits of logging companies, mineral mines and factories, the lone wolf was swiftly deposed by Philippine cabinet members who mounted a counter-offensive. As indicated in Babu's diary, he was aware of the malice directed toward mavericks who rocked commercial boats.

Much of what I have recounted in this section lies in hinterlands far outside the scope of the empirical and the rational. There has been a stupendous dose of hocus-pocus and conjuring in these pages. We have used cognitive springboards to leave Aristotelian and Euclidian concepts behind us. How are we to reconcile these irrational tensions? Was Babu really attacked by a constrictor? Or while sleeping under the tree, had he wrestled with his conscience and his betrayal of the Mandi women? Some readers may posit by virtue of Jungian analyses that Babu had unconsciously beaten himself black and blue and fallen gravely ill. Mayhap, this was when he stage-managed with Mali Da the waylaying of herpetologists to restore vanishing scruples? Or I am hazarding too far afield and grafting grace unto Babu?

40,000-years-dead in Bangladesh does not rule out the possibility that the *Liasis* tagged by Babu had verily violated him. In 2019, a hover of amphibians that were believed to have been extinct since Mesolithic times were rediscovered in the southern Sundarbans. And in 2023, for the first time in the twenty-first century, the saola, a mammal often referred to as the Asian unicorn, was spotted in the south of the country.

Conversely, are we obliged to concede to the Manasa priestesses, to their esoterica, legerdemain and their avenging serpent? My brother has substantiated that the shawl Dynamite had supposedly given Babu was in fact a gift from the Mandi matriarchs. Did I fantasize 'manas' into that bright shawl, or was it bewitched? Did the Mandis seriously intoxicate those at the China Friendship talks with psychoactive substances? Must we acquiesce that something supernormal transpired when Babu visited the cantonment? And what about the November rally? Did they transport away a stuntman, or was Babu some kind of an immortal, capable of sprouting more than a single head?

Perhaps all of this can be dismissed as the Bangladeshi penchant to weave superstitions and phantoms into the most mundane of events. There is no denying that for thousands of years, we have paired this dunya's worthlessness and unimportance with symbols, totems, rituals and ceremonies that hearken to the unearthly. Even when we profess it to simply reflect on heavenly spheres, we have warped and woofed for ourselves a thundering carnival of life out of dust, water, leaf and animal. To untwine from the Bangladeshi mind millennia of fabulist narratives that have sustained and defined us would be akin to going back in time to pull apart our very DNA. Can we separate our dreams of snakes from our primordial consciousness?

And what dreams they be! The earliest authentic record of ophiolatry (serpent-worship) is to be poeticized in the astronomy of Chaldea and China. The diffusion of this practice throughout disparate regions of the globe indicates that neither Chaldea nor China were birthplaces, but that both were offshoots of this idolatrous tradition. From the Mesoamerican Nagual to the coils of the Teutonic Midgardsormr, from the Korean Eopsin to the cults of Canaan, and from the Rainbow Serpent of Australia to the Sumerian Ningishzida, the reptile has wrapped itself around paradises, the necks of gods, and the human imagination. With its ability to induce hallucinations, the snake has often been considered one of the wisest animals with a hermetic connection to the afterlife and immortality. It has also played a central role in tying together our anima mundi.

If we are to rid ourselves of all things preternatural, would we then be required to lift our world off Sesha's thousand hoods, confirm the asp that killed the last true pharaoh, Queen Cleopatra, discount the Python of Gaia, and slay the two hundred serpents of Sistan? Must we decry all fruits for fear they are forbidden? Is there a moly herb or an anise seed we can imbibe, or prayers, mantras or surahs that can stop these spells from inhabiting our memories? Are these imaginings blessed Barakah, or are we shopping in some goblin market of the Shaitan's?

On my part, I have expended marked efforts in tackling the November speech. According to Babu's memoirs, it seems nothing all that fantastic transpired. He came, he delivered a speech, and he conquered a constituency. Even so, I have sought out people who lived in the area at the time. After interviewing guards, doctors and provincial employees, I have unearthed no definitive answers. But as luck would have it, one woman divulged a fascinating and unrelated recollection. She remarked that in the winter of 2003, a number of poultry farmers had been distressed. This clean-faced woman looked me straight in the eye and said, 'The chicken coops, all our chicken coops, had been raided by something brawny and heavy. It made round holes though our wires to get to the chicken.' She said they had reinforced their cages, but there was no stopping this animal. They were sure it was a snake – it had left behind enormous, symmetrical scales. But this was some kind of a brute they had never known before, something that was able to tear through thirty-gauge wire. She concluded, 'This happened for a few weeks, and then, thanks to Allah, our chicken stopped disappearing. It stopped bothering us. And there were no more holes after that.'

It has taken me years to admit the possibility that Babu may have been a tool as much as he was a wielder. Perhaps unseen puppet-masters had controlled his political ascent, chastised him when he slipped, and kept him secure in their assembly lines. Was he some absurd Monkey King who rehabilitated his errant habits or was he like Ivan the Fool, a goodhearted ninny that won against all odds? Or like some Loki, maybe the whirling taijitu inside Babu splashed splendid colours, but maybe there were nights when he tussled with the darkness of his soul?

In deliberating all this, I am once again reminded of all the holes in my narrative. Not unlike a snake that swallows its own tail, these narratives may nourish me, but they will almost certainly consume me if I do not cease to probe. And in the arsenic green of Bangladesh, who knows what shape truth may take?

IV

ISLAND

Everything was water and sea. These waters held the germ, and produced the golden light, whence arose the life of all the gods.

– Shatapatha Brahmana (XI, 1, 6, 1)

The earth was formless and void, and darkness was over the surface of the deep, and the Spirit of God was moving over the surface of the waters.

– Genesis 1:2

See that the heavens and the earth were sewn together and then We unstitched them and that We made from water every living thing.

– Quran (21:30)

Humans are amphibians ... half spirit and half animal ... as spirits they belong to the eternal world, but as animals they inhabit time.

– C. S. Lewis

IN ITS ELEMENT, THIS is a story that is as indecisive, capricious and shilly-shally as water. In this examination of the times that Babu inhabited, the narrative challenges we face repeatedly assume aquatic qualities. As when gazing deeply into an ocean, in probing into the submerged grottoes of the following anecdote, we find that things are living, growing, and that no landscape is immune from upheavals. It is much like life on terra firma, but everywhere teeming with movement and an astonishing abundance. Things unpredictably drift, with no certain sway, but turn, darken and thicken. Or become shallow, frozen and brittle. For is this not the true nature of a story told with water? Water – with all that it hides, and the regrets and rewards it leaves behind – is central to the telling of this specific tale. And as one who has resolved to walk into the ocean and not look back, one must proceed.

This section deals with a famous incident involving an island that submerged overnight, along with a state-of-the-art archaeo-genetic laboratory and a crew of global scholars. A previously unregistered landmass located inside Bangladeshi maritime borders catapulted into national hearts, imaginations, and into the mainstream media spotlight in 2010. The hitherto unnamed parcel of land was designated Samadi Island. The thirty square kilometre strip was located about 350 km from the mainland, in a 'danger zone' known for seismic disturbances, cyclones and electromagnetic anomalies. While Babu is not a dominant player in the events that unfolded about the island, examination of this cause célèbre will grant valuable insights. Through Samadi's periscope, we will be able to piece together how Babu had evolved since *Tricecatus domeli* had been discovered in the Madhupur Forests in 2004. Furthermore, we will also observe how enemies reshuffled their colours to resist political initiatives promoted by an increasingly influential Babu.

So, before we plunge into the details of it all, we must quickly apprise ourselves as to Babu-related activities since 2006. In 2010, Babu had been a parliamentary representative from Tangail district for almost eight years. As an independent candidate, he had resisted invitations and threats from AL, BNP and former JSD mentors. Defiantly, he scraped by and won his Madhupur seat again in 2007. When the BNP was forced to resign in October 2006, the chief advisor of the caretaker government had appointed Babu as Advisor of Environment and Forest. This was done due to the spectacular support Babu had recently drawn from foreign aid donors with his whirlwind of eco-friendly tourism developments and communal bridge-building.

Not only had Babu's constituency thrived economically under his conscionable piloting, but the fortunes that poured into the country benefited numerous other districts. Wherever indigenous woodland tracts remained, multinational pharmaceuticals dedicated finances and passion to nurture exotic growths back from the brink of extinction. Biotech companies invested heavily in universities and science programmes in all seven divisions of the country. A drive to conserve animal and plant species had rapidly gained domestic momentum. The Bangladeshi caretaker government that replaced BNP in late 2006 lasted much longer than the constitutionally mandated three months; with the prompting of army chiefs, it did not relinquish administrative reins for almost a year. This permitted Babu officially endorsed time and resources to extend his efforts far beyond the Madhupur and Ghatail upalizas that were normally under his parliamentary sway.

Buttressed by coffers overseas, he was able to establish test centres that specialized in examining patents registered by agri-business giants. This last noble endeavour, however, was exceedingly distasteful to genetic food-engineering czars, and I have uncovered evidence that there was at least one directive to have Babu assassinated in 2008. Given that he was already a figure of major repute, the plot I chanced upon involved Babu perishing in a car accident. If staged correctly, this would not have mustered any suspicion (Bangladesh has a very steep road accident fatality rate and official figures in 2008 indicated 90 reported deaths per 10,000 motor vehicles). Before opening Samadi's dossier, we will briefly examine this intrigue.

Apart from infuriated seed oligarchs, there were others that wished Babu deceased or, at the least, removed from office. Since Babu's tumultuous experiences with snake-worshipping matriarchs and his consequent abandonment of fiscal grafting for horticultural ones, Babu had cajoled commissioners, judges, corporate executives and generals into contracts which allowed no elbow room for embezzlement. Though the costly projects generated biodiverse triumphs and were fiscally just as successful, they exasperated many an autocrat. Babu brought whale-fisheries in the Bay of Bengal nearly to a standstill, along with the mass export of tiger shrimps. Choice deft manoeuvres similarly curtailed the rampant growth of commercial plantations in the floodplains and the appropriation of lands for military expansion (this aggravated Chinese and Russian weapons manufacturers, in addition to North American retailers).

Like a wily nine-tailed fox, Babu leveraged bureaucratic briefings at the Sangsad Bhaban, student coalitions at Dhaka University and mutinous officers in the navy to broker treaties. These pacts were most unfavourable to money launderers in Dubai, Singapore and London. International anti-corruption watchdogs recorded that, between 2006 and 2010, illicit capital transfers out of Bangladesh dropped by an unprecedented 19 per cent. Bangladeshi billionaires were in danger of losing club memberships in Costa Smeralda and being evicted from Pacific Avenue homes. As one sullen undersecretary put it: 'That Babu character is really out to squeeze every poisha out of our budget. If he has his way, I'll have to sell my house and buy a bicycle.'

This statesman was being unnecessarily dramatic: he had six motor vehicles registered with the Road Transport Authority and possessed numerous properties abroad. But there was little dispute that after recovering from Madhupur's spells, Babu zealously applied himself (and any available monies) towards ensuring sustainable trade practices in Bangladesh. And the buck did not stop there: common citizens had been inspired by the success of Madhupur's reclamation initiatives and increasingly held their administrators accountable. As a result, it became increasingly difficult for millions to simply disappear from governmental exchequers. Venal officials scrambled to concoct more creative laundering schemes as transparency and monetary sincerity became the order of the day.

The caretaker government held elections near the tail-end of 2006 and by February 2007 had surrendered command to a victorious BNP. Babu had once again won his parliamentary seat from Madhupur upazila, but his advisory position was reclaimed by BNP partisans. Nonetheless, the new BNP minister of environment and forest scored it as rewarding to follow Babu's counsel. This was due to benefactors abroad who made it clear that Babu was indispensable in the managing of their endowments. Despite warnings from Rafik Kaka, Babu started to petition for more stringent legislation to regulate industrial waste. This was when the camel's back gave. A coterie of businessmen approached CIA associates in Dhaka, disbursed bribes and threats to army officers and bureaucrats, and suggested Babu's imminent involvement in a crippling accident.

Despite the commercial influence of Rafik Kaka, the matronage of Babli Ma, and protection provided by constituents and affiliates overseas, in September 2007, a proposal detailing Babu's road-death ended up on the desk of a certain CIA puppet – Manzoor Iqbal. The blueprint involved a heavy goods vehicle colliding head-on with Babu's minivan on the Dhaka–Tangail highway. Babu typically used a cheap Isuzu motor to shuttle back and forth from his home there. Though most politicos of Babu's stature possessed sturdy Range Rovers, Mercedes Benz crossovers and Porsche SUVs, ever since his awakening at Madhupur village, Babu had eschewed material luxuries. In fact, Babu relied on public transportation whenever he could – a practice for which he was ridiculed by peers. This had no impact on him: Babu cheerfully expounded on the desirability of low carbon footprints and reduced road congestion, and on the health benefits of sweating (most public conveyance lacked working air-conditioners). Babu also shared conversations he had had with passengers and the revelations he had attained regarding obscure neighbourhoods and their residents.

Manzoor Iqbal assessed the proposal to be solid. Babu's rickety Isuzu lacked seatbelts, crumple zones and airbags – his death would be guaranteed if the truck driver they hired was any good. Post impact, the driver would hightail it from the stolen vehicle with associates on motorbikes, leaving no leads for investigators. Iqbal approved the operation: he had received missives from Washington notifying him that US corporations with Bangladeshi holdings had had enough of Babu's radical measures. The plan was approved for execution early in August 2007, when blueprints, businessmen and rogue trucks crashed against an unstoppable will; that of a young woman in her twenties. Minnie was twenty-eight, Iqbal's only child, and a beautiful woman with steel in her blood. On meeting Babu at a gala in March, sparks had flown between them and she became infatuated with his magazine-cover persona. Babu himself had been affected by her beauty, her curly locks and her toughness. All the same, he was well aware who her father was. In fact, Minnie had been an acquaintance of Babu's in his JSD years, before he had left the country for Dubai and New York. But in 2007, she felt very differently about him.

When the hullaballoo over Samadi started, Babu was invited to numerous fundraisers organized by the young jet set of Dhaka. Amongst them, he found the radical revolutionaries of the rich – the LVMH socialists. But it was very apparent to Babu, and to them, that they had nothing in common. They wore lungis as a statement, whereas he was unable to sleep without wearing one. They donned thick gloves before entering orchid houses, while he could sniff out the best dung manures for his jackfruit and gauge their mineral composition. They purchased organic toiletries from Shiseido, La Mer and Chanel; Babu brushed his teeth with neem twigs. Babu and Minnie renewed their acquaintanceship at one of these parties.

At the Radisson's Watery Garden, they eyed each other from the very beginning of the night. Both splendid youths, they carried themselves proudly, the air shimmering with pro-vitamin shampoo. But whereas one was draped in a smoky shawl under which one could see the hint of a coarse kurta, the other was decked in the latest Valentino evening frock with footwear provided by Blahnik. At his table were rebels from high-flying castes (as well as a sweaty and uncomfortable Munna), at Minnie's, wearing Cartier and Tiffany, were those that held the country in their tentacles.

While Babu was ideologically attracted to revolutionary women, à la Pritilata Waddedar, Angela Davis, Qiu Jin and Wangari Maathai, he was a sucker for curly hair. As his eyes met Minnie's, they realized from constrictions in their throats and flutters in their partially inebriated hearts that there was something very definite between them. They approached each other and talked, striking up where they had left years earlier. She took the lead: Babu was famously terrified of pretty women. But just as surely as they were aware that something unnameable was drawing them together, they noticed the gulf that separated them. There was no ignoring the unnavigable stretches of pungent manure, and the yards of fine furs, Nappa leather and bright lungi-checks. They parted company, each aware that they had once again defended the choices they had begun to make elsewhere, unknown to themselves. Nonetheless, they could not help but glance back: unable to take their eyes off each other, they knew that they had unfinished business.

When corporate and bureaucratic sentiments began to turn dangerously against Babu later that year, an astute Minnie was well aware that things were looking bad for him. One evening, Iqbal was seated in his office with an assembly of strongmen to finalize Babu's 'mishap' when Minnie strode in, went around his desk, and pulled the Havana from his mouth with perfectly manicured fingers. She was the only living person who could get past his security guards and had been listening to her father speak from the hallway. As Iqbal's thugs shrank back against the walls, their hands behind their backs, Minnie looked her father in the eye and said, 'By God, over my dead body will you lay a finger on that man.'

Minnie was the apple of her father's eye, and after a red-faced Iqbal shooed his men out, he tearfully promised his daughter that no bastard in Bangladesh would lay a hand on Babu. Just the same, over the ensuing months, many would try to apply feet, bullets, tainted cakes, chemtrails and hands on Babu, but in all fairness none of these attempts were endorsed by Iqbal. And miraculously, our Rasputin-like antihero endured them all. This account of Minnie and Iqbal's confrontation was provided to me in 2020 by a drunken ruffian who had long since left Iqbal's employment. The details provided were much too specific to have been concocted by a boozed-up goon – I am almost certain as to the legitimacy of his account of their illegitimate plans. Besides, we will witness how Minnie's trim silhouette would continue to figure importantly in Babu related proceedings over the following years.

Such lay the terrain when Samadi Island first commanded headlines in science, technology and big pharma thinktanks. The controversy involving Samadi had, coincidentally, familiar roots that involved the detection of new floral species. A group of six visiting scholars had stumbled across the growths near the shore of the small landform. Babu's position dictated that he expeditiously assemble a research base on the isle, replete with the research tools and amenities desired by eager logicians of plant ecology and biodiversity. After an uneventful visit to the capitol in Dhaka, Babu surprisingly obtained more than sufficient finances to triumphantly christen the New Horizon Centre on 4 May 2010.

Once complete, the facility was nominated as home to the professors and researchers who had first encountered the vegetal bonanza. They communicated weekly with the mainland via naval envoys; telecommunications and air travel were ruled out due to topographical and environmental peculiarities. The scientists initially declared the newly identified plant lifeforms to be of aquamarine varieties with great potential to assist in the fabrication of saline-resistant jute and rice strains. From their brilliant green stalks, the Bangladesh Rice Research Institute isolated a gene that could essentially allow submerged grains to 'hold their breath' for up to two weeks when salinity levels were undesirably high. Most of the island showed signs of periodic and extensive submersion, and botanists surmised that frequent inundations, atmospheric moisture and elevated methane levels had contributed to the evolution of the unique flora. This last factor was especially influential as zones near submarine hydrothermal vents are typically biologically rich due to high concentrations of nitrates and minerals.

After having been on the island a month, a report was issued that the southern edge of Samadi showed signs of recent human inhabitation. Excavations unearthed rudimentary shell and bone tools dating back no more than 4,000 years, yet strangely no trace of their manufacturers was apparent.

In fact, public curiosity with the island enflamed when, just a few days later, on 26 May, excited researchers from Samadi announced that they had found four partial skeletons of what appeared to be a previously undiscovered hominid. The zoologists on the base at Samadi requested additional pharmaceutical and medical apparatuses, which were immediately procured along with carefully selected genomic engineers. Soon, New Horizon staffers forwarded the results of genetic analyses and taphonomic examinations, as well as hundreds of 3D X-ray pictures of the skeletal remains, to scientific compatriots worldwide. Having correctly anticipated academic furore (the case of *Tricecatus domeli* from Madhupur forest still fresh in memories) the location of the island was concealed from the general public, while only a handful of specialists, along with a small contingent of electricians, caretakers and security personnel remained at the site. The Bangladesh navy cordoned off a fifty nautical mile radius and diverted any vessels heading toward Samadi.[65] The on-site researchers estimated the skeletons' age to be two hundred years, a date that was later echoed by laboratories on the mainland. Lineaments, including abnormally long legs and a flattened and broadened physique, differentiate these specimens from known hominids. The cranium for the most part is comparable to that of a *Homo sapiens* with a diamond-shaped nose. Though their upper torsos and arms seem typical of primates for the most part (the ribcage shape is more spherical than is standard), their long legs appear to have been attached at the ankles. This unexpected trait would make it impossible for them to walk efficiently or stand

---

65 They were so dedicated in their surveillance that not a raft or a catboat could slip by. In fact, a school of giant platypuses was mistakenly identified as a submarine vehicle. This itself dropped scientific jaws; the outsized mammals are extremely rare.

upright for long periods. Pre-fossilized impressions remarkably indicate webbing on the feet. In summation: while the specimens do possess markers that are unquestionably hominid, numerous unique features mark them as a distinct group.

Keeping the island off-limits to most, the government of Bangladesh uncharacteristically authorized a small fortune in machineries and technologies to be directed toward its shores, allowing the fascinating stuff to keep coming from the Centre. Genomes were sequenced, relevant environmental factors chronicled, and a fleshy picture of the four skeletons began to take shape. As the international media began to cover the story, and as planeloads of wealthy researchers, technologists and executives landed in Dhaka, street celebrations broke out in major cities including Narayanganj, Rangpur and Chittagong. The spontaneous festivities were propelled by a sense that things finally seemed to be changing for the national better, along with the fact that the capital that was funding these changes was once again falling like manna from the heavens. No lengthy infrastructural development or manpower training programmes were needed: as with the Madhupur miracles, citizens watched as buildings and jobs sprang up overnight.

There was also the proud sentiment that rapid economic advancement was taking place in a scenario where it was necessary to 'red-list' natural assets, and not uproot or murder them for sale. The celebrations brought commerce as usual to a grinding halt, along with the traffic that normally seemed to have been halted anyway (due to extreme urban congestion). Revellers overwhelmed even cricket and football stadiums. On 13 June, a smiling Babu boarded a ship to make an expedition to the Centre. Unfortunately, he was violently sick after braving the churning surf and returned spotty-faced to the mainland hours later, having refused to stay even for Friday high tea.

On 23 June, just days later, seismic disturbance in the Bay brought exploratory labours to an abrupt halt. Colossal waves battered the naval frigates, and while the ships managed to escape safely, coastal villages in India and Bangladesh suffered sizeable damage. In a cyclical tradition, scores of intertidal ferries and boats went under, leaving behind bits of painted sheet metal and bright saris used as sails. Emerging from their seat of death, these drifted inland – along with the bodies of men, women and children. Having spent lifetimes swimming, they only reached shore after death.

After the seas subsided, the Bangladeshi government dispatched vessels to Samadi with relief materials. Captains made multiple attempts, but failed to sight land and returned fruitlessly. Additional scouts were sent out with updated satellite feeds, nautical charts, and radar ranges employing ultramodern echo-sounders. No island was found. The government kept the status quo confidential as they requested support from the British Royal Navy, their Indian counterpart, as well as from US Marines posted in the area. After six days, the news finally broke: Samadi Island had submerged, despite the fact that official records issued earlier had it approximately a metre above the surrounding sea level. The incredible conclusion was corroborated by frogmen who had photographed a completely demolished New Horizon Centre seventy metres below the crust. Seismologists posited that tsunamigenic volcanic eruptions in the proximity of Samadi had caused it to slide into the ocean. This was not an uncommon occurrence – in 1762 CE, a violent earthquake raised the northwest coast of Chedua Island almost seven metres above the sea level while engulfing 155 square kilometres near Chittagong. This phenomenon caused riverbeds miles further inland to dry up, nudging awake dormant volcanoes in Sitakunda. The tectonic shift that had claimed Samadi was mild in comparison.

That said, the quake at Samadi had resulted in massive topsoil loss. Divers expended admirable efforts in attempting to salvage what they could of the island's suspected biological treasures, but strong currents (with surface velocities in excess of three metres per second) made this extremely dangerous. Furthermore, high levels of methane and sulphuric compounds medically incapacitated sailors. The project was officially abandoned by late August.

Swabs, records and samples sent from the Centre by boat to the mainland had made it into the hands of foreign medicinal directors, but because the disaster took place so soon after the facility's inception, most of the data that would have been needed to draw meaningful conclusions had gone under. Though a few independent researchers persevered in their attempt to retrieve more data from the now submarine landmass, tragic accidents snuffed their ambitions. The flora recovered from the area has proven to be of great value in biogenetic engineering, but there was insufficient evidence available to determine whether the four 'Fish People' represented a species or family distinct from modern humans, or whether they suffered from recessively inherited pathologies that had resulted in the observed syndromes.

While most scientists today accept the notion that we are the last humans standing, many posit that as little as 50,000 years ago, the earth was inhabited by at least three other hominid species. But this timeline is not beyond contest. One example is the 2003 discovery of *Homo floresienses*. Nine 'hobbits', smaller in size than any pygmy population of southeast Asia, were found together on an Indonesian island. Of the nine, one has been dated to be approximately 13,000 years old. Indonesian myth and folklore is coincidentally littered with the bones of *Ebu Gogo*, a resident hominid that was small, inarticulate, and walked with an odd gait. As regional tales would have us believe, the Ebu Gogo, like some wily jackalope, was alive as recently as two or three hundred years ago, and could be espied in remote jungles. In Palau, Micronesia, similar remains of twenty-five individuals were unearthed in 2008; one of these was just 1,400 years old.

In all instances – Samadi, Flores and Palau – it is contested whether the specimens were simply *Homo sapiens* with similarly altered DNA sequences (which made sense if they were congenitally related) or if they truly were a separate hominid species. Genetic disorders that result in bizarre mutations include microcephaly, the Apert syndrome, true hermaphroditism, progeria (where children age and die before their teens, a condition sensationally linked to the Elephant Man), werewolf syndrome and true human tail (vestigial tail). The scientific possibility also exists that on islands Samadi, Flores and Palau, mutant alleles had become desirable as per natural selection and thereby assumed dominance within a small, secluded population in a relatively short evolutionary timeframe. This is evinced in the phenomena 'insular/island dwarfism' and 'gigantism' where sequestered populations respond to provincial ecologies and nutritional resources by shrinking or becoming gigantic. Island dwelling creatures tend to follow their own, and very often bizarre, sets of evolutionary rules.

Another explanation involves the Aquatic Ape Theory (AAT). Also known as the Aquatic Ape Hypothesis (AAH), proponents of the concept argue that hominids went through an aquatic phase in the evolutionary process that produced humans. They point to distinctive attributes in the anatomy of recent humans to support their premise. The AAT proposes that during such an aquatic phase, our ancestral hominids settled in a water-filled habitat, explaining our mechanism of sweating (a waste of water for savanna-dwelling creatures), our rapid loss of fur, and our relatively thick layer of subcutaneous fat. The controversial notion proposes that it makes more sense that humans developed hairlessness and their unique glandular system for an environment where water was both plentiful and continuously available. Thus, many argue that the remains from Samadi lend credence to the AAH.

Over the past two decades since its inundation, Samadi has been forgotten by most. Though scientists occasionally debate over the scant skeletal remains, and while the natural potentials of the floral samples have been unlocked, the sunken property itself is hardly ever mentioned. Oceanographers and biologists have cultivated similarly unique vegetal sections from other small and secluded locations, thus few seek the fault lines where the island sleeps.

In studying Babu's diary to discern his sentiments regarding the entire affair, I have surmised that while he was enthusiastic about the medical initiative at the start ('By God, this fish-human is exciting stuff!') his attitude went through a drastic change once he made the aforementioned trip to the centre on 13 June 2010. In his diary, it becomes apparent that after his visit, he is loath to speak of the biotic venture at all. Babu scribbled, on 15 June: 'Bastard Muzaffar [home minister at the time, and Babu's superior] and bastard Hakim [most probably the chief of navy at the time, a certain General Hakimul Chowdhury] taking all this money for the bloody rubbish island. And people are starving on the coast. Bravo Sierra.' That is all he has to say about Samadi after his visit.

In my indefatigable quest to uncover leads about Babu's activities at the time, I kicked up enough seabeds to be noticed by an underground collective of sorts. This group of folklorists, historians, poets, ecologists, astrologers and anthropologists is still very interested in the drowned acreage. I will assign them the designation Samadi Secret Hundred (SSH) for our narrative – I estimate them to number about that many. Having heard of my task of piecing together the truth about Babu, they warily approached me. In time, I came to learn that they had acquired details of Samadi from Babu himself. Their consortium has existed for more than a century; before the birth of the nation, they had been working to catalogue natural wonders from the West Bengal region and the Indian subcontinent. In time, as I won over their trust, I became privy to the fact that au reste Samadi, there were many other subcontinental mysteries that demanded their attention.

When I first met with SSH affiliates, the majority of them were busy studying a clandestine tribe of Green People. This Bangladeshi order has for centuries prostrated itself before a 'verdant saint' who can supposedly endow one with miraculous faculties over plants and the ability to transform into trees. The SSH were exploring the notion that the sect had been established by wandering Sufi mendicants in the thirteenth century. Meanwhile, other SSH pundits were surveying a small riverine community in the south of the country that communicated visuals via songs and vice versa. This Arakanese tribe was rather similar to the Shipibo people of the upper Amazon. The latter encodes music within geometric paintings, but the Arakanese clique being (discretely) observed, could convey acoustic compositions via complex and often abstract illustrations. Theirs was an intricate interchangeability between light and sound. They flipped the coin on this translation while at sea. While navigating their fleets in the dark, instead of shouting instructions and warnings to other boats, this sect used ballads to relay topographical and formation details. Those in the command vessel would harmonize together and sing shorelines and naval lines into existence for those following.

These varied camarillas that the SSH busied themselves with, of course, bring into question the very appropriateness of naming SSH after Samadi Island, but for the purposes of our narrative, the appellation will suffice. Furthermore, members informed me that once Babu had divulged his insider's account of Samadi to them, he most wonderfully grounded a myth they had been investigating for years. Thanks to Babu's testament, Samadi Island became a star in their private crowns. It became a hidden and private gem, one that sparkled with beautiful colours and reflected the abundance of our dunya.

The men and women of the SSH include theologians, saints, judges, mayors, journalists and musicians. I recognized several of them immediately as nationally eminent savants and pundits in intellectual reviews of our subcontinent. In speaking to them, it became apparent that they inhabit a multi-dimensional and reticulating time that reaches into our collective animist past. They are decidedly non-conformists, with a peculiar synthesis of liberal religiosity and political activism. I was summoned for an evening that became a night and then a week at one of their communes. They had also invited musicians, tribal herbalists, poets and new recruits for a night of devotional merrymaking. In that week, I experienced an ecstatic state of consciousness; all matters of herbs and fungi were ingested, and fermented rice and milk beverages consumed by the gallons. Men with bells around their ankles acted out scenes from epic myths and made vows to Buddha, Krishna, Ganesh, the Zoroastrian Ahura Mazda, Christian saints, Allah, and to a multitude of homegrown tribal gods including Buri Ma (an archetypal Old Lady), Surya (the sun god) and Ola Bibi (the goddess of cholera). Natty-haired men with dreads went into euphoric trances as their shaven-headed partners thrashed about on the ground. Women, accompanied by drums, cymbals and flutes, sang powerfully to the skies as their vermilion forms whirled and expanded to fill entire rooms and then the fields outside, stretching to the horizons.

After days of this, of which I only have vague memories and possibly hallucinations, my head started to uncloud and I found myself in a field, seated under an enormous ashoka tree. Though it was night, I could make out the faces of a few SSH elders in the crackling firelight. They were playing a game of dice with bedda nuts. They fed me a milky gruel sweetened with molasses, and grilled me extensively on my handling of Babu's biography, on my spiritual views, my fears, my desires and my goals. I made subtle attempts to discuss with them the existence of another mysterious group, which I had arbitrarily branded the Sangsad Bhaban Group (SBG) in our examination of Babu and the national parliament. I utterly failed in eliciting a response: I was met with blank stares and receding backsides. But this mattered little when I was rewarded with the SSH finally opening up and sharing their incredible insights as to what they were told had transpired at Samadi.

According to the SSH, Babu met with them just two days after his visit to the New Horizon mission on 13 June. I will now paraphrase their description of his exposé.

On meeting with naval officers stationed on the base, Babu was debriefed that, a few days prior to his visit, three boatswains had been viciously attacked by an unidentified creature. One able seaman was found raked and clawed to death, and the other two were barely clinging to their lives. These men would succumb to their traumas a few days later – their burial is logged on the 19th of the month. They briefly spoke to Babu on the 13th. I was able to obtain details of Babu's meetings with terrified messmates and the two dying soldiers from SSH chronicles.

Babu had met the injured guards in their separate hospice chambers (the New Horizon sported an extravagant clinic) and was very disturbed by their reports. Both patients spoke of a daini (a female monster) from the water charging them. Each independently whispered a terrifying tale that started with a stroll under the full moon. They averred that they heard a commotion near the waterfront and, in going closer to investigate, were assailed by a mutant that was half woman and half fish. One of the delirious soldiers even used the colloquialism 'maal', native to Sylheti teagardens in the north. In their provincial dialect, a maal is a malevolent siren that drags hapless victims to their death (somewhat similar to the myth of La Llorona or Hera).

However, this man suddenly snapped out of his feverish stupor to confess details that his comrade had omitted to mention to Babu. As if overcome by a need to divulge a truth he could no longer deny, the dying crewman grabbed Babu by the hand and said, 'But it wasn't her fault. When we heard her singing by the water, we quietly ambushed her. You should have seen it; she was almost pitiful, tiny and squirming in the sand. But her voice, it was so beautiful. It was blessed, like a mother's lullaby, and I wanted to cry. She was timid and docile at first. But they grabbed her and started touching her everywhere; I told them to stop. She was naked, but she was not normal. It was obvious she was different, it was dark but I could tell that she must be diseased. She was crippled, her skin, her whole lower body ... and even her face was very unusual. She started crying and, in her own strange language, I think she was begging us to let her go. They didn't stop, and it was very dark, but suddenly I saw ... something like gills or fins flare out from the side of her head, and she changed, she turned savage towards us.'

The sailor was weeping as he continued, 'That sweet thing became horrifying, it turned into some monster that tore us to ribbons. She was not human any more, Allah, what did they do to her?' The man continued to weep, and as medics unlocked his hold on Babu's arm, the patient implored, 'Please help me, sir. Please, sir, get me out of this island, I don't want to die here. They don't want us here any more.' Babu nodded and placated the survivor, but it was evident that he was on his last legs and in no shape to be transported anywhere.

This unexpected admission from the enlistee struck Babu. In the passages of his dairies, Babu encloses the man's words within quotation marks. Babu only does this in his memoirs when considerably affected. His initial response on hearing the story was to dismiss the whole thing – perhaps the three had been drinking buddies – perhaps the centre's work had gotten to their collective imaginations. But upon closer inspection, bizarre facts begin to validate their version. Other officers had photographed the sand by the third body and there was a distinct imprint left by a figure that had neither feet nor flippers, but rather what appeared to be a tail-like appendage. The sand nearby was also scraped and gouged inches deep with a great deal of force. Littering the area where the struggle took place, and in the soldiers' clothes, were enormous fish-like scales. These scales were as large as windowpane oysters and could not be identified as per any ichthyologist manual.

That was where the matter paused for the time being. The case was left under the jurisdiction of the naval police (thus guaranteeing that no further progress would be made) and Babu was lead to the research canteen. SSH associates recounted Babu's cursory tour of the laboratories and his comment, 'I didn't really understand what kind of important work they were doing. I know it cost us a fortune though.' Babu had disenchanted the unconventional ethnologists by being overly anxious about the financial expenses of New Horizon. The SSH was loathe to place a pricetag on the socio-scientifically marvellous.

After the brief tour, Babu noticed that one individual kept catching his eye. This red-faced European communicated through violent twitches and facial gestures that he wished to speak to Babu away from the others. Babu's curiosity was piqued and he approached the man to the side. His clearance badge identified him to be a forensic technician. The man professed in a German accent, 'Do you know vhat? Dis damn sing dat bashed zee soldiers, I bet you my life, it's the same thing ve're studying. Zose creatures are still here, I tell you.'

He then requested Babu to come and inspect the corpse of the dead midshipman. He also showed Babu a black, fungiform growth taken from the sailor's fatal wounds. The German informed Babu that the doctors had identified it as *Aspergillus subterreu*, a dimorphic fungus that naturally grows more than three hundred metres under the water. He also related that the two surviving seamen had experienced blood poisoning from the very same agent. The SSH here recalled Babu mentioning, 'A Bengali nurse there told me she had worked with tiger attack victims in the eastern wetlands, and that the lacerations sustained by the three seadogs were *just* as bad.'

The German continued, 'You need to zee something. It will blow your mind. None of zese fools here know what iz going on. I ave heard ov you, you're za guy who saved the forests of Madhupur. You are exactly zee guy I need. You care about your country? You really vant to save your forezts and your indizenous resourzes, right? Very goot.' Babu nodded briskly as he knew well his burden of appeasing eccentric foreigners. But there was also something in the way the man appealed to him, an earnestness that brought out his best side, and Babu avowed, 'This country and my post, all the wealth they offer me, is nothing to me unless I can halt the plundering of our natural bounty.' He spoke in good faith, and the German heard him.

The non-national continued, 'Goot. You ave to come vith me. It vill take about twenty minutes, but ve have to lose zese dummkopfs.' Babu remonstrated tepidly, but the avid fieldworker was undaunted – he placed a firm grip on Babu's arm and Babu obediently followed. What ensued was almost an hour's ride on a Honda dirt-bike for two swarthy and sweaty men who had no choice but to cling on to one another for dear life. The German had decidedly lied about the estimated distance of the excursion. After the uncomfortable trek to a remote corner of the landmass, the agitated scholar pointed towards what appeared to be a primitive manmade mound. At this point the SSH members became animated themselves and their body language conveyed that what would ensue was significant.

The scientist (whom I will call Hans) made Babu alight from the Honda a few hundred metres from the construction and remove his shoes. Together, the two barefoot men skirted around edges and soft clay. Babu imitated Hans and took care not to leave any footsteps. Once closer, Babu could make out that a gentle slope had been shaped, and fortified walls constructed, to shelter an inner sanctuary. On passing tortuously carved pillars and totems, with a gasp, Babu made out beautifully intricate terracotta images adorned with sparkling stones as Hans recited, mantra-like and under his breath, 'Alluvial clay, double moulded and cleared, tempered vith husk and faecal matter … zemi-precious stones are amezyst, agate, carnelian … short-barrel hexagonal, peculiar hexagonal, those are convex elliptical beads … unperforated specimens are evidently to be used by gamezmen. Also, present, are unpolished rocks with a high concentration … of gold.'

Hans pointed to the heart of the shrine, an area decorated with numerous aquatic figures. Easily recognizable were whale sharks, demon fish, rainbow snakes, lotus buds, terns, and a horde of unnameable fantastical beasts. 'Chiselled, organic pigment, unfired and non-oxidized, clearly vater-resistant, sun-symbol disc, crescent designs look to be etched by soft matter … like long feengernails. Sea change, so rich and very strange, eh?' A stone statue was the obvious centrepiece of the altar. This statue had the torso of an ordinary woman seated comfortably on her beautiful fish-scaled tail.

Hans stopped speaking now. Only for a moment though. 'Dominant figurine, top alf woman … lower alf feesh.' Hans turned to Babu and drew his attention to the grounds around the shine. 'Look at ze soil, zere are no footprints. Look, zere are those same giant scales we found on the three soldiers, and see, are zis marks not like zee same prints ve found on the sand next to their bodies, no? Zis are not human. Zee facets in these carvings are like nothing in human history. Ve can hardly get ziss kind of detail, even with laser-cutters and marking machines. Nothing here is human, Mr Babu. And zis prints are all fresh, just two or three days old. I have followed them to the water, half a mile that way. And no, zere are no ships there, no alien spacecraft. Zis things just shuffle into the water. Zey never come when I am here though. Scheiße.'

And indeed, according to Babu, Hans's assertions seemed to hold true. Babu hastily snapped pictures with his smartphone and, as these were now in the custody of the SSH, an assortment of these prints were shown to me. According to the SSH professionals, Hans had done his homework and most of his archaeological analyses were accurate. Even from the grainy shots, I could see the eerie, ethereal splendour of the shrine, and something about the dimensions and arrangement just did not seem 'human'. It was grotesque in a unique way, completely unlike the anthropomorphic figures that have been found in Syria, Polynesia, Hohlenstein-Stadel, or on Gothic cathedrals from the Middle Ages. In the photographs, it was almost as if one were observing the world from underwater: things were recognizable but their logic and spatial rationality seemed warped in a most perplexing and inconsistent manner. SSH elders described how Babu had recounted the intense green of the undergrowth and the dark dense bushes brushing against the grey light inside the enclave – shiny figurines moving, blurring, sunbeam shafts piercing, sounds muffled, rocks plopping, air ripping. Streamed with red, an enormous bird with yellow eyes dives into the liquid and drags me out with its claws, and I suddenly myself on the floor being revived by an ethno-botanist. 'It's okay,' the SSH stalwart reassured me. 'It happens to all of us if we stare into the photographs. Nobody can look at them for too long; we all faint.'

After taking a few minutes to recover, I was told that Babu claimed to have collapsed too, as did Hans regularly, after a few minutes at the shrine. While I was not convinced that my dizziness was altogether unrelated to my earlier carousing, I temporarily held off from examining the photos further.

Hans and Babu apparently made a pact. They both recognized the importance of keeping secret the possibility that there might be an indigenous populace hiding on the island. Not only would naval soldiers be out for blood, but as was common procedure in cases such as this, the islanders would have no peace. As Hans put it, 'If zey find out, your generals, this will become their El Dorado. They will plunder zis island faster zan a continent.'

His argument was irrefutable. If Samadi's locals were simply ordinary people, with no fascinatingly floppy tails, they would be forced to the mainland, out of the way of valuable foreign interests. And if by some miracle, they were a specially evolved hominid species with non-functioning hindlimbs, they would be harvested and pinned down like moths for scrutiny. Hans himself was a rare find: a chemist and an empiricist who had qualms about invasive scientific colonization, one whose progressive scruples balked at the thought of this hapless tribe coming into contact with dominant alien populations. They both agreed that the best thing to do would be to let the scientists continue with their work on the other end of the island and keep this holy site under wraps. Babu promised that once he returned to the mainland, he would recruit assistance from prominent conservationists and social activists that could exert the political pressure required to limit New Horizon's operational carte blanche. Both Hans and Babu joyously agreed that they would cooperate to unobtrusively study the sentient beings that had constructed this primitive and striking shrine.

After they returned to the base, Babu concocted a hasty excuse for his absence, and had a hard time not letting his agitation show. He cut short his stay on Samadi and returned to the mainland. Babu knew it was vital that he approach the right people with his bizarre encounter, and he consulted with his most trusted aides in finally identifying members of the incorruptible SSH. He was told by an insider that they were a principled guild of scholars invested in subjects related to Samadi's enigmatic trophies. Babu wasted no time in requesting an introduction.

And thus ended Babu's narration to the SSH. Apparently, he had met with them under the very same ashoka tree. And after careful screening, the SSH were convinced that Babu's political struggle was just as sacred and endangered as my efforts to establish truth are. Babu shared his story only after undergoing their induction of psychedelic rituals and calculated revelry. In the flickering of recycled vegetable-oil candlelight (the SSH used electricity frugally), Babu won their support. As per the narration of SSH comrades, Babu had bared his chest in a fiery display of passion and courage. Pacing the room, he had smashed his fist into his hand in reiterating crucial realizations about Samadi. Option one of two was that the island was hiding an isolated tribe that still believed in wonderfully pagan deities, in addition to sheltering undiscovered flora and the remains of an extinct and apparently revered hominid species. Option two suggested that (in addition to exotic foliage) the island was home to an aquatically enabled hominid which was very much alive and had the means to build exquisite shrines to a deity in their own image. Option two seemed the most likely – there was nowhere on the island any trace of bipedal human presence; everything seemed to point to the delightful conclusion that there was rather a breed of intelligent, tailed creatures that fabricated temples on par with human aesthetics of the Palaeolithic period (excepting the superhuman carving skills indicated to by Hans).

On calming down, Babu begged the SSH not to expose him as the source of these observations. His bravado disappeared, and the thirty-nine-year-old man revealed himself to be terrified. He divulged that he was being watched by intelligence agencies, including the Special Security Force, to ensure that no secrets from the island were disclosed. Babu cogently reasoned that, if they ever deduced his complicity in bringing work on Samadi to an end, there was no telling what they would do to him. After all, what did they care about safeguarding a new species of hominid or an obscure indigenous tribe? Their primary objective was to keep multinational funds streaming in.

It was at this point that Babu stopped being a provider of information and became a recipient of wisdom. The SSH sat Babu down and notified him that he had struck gold in seeking their aid. They apprised him that they had been archiving minutiae about an island like Samadi long before the story about fish-people had blown up in the media. They admitted that once reputable scholars had confirmed the bones as genuine, SSH members themselves were panic-stricken that Samadi would be ruined. They explained that accounts of the fish-people had been logged for thousands of years, and while they were overjoyed to find that these annals were true, they were as fretful as Babu that irrevocable harm would be done to the island's treasures. They then pulled out certain volumes and imparted to Babu, as they did to me, a critical backstory.

This ancient Bengali saga sheds light on all matters pertaining to Samadi. But dear reader, you will have to be patient. This is strong stuff. It is nothing that Hans, Babu or ordinary folk like me could be expected to know. But before I can effectively share the legend of Samadi, I must first ask the reader to familiarize themselves with the role that water plays in the Bangladeshi topography. This is essential for us to understand the reality that Babu and SSH were facing on the ground. Then, we will track a thread, an aquatic motif that bobs up intermittently and floats through all mankind's histories. Finally, we will follow these timeless lines, these threads that vibrate with a thousand inherited stories, to Samadi. While these spools unravel rather erratically, entrust in me that, like an octopus, everything will tie together. Lend me your ears; there will be treasure at our journey's end...

FOR MILLENNIA, DELTAIC BANGLADESH has had a tempestuous relationship with the thousands of islands that lie within its territorial borders. Coastal Watch, a non-governmental organization, estimated in 2012 that an average of sixteen Bangladeshis lost their homes to rising tides every hour, as the Padma, the Meghna and the Jamuna (the three major regional rivers) refuse to flow the same course two consecutive years in a row. Princely stretches of property adjacent to the great rivers disappear and reappear annually. Erosion is commonplace and requires communities to constantly relocate or occupy boat-houses. It is estimated that boat-gypsies (the bedeys) may number almost a million; they spend their entire lives navigating the network of over 700 rivers and canals.

Holdings that go under during the annual floods give rise to fierce ownership clashes upon resurfacing. As in the Nile Valley in the time of Ptolemy, it is difficult to maintain claims over reformed and newly shaped demesnes. It is vital that administrators have knowledge of mathematical geometry in recalculating new demarcations. This is complicated by the natural processes by which eroded terra firma emerges further downstream and re-coalesces into new mesas, tracts and peninsulas. It is little surprise then that, in Bangladesh, redistributive processes involving riverine terrains are vulnerable to corruption and bloodletting.

One prominent territorial altercation involved India and Bangladesh locking horns in 1970 over a sandbar that emerged in the Bay of Bengal in the aftermath of a cyclone. The uninhabited landform, just off the coast of the Ganges–Brahmaputra Delta, was named New Moore by India and South Talpatti by Bangladesh.

Both India and Bangladesh claimed sovereignty over it, as the likelihood of it possessing oil and natural gas reserves was high. Unlike other long-running battles in the continent, the contention over Talpatti ended abruptly and naturally when, in 2010, the island once again submerged into the Bay. This specific conflict reflected a larger dispute concerning the eponymously titled Radcliffe Award methodology of settling boundaries between East and West Pakistan and India. It is noteworthy to mention that partitioning British India was the very first experience Viscount John Radcliffe had in nation-state forming. Hence, surgically demarcated borders have resulted in enclaves, exclaves and counter-enclaves (enclaves within enclaves) where an area of Bangladesh is surrounded by Indian territory, which is in turn surrounded by Bangladeshi regions. It is not uncommon to visit families in Cooch Behar on the eastern border, where a knot of homes straddle the border with living rooms on the Bangladeshi side and kitchens on the Indian side. Though fences are often built in an attempt to reinforce Radcliffe's Award, few value the British prize; they tuck their lungis under and jump over the enclosure when needed.

Far from these inner regions, on the waterfront, the perplexity of land proprietorship endures. Just as they wipe out discord and contested zones, the churning rivers spew forth completely 'new' lands. Fertile and virgin stretches randomly appear as a result of accretion, and new settlers and agricultural brokers rush to procure frontage. While powerful and elite mainlanders waste no time in flexing muscles to secure these lucrative assets, those privileged to reside further inland are typically contemptuous of the transient lifestyle of the island-dwellers. Inlanders refuse to even visit these 'barbaric' frontiers unless compelled by legal or political interests.

The island lifestyle is adequately summed up in an occupational census report from 2012: 60 per cent of island working populations consisted of agricultural labourers.

Labourers occasionally engaged in fishing activities. Another 8 per cent were employed in the transport industry (plying rickshaws, boats, etc.); 3 per cent worked in the service sectors (as doctors, teachers, government officials, etc.); 5 per cent were businessmen, and another 4 per cent were thieves. The remaining staggering figure of 20 per cent was distributed amongst the categories of 'musclemen', 'touts' and 'cutthroats'.[66]

It is argued with no little merit that the role played by water in the Bengali culture is matchless. While provinces in China, and others

---

66   These categories are all unique in their own right. Musclemen, my translation of the Bengali word 'lathiyals' ('henchman' or 'goon' are equally valid) innovatively flourish knives, swords, spears, bows and arrows, firearms and, yes, sticks, to participate in public and bloody land-grabbing brawls. Though they are indubitably ferocious and sometimes murderous, they are primarily a show of force and are employed to intimidate. Many musclemen augment their revenues with part-time thievery.

Touts (the Bengali equivalent being 'touts', once again compliments of the Raj) are a much gentler sort. They are persuasive and soft-footed men who navigate local power-poles to bribe or harangue players occupying key positions in the property acquisition game. In cases where force is requisite, they contact the musclemen. Touts are habitually derided by musclemen.

The last group, the cutthroats ('koshais' in Bengali), are cut from a very different cloth altogether. Feared by members of the two other categories, they are considered the dark and unpleasant underbelly of capitalist combat. While a number of embarrassed musclemen accept the role of tout in their golden and weary years, and while many a frustrated tout has adopted the way of the muscleman, the ranks of cutthroats are quite exclusive. These elite assassins take pride in their vocation. They specialize in inexplicable disappearances and gruesome deaths. Due to the secretive nature of their trade, their numbers are not easily ascertained. Their choices of weaponry are popularly believed to include poisons (when discretion is key) and a particularly sharp sword used to decapitate victims (when discretion is not key at all). Of course, they frequently resort to semi-automatic weaponry. Experts and statisticians argue convincingly that cutthroats must be active in other occupational strata, to better integrate into local populaces. If there ever were people living on Samadi before it went under, these were the men who would have damaged them the most.

proximate to the Amazon basin, suffer terribly from annual flooding and deaths, and while even central Europe is not immune to aquatic upheavals, it is especially poignant that, in Bangladesh, there is no such thing as 'higher ground'. In difficult years, 75 per cent of the nation can become immersed, as was the case in 1998 when thirty million were left homeless. Poverty, the yearly monsoons, cyclones and tsunamis from the Bay, and melting snowcaps in the Himalayas make things all the more difficult on the Bangladeshi floodplains, most of which now rest three inches *below* rising sea levels.

Water has blasted down, worn away and drowned out any resistance denizens have historically proffered. In emphasizing its sovereignty over all things Bangladeshi, water found expression in the earliest manmade creations of mud, stone and treated wood, functional and decorative. Water then willed that its role in the first human paintings be central. Long before ideas about nationhood, community, currency or even language had birthed, water was a master institution. It was from the very start an arché on which all else stood; it was a power elite, a dictator and a god.

Populations that are markedly subject to the whims of water realize early that they are in the presence of an intensity and a force that cares little for human sport. Near the ocean, they must put away their mannish pride, for this is her dominion. The sentiment of being in-between, of accommodating multiple suns in the sky and accepting the new, of knowing that no comfort is guaranteed and that suffering is inevitable, is well captured in Bengali traditions. Apart from poetry, dance, spiritual customs and song, the sentiment is also embodied in the Bengali practice of drying fish – Babu's beloved shutki. The toughness and grittiness of the salted sea-fare captures well the resilience of a people who inhabit a world in flux between creation and annihilation, each separated by a single watery breath. The protein reflects perfectly on a people who often have to accommodate to scarcity of land, nourishment and expectation. These people must condense their existences, clear out all sand and moisture, and season their darkening skins for hardship. Shutki can be added to just about anything edible, readily lending its distinct briny flavour. This includes vegetables, nuts, herbs, roots, fruit, lentils and dairy products. The toughened fish is easily transported and does not spoil. Even when exposed to heat or immersed in water, it can be eaten. It conserves its potency and patiently bides its time. And when that time comes, the pungent ingredient must be carefully consumed, brittle bones and all. For the Bengali survivor, the shutki is his wizened old spirit, fashioned by the meeting of water and sun, algae and soil, and hunger and hope.

Evidence of the supremacy of water in the region is ancient. To the west, Mohenjo-daro, a Harappan city which scholars date from before 2500 BCE, was destroyed and rebuilt at least six times due to great deluges. This was no mean feat, as the colossal city boasted a grid of residences, markets, storage facilities, public baths, as well as a highly sophisticated drainage system. Archaeological investigations of the Gupta Period (approximately 320 CE to 550 CE) have uncovered the existence of a ten to fifteen centimetre thick layer of sand-clay, suggesting periodic inundation. This appears to be an antiquated natural record of extraordinary floods in the Bengal region.

Babu notes in his diary the extraordinary work of Stephen Oppenheimer, a famous researcher at the University of Oxford. This polymath has posited that, in the tradition of Atlantis, a continent that was the real cradle of civilization went under in southeast Asia approximately eight thousand years ago. Pointing to genetic, paleontological, archaeological, anthropological and linguistic evidence, Oppenheimer spearheaded a movement to trace mythic flood myths of the Middle East, Australia and the Americas to a common origin – a drowned area now called the Sunda Shelf.

Oppenheimer contended that those who escaped this first great flood used stones for grinding wild grains as early as 24,000 ago, predating Egypt and Palestine by ten thousand years. He theorizes that the Sundalanders spread out to the Asian mainland including China, India and Mesopotamia, and aquatically from Madagascar to the Philippines and New Guinea, whence they later colonized Polynesia as far as Easter Island, Hawaii and New Zealand.

Oppenheimer's paradigm-shifting catastrophism concept lends supports to a claim the Tamil people have made for centuries. They indicate that, fifteen thousand years ago, Tamil scholars had sophisticated research academies (sangams) that, despite vigilant relocations, were eventually inundated. Many Tamil sages evoke how their country once stretched far to the south, including Sri Lanka and the Maldives, comprising a vanished Tamil continent variously known as Illemuria, Gondwanaland, Kumarinatu, Kumarikhandam, or as Lemuria to Lumerian occultists in Europe and North America. Of course, Sri Lankans too have their own long lost island, Irisiyawa, which is chronicled in the *Culavamsa*. In March 2009, marine archaeologists caused much excitement on exposing a submerged landmass southeast of Sri Lanka. Estimated to be between 4,50,000 and 4,75,000 square kilometres, it is about seven times the total land area of Sri Lanka.[67]

---

67 While sceptics may contest this notion of submarine continents previously populated by advanced civilizations, there is no extracting the preponderance of water from the South Asian landscape. Regarding the creation of the cosmos, the Vedas enunciate that Hiranyagarbha arose from churning and chaotic waters to generate all that we know as beautiful and terrible. In the Rig Veda, Ruta was an enormous sunken continent to the east of India and home to a race of sun-worshippers. Torn asunder by a volcanic upheaval and sent to the ocean depths, fragments remained as Indonesia and certain Pacific islands. Manu, the progenitor of mankind, and the very first Brahmin king, is believed to have saved humankind from a later universal flood.

The pervasive worship of water representations further established itself in festivals of pools, rivers and oceans. Saraswati, the Hindu goddess of knowledge and the arts, is often personified as an ever-flowing river. The primordial symbolism of water has resulted in many a story that addresses notable Bengali tribes, such as the Gauds and Palas, and their briny connections. In Goa, a state that legend holds to have been fashioned when the sage Parashurama pushed back the tides, inhabitants centre the matrix of their social lives on aquatic metaphors and idioms. Adi-Mising animist tribes from the eastern Himalayas venerate the river as a female god and take care to appease its Nippong essence. In fact, their very name is believed by select specialists to be a blend of man ('mi') and water ('asi'). Manipuri folklores narrate how the world was composed entirely of water. The Buddhist poems of the *Charyapada* (the very first text recognized to be Bengali and a favourite of Mrs Majumdar's) use the metaphor of water to regard creation, illusion, perseverance, malleability, grace and destruction. Further east, and closer home to Oppenheimer's pre-Indian focus, the cosmology of water flows freely in olden Khmer through a complex of wet villages, rice paddies and agrarian canals that are constructed around bodies of water, as are their social customs and the crux of their religions.

Thus, it is of little surprise, given the ambivalent nature of water's sway – its spiritual sacrament and its irrevocable horror – that waters leave behind a horde of mythical sea creatures. These, equally awesome and menacing in character, are fascinating in their physical variety. In Vedic literature, the goddess Ganga is usually represented as a beautiful woman with a fish's tail. She rides the makara, a frightful aquatic monster, as does the Hindu god of sky, sea and celestial oceans, Varuna. The makara, revered alike by Buddhists and Jains, can be depicted as an amalgamation of different animals. They may possess the torso of an elephant, crocodile, stag or deer, with the tail of a fish or peacock, or the flappers of a seal. All species of mammals, fish and reptiles intermingle freely. Rarer though, are the jala-turaga (fish-tailed horse) and the jalebha (part elephant, part fish). The yakshas, elemental nature-spirits, too, are customarily accompanied by their personal makaras. Babu, like all Bangladeshis, was well aware of these particular manifestations of our hydrospheres.

Water after all is a Quranic symbol for the essential unity of Creation. Hundreds of miracles involving water were narrated by companions of Prophet Muhammed (PBUH), including accounts of the revered Zamzam well in Mecca. Younus (the Biblical Jonah) was variously associated with sea-serpents and monsters, as well as his famous whale. In dated Islamic odes, deckhands reported that in passing certain Javakan islands, beautiful music was heard – the lute, oboe and tambourine were accompanied by the sounds of dancing and clapping hands. This saga is believed to be connected to the Golden Legend and to the mythical dragon that lived in a lake near Silena in contemporary Libya. In the *Akhbar al-Sin wa 'l-Hind* (Notes on China and India), a text dating to 851 CE, the mouth of a gulf at Arabian Larwi was barred by sea creatures upon whose backs grass and seashells grow. Sailors perished on attempting to dock there. Parenthetically speaking, these chronicles are believed to have inspired the authors of Sinbad's adventures. There are also historical references to the sacred fish of the Caspian mountain ranges. The Sufi poet Rumi is said to have encountered the water monster Su Essa at the Turkish baths of Ilghin. The Arabic Bahamut, from which the English Behemoth is derived, is a vast fish that supports the Earth and is sometimes described as having the head of a hippopotamus or an elephant.

Less familiar is the Greek genealogy of Ketea Indikoi from 2 CE that addresses multi-formed Indian sea-monsters. Some of these possessed the foreparts of land mammals such as lions, rams and

wolves, with reptilian and fish tails. It was as if we had conjured
immortals that returned in time to borrow parts from evolutionary
ancestors. Hiuen Tsang, a pilgrim who visited Buddhist Vasu Bihar
in 7 CE, reported his detection of splendid terracotta plaques
representing composite beings of a half man half fish nature. The
maal[68] from Sylhet was the creature mentioned to Babu by the
agitated sailor. The vaporous aleya is another Bengali apparition
that confuses fishermen and makes them lose their bearings and
drown. There is also the mecho, a fish-stealing undine that lives
near well-stocked village ponds. The Nagas idolize a mermaid and
merman that have a human torso with the lower half of a snake.
Further east, the supernaturally strong pi-hsi (also known as tien-
xia or ba-xia) is the Lord of the Rivers in Chinese mythology. It is
half tortoise and half dragon. Before the Karatoya river changed in
size and course, the inhabitants of Maghdesh (Land of the Fish)
used to depict its female goddess in the shape of a mermaid. Her
image, retrieved from ruins dating from the fifteenth and sixteenth
centuries, is half fish and half woman. [69]

68 A twist in the maal's dorsal hindquarters might lead some to Ramsagar lake
    in north Bengal, near Dinajpur. Songs capture how King Raja Ram Nath
    (1750–1755) prayed to the gods to relieve his people from the blight of a
    severe drought. The king was told to dig a lake and have his favourite consort
    pray at a temple in the middle of the lake. So it was done. As soon as she
    started to pray, the waters began to rise, and she prayed until she drowned.
    Till today the massive lake exists, and spirits guide the strong currents so
    as not to allow anyone to swim in the water, so fiercely do they protect her
    memory.

69 The worship of water (hydrolatry) and of fish (ichthyolatry), on a global
    scale, go far back into the human journey and are often inseparable from one
    another. There is the veneration of Mimi Wata in west, central and southern
    Africa. This continues in their diaspora in the Caribbean, and North and
    South America. There is the Nommos in Mali, the Mbói Tu'I from Paraguay
    and Argentina, the Amazonian boto, the Chilean sea-horse, the Incan
    Pariacaca, Daucina in the Fiji Islands, and the Nyami Nyami in Zambia and
    Zimbabwe. Once again, these god spirits capture perfectly the duality of

But now let us move even closer to Samadi itself, and to early stories that keep appearing in the Bengals concerning an enchanted island that disappears and reappears. The following parallels were pointed out to me by the learned SSH.

The first appearance in written literature of a mysterious island that swims four thousand bighas (approximately 320 kilometres) from the mouth of the Bay, is in ancient Bengali palm-leaf manuscripts retrieved from caves as far away as Nepal and Burma. These are dated to belong to the fourth century BCE. Songs in the manuscripts refer to an island of demigods that ride the oceans like

---

grace and wrath, the eternal flux in Poseidon, in Yin and Yang, in the stillness and motion of water, and its correspondence to matter and energy.

The Syrian deity Atargatis is said to have had sacred fish at Askelon, a seaport now in Israel. Certain Jewish scholars posit that the Canaanite god, Dagon, was a fish-god: recently recovered reliefs suggest a fish-god with human head and hands was worshipped by people who wore fish-skins. There were allegedly sacred fish in the temples of Apollo and Aphrodite in Greece, harkening to a fish cult. We have already encountered their Hindu and Buddhist counterparts.

The Bengali cults that idolized and feared water genies did not stop thriving with the advent of Islam in the thirteenth century. In 1303 CE, the great Muslim saint Shah Jalal fought the sorcerers, witches and soldiers of a Hindu king, Gaur Govinda. It is believed that, on defeating them, Shah Jalal metamorphosed Govinda's allies into catfish and cursed them to be born over and over, eternally, as the common bottom-feeder. The descendants of these fish can be found today in 'tanks of abundance' in Sylhet, Bangladesh. Located inside Shah Jalal's famous mosque complex, they are attended to day and night. A privileged few are allowed to visit them, and every evening when candles are lit, the huge catfish appear to dance. This legend, like most others, has a precursor: the Persian Sufi Bayazid Bostami is said to have converted evil spirits in Chittagong into turtles. This is said to have happened in the eighth century. A shrine there entombs his remains, and his black soft-shelled turtles are guarded like a miracle. There is also a rumour that the artificial lake that surrounds the national Capitol on three sides is host to ferocious and indescribable water nymphs. Hundreds have witnessed its waters surge unexpectedly.

fish and beckon the waters when in need of aid. The songs clearly indicate that the gods must not be molested, that they control the seas and storms, and that no man can hope to understand them.

Metered verses and sacred Vedic märchens refer to a sorcerous island of the sea that belongs not to God, not to man, but a special godlike race. Reference is also made to these demon-slayers' habitation – an islet positioned inside a gyre of milk in the middle of the 'eternal waters'. In more than one verse, it is mentioned that the demigods, when angered, beat the surface with their tails and generate fierce hurricanes. These date from between 1500 BCE and 300 BCE.

In the stone scripts found in Bogra province, a treatise on Ayurvedic and herbal medicines primarily addresses the need to eliminate the use of meat, animal-based products and intoxicants. This record also specifies that if 'the giant scales of fish-gods from the sacred island' wash ashore to the mainland, they can be boiled for the manufacture of tonics. The scripts clearly prohibit any attempt to search for the cay (in the 'stomach' of the Bay, which is not a poor metaphor for Samadi's general location) as the seas will 'rise and seek vengeance' on those that do. These scripts are dated to the third century CE.

Beautiful poems have been found from the Pala Empire that ruled from 750–1174 CE. Panegyrics were commissioned by kings in an early form of Bengali; several of these make mention of how the 'gemmed keys of the ocean nymphs' pale in comparison to the grand pavilions of the Pala emperor. Nonetheless, in other drafts issued by historians, it is revealed how no human king can ever make war against the fish-kings of the unwholesome seas. Contemporary scholars plausibly reason that these were most certainly private works and not contracted by royals.

Most thought-provoking of all are accounts from the Bengali Sultanate of the thirteenth and fourteenth centuries and their extensively chronicled interactions with a race of fish-people. Great rulers of the period were preoccupied with extending their immense empires, constructing fabulous buildings and mosques, and engaging in profitable international trade. Domingo Paes of Portugal, who visited for a year in 1540, described the citizens as being heavily 'bejewelled'. State treasuries were amply stocked with gold from the export of textiles, sugar, spices and indigo.

Many of these Islamic Turko–Persian monarchs understood the need to accommodate domestic Hindu and Buddhist power-players. They did so by incorporating new deities into their own pantheons, and thus governed peaceful and prosperous empires. Subjects were taxed equally and the sultans sponsored inter-faith and intra-continental art. For these enlightened trailblazers, the age was golden. Others that were not as judicious as these 'yellow emperors' persecuted rivals and commoners that did not adopt alien Islamic creeds. These kings were known to give themselves ridiculously grandiose titles, which became longer with each successive generation. Unlike their European counterparts, these sovereigns did not bother with styles, which would have facilitated official life a great deal. Palace guards and courtiers were bound to address their lieges by extensive titles such as Al Sultan Muhammad Mu'iz ud-din Iskander ibni al-Marhum Shah Ghazi al-Hasan 'Izz ud-din (Supreme King and Humbly Incomparable Servant of the Omniscient as Verified Truthfully by Everlastingly Good Governance) or Al-Sultan al-Azam wal Khaqan al-Mukarram Abul Muzaffar Muhiuddin Muhammad Aurangzeb Bahadur Alamgir-i Padshah Ghazi (Most Supreme Ruler Self-Subsistingly Demonstrated as Esteemed Favourite Servant to the All-Seeing as Opener of Heart-Enriching and Perpetually Rewarding Life). In fact, things came to a head when imperial viziers and sentinels finally began to lose their patience with their petty princes – history bespeaks how Abyssinian slaves united with frustrated court eunuchs to overthrow these self-involved Turko–Persian despots.

Prior to their usurpation, these bombastic specimens from the great Sultanate had famously gone to war with native populations that had fled to the hills and islets of Bengal, refusing to change their age-antiquated ways. These arrogant sultans, each an Ozymandias or a Qianlong, sent out tired armies to hunt down indigenous 'infidels'. Famous battles and victories are recorded as having transpired. However, there was one tribe of aboriginals that proved singularly difficult to conquer. They were believed to inhabit a number of islands '300 leagues (approximately 340 miles) out into the Bay' and were described as 'burning jinns of the water' that preyed on true believers and devoured trade ships. A legion of battleships was sent out to conquer them, and on returning, battered captains attested to submarine skirmishes with 'great fish-tailed soldiers of the devil'.

Their lords, in an attempt to appease dissatisfied subjects, issued impressive silver coinage embellished with wartime images. The most intricate of these depict a sultan quelling (with sword-raised arm) writhing half man and half fish silhouettes. These monies, as well as inscriptions and paintings illustrating the great sea wars are available for public view in a sprinkling of national museums. The representations of the devilish jinns is strikingly similar to the images that Babu snapped on Samadi of the 'mermaid' goddess in the shrine – they have the same chin-to-eye proportion and an equal neck space of a quarter head-length, with almost identical clavicle and shoulder lines. Furthermore, the chest and torso triangles that extend down to the space between the lower limbs match perfectly, as do their elongated lines. Much of this can be made out as the SSH had the photo pixels de-mosaicked for optimum clarity.

Despite grand works eulogizing victories over oceanic monsters, non-courtly testimonies from 1378 CE indicate that seamen from the dynasty of Al Sultan Muhammad Merah Ibni Ismail Petra Tuanku Yahya Al-Mu'izzaddin Hussein Kamel Waddaulah Omar Ali Saifuddien Sa'adul Khairi Waddien (Absolute Indeterminate Beloved of the Eternally Manifest and Governor Trustee to Superior Consorts of the Unique Protector of the All-Hearing) refused to fight the tenacious 'water-devils' any further. They countered that there was no group of islands as alleged by the sultans; there was only one small strip of land, and if those tenacious sea-dwellers wanted it that badly, then by Allah, let them live in peace. This occurred only weeks before the Abyssinian revolt. After the insurgency, the persecution of non-conformers ended and the Sultanate turned decidedly against any further naval hostilities. It is sad to note, however, that the 'black' Abyssinian kings cared little to maintain goodwill in their own ranks. In spite of having faced a common oppression, they soon turned on one another as lieutenants and governors engaged in treason and as eunuchs conspired against their own kind.

By far, these accounts from the thirteenth and fourteenth century are the most detailed historical registers in Bengal of a Samadi-like island being encountered in the Bay of Bengal. There was also a brief circulated among West Pakistan's naval chiefs in 1971, as they readied for war with Bangladesh, warning of a certain atoll within East Bengal's maritime borders that should be avoided at all costs. There is a longstanding rumour that Commander Zafar Khan, captain of the Pakistani submarine PNS Ghazi, had frantically reported being attacked by subaquatic sprites in the Bay. He then somehow incredibly navigated his vessel back to the Vishakhapatnam coast before it sank. This is considered by many to have been a turning point in the battle for Bangladeshi independence. This melee remains uncorroborated – no official records of the commander's last dispatches exist.

AFTER SSH HAD EDUCATED me on all of this, I became even more fascinated with the now missing terrain. Though I was aware of some of the sociocultural details, once they presented the accumulated data, it was difficult to remain sceptical regarding the amphibian-hominids. While the SSH's principal interest lay in defending the sanctity of the island's inhabitants, tempered with a yearning to inconspicuously study them, mine were primarily centred on Babu. The SSH had been approached by Babu in order to organize a national campaign to have the island added to UNESCO's World Heritage list. This would have been the speediest and most feasible way to halt activities on Samadi. The Bangladeshi key met four out of ten natural and cultural selection criteria published by UNESCO; they needed only one more to lawfully tether a safety net for the Heritage Centre. Had the island not gone under just ten days later, the SSH would have presented a case before the General Assembly, which was to meet in Lithuania that year. The SSH were also preparing to galvanize Bangladeshi environmentalists through a nexus established in 2006, in response to the Madhupur crisis. They were also to request allies in the Blogger and Online Activist Network (BOAN) and in the Bangladeshi Black Hatters (a sophisticated hacktivist consortium) to launch internet campaigns highlighting Samadi's plight.

However, after Samadi's submersion, they shelved these plans and moved on to other problems. Ironically, the SSH believe that the 2010 tectonic shift and the sinking of the island were inevitable. They had come to the realization that, with or without UNESCO, the inhabitants of Samadi knew how to fend for themselves. They had been doing it for millennia: all the literature and sculpture unequivocally affirmed that the amphibian-hominids had the power to 'call on the waters' when needed. The SSH firmly trusted that the strange race of non-humans had access to influences we cannot understand. In their opinion, while it was a blessing that Babu shared his knowledge with them, action on their part was unnecessary. Human logic and empirical cogency, they say, cannot access the truth of Samadi – its miracle lies outside the domains of our rationality.

True to my nature, I began to run down the historical references the SSH scholars had provided me and found them to be precise. I also exhausted my contacts in the navy to locate anyone that had visited the famous island in 2010. After months, I finally tracked down one petty officer who would talk to me. Now dismissed from the force, this fearless individual divulged certain facts to me that have once again thrown everything out of jamb. He would not meet in person, but agreed to a video conference call. I was hardly able to get in a word edgewise, but I will include here a transcription of our conversation.

This man claims that he was aboard the ship that had sailed Babu to Samadi Island on 13 June. 'You know the truth, don't you?' the man asked me, inspecting me searchingly through the camera, before looking away, unsure. 'Oh well, there's nothing to lose if I tell you now, they have all left anyway. Don't interrupt me, just listen.

'Well, our directive on 13 June 2010 was to pick up a unit of civilian politicians from Chittagong Port. We were on *BNS Bangabandhu*, a frigate with a crew of 200. We were rigged with quad-Otomat launchers, that's serious firepower, man. Anyway, this was one of our best ships and we had a few naval bigwigs on board: a rear admiral and two commodores. This wasn't usual; for the past month we had been patrolling the danger zone without any senior officers on board. We were a total of three frigates, *BNS Osman* and

BNS *Umar Farooq*, and all of us on board knew what was going on. According to the media, we were supposed to be protecting Samadi, supplying it with resources, but none of us did anything more than drift around and refuel. It was all made up, man – *there was no island, no real AOR.*[70] Well, no real responsibility. The big guys in the navy were pocketing the money; they must have been working with others in the government. All that money for the equipment and research centre? It was lining the pockets of these greedy public servants. *There was no Samadi Island.* Those scientists that were supposed to be working on that island, we dropped them at Vizag Seaport in India. They were clutching suitcases and airplane tickets, I heard they were bribed from the start and were flying off to the Caribbean or the Mediterranean or something. I don't suppose you'd know?

'Anyhow, as no planes ever flew over the danger zone, our only job was to deter ships and smugglers from getting too close to the area. We maintained a triangular formation for the whole time the so-called island was hot in the media. I guess our bosses didn't realize that the fish-people thing would catch the world's attention the way it did. I heard the fools had collected real bone samples from somewhere and sent them to scientists on the mainland. They didn't realize that what they were sending in was dynamite; they sure as shit didn't expect all that attention.

'On 13 June, at daybreak, we docked at Mangla and picked up Babu; I think he was with a staff of eight or nine in civvies. I was a petty officer on that ship, but I've always managed to make my way around. About an hour after we had embarked, I was near the captain's quarters, when I witnessed an encounter between the officers and Babu. From a dark spot, just about thirty feet away, I watched the two commodores, the admiral and two other officers

70 Area of Responsibility

talk to Babu. Babu was alone: his staff had been sequestered in the quarters below.

'They basically explained to him there was no island. He hadn't known about this; he actually thought the whole thing was for real. They gave him a bunch of documents that described the island and the centre. He and his staff were to use those briefs to report on their visit to the New Horizon Centre. The bigwigs were pretty frustrated; apparently Babu had been giving them trouble. One guy, I think it was a commodore, leisurely alerted him that, as they had received nothing from the Madhupur funds, they had brainstormed Samadi to earn revenues. The brass hats were definitely not happy about how difficult it had become to make extra monies for themselves. But as I was saying, they didn't realize the data they provided the foreign investors was such hot scientific property. They had searched extensively, on real islands and near the coasts, for more fish-people skeletons, but they had failed. They stressed that the fish-people remains were genuine, one of them said something like: "So Babu, even if you obviously frown on us trying to make a decent living, you must admit, we really did give the world *something*, man, we gave them real samples of something the world had never seen before. You know, they say this will even change all that heretical shit, astaghfirullah, they believe about evolution and everything."

'They made sure Babu understood that he had to return to the Sangsad Bhaban and help maintain the status quo. Babu tried to object, but these guys were serious, man. It was clear if he and his staff didn't follow orders, there'd be trouble. They kept saying that nobody could safeguard Babu from them, not even his foreign supporters. They also reasoned with him that they were to end the whole Samadi Island thing very soon, and that there was no point in his getting all riled up. Babu's assignment meanwhile was to do diddly. He only had to maintain before others that research at the centre was running like clockwork. As long as Babu toed the line, they assured him they would shut down the operation without anyone being compromised.'

The former naval serviceman then took a deep breath. 'Brother, that commodore had some scary eyes. Babu looked terrified. I myself was shaking and left the quarters then. I had heard enough. I suppose all of us on the three ships knew this was going on. But to hear those stiff suits quibble like greedy bandits – the whole thing was sickening. There were several of us who felt we should do something, maybe report the whole thing. But to whom? There wasn't squat we could do: nobody would believe us. This conspiracy was too big for a bunch of petty officers to change anything. If they could threaten a civilian minister or whatever exactly Babu was, just think what they could do to us?

'That whole day, we sailed out into the Bay and anchored near the danger zone. Later in the evening, we returned Babu and his staff to Chittagong port. Short of shooting Babu in the leg, they made it clear that he was their bitch and that all he could do was issue their report. When we returned to shore, and Babu was released along with his team, I watched him carefully. I think Babu had one of his cousin brothers or something with him. He had been detained with the other staff members when they took Babu away for the briefing. My friends later told me that this enraged Babu's cousin, I think his name was Omar or something. He tried to fight four petty officers and a lieutenant, even though they had him at gunpoint. I think they eventually had to tie him up.

'Anyway, those high-ups, I don't think they feared anyone. It would never occur to them that Babu might disobey their directives. But I swear, when he walked off that ship, I was sure he would rat them out. But I guess they were right, huh? Just days later came the giant waves, and they took the chance to clean up the whole island fiasco. I guess your Babu did jack shit – as they say, even pearls will yellow. The officers on our boat, most have retired and left the country. I hear they all live in mansions abroad. Nobody cares about this shit any more; it's an old story. Even so, I would advise you not to poke your nose into all this too much. You could piss off someone. I'll be fine. Nobody will find me. I live on the waters. I still liked your Babu, though. He reminded me of myself, a lonely man "alone on a wide, wide sea". And no, saints do not take pity on our types.'

Before I could ask any questions, he disconnected our remote session.

Dear reader, you can understand my perturbation at the conclusion of this boatswain's rime. In just twenty minutes, he had shattered months of my work. The whole Samadi thing, the SSH and all their files and historical parallels, was it all false? I have pondered the matter from every possible angle to try and figure out where the lies end and the truth begins. Did Babu lie to the SSH? Why would he? And was there any way he could have stumbled across the historical details necessary to coerce the SSH into motion? I have looked into their research, and it is irrefutably backed by academic papers. Or had the SSH lied to me about receiving the insider (Babu) glimpse into Samadi? Why would they gaslight me so? Was theirs a case of schadenfreude, given that they weren't exactly asking for royalties from my biography or pretty acknowledgements in the foreword?

Or had the petty officer lied to me? Why? In spite what he said, he was taking a risk by disclosing his insights as to what had happened on 13 June. He had been discharged from the navy years ago due to insubordination, and survived since as a fisherman. All the same, he seemed quite happy: he had no illusions from what I could tell. His psych profile did note that he was inclined to 'lie pathologically'. But had he lied? In fact, I later found another sailor who admitted that he had also been on one of those ships and that there had never been any island. He insisted on being off the record, and made it clear that he would deny having met me if the story broke. And on poking my nose even further in, I came across a coterie of accountants who found my confusion rather comic. According to them there had never been any receipts of advanced technologies being imported in 2010, and the Samadi Island expenses had always been wishy-washy. Apparently, the high-ups from the government and navy had not done a thorough job of satisfying bureaucratic bookkeepers with their accounting of Samadi expenditures – the whole island thing had been fabricated by brassy thieves. But with the furore over the fish-skeletons, all this had been swept under the rug. I suppose Babu had not been the only one in the know who had been too afraid to speak up.

In turning the matter over and over in my mind, I am left with nothing but threads. Yes, the threads thrum and vibrate with energy, but I am as confused as a kitten as to what to do with them. It seems that I must choose between truths that are mutually exclusive. One way it can make sense is that Babu had lied to the SSH. Why? The best I can come up with is that he had hoped they would reveal the 'real' lies about Samadi to the world. Maybe, on learning of the kooky group that was interested in just this kind of historic saga, Babu had pictures professionally photoshopped, invented an enthralling shrine-story, added a dash of thorough research, and seduced the SSH to commit? If these scholars were the ones to draw attention to Samadi, or the lack thereof, Babu would likely get away with having to dodge bullets from the two men who drank a dozen cups of tea daily at the shop located just outside Babu's Madhupur village compound. One had not even bothered changing his army-issued boots, and whistled in a sinister manner whenever Babu walked by. Munna and Amar had noticed them as well, but Babu begged them not to do anything reckless.

But why had Babu not mentioned any of this in his diaries? Was he so very afraid of the fraudulent statesmen? Could they access Babu's village estate, his electronic devices, cloud drives and textbooks? It is likely they could; after all, they commanded professional assassins and rigorously trained personnel. And if their global allies and Langley brothers-in-arms could pluck a Torrijos Herrera from the skies, a General Ahmed Dlimi from a military motorcade, and a Patrice Lumumba from within a ring of UN Peacekeepers, what chance did Babu have?

At this juncture, I feel a compelling need to sketch details of Babu's domiciles and general lifestyle. For the reader to better gauge if Babu were being overly cautious, or whether real threats existed, additional tidings are compulsory.

Since the miraculous Madhupur snake episode, living arrangements at the compound had been significantly revised. Despite their objections, Babu had signed the title for 22 Kalabari Road over to the Madhupur Upazila Women's Committee. Babu had left his spacious, teak-accented master bedroom for a storeroom in the kitchen garden, in a standalone, single-pitch brick building which was several hundred metres from the main wing. The Women's Committee elected to convert Babu's former rooms in the main hall into a guesthouse for visiting dignitaries and scholars. They promised Babu he could live in the storeroom for as long as he wanted, and that for all intents and purposes, they would treat it as outside the jurisdiction of the guesthouse grounds. They also set aside a grassy stretch, contiguous to the outhouse, for Babu to garden. This was almost two acres in size. Babu refused it at first, protesting that it was much too commodious for his needs. Sure enough, as it lay unused over time, Babu started to weed, irrigate, till and plant. Within months it was overrun with organically farmed vegetables and fruit that were capable of feeding dozens per annum.

The fortified shed had four equally sized rooms, placed alongside each other, side by side. In each one, mosquito nets were strung, methane lamps placed, and thick straw mats laid out to serve as beds. Delighted with his new accommodations, Babu cooked enthusiastically, and invited guests to sit and talk for hours on the veranda. These hours sometimes turned into long nights. Companions included writers, painters, philosophers and political radicals, some established, others struggling. At one point or the other, in the twenty-odd years that Babu squatted on the plot, some of the greatest minds to ever pass through Bangladesh rested awhile on the red-slate verandas of that outhouse.

Regulars, of course, included Munna, his two fraternal brothers, and a young man called Partho. Just two years younger than Babu, Partho was already a teacher at a nearby science university, in addition to being the grandson of a renowned magician. Despite the famous forebear, Partho was a figure Horatio Alger might have written of. His parents had no money, and Partho had risen from dust to remake himself.

Soon after the reorganization of Babu's residence, Mali Da dropped in, literally – he did not use the front gate, but a tree that run alongside the compound walls – to chat with Babu. Mali Da was delighted with the new habitations. He confided in broken Bengali that loosely would translate as: 'Babu, when you were sick before, and I spend the night in that big room in the big house, I watch you cling on to life. Inside you – *you* – I hear things thrashing about, and I see big shadows. Grand house, all carpet and paint, you were dying… caged bird. Here in garden, you fly.'

Hearing of renovations in 22 Kalabari, Rafik Kaka had visited with Mr Majumdar. They installed ceiling fans, high bookshelves, and even equipped one room with a hefty Samsung desktop. Since Babu's teenage years, Rafik Kaka had regularly gifted Babu with boxfuls of books; he had never forgotten the thrill of making others read. These books now lined the shelves. Munna, for his part, devised a respectably fast internet connection for the computer. In his downtime in Madhupur, Babu could invariably be found in the single-storey brick house.

Despite Minnie's appeals that he forward her his memoirs via the Samsung, Babu preferred putting everything to paper – a habit which meant that nothing could be electronically locked away safely. Amar was quite paranoid about this, and would oftentimes conceal Babu's writings in locations he would later forget the whereabouts of. Munna, characteristically, took to weekly sweeping the galley and service premises for bugs and espionage devices. He never found anything, until a day in November 2008, when he uncovered a neat packet of radio-controlled PE4 that was too sophisticated to be anything but military. As everything was in perfect working order, it was surmised that whoever had planted the explosive had not triggered it yet.

The Women's Committee comprised fourteen elders from the landholding machong (motherhood). For the most part, they kept their promise and never bothered Babu. Except when it was for his own good. They regarded Babu as a son, and kept an eye on his workload, diet and welfare. In another stopover after Babu's move, Mrs Majumdar stayed over for a week. She had been grilled by the women as to Babu's food and hygiene rituals. Afterwards, the matriarchs had hugged Mrs Majumdar and forbade her from worrying about him. They promised to keep Babu in line, and in good health. In fact, it was probably due to these formidable women that those who wished harm upon our nervous protagonist never succeeded. Several of the committee associates were head priestesses in a Manasa-worshipping sect; they could be righteous and terrifying guardians. It was probably due to their efforts that the two 'undercover' soldiers who shadowed Babu soon became violently sick. Though the agents blamed the tea-stall owner and his cost-cutting ingredients, they had argued with the Manasa devotees a day prior to their incapacitation. Their replacements were more respectful, and sat a half mile down the road, wore sandals and did not seem to be musically inclined.

Despite the blessings of vigilant well-wishers, Babu did not have a security detail (he repeatedly dismissed them) and was vulnerable. A protective Minnie had a gold-plated Colt .45 custom-ordered as a gift, but on attempting to coach him on its use, found that Babu would not even touch the thing. He was probably most safe when at the Capitol, given his ability to consult the wizardry of the building's architecture. But Babu was hardly at his quarters while in the capital city at the time Samadi chicaneries reached their zenith.

An initiative that Babu had launched in April 2010, in conjunction with the Dhaka City Beautification Cell, had gathered momentum and required constant travelling on his part.[71] Babu used public transportation whenever possible, and while he was typically accompanied by an acolyte or two, he occasionally commuted alone.

In fact, I know of one anecdote where four men ganged up on Babu in a crowded bus near Savar. Two attempted to stab him, but when the bus providentially crashed into a fallen mango tree, Babu was able to make good his escape. I have no affidavits as to who the thugs were, but Boro Ma (from whom I obtained the scoop) recounted how a terrified Babu sought refuge in her home for many days following the incident. When he had recovered sufficiently to venture out again, she directed her hardiest subordinate to accompany him to the Sangsad Bhaban, where an anxious Amar

---

71 In this project, Babu had encouraged industrialists to naturally grow vegetable gardens on factory and business properties. These gardens were tended by employee-offspring; once it was announced that the produce would be distributed to the families of volunteers, there was no dearth of eager young hands. Once business magnates realized the benefits of the programme (not only were their workers happier and healthier, but the publicity was great as well), many subsidized costs in addition to offering use of their lands.

awaited. Amar had a group of plainclothesmen positioned in the area; they were variously disguised as rickshaw-wallahs, cigarette vendors and indigents.

It is perhaps due these menacing occurrences that Babu had never made official statements that exposed the hoax. There was only so much that his family, Munna, hot-headed friends, or Manasa matriarchs could do to shield him. It makes sense that brave Amar (what Partho lacked in aggression, he made up for with his guile) was with Babu on the *BNS Bangabandhu* but, if push came to shove, those who were pulling the strings behind the Samadi heist would likely pull out automatic rifles.

Did Babu truly leave that ship with an intent to defy the soldiers, albeit via the SSH? I am inclined to agree with the discharged seaman's instinct on this one. After the lesson he learned from the matriarchs, most everyone would agree that Babu had become a staunch and wily defender of public good. From my own translations, his diaries and journals post-snake-attack indicate a sustained concern for coastal populations, poverty and environmental degradation. In 2010, I am almost certain that Babu was fighting for national needs, and challenging corrupt and debased power-pyramids howsoever he could.

If Samadi was a bureaucratic swindle, the SSH would have been able to draw intercontinental heat in a manner that no global environmental celebrity would have been able to. It would have been a smart move on Babu's part to enlist their aid, not a cowardly one. When I cautiously approached one SSH member with my doubts as to the account of his incursion to the New Horizon Centre on 13 June, I was once again ridiculed.

Apparently, the photographic evidence Babu provided confirmed the truth of his narration of the shrine and its architecture. 'Those pictures, we have had them studied and magnified and pixelated to the point that every detail is visible. There is no way they were fakes. Babu's snapshots catalogued a shrine constructed perfectly, according to the historic and literary works we have studied. It has taken us decades to draw these conclusions. If you believe he had made the whole thing up for us to uncover government corruption, where did he get those pictures from? There is no one alive, other than our group, who has the knowledge to really understand the primordial tribal details; Babu could not just have chanced to get it all correct. And the DNA samples of four amphibian-hominids? This has all been systematically verified; they are real. These are not things that can be concocted in a lab; it is science, my friend.' In fact, this academic referred to a little-known artefact from the Sultanate – a terracotta pillar depicting carvings that are almost identical to images from Babu's Samadi shrine. 'That artefact was pilfered from Bangladesh National Museum in 1929. Nobody really paid any attention to it; there are no records or pictures of it other than the ones we own. It just happens that we had come across it, long before Samadi Island, before Babu's grandparents were even born. Before we knew anything about vanishing islands, a group of our now deceased colleagues had found it remarkable. That whole fainting thing happened to one of them when he studied it. But soon after we became interested in it, it disappeared.

'We know a private collector in Paris took it: he must have stared at it too. We have been watching it for eighty-one years, and the piece has never left his estate. His daughter currently owns it. She is even richer than her father was, and has the item guarded day and night. She is a Lumerian "channel" and believes in the Dolphin Tribe. There is no way Babu could have gotten access to the pillar and had images copied from it. Do you understand? Two of our team almost died trying to do so. The photographs that Babu gave us stand up to the test of centuries of poetry and paintings. The scholarship that would have been required to fool us with replicas, my dear biographer, no one can accomplish. Anyway, Samadi and its spells have been around forever. Yes, it's vanished now, but wait two hundred or seven hundred years, and it will punch through the ocean after another earthquake. It will be here after we're long gone. You're wasting your time in investigating the colour of this kraken.'

Once again, I find myself at a crossroads where two firmly established truths seem hell-bent at colliding into one another at full-tilt. Both groups, the Samadi scholars and the veteran government employees, are convinced they know the truth about Samadi. If I were to bring them together, would they collide to leave us a scalding soup of antimatter? Would dazzling starbursts illuminate what really went down?

I am unsure what lesson to draw from this exercise as I search for meaning. Is Samadi truly beyond understanding, as so many have warned? It seems that 'truth' is irrelevant: the story of an enchanted island exists whether we like it or not. To discredit it, I would have to unstitch history, return in time to battle old dreams, and reverse what water has impressed on our human minds. As with Babu's photographs, should I not stare too intently?

Despite my litany on the gods and demons of water, I feel that I have not conveyed successfully the absolute awe that water commands in Bengali souls. As giant turtles, umbrella-mouth eels, duckweed, crab-eating frogs, parrotfish and coral debris block our roadways, crocodiles take to the water in numbers enough to halt super-tankers. In Babu's absence, we chop down the last of our Bangladeshi rainforests, but behind us, we hear the hiss and gurgle of a tidal surge assuming shape. Devastating hydro-systems overcome our sturdiest embankments and loftiest towers, strewing palaces and monasteries with *Sargassum* weeds and whelks. As we return to flooding our lands with fertilizers and insecticides, and harvesting to extinction our dolphins, whales and devil rays, in the tradition of Lazarus taxa dead species return to life and stun our scholarship. Meanwhile, cryptozoologists locate new breeds of mudskippers, goblin sharks, dugongs, sea horses, mantis shrimps and sacred chanks. And mariners return from the waters, unable to speak, their eyes pointing wildly to the skyline.

Beneath the assorted parables of this chapter, I forebode there lays some noteworthy and evocative moral. I remain convinced that there festers an undigested lesson in its entrails, enduring like a knot of gritty fish. This sentiment is heightened when I review how olden kings had ruled Bangladeshi lands. Their speckled regencies showcase the irresolution to which the human animal falls prey.

Given the great prosperity of our sultanates, what spurred certain rulers to tyrannize their own subjects? And why had Abyssinian slaves revolted against overbearing masters only to continue in palace putsches and regicide? Do Bangladeshis today even remember of these black kings? If so, why do they regard the dark-skinned among us as any less than sovereign and beautiful? Why cannot we follow the examples of great leaders such as Alauddin Hussain Shah, Ghiyasuddin Iwaj Khilji or Jalaluddin Muhammad Shah? Instead, our political treatment of Bangladeshi 'others' is to rob them of their belongings and stamp on their foreheads the mark of second-class citizenry. If we were able to clear from our foggy minds three hundred plus years of British colonization, would we stop keeping girls indoors, away from the darkening of sunshine? Would we yield to the flower every human carries within, or would we beckon at our own reflections, like a silly narcissus about to drown?

As humans, we do not seem to do a very good job of learning. As strings uncoil and fray, it seems we are bound to repeat past errors. Did one of our early ancestors, in a moment of clarity (here the Sanskrit notion of 'samadhi' stares me down the nose) decide to name such an island, fictional or real, after the Buddhist transcendental state? Was the choice of the name 'Samadi' a recognition that the island could serve as a fable, with a clear moral message? Does it perhaps emphasize how futile human aggressions and attachments are? Was the name meant to draw attention to our failings, and our inclinations to persecute islanders and foreigners? Does it protest how we label those who sing, love or worship dissimilarly from us as freaks? And how, even when those differences are lacking, we find others within our own ranks to single out?

The myth of Samadi is testament to our proclivity to accept difference, and to regard the unfamiliar with compassion and wisdom. Samadi, with all the fury of nature, dashes our attempts to strongbox prejudice. It frustrates our attempts to design an imbalanced science. Swimming in the periphery of the Bengali imagination, the island sings to us warnings of bloody, and apparently still attractive, rocks. But it evaporates when we approach it too closely, when we probe at it with our tools. In this, perhaps, it is a lamp whose wick should not be touched.

After Samadi's departure, and after the fading of its songs, we return to battering ourselves and to drowning in Lethe-like waters. In refusing to coexist graciously, and in foregoing kindness and empathy, we have not been much smarter than catfish or turtle.

In trying to tie up this tale, in turning the final knots, I find myself as a seafarer who should have been discharged. I am unable to restrain the ropes, make ends meet, or secure frayed loops. My lines do not hold, and they bear anchors of little significance. But I have reconciled myself to this. If I endeavour to try to deliver unto you a neatly tethered package, I may as well try to lasso the waves. In sitting on the lap of the Bay and in gazing into her vast face, I find myself at the margin where life transpires for many of us. On the shore, that edge between man's constructions and nature's dominion, I am reminded of her sheer fertility and immensity. And as algae turns from brown to blue, and then green, my doubts ebb, and I hear a bygone song from a nearby ferry...

> You've set me adrift
> You've sunk me
> These endless waters have no shore
> Limitless, with no shores, the waters have no banks
> O boatman, row with care my riven boat...

V

BIRD

Faith is the bird that feels the light when the dawn is still dark.

– Rabindranath Tagore

Some birds are not meant to be caged, that's all. Their feathers are too bright, their songs too sweet and wild. So you let them go, or when you open the cage to feed them they somehow fly out past you. And the part of you that knows it was wrong to imprison them in the first place rejoices, but still, the place where you live is that much more drab and empty for their departure.

– Stephen King

Look, how an uncanny bird flits in and out of the closed cage!
If only I could contain its mystery with the fetters of my reason.
O mind, you are a bird encaged! Of bamboo
is your cage made, but it too will one day crash.

– Lalon

THE THREADS OF THIS section on Babu require our traversal from February 2013 to November 2021, when Babu vanished from the public eye. He did so in a fashion that most find inexplicable: to the general public, it was as if Babu just upped and left. I have, however, uncovered fascinating details that tie his departure to a 'theft' that took place when the ministry of culture found itself missing a large sum of money. This money was disbursed, without prior authorization, to struggling artists who had never before seen green nor gold from governmental exchequers.

Stage-centre in Babu's disappearing act jostle two enigmatic personages. One, an elderly mentor, is introduced in Babu's diaries as YS. Babu writes of this senior in great detail. Babu claims to have met YS in 2013 and, as becomes evident in his daily routine, the two became inseparable. More accurately, Babu regarded YS's wisdom as a blessing and held the man as a standard by which the world was to be interpreted. This is not an exaggeration – before Babu's diaries unceremoniously cease in August 2015, they plainly convey his high regard for YS.

YS was known only casually to Babu's coterie and relatives. From the interviews I have conducted, I have gathered that Babu simply introduced the elder as YS. Nobody I have spoken to knows details of his personal life. YS, in perpetual sotto voce, seldom engaged with conversations with anyone but Babu. After Babu's unexpected withdrawal, many, aside from friends, family and well-wishers, attempted to locate YS. No leads led anywhere. YS rolled up a mat, picked up a bag and turned around corners that no one was able to follow. Current biographer excepted.

The other person of vital importance in this account that Babu is linked to, near about the time of his disappearance, is a man named Mohammed Younus Shah. This man was identified by investigators as the prime suspect in the alleged theft at the Bangladeshi ministry of culture in 2021. I will contend that Babu was in close touch with this man at that time. When forty-five-year-old Babu escaped our narrative frame in 2021, this wily bookkeeper disappeared too. As ministry sleuths identified him as responsible for the larceny and gave chase, Younus Shah fled for places unknown at almost exactly the same time that Babu took his leave.

Babu makes no mention of Younus Shah in his writings, and the two were never seen in public together. While my contention that Babu knew the man is supported by testimony that is spotty at best, a number of circumstantial pointers make it highly probable that they were in cahoots.

As Babu's diaries do not continue past August 2015, I will have to fill in a great deal with the aid of informants previously encountered, namely the SBG, the SSH, Boro Ma, and a consortium of the usual disillusioned bureaucrats, intoxicated ex-goons, retired schoolteachers, JSD compatriots and former street urchins. While Babu's memoirs provide some backstory for our biographical tapestry, I have found it exceptionally challenging to undo the knots that time and a secretive Babu have left us with. Despite our hero's continued importance in public arenas, with his thousand faces, he succeeds again in manoeuvring undetected by space radars and infrared surveillance satellites.

Like YS, Mr Shah too provides little to work with. In 2021, he had been working as an accountant at the offices of the ministry of culture for two years. After his flight from lawmen who had little that was lawful on their minds, he left no geographical footprints, no family references, and no trail, paper or cyber. Younus Bhai, as colleagues described him, was a quiet and unexcitable man who kept to himself.

Moreover, by sheer chance, I believe I have uncovered facts that indicate that YS was none other than Mohammed Younus Shah. Perhaps, my reader, the initials have already revealed so and you have seen this coming? As this can only be inferred, and not proven, our account will treat them as separate individuals for the most part. I will, however, share snapshots and instances where their contours seem to merge as one.

As Babu disappears on us at the tail end of this account, we will have to surrender our biographical mission. As YS and Younus Shah also fade away before our eyes, they do so with little regard for the dead ends they leave us. Our loss is quite abrupt. This chapter has been an emotional rollercoaster, one supercharged and boosted. In the process of conducting research into notions of divinity, mortality, death, and the enisling of Babu, I have often had to clutch at boxes of tissue paper. In this chapter, you may feel me to abruptly cross genres. You may reason that the work in hand digresses from being a biography of Babu to an autobiography of myself. If so, I seek your forgiveness. I also offer the tentative defence that to understand Babu's disappearance without the crutches of his diaries, to fathom his motivations at the time and to differentiate what was accidental and intentional, requires the recreation of his mindset. The sublime investigations that frame this story have also affected me in a way that none of the previous accounts did. If I were to conceal my own emotional passage, I would disallow the reader from identifying potential biases. My cards need to be on the table. Only this allows an informed appraisal of the content I jockey.

In these concluding logs, perhaps more than ever, I have experienced the biographer's harrowing climb. Typically, this exile from his own world must climb two flights of stairs – his own, and his muse's – before reaching his, still alien, front door.

But in this chapter, due to the triumvirate of Babu, YS and Younus Shah, and the imbrication of their authorities, I have found myself illuded by logical mirages. I have picked my way over gritty floorboards only to find that they are warped by rough compasses, and gangplanks have twisted and wound to deposit me in formerly navigated and checked thresholds. In this, I have caught the scent of repetition, one not far from the spinning of madness ... from the neural spinning of a mind that finds itself doomed to circular wastelands. Like some primitive draftsman, spurred by the desire to emerge intact, I have scored my errant pages and creased their edges. There is little surety, however, that my transit will not end before an unmarked entryway, before some chamber with no pointers for inclusion, exclusion or identity.

There is also a great deal of weeping and sniffling on the part of those who figure prominently and tangentially in this account. However, resulting from the distribution of ministry funds to a wide range of national artists, we are left with a sweet aftertaste, that of an altogether unexpected Bangladeshi renaissance. Even though Babu vanished like a bee, the time was joyful for those who celebrate Bangladesh and all her peculiar and creative people.

In 2012, though Babu was still travelling globally to maintain a degree of participation in green initiatives, from glances that are more than cursory, one finds evidence that Babu was putting these transnational trips to multiple uses. Invited as a consultant in efforts spread out over five continents, Babu did not lower his high-flagging assault on nepotism, wherever in state apparatuses it could be found. However, there are also indicators that, on these overseas forays, Babu took significant pains to touch base with reclusive Bengali intellectuals. There is ample evidence that Babu used these tours to compile rare travelogues, dusty ledgers, and musings from living repositories of times gone by. A lifetime of digging about in the past had made Babu a very resourceful bloodhound. As I have learned from my own explorations, it must have taken a great many trips to geriatric wards, retirement homes, prisons, mental asylums and deportation centres to gather the data he exhibits in his sociological treatises.

One particular storyline seems to have hooked Babu more penetratingly than any other. Babu's diaries, from 2013 to 2015, refer repeatedly to a secretive Bengali community that venerated birds. While bird veneration is not a secretive matter in Bangladeshi-necked woods, the lore that fascinated Babu pertains to wizards who are believed to shapeshift into birds. Babu waxed loquaciously on these marvellous savants and their so-called ability to glide between trees. In August 2015, nearly two years after he made the acquaintance of YS, Babu astonishingly reveals that he had unearthed signs that this marvellous sect had incorporated the traditions of Yazidi wanderers who arrived in Bengal in the tenth century. Even more astonishingly, Babu reveals that he had come by this startling discovery by way of YS, whose forebears were guardians of this syncretic tradition. In time, we will address the specifics of these alleged avian connections.

As outlined already, we will start our factual rummaging in 2013. Early that year, Babu resigned from his Tangail-3 parliamentary seat. In a widely telecast Ghatail address, Babu smilingly explained that his contributions to Tangail's prosperity had plateaued, and that while he was grateful to the people for endorsing him for a third term, there were others who could better carry Tangail's torch.

We will peer over his shoulders in 2013, and as he sheaves through tomes in search of divine birds. Later that year, YS will join us and we will accompany them as they browse libraries, visit madrasas, retreat to ashrams and maths, and voyage with singing river folk. We will chart how YS influences Babu in 2014, as in 2015, and how our titular subject ripens, transcending the profane and mundane wrinkles of worldly attachments.

I will interrupt the timeline at this juncture to share an experience of mine from late 2025. This particular affair led me to first discover the likelihood of a connection between Babu and Younus Shah. Subsequently, we will dig into dirt to surmise how Babu and Younus Shah may have known one another.

After expounding on my suspicions, our time with Babu, YS and Younus Shah will be suspended as I narrate a journey I made to Romania in October 2025. I did so in an attempt to uncover YS's past. On completing this chronologically wayward account of my trip abroad, we will gather again our threads from 2015 to discern how Babu and YS persisted in their scholarship. We will also look deeper into lines that bind Babu to Younus Shah and to those that squeeze the contours of YS and Younus Shah into one.

The taproots for our plotline permit Younus Shah to enter our biographical frame in 2016. My findings indicate it as being the year Younus Shah and Babu would have most likely met. As mentioned previously, though Shah and Babu were never seen in each other's company, inquiries and probes have yielded anecdotal evidence that they did know each other. Again, though I believe YS and Younus to be one and the same, a lack of cast-iron proof and the difficulty of concluding which might have been the alter ego require that I treat each as an 'unattached' individual.

After surveying Babu and Younus Shah's camaraderie, we will proceed to the theft at the ministry in 2021. As Babu and Younus Shah pass from our sight, and as YS too cannot be found, we will engage in forensic examinations to determine what transpired at these fateful crossroads. I will repeat here a redundant disclaimer: there is no guarantee I will be able access the whole truth. Everything we know about the time might as well have been obtained by way of forged documents. I cannot promise that we will reach authentic dimensions where celestial birds suck sugary cubes.

Let us start with Babu in 2013, and with the speech he made to his Tangail constituents. Babu begged thousands who had gathered for his speech that day in Ghatail to forgive him for abandoning the post mid-term. He insisted, however, that he felt it unethical to continue to draw a salary from public treasuries. Drawing attention to the two politicians who would almost certainly contest his seat, Babu praised both of them at length, referring to their exceptional track records. One candidate, a Khasa male, was a renowned doctor of law, while the other was a Bengali female with a distinguished track record of public service. Both presented new ideas for the Madhupur biosphere and were more than capable of assuming command.

Babu explained in the 2013 speech how he could better serve the country by applying lessons he had learned from the rebuilding of the park to newer operations. He pointed to the great strides the nation had made economically, and how bands of young and ethical investors had fashioned an adhocracy where few went hungry, where healthcare systems had improved dramatically, and where the media had more freedom than ever before. Considering these positive developments, Babu advanced that his efforts could be better directed towards the promotion of Bengali arts and culture. He stressed that it was time for everyone, including 'brothers and sisters in other nations', to witness the brilliant beacon of Bangladeshi creativity emerge from baskets that had formerly been gauged as empty.

His speech was called passionate, humble, and even somewhat sad. On completion of his delivery, however, the crowd cheered him with wild cries of 'Babu is always our brother!' and 'We love you, Babu Bangladesh!' This made Babu weep, but as those present corroborate, they were happy tears.

Babu's speech had done a good job of setting up things as they truly were. What prompted his abdication of post and salary was that, since 2011, Babu had become mostly irrelevant in the protection of Bangladeshi flora, fauna and biospheres. A bevy of resourceful Bangladeshis had stepped up to ecologically centred plates, armed with stronger and lighter bats. This fresh generation had borrowed from the past to innovate greener and more profitable infrastructures.

Sensing that socio-botanical matters were in good hands, Babu had increasingly involved himself in literary circles. He was finally able to indulge his yearning to advance in his work with Bengali fringe literatures, and in recording the dying echoes of subaltern myths and registers. Perhaps the dangers he faced in the Samadi affair, too, had cooled his ardour for bureaucratic legwork and genuflections. It was also possible that the island's legend had triggered anew his zeal for Methuselian backstories from the subcontinent. In 2010 and 2011, as he steadily removed himself from Bangladeshi governmental affairs, it was undeniable that Babu had become noticeably active in Bengali artistic circles.

There is also no getting away from his immersion in the age-old fascination with birds. Babu writes in this vein until the very last pages of his journals. As we shall see from extracts I have translated, this obsession propels him from Paleolithic man to Plotinus, from the Egyptian 'bird of light' to the Mongolian Garuda, from the Mesoamerican Kukulkan to the Celtic Swan, from the Catholic Holy Spirit to Abu Bakr. Babu focused on particular birds including the swan, the dove, the eagle and the peacock. The list of sacred birds, however, goes on and on. Other rara avis would include the crow, the quail, the heron, the owl, the cock, the hawk and so on. But at this juncture, let us read an extract from Babu to acquaint ourselves with what figured primarily in his mind. The following translation is from an essay which was written in early 2014; Babu titled it 'An Eternal Flight':

'When man first climbed down his sturdy trees and exited withering savannahs, he taught himself to construct abodes. These were humble in the beginning, but man soon learned the art of exploitation. He would then labour others to elevate columns and arches in his name, and raise walls that receded godlike into the horizons. Yet, no matter how many thousands died in assembling his visions, early man was acutely aware that no pedestal he built would permit him to clutch the heavens. Emperors sepulchred themselves in gems and rubies, revered by millions, their armies girded the earth, but never were these monarchs able to rise through the cracks in the skies. Rather, they watched the most common of birds shoot into the ether, into celestial mantles that looked down upon their monuments. The most powerful of men watched with heavy hearts their pyramids and temples fall, as birds continued in their eternal flight.

'This was a source of things both good and bad. Many learned humility and to long for the divine. Others let their ambitions soar in the trails of disappearing birds and began to count the nine billion names of God. This type of man, though aware that his palaces would crumble one day like clay tablets, took pride in the fact that he had managed to conquer most every rival that stepped on to land. An Akkadian text captures this sentiment well:

Once upon a time, there was no snake, there was no scorpion,
There was no hyena, there was no lion,
There was no wild dog, no wolf,
There was no fear, no terror,
Man had no rival.

'Birds, however, eluded man's clasp. The awe that humans developed for birds, always carried with it an admixture of wistfulness, respect, envy and fear. The earliest men had looked to birds, they did this long before the advent of any societal architecture. Birds predate humans by a hundred million years. When man stood up in a field, newly minted, birds glanced down at him, discerned his origins and his forebears. And the human being, new born and still covered in down, looked up to the bird.

'Prehistoric men continued to follow birds in seeking food and water, and in identifying the turning of the weather. As passenger pigeons blocked out the sun, many came to believe that birds caused the phenomenon of wind, created water-spouts and controlled cloudscapes with the agitation of their wings. Communities thus came to recognize birds as couriers, as harbingers and diviners, with secrets both angelic and terrifying. Some believed that the patterns and symmetries created by winged messengers in flight communicated omens and oracles. Much later, as human cognition turned to erudition, scholars would recount that the heavens had poised cranes in the azure to convey them the alphabet.

'When birds assembled, in times of abundance, at harvesting festivals or in the verdancy of spring, bards sang of how the gods dove down to confer earthly blessings. While some tribes singled out certain species to revere, other clans hallowed all birds. Man and man, in amity and enlightenment, pressed together their hands to release jubilation, colour, feather and wing. They marvelled at the manner in which birds, concrete and tangible, suddenly rose, and opened their wings and breasts to return to the white nothing in the sky. For these blessed few, there were no false birds of paradise.

'Even in the midst of these celebrations, others felt an inexplicable agitation. They could not shake their desire to master birds and the visions they possess. In arrogant impatience, they tore apart bird nests to look into the future. Soon thereafter, cabals developed the practice of haruspicy, where they bared their canines and tore into the entrails of birds. Drunk with victory, many declared themselves prophets.

'When man took to caging birds, he forgot the beauty of their silhouettes against the sky and shackled his own sense of marvel and wonderment. This departure has cost us dearly; we find ourselves enclosed within our own constructs. And when we perceive silence descend into the breasts of imprisoned birds, we lament, even unknown to ourselves, our loss of turning points. We mourn that we can no longer recognize the pivot about which our soul gambols. For without this still point, how are we to take flight and return to the Alone?'

Babu's preoccupation with the class of aves has in part infected me. I too have spent months immersed in research, and must admit that the beauty of birds has not left me untouched. Irrespective of how one rationalizes their symbols, idols, totems or insignias, there is something uncanny about birds in flight that has haunted all mankind.

Now, we will welcome YS into our storyline. YS first appears in a note Babu jotted down on August 2020. Babu mentions that, while lunching with colleagues at the Saju Gallery in Dhaka, a man seated a few tables over had caught his attention. Babu recalls having spotted this person just a few days ago on the Sangsad Bhaban grounds. This senior was striking to behold. Babu writes that while no one thing singled him as exceptional, the old man's posture and manner of walking lent him a quality of ethereal grandeur. He was dressed in a loose-fitting kurta with long billowing sleeves. His head was draped in a light cotton scarf which he had knotted like one would a turban or a pagri but, like a keffiyeh, it flapped and fanned about him. He was not wealthy, judging by his threadbare sandals and his jute bag, but the air of dignity he carried was regal. Babu recounts how the curiously dressed figure 'pecked at his food like some strange and blessed bird'. While one may be inclined to read this simile as a comical offshoot of Babu's fixation with fowl, comedy leaves the picture as Babu perseveres in this vein over and over again, over the following thirty pages.

The next mention Babu makes of YS is in October, barely two months later. This sighting, too, was in Dhaka. Babu had stopped by his alma mater, Dhaka University, to attend a conference. When exiting the seminar room at the department of anthropology, Babu espied again the gaunt yet elegant man floating down the hallway.

On this third chance meeting, Babu introduced himself to the man with the remark that they had run into each other too many times to remain strangers. They talked awhile about Saju's newest collection. Babu writes: 'It was quite difficult to hold a conversation with him. He was quite skittish, and tough to hold down. It wasn't because he was nervous to meet me; he was that way before I introduced myself. He spoke Bengali with an accent I'd never heard before, but he indicated his hometown to be Rangamati. YS had this great aura of staidness about him, but he didn't seem to want to engage in small talk. It was like he'd rather stand there and smile benevolently, without having to rely on words.'

Despite these challenges, Babu's instincts told him there was something about YS that was worth pursuing. Babu talked YS into promising to accompany him to the annual Langalbandh festival that was being held a few days later. Babu suggested that he collect YS from his residence for the twenty-seven kilometre drive to Sonargaon. YS assented and provided his address.

As planned, they made the trip to the festivities at Sonargaon. Babu brought no one else along, and personally piloted his cherished Isuzu. Babu reasoned that it would be more likely that YS might emerge from his shell in the absence of others. And YS did open up, hesitantly but steadily.

Sonargaon ('Village of Gold' in Bengali) was a historic administrative, commercial and maritime centre in Bengal. Sonargaon had been extolled by numerous historic travellers, including Ibn Battuta, Ma Huan, Niccolò de' Conti and Ralph Fitch, as a thriving centre of trade and commerce on the silk route. The Langalbandh festival was held on the banks of the Brahmaputra river. The site was holy to thousands of Hindu pilgrims, but they were customarily accompanied by friends of all denominations. After Hindus ceremonially bathed in the river to cleanse themselves of all sins, more festive activities followed, with young men playing drums, and much merriment. In the backdrop of Sonargaon's striking and aged architecture, Babu and YS sat at the stalls in the sweetmeat corner.

Babu wrote of YS: 'While it became obvious that he is sparing in his verbal interactions with others, he is ethereally gentle and generous. After I picked him up, he described my rickety car as a "splendid chariot of God". YS is intelligent too, and unquestionably an expert in the arts. Given that I had kept bumping into him at art shows and literary talks, this was predictable. Yes, YS is reticent, but there's definitely something stirring in there.'

While Babu was partial to compliments directed toward his 2001 Japanese minivan – he had learned how to maintain and repair the vehicle himself – YS was to provide Babu with more meaningful fodder for psychoanalysis. As they struck up a friendship, they met several times a week to travel about the capital and deliberate its historical marvels. They trekked on weekends to different studios and art collections, watched dance recitals at Jago Art, debated predestination at the head office of the Islamic Foundation, and rummaged for books at the Dhaka Art Centre, Bengal Boi and the Bangla Academy Library. Their cultural horizons were expanded with visits to the Russian Centre of Science and Culture, the Indira Gandhi Cultural Centre, the Annisul Huq Gallery, and the Archer K. Blood American Centre Library. They were usually unaccompanied on these trips; Babu enjoyed having YS to himself. By the end of June, they were planning weekend expeditions outside Dhaka. They made it to the Bandarban Golden Temple in Chittagong, to the Central Library of Shahjalal University, and Tagore's Shantiniketan in India.

Babu says in his memoirs: 'It has become apparent to me that YS's detachment does not stem from a lack of warmth or amity. YS's gaze is distant and kindly, and has transcended mundane attachments. Like Kobayashi's world of dew, reality to YS is fleeting. But he is still attached to the here and now. To YS, our actions do have their consequences. Yet, he does not hold any particular scripture or canon as superlative; he quotes from the Upanishads, the *Sutra Pitaka*, the Gospels (including those branded as 'secret'), and from obscure sources in the Tanakh and the Tafsīr. He is familiar with rites from every tradition, and I have been fortunate to stand behind and follow his lead at numerous prayer houses. He has effaced himself of doctrinal rigidness; anyone will consider him holy. He is vegetarian (he has complimented my cooking repeatedly), an incomparable ascetic, humble and infantile simultaneously. All the same, YS has a sense of purpose. There is some task he has devoted himself to; I remember reaching this conclusion after our first lengthy conversation. It is my hope that, as he learns to trust me, he will reveal his mission. Perhaps I will be able to aid him. I have forgotten the exact context, but YS quoted to me, in our second or third meeting, the beautiful and enigmatic lines: "In our abode of inconstancy one must mind one's deeds / For a sea's existence could turn to bubble in a breath."'

It was this admixture of knowledge, grace and purpose that kept Babu barking up the mighty tree that was YS. Babu records how they spoke of a great many theological matters, about art, architecture, and the syncretic traditions that Bengal had developed. YS had apparently taught Bengali literature at a national university, he was now living off his savings, a small pension, and from the income received for poems and articles he published in local gazettes.

YS's erudition was broad and deep, and Babu lauds him constantly. A paragraph translated from his annals of March 2014 amply demonstrates this: 'I thank the heavens for sending this retiree my way. This hunched man, this winged man – he must be an angel. He speaks to me of times interminable, and of the days humans walked crablike. He tells me of the wandering mahatmas, and how their descendants still live among us. He is so much deeper than his sixty-odd human years. He is both anthropologist and poet-seer. He has taught me much about how our antediluvian religions first brushed each other, how they extended benedictions to one another, and how they collectively danced to rejoice in the divine. While I owe so much to the uncles, aunts, grandmothers and grandfathers who have educated me, and supported me in distressful times, there is something special about YS. Amar, my parents, and even mighty Boro Ma, all of us would bow to touch his feet. A week ago, we talked from supper till dawn; the next morning, I mused over whispers about the mountain-village, Habalah: if a guest can last a night in YS's resplendence without becoming insane, one would emerge a poet or a *mufti*. And to me, this man is not human – he is more a bird. I mean, just look at him. The way he holds his head upright, and the way it bobs back and forward when he walks. And the way he turns his neck suddenly. When he stands before the light, his frail body becomes translucent, vanishing before the eyes. I swear, his thin bones shift quietly under his skin and clothes. This man of light has to be one of God's own.'

However, in an entry dated 20 May 2014, Babu is palpably frustrated by the fact that YS showed little interest in speaking of birds and their emblematic standing in various creeds: 'I cannot understand why YS never wishes to discuss the holy birds I keep bringing to his attention. It makes him uneasy when I do. I've tried to speak to him of Persian myths and the notion that the Simurgh lives in the Tree of Knowledge. We once spoke of the 360 different deities that idolaters displayed in the Kaaba before Islam arrived in Mecca. When I endeavoured to steer the conversation towards the great bird Awf, he spoke no more. He is similarly uninterested in discussing the Hindu chakora, double-headed eagles, or the Mesopotamian Anzu. In discussions of epic battles, I've tried to edge in references to Prophet Suleiman and his ability to communicate with birds. When we were admiring calligraphy at the Abinta Gallery, I referenced the Language of the Birds, and the Green Language. But YS refuses to take the bait. I also tried to circuitously bring up Ibn Arabi's Universal Tree and the Four Birds, and in other debates, the Korean sotdae, and how St. Francis preached to the birds. But every single time, YS has clammed up and withdrawn to himself.'

However, this was to change three months later. In August of the same year, a jubilant Babu summarizes: 'YS has finally broken his silence regarding birds! For the umpteenth time, I was trying to talk to him about the secretive bird clan that hides in Dinajpur, and this time he did not retreat from me. This time, YS turned to me and said in a sudden songlike voice, "Babu, my dear boy, I know exactly what you speak of. It's not just a story, you know? These things are real. You've tried many, many times to question me on the matter of birds. I have been reluctant; this is the only subject I have avoided ... This is because, you see, this is a personal matter. That tribe in Dinajpur, it is real. I do not think you will be shocked by what I have to say. I sense you already suspect it, Babu, but I myself am of that community. When I am positive your Din is ready, I will tell you more.'"

YS began a series of sermons and musars that lasted months. Babu recorded them cursorily. In these exposés, YS talked about the great Sufi travels and how the dimension emanated from the steppes of Central Asia, absorbing a range of mystic influences. He examined the belief that precursors of Sufism had been among the first that crossed Beringia to spread into the Americas. The elder drew Babu's attention to those that settled in temples in the Hindu Kush mountains, and how Sufi tribes took to practising holy sorcery and baraka. For the first time in their relationship, YS addressed how the bird was a central motif to many, and how the caged creature symbolized the essence of an unawakened humanity. He addressed subjects Babu had broached earlier, including Attar's *Conference of the Birds*, Aristophanes' play *The Birds*, and Al-Ghazali's *Epistle of the Birds*. YS exposited on Rumi, praised Al-Buraq for carrying Prophet Muhammad, and radiantly reflected on The Valley of Unity. However, YS stayed well clear of the tribe that originated from Dinajpur.

Babu was silent through these orations, although inside he had dried, pickled and bottled inquiries. One day, in March 2015, as YS started to expand on the nullification of selfhood in the divine presence (fanaa), Babu became visibly impatient. As Babu acknowledges, 'I truly did not want to hear him ruminate any further. My agitation for YS to share more about his connection with the Dinajpur wizards must have been obvious, because YS gradually stopped talking. He then looked at me searchingly and thought awhile. He continued, "Babu, there is a story I must share with you. I need you to think about this before I can be sure you are ready. I do not think you know this particular legend, but it is a time-touched one about our beloved poet Attar.

"'As the tale goes, before his great spiritual awakening, Attar worked at his father's perfumery. He was a wealthy young merchant and, like all entrepreneurs, he was attached to his wealth. But there was something inside him, some dormant germ-seed of enlightenment that the special could sense. One day, a wandering monk walked into Attar's store. Apart from his tattered robes, the empath possessed only a bowl. This fakir marvelled at the opulence of the store, making Attar uneasy. Attar directed the fakir to leave. Looking the owner and the well-stocked shop over, the fakir said, 'I have no difficulty with that; with my lack of possessions, I can leave any time. But you, how are you with all this finery, planning to leave?'

"'This troubled Attar. The young man responded to the mendicant, 'Why, I can leave exactly as you would.'

"'The fakir pressed on, 'I possess nothing that holds me down. You see, this is all that I have – this alms bowl and the garment I am wearing. Will you really be able to exit the world as easily as I?'

"'Angered further, Attar shouted, 'I have already answered your question. What do you want from me? If you are not attached to this world, well ... why don't you just die then?' It was obvious that something about the monk's demands stirred the young merchant pointedly.

"'Then something happened which left Attar stupefied. The fakir smiled peacefully at Attar, lay down on the ground in front of the perfumery, rested his head on his bowl, and departed this world. Attar was left aghast. The event had such a profound influence on him that he immediately shed his luxurious clothes, abandoned his shop, and set out in search of truth and love. The fakir had rightfully intuited that Attar would indeed become a great poet and teacher for the centuries to rejoice.

"'Babu, I tell you this story because I feel that you are sometimes too attached to this dunya. I know you do not care for wealth or fame, but maybe you are a little too concerned with understanding things, with trapping facts and knowledge into boxes. You want to know my secrets, but I would rather you breathed in the wonders of our world, not hunted them down like some prey.'"

According to Babu's notes, YS had him in tears at this point. From here on, Babu seems to undergo a transformation. No longer does he obsess over the importance of birds, but it seems YS was training him to see with some inner eye, for some inner creature to unshackle itself. Babu's tone changes significantly in these pages of his diaries. He continues to write, but there is no longer a sense of urgency in him. There is, rather, a sentiment of serenity and a tranquil delight in his learning. He reveals how YS trains him in hamsa, and in attaining the Holy Breath or Spirit. Babu rejoices in this new insight.[72]

Babu reflects on the glory of this practice, and its possible reflection in the Persian 'huma', which in Old Iranian was 'humaya'. In Sufi traditions, one who catches sight of the huma bird, or even a shadow of it, is sure to be happy for the rest of his or her life.[73] YS encouraged Babu to strive to attain this regal bounty for himself. He pointed to areas of congruence in Ibn al-Arabi's treatise that the 'perfect man' is endowed with extraordinary spiritual energy, or 'himma' in Arabic. YS stressed that this enabled awakened ones to bring 'creatures of energy' from the world of images into the world of bodies.[74] Thus instructed, Babu diligently listened to his own breath, for what was kingly and perfect in his own soul.

Irrespective of hamsa, huma and himma, and their connectedness or lack thereof, it is undeniable that YS had considerably altered Babu's perspective on things. Babu's acquaintances, both casual and close, have confirmed for me that those days were particularly wondrous for Babu. These sources conveyed to me radiant portrayals of Babu in 2015, not unlike those Babu provides of his ephemeral YS, or I of Boro Ma for that matter. YS had indeed stirred deep pools within Babu, which over months floated to the top inestimable treasures.

---

72 'Ham', literally meaning 'I am' in Sanskrit, is the 'in-breath'. It refers to the individual and mortal ego. 'Sa', meaning 'that' is the 'out-breath' and refers to the universal immortal Being. Its alternative Sanskrit version is *So'ham*. Hamsa and So'ham both signify perfect balance, harmony and a union of dual opposites, the oneness of the human and the divine. That is to say, the immortal-mortal.

73 The stellar sage, Inayat Khan, lends the auspicious bird legend a spiritual dimension: 'Its true meaning is that when a person's thoughts so evolve that they break all limitation, then he becomes as a king.'

74 Arabi, an Arab-Andalusian mystic commonly dubbed by Sufi practitioners as 'the greatest master', emphasized that the purity of himma's force and miraculous powers must only be employed when God commands so.

This was best captured for me in an interview with Boro Ma. The last time I spoke to her was on 14 February 2020. It was Valentine's Day, and I had to visit my beloved Boro Ma. She had been struggling with diabetes for months, but I was shocked that day to see how sickly she had become. I had not seen her in three weeks. I blamed myself for my carelessness. I had been wrapped up in my own world (well, in Babu's world, to be precise). As I attempted to articulate my regrets, Boro Ma shushed me. She told me she had more nurses than she needed, that there were more hands about her than necessary. She went on to add, 'I did not want them to disturb you from your work. I want you to finish this wonderful book you are writing. But I am glad you are here now. There are some things I have to tell you. They are about Babu, but I guess they are also about me in a way. So stop being angry and listen to me, you silly boy.'

As I smiled through my tears, she continued. 'You know, Babu never had it easy. He always hurt from trying to do the right thing. I don't think he was always happy in his adulthood. He was too much of a thinking man to be content with the world as it was. The other day, I came across a letter written by a young Mexican woman who was struggling to change things. She wrote on the internet about poverty, pain, and then of the "twin curses of agonizing empathy and belly-deep hatred, the two beating hearts that keep every warrior alive". I think those were her exact words in English, such bold beautiful words. I wish Babu were here – he would appreciate the thought. My days as a warrior are over now. Babu too stopped fighting after 2015. I mean, the fight never really stops, but its character changes. Your belly empties itself of anger; the hatred disappears, and all you have is the great illogic of limitless love.'

I had never seen Boro Ma like this. My sturdy, tenacious and kind Boro Ma was dying and we both knew it. She had turned to poetry in her last days, and I could see the light it filled her with. She asked me to fetch a book from her shelf and she turned to a page, worn with visiting, to read to me of 'the lightless edge, where the slopes of knowledge dwindle. And love, for its own sake, lacking an object, begins.'

She continued to say, 'Babu had passed those slopes, I understand that now. He had gotten to a point where all he saw was the face of his Beloved. I was so happy for him. Now I enjoy that peace myself. Tell the world that. That at the end, in our leaving, there should be nothing but amity. But it should have always been about love, no?'

I nodded in agreement, and continued to weep that day and the following week – Boro Ma passed away four days after my bedside visit. She had been everything to me. She had impacted me physically from the moment I met her. She had touched the stuff I was made of, cupped it in her brown and scarred hands, and whispered encouragements to it. Her faith in me, her Leviathan presence, her standing, the branchiness of her reach, the winds she brought with her, all of these had directly informed the shape my body holds today. She brought me chicken soup when I was starving and did not know it. She brought me poetry when I had become deaf, and even when dying, like a supernova, she left iron in my blood.

There is a painting I admire titled *In Birth and in Death the Generations Embrace*. When Boro Ma passed away, though I felt this huge emptiness inside me, I felt honoured to have been privy to some great and satisfying union. In a vicarious manner of sorts, I sensed that she and Babu were perhaps meeting again. While there was no guarantee that Babu was indeed dead, there was also the feeling that maybe Boro Ma, Babli Ma, Dynamite Ali and Mali were meeting in some unearthly field. That day, when I had been seated by her, there were moments when she gazed into nothing. I felt she was seeing and listening to things that were closed to me. I remember clearly the halogen glow, and how the half-drawn curtains cast an anthelion around her. But the light had always been on her side. I believe that, like YS and Babu, she too had reached out and grasped the substance of her inner perfection. The atmosphere around Boro Ma, and excuse here the purple of my prose, was dense and heavy. I have heard others describe similar deathbed encounters as the renting of earthly veils. This place Ma looked into, perhaps it was populated with faces from the past? From that crowd, perhaps Babu himself was peering at us?

The fact that Boro Ma is buried in the same grave as her mother, in Mirpur Intellectual Graveyard, adds to my sentiment that she had attained a final great union. Surrounded by compatriots who had died in the war, with her bones powdering into her mother's, I rejoice that she has found a fitting resting place.

I WILL NOW RETURN TO examining the notion that Babu had indeed passed the slippery slopes of human attachments. An illustration of how our titular subject blossomed in this period requires us to rather paradoxically deliberate a tragic incident from July 2015. On 17 July, a town named Ramu was devastated by a mob Of 25,000 rioters. They left a trail of destruction as they torched Buddhist pagodas and homes there. Merely kilometres from the serene beaches of Cox's Bazar, demonstrators chanted 'Allahu Akbar' as they set fire to the largest Buddha statue in the country. These hardliners had coordinated the onslaught to allegedly decry a Facebook post that offended their pious sensibilities. The cyber-posting was believed to have been made by a Buddhist man from Ramu.

Violence spread to neighbouring upazilas within hours as reactionaries targeted all prayer houses not of the crescent moon and star. National Security Forces ambled into troubled areas later that night but were, of course, far too late to halt the damage. They contented themselves with visiting hospitalized victims and taking down details. As public outrage mounted, they eventually charged a hundred or so of 'miscreancy'.

As the home minister vowed to bring perpetrators to justice, it was uncovered that no insulting posting had been made on Facebook. Babu, along with an improvised gang (including his parents, Amar, Ali and SSH members) had already rushed to the devastated areas to condemn the violence, help with the rehabilitation of survivors and demand fuller investigations. There, they joined hundreds of other human rights advocates who had responded to the crisis. In Dhaka, spontaneous and massive street rallies organized against right-wingers. On Babu's part, involvement in counter-protests nearly cost him his life.

In the midst of all the confusion, something tangential and very peculiar was reported by a group of men who had engaged in ransacking non-Islamic homes. As hardliner gossip had it, these men had discovered, at a rendezvous four kilometres west of Ramu, household shrines in which traditional Vedic figurines had been replaced by what looked like blue-tinted photographs of Babu. It was clear from the placement of flower garlands, fruit offerings, lingams and oil lamps that Babu's representation was central in these devotion rituals. Startled by this unforeseen idolatry, the rioters made sure to inform organizational heads about the discovery.

As illustrated in prior chapters, Islamic fundamentalists in Bangladesh had nothing but contempt for Babu. Since HUJI's disbanding in 1999 after the disastrous bombing at the Sangsad Bhaban, these men had followed Babu's secular career over the decades with frequent and macabre attempts to end it all for him. They had failed time and again. Babu had escaped numerous feints by the skin of his teeth as sympathizers, crossfire and fortune interceded. In other instances, when religious zealots had Babu cornered, they had been ordered to retreat by superiors. On these occasions, Babu had been protected from their wrath by the international approbation he drew. In July 2015, as Babu publicly pressed for the detention of extremists, he was no longer immune to their ire. Having given up his government seat two years ago, Babu was not the entrenched politician he used to be.

Architects of the 17 July outrage convinced their disciples that Babu's decrial of their Ramu campaign was motivated by a desire to protect his blasphemous cult-like followers. I have befriended two Bangladeshi Muslims who were formerly recruited into domestic terror cells. I will tag these men as Abed and Bilal. Both, in their thirties now, have made 180 degree turns in their religious outlook.

Regretful of their youthful transgressions in the spiritus mundi, both have consequently dedicated themselves to espousing peace and tolerance. Abed and Bilal do not know each other; this strengthens my confidence that their nearly identical testimonies are genuine.

In seclusion, Abed related to me memories of how prominent mullahs had denounced Babu as having raised pantheons to bask atop. Abed paraphrased one such speech for me; following is my translation of an ultimatum pronounced by Sheikh Sayyid Ahmed in a closed meeting:

'Brothers, my dear pious and God-fearing brothers, how can we allow this sort of profanity to carry on? He has been a thorn in our side, for what, twenty years now? He must pay for his misdeeds. This cur, who calls himself Babu Bangladesh, has waylaid the most noble of our efforts repeatedly. Babu has stopped us from shining our beacon of wisdom and light on to the people of this nation. He and his impious supporters have stopped the blessing of Allah from raining down upon this nation of needy and desperate ghosts. He has no beard. I hear he is vegetarian, wears tight-fitting robes and does not regularly trim his nails. What kind of a scoundrel is he? Those blasphemous pictures we found of him on those infidel shrines, we know the studio where they were shot and printed. We can vouch that Babu paid for them to be distributed. I hear he calls himself a prophet. There is nothing more to say. We will weed out this scourge immediately; he is a threat to our faithful ummah. All those who agree with me, raise your hands now, let me see your swords!' Though no one in the room actually carried swords, they voiced their eager support.

Abed detailed how an alliance of assassins quickly assembled, with members drawn from three organizations. A squad of nine was drawn from Jamaat-ul-Mujahideen Bangladesh (JMB), a group which had absorbed many of Babu's former adversaries from HUJI, Jagrata Muslim Janata Bangladesh (JMJB), a society which generally confined its activities to northwest districts, and the quixotically named Ansarullah Bangla Team. Just days after the plunder of Ramu, their attentions turned to Babu. Abed was not chosen for the mission although he had volunteered. My other friend Bilal, however, was.

Before we reconstruct their operation to end Babu once and for all, I must interject a brief annotation about the Babu-revering 'cult'. After a comprehensive sweep of villages in Cox's Bazar district, and after having interrogated dozens of locals from the time, it appears that there was some truth behind the fundamentalist claims. In 2010, Babu had introduced to the area a technology that desalinated voluminous amounts of saltwater for agrarian purposes. Babu, along with a set of collegiate types, introduced to residents a solar-powered 3D printer that shaped components which attached to water pumps and enabled thousands of tons of crops to survive when embankments overflowed in the monsoons. Start-up groups replicated these efforts elsewhere, but in the upazilas neighbouring Ramu, Babu was honoured as a saviour.

One especially grateful community was comprised of Mohyals, a historically overlooked community that had served under Islamic leaders in the past. While most Mohyals are Hindus, many are Sikhs due to their tradition of raising the eldest male child as a Sikh. Quite a few Mohyals are also converts to Islam. These warriors settled on plains that were to later become part of Bangladesh and surrendered their martial ways. In the village near Ramu, the Mohyal homes that the mobs had vandalized were Hindu in most aspects. However, their history of service under chieftains of different faiths was a source of pride to them. In appreciation of Babu's efforts to better their lives, they venerated his image as per aboriginal practices. The villagers informed me that, in the past, they had similarly paid homage to other benefactors. These had included the poet Kabir, Mahatma Gandhi, Mother Teresa,

Michael Jackson, and the actor Rajesh Khanna. In fact, one Mohyal insisted that some of the photographs that riot-mongers had identified as Babu's were most likely airbrushed representations of contemporary Bollywood heroes. After all, Babu could, with a dash of fancy, be said to resemble more than one mascara-eyed and star-dusted film legend. Nonetheless, some of the images were of Babu. Whether he was aware of the snapshot supplications remains unconfirmed. I would wager that such blatant hero-worship would make our increasingly humble Babu very uncomfortable. My estimation was quite definitely not shared by ringleaders that conspired to cut Babu down to size.

Zealots from a miscellany of Muslim organizations clinked sabres, linked arms and devised a plot. The operation they came up with was not particularly complex or subtle. Their plan was basically to surround and overwhelm Babu at Ishwaripur village the following week. The historic village, which had recently experienced a resurgence in public interest, was holding a musical night featuring numerous folk singers and gypsy crooners. Babu had been asked to deliver a keynote address at three in the afternoon.

The village was renowned for its religious sites, including temples, monasteries, churches and mosques, all in close proximity to one another. Babu's slayers-to-be had very purposely chosen the religiously diverse Ishwaripur. Their intention was to decapitate Babu and damage the village's secular reputation. By their reasoning, killing a formerly famous politician in broad daylight would strike fear into religious deviants everywhere. The squad was aware that there would be a police presence. Institutional heads had already informed the volunteers that, due to media presence, it was likely that members of the squad would be arrested. Bilal, the martyr chosen to cut Babu in two, would face the severest charges. If Babu's murder was picked up by international news outlets in the absence of more compelling broadcast materials, there was a good chance that Bilal would be convicted and sentenced. Bilal later avowed to me that he'd had no problems in forgoing his life to end what he had perceived to be Babu's unholy sway over vulnerable minds.

I consider myself extremely fortunate in earning Bilal's confidence. In April 2025, I established contact with Bilal. After the failed assassination attempt in 2015, Bilal had been remanded by the police for fourteen weeks. Once released, he faced the wrath of the Ansarullah Bangla Team; he had been their conscript. When introducing myself to Bilal at a Dhaka mosque, I mentioned to him that I was working on chronicling Babu's life. Something in his eyes, an immediate softening and surrender, communicated to me that he might be amenable to aiding me.

Without Bilal's revelations, this story would be missing the central component of how even sworn enemies recognized, in 2015, saint-like qualities in Babu. Bilal is a very peaceable thirty-four-year-old today. I have known him for three years now, and value him as a close friend. Though I had initiated contact with him due to his role in the failed murder attempt, I am grateful that our relationship has developed stronger bonds. Bilal opened up to me gradually; we met multiple times before he was willing to share the details.

This is what he told me: 'As you know, 26 July was the day we followed Babu Bhai to Ishwaripur village. I remember everything about that day clearly, for my life was transformed after that incident. Babu Bhai had gone to the show with three companions. At that point we had been tailing him for days, and did not expect him to have a deep entourage or anything.

'Of the three men with Babu Bhai, one was the gigantic Munna Bhai, one was Partho, and the other matches the description of a man you have already questioned me about, the man you call YS. After Babu Bhai had given his opening talk, all nine of us were visibly shaken. This was the first time we had seen him in person, and we were all affected by his composure, by the calmness and equanimity he radiated. There was nothing evil about this man. He was nothing like what we had been told to expect.

'All the same, the nine of us had our orders, and years of indoctrination weighed heavily under our belts. We would not be that easily swayed. We proceeded to surround Babu Bhai and his companions. After debating on the use of firearms, our group finally decided that working with blades would be the honourable choice. Of the nine of us, six were to form a chain and stop anyone from the crowd interfering with our objective. The remaining three of us would charge at Babu Bhai. I had been chosen – they already called me a great Sayeed – to kill Babu Bhai and sever his head. The other two by my side were there to step in if I failed, or in case Babu Bhai or Munna Bhai put up a fight. We were not worried about the man I believe is your YS. He was too frail to be a threat.

'Babu Bhai was sitting on a chair when I approached him. I wanted to look him in the eye when I struck. He was turned towards the stage when I pulled out my sword from under my kurta. Munna Bhai had his back to us; he was engaged with someone in the crowd. When I was just four or five feet away from Babu Bhai, I raised my sword and Babu Bhai turned to me. We gazed at each other for a few moments.'

Bilal stopped here and started to cry. I did not console him.

After a minute, Bilal continued: 'When I reached Babu Bhai, when I looked into his eyes, it felt like time had stopped. It felt as if we stared at each other for hours, but of course, it was just a few seconds. I could not move. I was trembling violently; I had never hurt anyone in my life and was overcome with pain and confusion. Babu Bhai saw this. He smiled at me and spoke – it was almost like he was singing, or intoning a surah. He said:

It is okay, come to me.
Bring your blade; bring yourself.

You are welcome here; you see
the knife is already dancing inside me.
I am the knife.
You are also the knife, and you too are me.
There should be no fear in our union.
I love your knife, and I love you.

'On hearing this, I dropped my sword. As it struck the ground, it tinkled like music.

'When I recovered from my shock, I beheld that both my associates had discarded their weapons as well. All three of us bowed with shame. But ... it is difficult to express our emotions ... we were simultaneously euphoric. Our heads were spinning with some kind of intoxicating delight. Till date, I have remained friends with my two aides from that day. I know they felt the same way I did. I cannot explain why, but we experienced joy and a sense of unbelievable lightness after Babu Bhai had spoken. After thinking of this for months, one way I can explain it is that the contentment we had obtained from the Ansarullah Bangla Team was tawajud. It was an inauthentic harmony. The way we felt when near Babu Bhai was wajud: real ecstasy. And all of our lives changed. We have never been the same, Allahu Akbar.

'The infuriated crowd descended upon the three of us, while our six helpers escaped in the chaos. The crowd started to beat us; the police and Babu Bhai stopped them. They would have killed us otherwise. We were taken to the hospital emergency ward. But we deserved the beating.

'We were released by the police five weeks later. Babu Bhai had them drop the charges; he pulled strings. But nobody could protect us from the seniors in our parties. The Ansarullah Team tortured me for two weeks. I almost died. I don't know how exactly I survived, but I had this new sort of strength after what had happened on 26

July. My two colleagues were also tortured. We all lived – though our bosses wanted us dead. I'm not sure why they didn't execute us. Some say they let us live because we were still in the public eye.

'After the three of us were released, we stopped being soldiers for the group. My two former colleagues also feel that Babu Bhai had given us some kind of a new strength, a new kind of devotion. Now we work for peace and forgiveness, as you know. We are changed men.'

Though Bilal is a pseudonym, my friend's identity is not inaccessible. Anyone determined enough can retrieve legal records and access his name. Nonetheless, I have accorded him a false name to spare him from unwanted attention. It is not unthinkable that some radicalized student, even today, could want Bilal assassinated for his failure to silence Babu and for his renunciation of Ansarullah Team ideologies.

In the course of the past three years, Bilal has discussed with me why he initially joined a party like the Ansarullah Bangla Team. It is important we consider his observations. Bangladeshi fundamentalism is too much a part of this book, and too influential a force in the telling of Babu's life, to ignore.

The story Bilal shared with me is one that many Bangladeshis know all too well. Growing up, Bilal was an affectionate and gentle boy. On attending college, this changed dramatically. Disillusioned by the hypocrisy, pettifoggery and violence around him, he sought protection in religious cliques that, by and large, appeared to be sincere and dedicated to a higher cause. In retrospect, he believes himself to have fallen prey to hardliners and their pledges to Islamically overhaul flawed Bangladeshi systems. Bilal feels that some of these leaders manipulate religious sentiments to achieve their own career ends. Bilal, without any hesitation, emphasized that the major failing of Bangladeshi Islamic groups lies in the manner in which they force theological doctrines on others. As Bilal put it, fear mongering and violence ultimately prove to be less than spiritually satisfying to those seeking a true Din.

More disturbing however is Bilal's observation that extremists lower in the chain of command often turn to violence to vent their fury over being battered and trampled on. This analysis is nothing new. Over time, Bangladeshi youths who are injured by national institutions resort to violence to strike back at a merciless world. This self-destructive cycle perpetuates itself in the absence of social reform. Illustrations can be observed in impoverished neighbourhoods anywhere in the world, whether they be in Ferguson or San Salvador. Of course, when religion is introduced into the picture, things get a little more muddled.

As Bilal reasons, Bangladeshis conscripted by Islamic fundamentalists are duped into channelling their longstanding grievances into movements against domestic minorities, against regional figures that are outspokenly secular, against Indian and 'anti-Islamic' Western hyper-puissance, and against those perceived to be at odds with theological allies. They battle almost everything but the native forces truly responsible for their economic and political victimization. This is partly due to the fact that economic tyrants have military guns on their payroll. This serves leaders of radical political groups well, as party chieftains are often part of the reprehensible system which generates the suffering that creates these recruits in the first place. Such is the nature of the hegemony maintained by those that head money-chains.[75]

---

75 This troubling sociopolitical development in the ummah is observable in Malaysia, Indonesia, the Philippines, Mali, Burkina Faso, Niger, Cameroon, Northern Nigeria, Tunisia, the Democratic Republic of the Congo, Uganda, Sudan, Egypt, Eritrea, Somalia, Iran, Uzbekistan, Afghanistan, Pakistan, Tajikistan and Kyrgyzstan. While Bangladesh is considered by savvy analysts to be more secular than most names on this list, and while many a Muslim body in Bangladesh has engaged in tangible societal amelioration programmes, the pattern of duplicity persists in fringe consortiums. In order

As Bilal and I concur, for the powerless and oppressed in Bangladesh, right-wingers package Islam as a Procrustean axe with which to hew conformity on to a monstrous and mutating world. To this, they channel in other disenfranchised Muslims from overseas. Devotees who fall prey to this spiritual abyss carry bleak and grieving souls. The twisted and malformed piety that marks these unfortunate and damaged individuals offers little in the way of love or solace. In Bangladesh, this need to instil terror is partially rooted in the fact that pivotal figures in the Islamic parties dread being tried for the crimes they committed in 1971. Hence the need for men with sabres by their sides. Once these old criminals are gone, the nature of Islam in Bangladesh will change.

It is time to leave Ishwaripur and the failed plot behind us now. We must, however, carry with us the picture of a Babu: wise, angelic and, perhaps, a little blue-hued.

---

to blind those that suffer, vested leaders in these factions drape legitimate grievances under 'Islamic' shrouds.

WHILE BABU DOES NOT mention the 26 July aggression, he transcribes in the second week of August 2015 fruitful conversations with YS. The senior now resumed to confide in Babu the history of his Dinajpur peoples. I believe this to be a direct result of the humility and selflessness Babu demonstrated during the assassination attempt. Bilal has all but certified for me that YS witnessed the sublime moment himself.

YS, satisfied with Babu's new way of breathing, picked up where he had left off before. The following is a translation from Babu's text of YS's disclosures: 'You see, Babu, I avoid talking about my western lineage because there are many here in Dhaka that would have me burned at the stake. I know you've often wondered if I am a Muslim or an amussulman. The truth is I cannot really answer the question easily. You know I use a pseudonym for the articles I publish. If the right-wingers could find me, it'd be the end for me. Not that I'm afraid of an end, but there is work I have yet to finish here.

'To answer the question you've undoubtedly been pondering, no, I suppose I'm not really a Muslim. I am some kind of a hybrid. But never, even for a moment, do I ever feel that I do not belong here. My Yazidi roots are very unique. We incorporated bits and parts of many religious traditions, and while I have personally come to embrace a great deal of Islam, I will almost certainly be eschewed by other Muslims. The divisions within Islam are ancient. You and I cannot single-handedly change them.

'As you know, there is a legend that the schisms started just after Prophet Mohammed's death in the sixth century, when the Companions circled to deliberate what should be done next. Then, suddenly, the Prophet's confidant of just two years, Abu Hurairah, stepped forward with 5,374 quotes and observations of the Prophet's life. There was an immediate uproar when he produced all these hadiths. Abu Baker, who had accompanied the beloved Prophet for about twenty-three years, had just 142 hadiths to share. This, of course, is common knowledge. You know, Babu, how certain chiefs accepted Abu Hurairah's writings as true chronicles, while others abjured him as an impostor.

'But what few know is that as caliph turned against king, as Abu Hurairah stood before the circle and thunderously discounted Imam Ali and Imam Hussain, three distinguished men stood up with a sigh and began to walk away.

'Others from the venerable circle called to them, "O Fathers of the Birds, wherefore do you wander?"

'The three replied in song, "We leave you old dears, because we hear now the tinkle of gold and everywhere about you descends a cage."

'Babu, my particular Yazidi family descends from these three men. When all of Islam broke into kingdoms and wars, these three leaders of our tribe cast away their weapons. The stars overhead started to go out silently as they were attacked for being deserters. And in many cases, that is exactly what they had to. They sought refuge under the veils of varied clans. Over the centuries, they incorporated some of the ways of these other people. One particular tradition my forebears embraced was the exaltation of a divine thousand-eyed cosmic bird. This bird, a blue peacock, is the Melek Taus, our Peacock Angel.

'In continuing to flee abuse, precursors of my bloodline made their way north to Kurdistan in the tenth century, the cultural zenith of the Islamic world. Some headed west from there, for the Taurus mountain ranges. They continued as far as Armenia. In the eleventh century, when wandering Sufis drifted by, a number of

Yazidis who had remained in Kurdistan joined them to travel east. They crossed over Turkmenistan and Afghanistan to settle in the Kush Mountains.

'My western ancestors, however, journeyed all the way through northern India, to Bangladesh. They arrived here in the thirteenth century. But something had changed over their travels; my forebears no longer idolized the peacock, but had at some point replaced its image with that of an emblazoned and immortal crane. They could thus no longer be considered true Yazidis. Local Dravidians who deified the peacock were divided on how to receive our crane idol. Some accepted us and, as with the Sufis, married with us to start new families.

'My clan was fortunate to be adopted by kind trusters in Dinajpur. We have been here ever since; there is no way for me to say which drop of my blood is from the west, and which belongs to those that arrived here long before. We call ourselves Agnau Janah, those of the Holy Fire. I know you are fixated on the fact that we hold our crane deity in esteem but, for us, the crane is inseparable from the Holy Fire that constitutes it. There is also little point in debating what we really are, or which religious building we belong in. We actually take our name from something that happened in the fifteenth century. When our great guru Jalla Didi passed away, three different sects started to fight over her dead body. Each wanted to bury Didi as per their particular mortuary rituals. While they argued, the legend has it that Didi's remains were suddenly engulfed in a burst of flames. Miraculously, no one was hurt and the explosion lasted just a few moments. After the fire died away, there was no body, there were no ashes, no charred remains. Where the body had lain, was now a bed of flowers. And as they scattered into the breeze, we learned to stop fighting amongst ourselves. We learned to embrace the Holy Fire that burns within.

'Of course, there are many who never accepted us. They would kill us on sight; there is no space in their hearts for our syncretic faith. The danger they pose to us has gotten worse over the past few years, as you know. We must hide ourselves and our mixed-up ways. With the help of well-wishers and supporters, we have held on till today.'

Babu's diaries stop just a few days later. While there is no mention made of shapeshifting or aeronautical abilities, Babu does indicate that he was to visit Dinajpur with YS and meet others of his clan, but we cannot be sure if he ever succeeded in this. I have reasons to believe that YS did acquiesce to such a trip, but we must wait until later for how I have surmised so.

Having conducted considerable scholarship of my own, I have corroborated that the Yazidi of Kurdistan do indeed revere a thousand-eyed cosmic bird. Their syncretic oral tradition traces its roots to antiquated Sumer and Assyria, where bird-supplication dates back as far as six thousand years. The religion holds itself to be distinct from Zoroastrianism, Mithraism, Hinduism, Christianity and Islam, but displays flourishes evident in all faiths. I refreshed myself on crane adulation in the South Asian peninsula, and include here a paragraph-long synopsis:

The sarus crane is the species most venerated in India. As legend has it, the epic Ramayana was written after its author, Valmiki, had contemplated why the killing of a sarus crane had affected him so profoundly. The meat of the sarus is considered taboo in the earliest Hindu scriptures. Among the Gondi people, the tribes classified as 'five-god worshippers' consider the sarus crane as sacred. Found everywhere in the Gangetic plains, it had enchanted the Mughal emperor Jahangir in the seventeenth century, prompting him to engage in studying them.[76] Hundreds of years later, in 1963, the

---

76 British taxonomists, intentionally or otherwise, made a rather profound choice in designating the sacred crane the epithet *Grus antigone*. On encountering the bird in the 1700s, the British had no qualms in hunting it. In doing so, they trampled over local superstitions and traditions. Their decision to name the species after a rebel from Greek tragedy inadvertently

species came in a close second to the Indian peafowl (*Pavo cristatus*) in the nomination of the Indian national bird.

As I could find no records of the Asiatic voyages YS accords to them, in 2025 I decided to start with Dinajpur and work my way west. I spent three months there searching for leads.

Shedding my city ways, I spent this time in a mud-baked clay hut with no electricity. As I continued my work, tramping along village roads and following forest-men down thorny trails in the infernal heat, my sacrifices for this work rose to new heights. I suffered long nights in kerosene lamplight, swathed in mosquito nets, and delirious with heat exhaustion. I suppose, though, personal sacrifice is key to this chapter, and the tribulations exposed to me the rewards of surrendering trivial comforts. But not immediately. I exited Dinajpur having uncovered neither hide nor Yazidi hair.

On returning to Dhaka and my snug apartment, I realized that the experience had trimmed fat away from my soul and shaken the soil off my shoulders. It had even reduced my water-weight. After the Dinajpur trek, I felt light, possessing an inner calm that was key in seeing through everyday ash, seeing through to the beautiful fires that burn just behind. My work consequently became more productive and joyful. And good news soon followed. As my next breakthrough did not bear directly on YS's lineage, our efforts to unravel his heritage will be shelved briefly.

I struck unexpected gold when a trusted source and Babu-insider provided me YS's address. This individual had accompanied Babu and YS on two jaunts they had made about town. The kindly governmental employee led me to a block of rundown flats in Dhanmondi. Overcrowded and overrun with refuse, sewage and pests, it was a typical middle-class Dhaka residence. I was able to

---

reflected sentiments harboured by many subjects, Indian and avian, that held the patriarchal Crown in low regard.

obtain permission from irate tenants to take a quick walk around YS's former chambers, but there was little that held me inside.

Adjacent to the flats, however, was a small but inviting grove of trees. This brief stretch of grass had in YS's time been a park. Tired from the day's investigative efforts, I made my way to the trees to rest awhile and browse my notes. Three elderly men already seated there were smoking from a shisha and invited me to join them. Tempted by the fruity fragrance of their smoke, I sat with them; we made small talk while enjoying the minty tobacco mixture. Before long, I felt myself falling prey to the cooling breeze and the babbling of fowl. With two ravens peering down at me, I leaned back against a tree and napped.

The following reveries of mine from that humid August day in 2023 are not dissimilar to Babu's encounter under the Madhupur acacia two decades earlier. While I was not mauled by any giant serpent, a loquacious bird was to throw my work into a tailspin. I believe this account has emerged intact from the confusion, indeed, I would contend it has profited from avian tidings but, similar to Babu's reptilian escapade, I cannot corroborate the veracity of my ensuing account. Whether what follows is dream or reality is open to interpretation. I will leave it to you, dear reader, to connect the missing dots.

As I drifted in and out of my slumber, I heard the unmistakable voice of a mynah. The specimen at hand – well, it was actually lodged high up in the branches of a tall jackfruit tree – was particularly chatty. It regaled me with previously registered snatches of conversations between bickering housewives, with playground songs, and with the strident calls of rickshaw-wallahs, street vendors and radio personalities. I smiled lazily at the talents of this starling, it boasted an unusually gifted ear. As the talking bird continued to jabber, I began to doze off again when, unmistakably and astonishingly, the mynah began to speak in Babu's voice.

I bolted upright to listen. The men with the shisha had left, so I was able to concentrate fully. The bird repeated words and phrases as per its personal inclinations and proceeded with inexplicable loops and digressions. I was sufficiently lucid enough to start recording the hill mynah's vocalization on my phablet. After imparting the content I include here, the mynah reverted to screaming insults, selling guavas and reprimanding schoolchildren. It then flew away.

In that very grove, I replayed and analysed the bird's delivery umpteen dozen times before jotting down the structure of the subsequent dialogue. In doing so, I had to omit redundant utterances, distinguish between numerous voices, and impart sentences a grammatical format. The bird had, unmistakably, transmitted part of a conversation between Babu and a man named Younus.

Babu's voice had emerged from fruity branches: 'Bhai, have there been developments? Did you access the account? Have the hatters any good news? Younus Bhai, please let me know if there is anything I can help with.'

A voice, unknown to me, responded to Babu. In recreating this counter-tenor voice, the bird had raised the volume of its delivery several notches, 'My dear fellow, thank you for your concern. Things are well, nobody at the ministry suspects anything. In two months, Abdurahman will, as usual, begin to transfer the money. It will then be an excellent time to proceed.'

As I sieved this conversation from the bird's scattered utterances, my mind was a whirlpool of thoughts. The bird had clearly pronounced the name Younus. In fact, it had screamed the name out in raucous and erratic voices. If the bird had overheard Babu and YS talking in the nearby apartment, perhaps YS's real name was Younus Shah? The only other possibility was that Babu had met Younus Shah at YS's residence.

The references to the ministry, the person named Abdurahman, and the money transfers, however, meant nothing to me. Hence, I used my smartphone to look up the names the mynah had dropped. This led me to Mohammed Younus Shah and the theft of 355 million takas (42. 4 million dollars) from the Bangladeshi ministry of culture in 2021. Abdurahman Rashid had been state minister that term. While I was, of course, well aware of the scandal and how the money had been, incredibly, distributed amongst the neediest of domestic artists, until that arboreal encounter I had no reason to link Babu to the affair.

Had Babu played some role in the emptying of ministry accounts? In the years since the Samadi hoax, he had continued to face antagonism from rankers in political totem poles. Though he was invited abroad to numerous eco-conferences and to workshops in good governance, Babu never again attracted the recognition he had commanded with the Madhupur sensation in 2004. Perhaps Babu did assist Younus Shah? We already know how involved he had become with local artisan efforts. 355 million takas was no pittance. The distribution of that stolen money would, in fact, revitalize the arts scene in Bangladesh.

In 2020, the first surge of new works to appear in national venues caused quite a stir. Many previously unrecognized painters, sculptors, weavers, writers and musicians, as well as a miscellany of other craftsmen were, unofficially of course, beholden to Younus Shah for his actions. The funds he had 'anonymously' distributed via intermediaries had taken a week to reach a motley of beneficiaries.

Younus Shah primarily relied on officials in the Bangladeshi national banks whom he had bribed to conduct the initial transfers. These officials were by no means unaccustomed to felonious and king-sized transfers. They simply assumed that the dubious withdrawals had been blessed with the consent of the state minister, and were part of his shady business operations. Once they had moved the monies to local microfinance BRAC banks, there was no way they could retrieve the funds. Before governmental officers could unravel Younus Shah's mass of fiscal exchanges, itinerant artistes, baul troubadours and gypsy dramatists had scattered with the bounty. Additionally, Younus Shah had seen to it that the majority of the transfers could not be tracked. Thus had he meticulously pieced together a windfall that, within a fleeting interim, yielded masterpieces celebrated by curators, publishers and agencies worldwide.[77]

I needed no biometric voiceprint examination to confirm that the bird had been mimicking Babu's voice. Years of listening to his recordings have imprinted on my mind the inflections and manners of his speech; the mynah had emulated some of these. The bird had also played with the word 'hatters' (it had shrieked 'hatt', 'hatterers', 'hattershattershatters', etc., etc., unnervingly) for a spell. I remember deliberating under the tree if this was perchance a reference to the Bangladeshi Black Hatters (BBH), a group we briefly encountered in the Samadi Island conspiracy. They were a consortium of hacktivists who had openly endorsed Babu in numerous affairs. While contemplating this, I was once again overcome with fatigue. The two hours of feverish work on my phone had me, once again, slipping into a stupor.

---

77 In 2022, Dhaka hosted a newly revamped National Art Summit which attracted a number of corporate sponsors and kickstarted an unprecedented level of engagement in curating and displaying paintings, photography, sculptures, installations, digital art, video art, etc. The same year, Bangladesh 21, a conglomerate of various musical foundations, hosted a week-long seminar which addressed a number of concerns, including the need to integrate musical training into the educational system, the availability of instruments, and access to studios. The seminar took place simultaneously in three major cities and showcased new talents. Executives from the recording industry provided open-mike facilities for complete unknowns to emerge. In 2022, a similar conference, named Jatra Bangladesh, invited troupes of itinerant actors to participate in four days of thespian competitions. Gayatri Chakravorty Spivak cut the ribbon for this initiative.

I awoke approximately three hours later with an excruciating headache. The sun had set, and I quickly gathered my papers, phone and self to head home. My mouth was dry and full of a no longer pleasant taste of tobacco. On reaching my apartment, I downed some painkillers, brushed my teeth with neem bark, and brewed some tea. After refreshing myself, I returned to studying my data. Then, on attempting to retrieve the recording from my mobile, I found to my consternation that the recording of the mynah had disappeared. I must have mistakenly pressed the delete key when overcome by the second bout of lethargy.

Furious with myself, I also began to puzzle over why I had, not once, but twice, fallen asleep in that grove near YS's former domicile. It was unusual for me to seek repose anywhere but on my trusty bed. I contemplated the contents of my breakfast and lunch menu from the previous day. Had those two men maybe added a little something extra to their tobacco mixture? Why had I collapsed like some marathon runner, like some Pheidippides or Sammy Wanjiru? In spite of my misgivings, there was little point in lamenting expired milk. At least I had my logs and my memories of the bird's oration.

I did, however, return to search for the mynah the next day. On failing to spot the creature, I continued to visit the copses on random mornings, afternoons and evenings over weeks, but was unsuccessful. To add to my distress, after having questioned various neighbourhood residents, I could not locate a single person who was familiar with the remarkable bird.

In the meanwhile, my efforts to ascertain a possible association between Babu and Younus Shah proved less than productive. After obtaining his photograph from governmental records, I made my rounds with them, consulting those intimate with Babu. The only probe to strike bone was provided by my former fishmonger. The retiree wagered that he had spotted Babu on two occasions with a man that might be Younus Shah.

He revealed: 'I didn't want to mention this earlier to you, but yes, I really believe that I had seen them together. Once the whole story about Younus Shah had been picked up by media outlets, I recognized his televised photograph. I'm quite sure that I saw him with Babu on two different occasions in 2016. You know that my store was on the same street as Munna's flat. Both times, I saw them from my chamber above the shop. It had been very late at night both times, but they had to pass by the streetlight in front of my building. I don't think anyone else saw them. It was insomnia that had me up so late. And the way they walked, quietly, with purpose ... I was quite sure Babu was trying to not be noticed.

'I remember this Younus fellow because he cut a very striking profile. He was draped in some kind of long and flowing kurta. He also walked rather beautifully, like a supermodel or something. But most interesting of all was his face. With those eyes and that enormous forehead, you can't forget a face like that.

'I never mentioned anything when I heard about the theft. And then, sadly, Babu too disappeared. I had suspected there was a connection between both of them going missing at the same time. It was too dangerous to talk to anyone about it then. I also didn't want to tarnish Babu's good name. But when you called me yesterday asking me if I knew about any connections between them, I decided it was time to come clean. Since you have come so far in your work, I will not hide anything from you. I am sure you will be wise in choosing how Babu will go down in history. Am I correct?'

With that, the septuagenarian glared at me, raising his eyebrows in a most histrionic and unnerving manner. I hastily assented, muttered my thanks and prepared to leave the bazaar we were meeting at. Before I left, my erstwhile fishmonger pushed an envelope into my hand. It contained three Polaroids of Younus Shah. Apart from the one from government records, the other two were new to me. Though the photos were relatively blurred, there was indeed no denying that Younus Shah was a remarkable looking man.

In interviewing a number of Mohammed Younus Shah's workmates, I found myself persuaded that he and YS were one and the same. More than one comptroller has confided in me that Younus Shah was 'pure', that he was kind, and that people could straightaway sense an enormous tranquillity within him. While higher-ups in the government speak disparagingly of him as the miscreant who escaped after burgling the 'people's money', those who worked with him hold him in high regard.

While no co-worker admitted knowing Younus Shah on a personal level, they uniformly spoke well of him. Until the theft in 2021, Younus Shah had been universally recognized as being exceedingly honest. In fact, this had been seen as a handicap by higher-ups in the corrupt ministry. Younus Shah had actually been marked for dismissal, but colleagues had rallied to keep him on the payroll.

Off the record, one female bookkeeper explained, 'Whatever they want to say about him, he is still like an idol to us. Yes, he was a very quiet man, and acted older than he was. He did not have to be a big talker – in the two years he had been with us, we all came to like him. Everyone who met Younus Bhai instantly recognized they were in the presence of someone clean. You know, he was a devout and peaceful man, and he never missed his prayers at the mosque downstairs. The bastards in the ministry who don't like him, they are the real thieves. They have been robbing the ministry accounts for decades; I mean how many painters or singers or jatra performers have they ever helped? I mean, we all take a little extra when we can, what can you expect with our salaries? But our bosses have stolen so much, they have so much, but they don't stop taking.

Younus Bhai … God knows how he did it, but he got that money out and spread it to the poorest and most talented artists. This was the first time anyone did something like that. Alhamdulillah.'

The fact that Younus Shah was allegedly a Muslim does not rule out the possibility that YS had been moonlighting in disguise at ministry offices. As descriptions of YS and Younus Shah overlapped in my Bangladeshi inquiries, I found myself rejecting the explanation that Babu had met with Younus Shah at YS's domicile in favour of the theory that they were one. This notion of mine would be further supported by events that followed my receipt of an email in December 2023 from Romania.

I had been looking into the prospect of a trip through northern India into Pakistan, and then perhaps Afghanistan, to retrace YS's Yazidi trail. To plan for this undertaking, I wrote to dozens of historians, philomaths, post docs and spiritual leaders for pointers. However, just as with Dinajpur, not a single bob went under. Not a body could credit the Yazidi as travelling any further east than Turkmenistan. As I was on the verge of chucking out laptops and seedy bathwaters, I received a polite email from a priest in Romania. He wrote to me from a small town named Slatina. A friend from the University of Bucharest had forwarded him my queries regarding the Yazidi tours. The man, who identified himself as Sheikh Halil Masafel, stated that he could be of assistance to me. A few of his ancestors had indeed made it as far as the Kush mountains, and he had letters and drawings to warrant the hypothesis.

I was overjoyed, and while the work on my desk, the kind that fiscally fired me, was stacking, I booked a flight for just three weeks later. In the interim, further correspondence with the Yazidi sheikh revealed his possession of carefully preserved letters. These, he maintained, certified beyond doubt that his ancestors had reached the towering Afghan ranges in the thirteenth century. If his claims were true, the letters would go a long way towards demonstrating the credibility of YS's chronicles. To Bucharest it was, in the very first week of 2026.

In preparing for the trip, my hasty research yielded little in terms of what I could expect in Slatina. While I learned the fundamentals of Yazidi traditions, they were quite a diverse and ever-evolving group. It was next to impossible to know what sort of a mixed bag these settlers may have alloyed in Romania. I did not know if they identified themselves as Muslim as many in Iraq did, or what their native tongue was. More practically, my research left me with qualms about appropriate attire and cuisine. Many Yazidis did not permit the eating of cabbage, or the wearing of yellow. And Sheikh Masafel, being a member of the prestigious Sheikh caste, would he expect me to genuflect and kiss his hand?

On landing in Bucharest, it was only a two-hour train ride to Slatina. The sheikh had given me the name of a small hotel – I found that Hotel Bulevard Prestige adequately lived up to its name. On touching ground in Slatina at ten in the morning, I slept until four in the afternoon. Sheikh Masafel was to meet me at seven for dinner.

I made my way down to the hotel foyer at half past six. I carried with me a binder of photographs that I thought the sheikh would enjoy. I had handpicked snapshots from hybrid Bangladeshi communities to showcase a variety of physical features, as well as of attires. Of these, many were quite visibly rooted in western Asia, in forefathers who had arrived centuries ago. It was undeniable that many Bangladeshis looked Arab and even Mediterranean.

I passed my time in the lobby translating the hotel menu with the help of my smartphone. I was famished. Just before seven, a man wearing an Arafat-style keffiyeh walked up to me. Sheikh Masafel, a man in his fifties, possessed an impressive black beard that spread out over his wide chest. While his pocked face looked rather grim, his eyes twinkled kindly as he seemed to look me over approvingly. I was clad in a suit, and had purposely not shaved for more than a week. After a firm handshake, the spiritual leader introduced himself in reasonably decent English. He then removed the menu from my hand and said, 'Let us leave here. The food is kind of lousy.'

A few dark blocks later, we quit the icy streets for a warm restaurant. Ensconced in European walnut and dark brown leather, the place felt alive even though there were few customers present. Speaking in what sounded like Romanian, the sheikh placed two orders of ciorbă de legume. I noticed at this juncture that the sheikh was carrying a small steel folder. As he gravely placed the sturdy case on the table before us, he handled it as if it were a mandala of some sort, as if it were a kingly sceptre or a darling chalice that must not spill its contents. Leaving the elephant on the table, we had hardly exchanged half a dozen sentences in pleasantries before a young man brought steaming bowls from the kitchen. I was grateful for the distraction – I was not altogether mentally prepared for the discussion.

The ciorbă was an appetizing soup of vegetables, and just a few spoonfuls coaxed me from lethargic passenger to inquisitive historian. While I ate, I curiously watched a woman two tables away strangely heap ketchup on her pizza. Sheikh Masafel emptied his bowl as fast as I did. He then spoke to the young man and a brass hookah appeared. It was positioned between the sheikh and me, yet well away from the sheikh's steel binder.

Tending to the pipe, Sheikh Masafel asked questions about my work. Though I had already emailed details regarding my project and intentions, small talk is always essential in establishing trust. I fielded his questions respectfully, making sure to place emphasis on my fascination for ancient travels. I spoke of how Bangladesh itself had been visited by waves of Sufis, both Middle Eastern and African, and how our culture was a complex mix of many traditions. The sheikh smiled at me, and now that the pipe was smoking, passed it my way. I did not refuse the offer, but it cannot be truthfully said that I actually inhaled smoke.

Sheikh Masafel now spoke, 'You do not have to explain any more. I understand what you need. I know a fair amount about your country. You know, we too have our musical preachers and tumbling dervishes. We are not so different in many ways.' He laughed.

I nodded gratefully, relieved by the collapse of cultural bridges. I sensed this may be an enjoyable conversation after all.

'We Yazidis also have adapted to many different places, different leaders and different challenges. You know something of the hardships we've endured? Ah, yes, everyone knows nowadays. We have suffered a great deal. But why I am willing to help you, even share our private records and documents, is because I am proud of how my foremothers braved all oppressors, the dunes, the ice, the mountains, and survived. There are many that focus on the divisions between groups; some say if you eat pork you are a heretic, another says if you do not grow a beard, you cannot be a sheikh. Others say we cannot let females inherit Yazidi priestly offices. What a big joke.'

Here, the sheikh paused and looked me over quickly, smiling. 'You know, some say we are not supposed to wear green or yellow, others say blue.' As I started to fidget in my very clearly blue wool suit, Sheikh Masafel laughed and reassured me, 'Don't worry, I do not agree with this sort of factionalism. With all these rules, we would all be walking around naked. This kind of you-cannot-eat-this or you-cannot-drink-that, that sort of thinking has brought us nothing but grief.'

Here I vocalized my wholehearted agreement. I had studied in dismay how the Yazidis had endured centuries of appalling persecution. Internal dissension had only added to their woes. The sheikh took a deep puff and continued, 'Today, Yazidis are scattered all over the world. We are in Luxembourg, in Sweden, in the Netherlands. You can find us in Denmark, Switzerland, France, the

UK, the US, Canada. Perhaps you may know, we even have temples in Australia. In some places, we call our prayer houses mosques. But it does not matter. In this, I am unlike most others in my position. I do not think of those who have changed previous traditions as evil. They have had to do many things to survive, but what's in their hearts, that's what counts. The rest is all surface.'

The sheikh must have signalled the waiter without my noticing – he arrived at our table with two small glasses of a strong smelling liquor. Sheikh Masafel picked one up and appealed, 'Join me, let's toast to clean visages.'

Brushing aside reservations, I downed the fiery liquid. It was a type of brandy. I would later learn that this was the famous țuică. The alcohol kicked into my stomach, and I sat up.

The sheikh spoke a little about Romania, he explained he had been born here. We talked a little about the Rom people; he was well knowledgeable regarding their origins from the deserts of Rajasthan, and how they had persevered in heading westward. It soon became apparent that the sheikh was indeed informed about the great walks of mankind.

The sheikh then shared select Yazidi stories that had been passed down over the centuries in song. While these were intriguing, it will not be in our interest to list them. After a spellbinding hour or so, Sheikh Masafel opened his bag to produce a hardbound file. From this heavy-duty folder, the sheikh pulled out an attaché of documents that were laminated in high-quality plastic. He indicated that these were the records he had mentioned in his messages. I scooted up in my chair and listened carefully.

There were about thirty laminates. Most contained vellum-like parchments with ornate Arabic script. There were a few sketches and portraits that looked like ink drawings. Sheikh Masafel drew my attention to a particular letter, 'This is, of course, written in classic Kurmanji, using the dated Persian script. We have been using the language for almost a thousand years now. This first letter is dated year 5975 in Yazidi, which equates to 1225 CE in the Gregorian calendar, and approximately 622 in the Islamic calendar, depending on the month. So this letter is eight hundred years old, and is written by Sheikh Aswad Bashiqa, an ancestor on my father's side from thirty-three generations ago. Sheikh Bashiqa was a prominent leader who traced his lineage to the first three who walked away from warring caliphs.

'This dispatch is marked as having originated from the Khyber Pass, halfway between Kabul and Islamabad. In the winter of Yazidi 5975, this forefather of mine writes of how a group of them, numbering one hundred and forty, had been travelling for six years. They had started from a place in western Iran today, across northern Afghanistan, to arrive at the pass. This letter is numbered as the seventh one that Sheikh Bashiqa had sent to relatives in the Tigris Valley. But I do not have the initial six; they probably never reached us. This one was delivered, according to the prefatory memo affixed at the top, by a Mongolian trader. The Mongol rested with our relatives in the Tigris for a week and shared many stories of our one hundred and forty Yazidis who had made it to the Khyber Pass. He was also carrying pictures sent by our family. Someone was quite a talented artist; here are some of them.'

I followed the sheikh's example in holding the thick sheets of plastic at the edges. The intricate calligraphy of the messages and the artwork were exquisite. It must have taken weeks to prepare them – to perfectly apply the exact amount of ink to skin and not flood the nib.

As I could not read old Persian, I was chiefly preoccupied with the illustrations. There were a spread of campsites, horses, impressive peaks and portraits of elders. Sheikh Masafel must have sensed my enchantment and had been silent for minutes. When he spoke, he added, 'So these came with the letter from 1225. Also, these drafts prove that they had truly reached the Kush. If you compare the mountains in the drawing with these present-day snaps from the ranges, you can see how all these peaks line up almost exactly.

'Though I have already shared the gist of the messages with you, you are welcome to have someone come with you on another visit and check what I have said. The documents will stay with me, of course; I also cannot allow you to photograph. We have had many problems in the past with people forging Yazidi writings. But yes, if you wish to bring someone trustworthy, I can show these again.'

I readily assented to his proposal as there was no other way for me to corroborate dates and locations. While I had no reason to distrust the sheikh, it was my policy to double-check references whenever possible, for purposes of biographical authenticity.

Sheikh Masafel then laid out a second series of laminates. 'These are from twenty-nine years later, from Yazidi 6004, or 1254 Gregorian. They were sent from the city of Skardu, not too far northeast of Kashmir. Also written by Sheikh Bashiqa. He mourns that of the one hundred and forty clan members, only eighty had survived by when they reached Skardu.' Phablet in hand, I furiously Oogled the location. I was delighted to find that it lay well over the mountains. After having endured the icy death-traps of the Kush ranges, the path to Dinajpur from Skardu would be a mere stroll for the remaining Yazidis.

I am not new to fine quills from Ottoman and Persian eras, and the samples Sheikh Masafel had were truly magnificent. It struck me as a shame that much of the correspondence had been lost. Now entombed under snow and rock, or perhaps used as fuel or fodder, they could have described to us the fantastic airs of the 1300s. What a time it must have been, with scholars and saints of countless hues, each selecting their wings and choosing their horizons. The time was populated by a thousand and one believers, with people worshipping and loving in an abundance of ways, but even so, worshipping and loving all the same.

The sheikh began to lay out the artwork that accompanied this second message, and the moment my eyes rested on the portrait of a certain man, I almost slipped off the edge of my chair. Reaching for my own binder, I furiously shuffled through its contents. I had carried copies of Younus Shah's photographs for the sheikh, he was after all a Bangladeshi who undeniably invoked remembrances of sojourners from the west. On finding the images, I spilled them on to the table, and it now was Sheikh Mafasel's turn to swoon.

The illustrated man who had struck me from Sheikh Bashiqa's second dispatch bore an uncanny likeness to Younus Shah. The sheikh obviously concurred – he instantly placed the images side by side and exclaimed unintelligibly. He then asked, 'Where did you get this photo? Who is this man? Do you know him?'

I quickly summarized Younus Shah's story and inquired about the identity of the man in the drawing. The sheikh informed me the picture was of Sheikh Bashiqa's father, Sheikh Jamil, who was a revered elder. Sheikh Masafel and I were silent awhile, staring at the practically identical faces.[78] Both possessed the same bizarre vaulted forehead, extraordinarily wideset and penetrating eyes, and fragile chins. Even their similarly slender necks supported their heads at the same bent angle.

Sheikh Mafasel and I talked for hours as the țuică kept coming. After walking me back to the hotel, the sheikh and I embraced and made an appointment for two days later. That would give me ample time to locate a scholar in old Persian.

---

78 Later that week, the sheikh and I consulted a facial recognition expert. While the poor resolution of Younus's photographs and the image of Sheikh Jamil being a human painting ruled out biometric measurements, the scientist averred that the two could have been identical twins.

After a week of gainful meetings and consultations, I bade farewell reluctantly to the sheikh and returned to Dhaka. Head spinning with new scores, I reexamined my deductions. Things were neatly rearranging themselves. While YS's description of Yazidi travels had certainly been endorsed as a historic possibility, even more importantly, I was now almost positive that YS and Younus Shah were the same person. Sheikh Jamil's likeness to Younus Shah supported this, in addition to giving strong credence to the notion that YS, aka Younus Shah, was a descendant of his family.

THUS RECONCILED, I RETURNED to my efforts to tie Babu to Younus Shah. While YS continued to flit in and out of Babu's life according to the latter's confidants, Younus Shah stubbornly refused to turn towards the spyglasses I directed at the matter. My next lucky break came by way of the Bangladeshi Black Hatters.

In trying to make sense of how the fourth-tier employee, Younus Shah, may have orchestrated the heist, and if there was any room to add Babu's influence in the undertaking, I referred to accounting and digital forensic gurus. They assessed that Younus Shah must have had access to, and a working knowledge of, sophisticated hacking programs and software. While governmental offices in Bangladesh are not exactly boned for impregnable firewalls, experts unanimously emphasized that the complexity of the breach, and the subsequent dispersal of the funds, required a rare set of skills and equipment.

While my natural instincts would have led me to bark up the mighty Munna tree, I tapped my resources to contact figures who lurked in the virtual and clandestine mesocracy that was the BBH. Sure enough, it took but two weeks of cajoling, whining and whingeing to finally bare a live wire. In February, my brother produced what was most certainly a decoy e-address for a man who went by the handle of BZR7687. This systems analyst had been a leading Bangladeshi hacktivist for over a decade now, and if anyone would know of BBH's possible involvement in the ministry scandal, that person would be him.

My own foot and finger work had revealed that cyber warriors in Bangladesh were by no means to be taken lightly. Their national christening had not been far removed from the creation of the first computer virus ever – Brain. This prototype had been unleashed on the world in 1986 by Pakistani siblings from Lahore (a full three years before WANK). Their Bangladeshi counterparts had participated in a miscellany of global campaigns; migrant techies were conveniently spread out in multinationals covering five continents. Most legendary of these operations had been their association in 2012 with the now defunct international network known as Anonymous. Software developers from Dhaka and Bogra had allegedly played a role in Barack Obama's victory in the 2012 US presidential elections. Banding with allies, these shadowy programmers were said to have foiled Karl Rove's attempt to use the GOP's ORCA system to steal the election in Florida, Virginia and Ohio.

BZR7687, a founding member of BBH, had more recently spearheaded campaigns involving Bangladeshis in Saudi Arabia, Kenya, the United Kingdom and Malaysia to disable more than 35,000 Indian websites. These domains mostly belonged to the Indian government and right-wing media outlets. The Bangladeshi consortium announced via social networking sites that the cyber-sabotage had been in protest of India's refusal to honour the Teesta water-sharing treaty, and their building of the disastrous Tipaimukh Dam that violated numerous mandates they were signatory to. BZR7687 had also been connected to the disclosure of criminal financial transactions made by prominent Bangladeshi politicians. This disclosure had been broadcast live over national television channels; the Anti-Corruption Commission had no choice but to audit and prosecute the corrupt representatives. The BBH did not just stop there, they stuck with the cases, following them through courts, covertly recording Vype sessions, furtive conversations, and crypto-transfers between disposable accounts, to expose judges and officials who attempted to thwart fair and thorough trials.

Needless to say, BZR7687 was very wanted and took elaborate precautions to conceal his/her/their identity. While the only line I had to BZR7687 was an untraceable webmail destination, it evidently took him no time to access the scoop on me. A rather terse response to my fourth pleading e-transmission finally acknowledged my messages with a warning of sorts. The entity on the other end brought it swiftly to my attention that he/she/ they knew of my favourite restaurant for kari ayam, my preferred brand of laundry detergent, how many suits I owned, and even the songs on my favourite Zune playlist. The response included a list of my confidants and informers, dusky figures you have encountered earlier in this text, alphabetically organized by their current passport names. BZR7687 then made it clear that 'he' had decided to share data with me, but might one day ask me for a favour in return. I eagerly accepted the offer. I fancied that BZR7687 was located somewhere in Southern California, a fan of vintage NBC sitcoms, and the owner of a black 1965 Stingray.

Over the next several correspondences, BZR7687 sent me records, logs, files and memos which indicated that Babu had indeed relied intermittently on the services of the BBH. I had suspected this for years. My hunch that Munna had played a role in the introduction was also borne out to be true: BZR7687 confided that Munna had been pivotal to their work between 2012 and 2018, and had convinced the organization that Babu's causes were worthy of their mettle.

BZR7687 could not advise me whether anyone in the network had ever made contact with Younus Shah, but on my request revisited BBH records from 2021 to check on logs pertaining to Babu. BZR7687 and I had reached the point where we were regularly chatting online. It was in one such conversation, held before he accepted the commission of opening up BBH logs to investigate Babu's activities in 2021, that BZR7687 mentioned in passing: 'I remember that we were monitoring Babu-led protests against the Saudi "Rusted Sword" project. When Babu vanished, I was personally sure that it had something to do with that. They said Babu had evidence that the drilling licence was auctioned by government honchos. With the media scandal about the effects of mining on the Sunderbans, Babu had made some powerful enemies. BBH ploys to track Babu, even with Munna's help, fell short of confirming if Babu had fallen to mining bosses because of Phulbari. We gave up finally.'

After grilling comrades and mining remote logs, BZR7687 wrote me a long and excited message just four days later. He reported that a group called Bangladesh Cyber Army did indeed possess data which indicated that Babu may have been involved with the seizing of assets at the ministry of culture. BZR7687 explained that friends in the group had data-feeds from the ministry they had never reviewed carefully. Technologically gifted activists had instead been focused on Babu's labours directed towards shutting down the controversial mine. My conjectures involving Babu, Younus Shah, and the appropriation of national monies for the arts, was completely new to them. Just as I have assembled this account, many others concerned with Babu's legacy and whereabouts have explored scenarios where Babu had been assassinated by petrochemical oligarchs, gone into hiding from a deathly jealous Minnie, or absconded from the hotbeds of Bangladeshi politics once again. Some have him running a restaurant in a remote Balinese island, while others place him in a hamlet near the Mediterranean. There have been multiple sightings of Babu in Argentinian jungles – images on the net substantially reinforce these claims. Still others swear the former reactionary has grown a beard and shacked up on a sinking Marshalls islet.

However, BZR7687 encouraged me by insisting that my hunch regarding a Babu-connection with Younus Shah was the most convincing theory he had heard till date. He gauged that the very precise requests that Babu had made of programmers, and the specialized equipment he had been collecting, perfectly aligned with my theory of him collaborating with an accomplice in the accounting department of the ministry. BZR7687 averred that congruencies in the timeline obtained on Babu's engagements in 2021 via the cyber army, the theft of ministry funds, and the ultimate disappearance of Babu, were too numerous to be written off as mere coincidences. Taking several weeks to validate his conclusion, BZR7687 contacted me again with the announcement that he had found three computer analysts who revealed that Munna (most likely on behalf of Babu) had worked with them in tailoring port scanners to detect vulnerabilities in governmental firewalls. BZR7687 also ecstatically exposed that Babu had actually met with one of these programmers for training on router protocol and security auditing tools.

The final gift that BZR7687 was able to provide me, this wonderful man/woman/cyber-intelligence that drove about in a shiny vintage Corvette in my dreams, was video footage of what appeared to be Babu entering and exiting from the ministry of culture building on 4 November 2021. This was the very day that detectives at the ministry, after scrutinizing the electronic signatures of the case and the dispersal of the ransacked funds, and after running background checks on all key personnel, had surmised that Younus Shah had been the one responsible. It had been almost six days since the monies had been criminally directed into the pockets of needy beneficiaries. As investigators reported their find to the

minister at 5 p.m. that afternoon, the infuriated autocrat roared
at them to go seize Younus Shah. As we shall see, though swarthy
detectives immediately gave chase to him, they lost Younus Shah in
the winding roads of Dhaka that tempestuous afternoon.

4 November 2021 was the last day that Younus Shah was ever
seen. It was also about the time that Babu indecorously withdrew
from our dunya. In fact, since about 24 October, no one could
categorically confirm Babu's whereabouts. The video recording
that BZR7687 somehow obtained was, in fact, the very last visual
of Babu that I personally believe to be genuine.[79] The previously
unseen footage was captured by a security camera in an adjacent
building. It is a bit of a mystery why government mouthpieces
never aired the evidence that Babu had been in the building on
that memorable day. As BZR7687 conjectured, it was possible that
investigators had never gotten around to checking neighbourhood
surveillance cameras for what was obviously an inside accounting
heist. Of course, it is also possible that excited officers injured or
killed Babu that afternoon. This would be plausible if they spotted
him in the company of Younus Shah. They would then have good
reason to conceal any substantiation of Babu having been in the
vicinity.

The digital video recording showed Babu entering the premises
at exactly 3.23 p.m. It then shows him leaving at 5.09 p.m. Babu,
wearing a long kurta, was rather hurried in the second instance; he
almost trips over in crossing the street. Just moments after Babu
departs from 53 Mohammadpur Road, he is followed by what most
certainly appears to be Younus Shah, serenely flowing robes and all.

This recording was crucial in my amassing the ensuing
explanation of what may have transpired. As intelligence personnel
and lawmen gave chase to Younus Shah, Babu and he made their

---

79 I remain unmoved by the blurry Argentinian photographs.

way through the crowd to turn right on to Ring Road. According to station records, pedestrians advised the constables that the two men had hurried into 23 Ring Road, a high-rise located at the corner of the street. The officers rushed into the building and were directed to the roof by groundskeepers who confirmed the two had rushed into the elevators and asked to ride to the top floor.

Once the detectives reached the roof level, they smashed open a jammed door to find themselves in a completely vacant concrete space. Three of the lawmen mumbled something about a bird before the whole group was mesmerized by a breathtakingly beautiful sunset. Many others in Dhaka recorded the sunset that day; it appears that the province had experienced a rare instance of an aurora australis.[80] In the twilight sky, it appeared that a glowing halo had descended over the area, diffusing the men's vision.

On overcoming their amazement, the policemen scurried back to the lobby to badger and beat building staffers who refused to retract their story that two individuals had indeed made their way to the highest floor. As other officers exited 23 for the road, they found traffic to have halted as the city turned its gaze to the sky. Sub-inspectors and captains were unable to obtain further leads as awestruck citizens paid them no heed.

The shamefaced lawmen were reported to have returned to the ministry to report to a livid head. Further inquiries led them to the conclusion that pedestrians had lied to them or misdirected them unintentionally, as Younus Shah had fled with an accomplice. Three sergeants publicly referred multiple times to having seen two enormous birds fly from the summit of 23 Ring Road just as they had smashed their way on to the landing, but after being

---

80 The Cree call this phenomenon the 'Dance of the Spirits'. In Europe, in the Middle Ages, the auroras were commonly believed to be a sign from God.

sternly warned to stick to the case, they eventually went silent on the matter.[81]

This, dear reader, is where our story ends. As Younus disappears, our hero becomes zero. Once more, to search for Babu we must fathom beyond what appears at the surface, to peer deeply into things that lay inside yet other things. Supernumerary minds, like Prophet Suleiman, have shrewdly observed that there is nothing new under the sun. But what about moonlight? Or dawn, or dusk? It can be universally perceived that when solar dials are turned down, the quotient of the familiar to the unascertainable turns in counter-revolutions. In half light, the uncanny is free to leap, no longer constrained by the fear of solar flames.

To chart Babu's life and his leaving, we must look into the abyss of human history, into its darkness, its dark green emerald, and into its brilliance and daylight. We will resist certain visions – some of what is uncovered will appear exhausting to us. There will be much to reconsider, rearrange and to file away for future returns. To measure the past, even if it does not wholly belong to us, is a tedious thing. We inevitably find ourselves thrashing about in the belly of intimate moments we thought long since disappeared. We will awaken inside desolate crypts populated by forgotten demons that roam untethered. If we are able to bear these most harrowing of reckonings, we will be rewarded with new growths, and peace and light.

All the same, just there is no way to own the freedom that lies within a feather, there is no way for us to weigh exactly what happened in those last days. Were YS and Younus Shah truly one?

---

81 There are indications that two policemen approached local ornithologists with an enormous feather that could not be identified. Based on its dimensions, experts indicated that the feather must belong to an animal larger than the Philippine eagle, which is the only living species to exceed a twelve-foot wingspan. The feather is nowhere to be found now.

Did the Yazidis really integrate with those that esteemed the crane? Could I trust all I had learned from Sheikh Masafel? What mynah had spoken to me under those tree groves? What were the chances that Younus Shah and Babu's disappearances were followed by a magnificent aurora, or by the flight of two huge birds? Did the officers rightly find no one on the top floor of that building? Or did they, in their exhilaration, mistakenly kill both Babu and Younus Shah, and conceal their deaths?

Is BZR7687's recording to be trusted? 'He' clearly has the means to concoct footage to deceive me. But to what purpose? What am I to make of all this? Had YS really trained Babu on the flight of the alone to the Alone? The sarus crane has been observed to mate for life. They are considered symbols of marital fidelity, and pine the loss of their mates even to the point of starving to death. Perhaps Babu and Younus Shah had both reached the point where they no longer wished separation from their beloved, perhaps they too had returned into its embrace. Perhaps their work on this earth was done. Perhaps their crusade at the ministry captured their swansong, their piece de resistance?

But was Babu, still in his forties, truly ready to leave this world? Or did he perhaps leap into the ether behind Younus Shah on that rooftop, only to flounce about and land on some treetop in Bali? Was Babu truthfully ready, like Boro Ma, YS or Younus Shah, to depart for the skies?

To extract the true value of this chapter and gain insights from what transpired, we must, like a three-headed Hecate, simultaneously look down different paths: one from the past, another of the present, and one into the future. But then, we have had to do this throughout our account. Can we accurately hear how reverberations from former journeys travel through present times, into a future that is unknown to us, yet shaped by our collective resolve? In trying to bridge what has been folded into the blankets of the sky and the soil we dwell in, we have rotated like a dervish, with one finger pointing towards the azure and another pointing towards the ground. At times we have whirled beautifully, but at other moments we have tumbled over our heads. That is perhaps the very best one can say of our journey.

Farewell, my friend.